Prophecies have a way of coming true.
Whether you want them to or not.

She drew her sword.

She didn't question why. It was an act as necessary as breath, and every nerve in her was insisting on it. As soon as its comforting weight was balanced in her hands, Ainhearag shifted to a wider, more dangerous-feeling stance and turned one white-rimmed eye back toward her rider.

"Easy," Kyali murmured to her horse, listening hard. "Be easy."

Far off, a branch snapped. Closer, the bushes rustled.

She took a slow breath, willing herself calm, and pressed Ainhearag gently forward. Then the brush behind them spoke and she hissed a curse and kicked her horse into a run, not questioning that instinct either. Ainhearag bolted forward. Branches whipped into her face and eyes. Suddenly, a bow seemed like a very useful weapon.

Behind and all around them, the woods were coming alive.

It wasn't a lesson. It was an ambush, and it was deadly...

Sword

Amy Bai

Candlemark & Gleam

First edition published 2015.

For information, address
Candlemark & Gleam LLC,
104 Morgan Street, Bennington, VT 05201
info@candlemarkandgleam.com

ISBN: 978-1-936460-61-8
eBook ISBN: 978-1-936460-62-5

Cover art, design elements, and illustrations by Jenny Zemanek
Seedlings Design
www.seedlingsonline.com

Map by Alan Caum

Book design and composition by Kate Sullivan
Typeface: Alegreya

www.candlemarkandgleam.com

To Art:

my rock, my goad, my shoulder, my always.

Lardan

Dark the wind that brings the storm
and lost, all, to its breaking,
Yet firm shall hold Sword, Song, and Crown
A land of their own making.

Sword shall guide the hands of men
and Song shall ease their sorrow,
Crown shall harbor all their hope
And lead them to tomorrow.

BOOK 1

THE GENERAL'S DAUGHTER

"*M erry we'll meet till the tides they all turn, then dance with the blades as the shadows return...*"

Children skipped and sang an old nursery rhyme in the parched air of the late afternoon. Their shadows fell strange in the slanting light. In the shadow of an oak thick with age, a girl crouched glumly on her heels, drawing aimless lines in the dirt with a battered practice sword. She was noble, this girl, a scion of the great House of Corwynall, whose oak it was: the oak and a great deal more. The silver locket at her breast declared it even if her patched dress did not.

> "*Sing we a new song, for sadness and woe,*
> *kings and queens all shall the darkest road know—*"

The children, passing under one another's linked arms,

stared at her and interrupted themselves with whispers. The
girl never spared them a glance. Only someone who knew her
very well would have marked the way her gaze held them always in its periphery, how her face tightened when a gust carried their words across the yard.

> *"Rise shall the earth and the heavens shall fall,*
> *fire can guard from what water can call..."*

It was the most senseless thing she had ever heard. Why
couldn't they sing "Skip to the River" or some other silly rhyme?

The tip of her sword dug into the earth. She blunted the
only weapon her father would allow her till she had proved
herself worthy of better, and recited the Five Tenets of Siege
Defense in her head, hating that she hated their stares.

They were too young to help in the fields, barely able to
toddle. But they learned it from their parents, who were too
far away right now to stare. *What did the general's daughter do
today?* those parents would ask when they were home in their
cottages over supper. And their eyes would follow her in tonight as they headed home to talk—she hoped—of something
more significant than the state of Kyali Corwynall's gown or
the battered old sword she carried everywhere.

Bold thoughts, coming from a girl crouched under a tree.

She pinned her gaze on the far hills, refusing to notice
the sly looks of the children. The mountains were wrapped in
a haze of summer heat, little more than shadows against the
sky. The soldiers always teased her when she looked in that direction: the mountainfolk taught the Gift and the sword to all
who proved both worthy and Gifted... and they took girls and

boys both for study. *You ought to go,* her father's officers often jested, secure in the knowledge that no Corwynall of the royal line ever left the family estates. *They'd like you up there.*

Síog girl, fae child, her brother would usually add, being less wary of her temper and endlessly amused by how those names made her blush. *Surely they would have you, you look enough the part.*

Sometimes, like now, it almost seemed like a good notion. Up there, the air would be cool and there would be snow in the winters, which she had never seen. Up there, no one would know her name, or stare at her.

Bind them together with holly and rue, the next lines of the song were, and she heard it even though they didn't sing that one. Kyali bit her tongue, annoyed that they had managed to fix the silly thing in her mind. *Those that will follow the heart's voice be true.*

This was the last time she tried to be helpful to the estate staff.

The headman's niece, whose rightful custody these little imps were, was probably behind the barn with one of the soldiers, looking to get herself a marriage the old-fashioned way.

That was unkind. Arawan was not a fool. But Arawan was not here, *she* was, minding babes with eyes like pointing fingers, and likely providing considerable amusement to the soldiers of the Third Battalion, who were scattered about the estate on boring guard duty today. Those men didn't find her odd, if only because she'd tagged after so many of them in her younger years. They weren't above a jest at her expense. But jests she would take from them, and from her brother Devin, as she took orders from her father and her father's officers... and neither from anyone else. Even now the men posted at the stables were sneaking looks at her, grinning. It was almost enough to make her smile back.

In the sunlit yard, the children sprawled like puppies, panting in the heat, and argued over what to sing next. Their voices hung in the air like dust.

> *"Dark the wind that brings the storm,*
> *and lost, all, to its breaking;*
> *yet firm shall hold Sword, Song, and Crown*
> *a land of their own making—"*

Fierce shushing from one of the guards stopped that rhyme, which was senseless but lately seemed much less silly. There were no smiles on the soldiers' faces now. There was a scowl on hers. Now nobody ventured a glance toward her. Somehow that was worse than the stares.

A shiver twisted over her and Kyali bent her head to look at the ground so nobody could see her expression.

Arawan would have to come back soon.

Hopefully her father and her brother would come back soon, too: they had braved the court to meet with the king on some matter or other, leaving her here to manage the estate and be skewered by the ungentle curiosity of children.

She made her way across the yard with the sun setting fire to the tops of the northern hills. Behind her, the fieldhands stacked their hoes by the oak and gathered their children for debriefing. She had no appetite, and no interest in the book on siegecraft her father had pointedly left her. She decided, since her father wasn't here to forbid it and her brother wasn't here to poke fun at it, that tonight she would sleep in the root cellar, where the earth was still cool and damp. Sleep was an attractive alternative to watching the candles drip and pretending to study. Or to sharpening her sword, which definitely needed it now. She wished Taireasa were here to prod her out of her moodiness. But with Taireasa came the bodyguards that were always in the princess's presence, and a witness to the bothered state she found herself in was the last thing Kyali wanted.

She was out of sorts, and annoyed with herself for being annoyed.

It's youth, her father would tell her, with that dry impassiveness she never could quite manage. *You're fifteen*—and then she would snarl, and he would raise one wry eyebrow, and she would trip over her own feet in sword practice and look like a fool.

Her limbs were growing longer, and banged into things at the worst moments. Her dresses fit badly and her head ached, and she knew her temper showed in her eyes, which sparked with an odd golden sheen whenever she was upset. That was her father's heritage, passed down from some questionable relation or other, and it was extremely awkward when she was trying to keep her face still. There was a grim irony in the fact that her private inconvenience had half the kingdom convinced she was fearsomely magical—and yet, unlike her brother Devin, she could claim not the slightest smattering of the Gift her House was known for.

It wasn't particularly amusing at the moment. She was a daughter of House Corwynall. She had duties, and things to be that she wasn't, and didn't yet know how to become. She stood in the midst of brocaded chairs and tapestries holding a sword, scowling at nothing. She didn't need the mirror on the far wall to know how out of place she looked at the moment.

"Damn," Kyali said aloud to the walls, and felt a little better.

Devin and Father should be back tonight, and if she couldn't manage a better balance than this, she had better be asleep before they arrived. Her brother was quick to scent a moment of uncertainty and turn it into a prank or a gibe, which would either improve her mood or worsen it considerably. Plotting an extravagant retaliation to this imagined slight, she descended the cellar stairs completely occupied, and so she noticed nothing odd until she reached the bottom. There she froze without knowing why, as every hair stood on end.

An arm reached out of the dark and wrapped around her neck.

She saw it coming from the corner of her eye but only had time to twitch uselessly sideways. Another arm immediately followed the first one, muffling her startled cry and stealing her breath.

Too shocked to be afraid, she bit down. The hand over her face jerked away. Her elbow drove backwards and her heel went up into a knee. The awful crack of bone that followed drew a pained groan from behind her and brought her panic in a thundering flood. Her attacker staggered, pulling her with him. The dropped candle sputtered on the floor beside them, throwing huge shadows everywhere. Spurred on by the thought that she might have to finish this struggle in the dark, she shouted. It was a much softer sound than she'd intended, but the floorboards above them creaked ominously, the arms around her fell away, and her attacker screamed as though she had burned him.

Leaving this mystery for later consideration, Kyali flung herself at the steps and scrambled up, leaving the back panel of her skirts in his fist. Her sword clattered on the floor as she snatched at it. He came hard on her heels and, as she turned, drove himself obligingly onto the blade for her. Stunned, she froze again.

Her blood sang in her ears. By the look on his face—a fair face, some much colder part of her noted, with the Western short-beard—he was at least as surprised as she was. He drew a bubbling breath. A dagger dropped from his hand and hit the floor between them.

They stared at one another.

He made an odd face then, and coughed a gout of blood all over her. She blinked through the drops. She knew she had to move—*not dead till they stop bleeding*, Father would say—but she couldn't. For all her years of study, all the secrecy and sword-play, she had never killed a man. She supposed, watching his face in a perversely distant way, that she still hadn't quite managed it. But he fell forward onto her then, going limp; after the instinctive terror of having him land on her subsided, the sight of his glassy gaze, of her old practice sword sticking out of his ribs, made it clear that she had done it now.

She watched his face closely while his blood dripped down her cheek. He didn't move. He seemed not to be bleeding any-more, though with all the blood on him already, how could one tell? She didn't intend to get closer to check. She couldn't hear anyone else in the house. Through the haze of shock, she was grateful the soldiers weren't here to witness this bizarrely per-sonal moment.

"Well," Kyali said, beginning to be pleased at how well she was taking this—and then threw up on him.

Damn.

New lessons were the result of the ordeal, which was not shocking: new lessons were the result of nearly everything.

Devin, when her family had arrived to find her scrubbing blood out of the floorboards, had predictably deemed her hopeless, right before he slipped on an overlooked puddle. Their father, also predictably, had directed the House guards to bury the man in the south field, made her drink half a cup of unwatered wine, and sent her to bed.

Kyali spun and parried as her father's sword came at her. The jolt when their blades met made her whole arm ache. Sweat pasted stray tendrils of her hair to her face. Her leather armor creaked with every move. She wobbled back on guard, her arms and legs trembling with fatigue.

It was both comforting and disturbing that she was not the only one out of breath this afternoon: beads of sweat stood on her father's brow and his armor was creaking, too.

He waved a hand at her, meaning, she hoped, that they should rest. Prudently, she waited until he leaned against a tree before staggering to one of her own, pressing her back against its bark. Her legs were barely able to hold her weight. Every time she grew accustomed to the lessons, he would add some new element and she would spend a week sore and winded and stumbling before she began to get the hang of it again. These lessons were both harder and easier than the other things he taught her: the movement of troops across provinces, the tricks of supply lines and alliances, the careful use of spies. An odd sort of childhood—but as the alternative was learning to sew and do accounts, she wasn't about to complain.

Except now she had killed a man, and she could no longer pretend her father was merely amusing himself by teaching her.

Her father sighed, and Kyali darted a worried glance at

him. He'd been very quiet since last night, which in her experience meant she'd done something wrong. But he avoided her gaze and so she looked elsewhere, determined not to be seen as a child today.

The wheat fields stretched out below them, brown stalks peppered with kerchiefed heads and teams of dray horses, and in the distance, the wide expanse of the Sainey River sparkled back up at the sun. It would have been a far more peaceful view if the fieldhands weren't watching them so closely.

By now rumor would have reached the capital; there was no way the soldiers who had found her in the aftermath of last night's little debacle had kept silent about it. She glanced over again. Her father seemed to be contemplating the same view. But she had learned the trick of staring at things from the corners of the eye from him, and she knew it was her face he really watched. Caught between gazes, she pretended to be absorbed in a rock under the toe of her boot. Her shoulders drew up.

"It bothers you, then, does it?"

There was no curiosity in his question; the answer was probably plain on her face just now. She shrugged. He sheathed his sword and folded his arms, looking a bit like a statue of himself as he considered the expanse of his fields.

"No," she said, which they both knew was an outright lie, but her father let it pass with mocking civility and spared her having to invent a justification.

"It'll only get worse, now that they've evidence it's not play we do here," he said.

She glared, feeling a rush of heat in her eyes. There was no hiding it; he knew exactly what it meant, having the same trait himself, though it almost never showed in him.

"What *is* it then, exactly?" she asked. "You're not preparing me for marriage, unless you were planning to marry me to an outlaw. Why—"

She choked the words off, flinching away from her own anger. There was more of it than she had believed.

Why are you teaching me to be you?

She could never ask him that. Just thinking it made her heart thump.

Her father tipped his head like an old battle crow, looking like he'd heard the words she was holding behind her teeth. "Don't you like it? I was perhaps mistaken."

Gods, there was no way to win with him. She wasn't even sure she *wanted* an answer— ten years at this; it couldn't be a whim that the Lord General chose to teach his daughter the sword. Surely not.

But what if it was?

"You know I do," she said, and they stood a moment, listening to the distant shouts from the fields. "But," she added, having recovered her argument, and he cast her a weary sideways glance—he hated that word. "But I've put this practice sword to a somewhat different use than you intended now, have I not? The villagers may find it a good tale to tell, but I doubt the gentleman's kin will. And others who have found my... hobby... amusing will think again. Won't they?"

"You've the Gift now, yes? You've used it—against, dare I guess, young Lord Alusyn in our cellar last night?"

How could he tell? She'd said nothing of the strange effect of that shout, or—

Wait. *Lord* Alusyn?

It was one of his strikes from the side. The surprise made

it to her face; she could feel it there, widening her eyes. Kyali thought hard. She knew the name; a moment's thought gave her the lineage and the location, and her knees went weak.

She'd killed a baron's nephew. A *Western* baron's nephew.

Her father gave a grim smile then, seeing her understanding dawn. "I need not explain to my daughter the repercussions of this," he said, looking her steadily in the eye. "Need I?"

He had explained it enough already, in lessons and lectures. Relations with the four provinces of the West were difficult: the rule of the kingdom sat in the East, on the other side of the Deepwash River, and all sorts of things from trade to taxes to the old names of the seven gods were points of contention—but the real issue, she suspected, was simply that the throne sat in the East. A girl raised in House Corwynall, the more martial of the two royal lines of Lardan and the one on whose estate the Eastern provinces' soldiers were trained and housed, could hardly be unaware of the tension. A girl who sometimes couriered orders to troops stationed near the Deepwash's winding border as part of her training was aware of a bit more… like that the men on their side were matched precisely in number and location on the other. It was not common knowledge, and her father wanted it not to be.

She was of the Blood, as was her brother: as eligible for the throne as Taireasa was, though nobody had voted a Corwynall onto the throne in so many generations it was just history now, something to read in a book. She was of the Blood and she'd killed a *Western baron's nephew.*

A Western baron's nephew had come to kill *her.*

Kyali shook her head, swallowing a thousand questions, beginning to be truly afraid now. She sensed in a vague, star-

tled way that her whole life had just turned on this point. Her
father watched as though every thought in her head was already known to him, and they probably all were. He was the
Lord General, after all, and troops moved at his orders, as did
she. "Good enough," he grunted.

It wasn't; not nearly. But she held her tongue and stared, a
tactic that sometimes worked. He laughed without much mirth
and tipped his chin out, toward the fields.

"Just look," he said. "Look at it."

She did. The habit of obedience was too ingrained in her
not to: she heard his voice and her muscles moved before her
mind caught up. Devin, older by a few years and having studied music instead of warcraft, had escaped such thoughtless
compliance. *Why* was Devin's question, generally before one
was done speaking, and his flighty attention skipped over half
the explanation anyway unless you caught his interest. *Changeling*, he had called her last night. Outside of *Síog girl*, it was his
favorite to throw at her, because of her eyes and her hair. (And
because she hated it. But he had given her the best of the pancakes this morning without a word, and that was Devin too.)

"Change in the wind," her father murmured, dragging her
attention back to this strange morning and all the things she
didn't want to think about. He nodded at the distant fieldhands. "They know it. They watch because you're part of it,
daughter. They're looking to see which way it blows, and what
it brings. Allow them that with whatever grace you can."

Well, *that* was hardly comforting.

"*Look at it*, Kyali Corwynall."

It was utterly unlike him. Kyali gave up obedience to stare
at him, finding his face as impassive as ever when she turned,

but there was a haunted look to it just the same. She frowned, worrying, waiting for him to tell her how to mend this mess she had made.

His eyes wouldn't quite meet hers, and his mouth tightened.

"Time I told you a few things," her father declared then, and turned to gather his sword and walk down the hill. Kyali followed silently, in confusion and dread.

2

aireasa's face was unusually impassive, for Taireasa.
A strand of curls wafted into her eyes, which darted to
the river, then to the bramble on the far side, and finally
came to rest on her hands, tying knots in a blade of grass. Even
when she was trying to be as stone-faced as her father, Kyali
thought, some part of Taireasa always gave her away.

"You already knew," Kyali accused, and watched those fine-
boned knuckles whiten. Taireas's hands stilled a moment, then
tangled into her skirts, twisting into fists. Tailors and hand-
maids were on hand at every court event: good cloth suffered
whenever the princess's nerves did.

Taireasa sighed. "Not about Lord Alusyn, Ky, I couldn't
possibly."

A poor attempt at misdirection. "And this stupid rhyme

that's been around for gods know how many centuries, that everyone's now calling a *prophecy*? When did you hear about that?"

That earned her a glare. "Oh, *say* you're surprised, Kyali Corwynall, and I'll know you're a liar. We've both known since we were old enough to skip to it that *that* one was more than whimsy. What else do folk do when the gossip gets stale and they need something to whisper about in the night? They've whispered about this one forever. Are you about to claim otherwise? Do you say you weren't whispering with me, when we'd run out of mischief to do and the shadows in my bedroom all had teeth?"

Taireasa had a very sharp tongue when pressed. It was normally one of Kyali's favorite things about her friend.

Kyali felt a flush heat her cheeks and knew her eyes were admitting everything for her. "You still could have said," she snapped. "Or are you about to tell me you've never known more than what we scared each other with when we were ten? Say that and I'll know *you* for a liar, Taireasa Marsadron."

It served to bring a matching flush to Taireasa's cheeks, if nothing else. Which she was immediately sorry for. Kyali softened her tone, trying to be more patient. "When did you know... more?"

"You never come to court anymore—"

"Gods, what has *that* got to do with it?"

"If you'd come, you'd know!" Taireasa's eyebrows rose as if even she were alarmed by the outburst. Kyali used the small silence that followed to gather the remnants of her composure. Nothing ever went as she planned with Taireasa.

Well, to be fair, things rarely went the way she planned *without* Taireasa.

Taireasa cracked her knuckles, then winced at the sound. She made a face. "Not that I blame you. Who wants to have their hands stared at for hours by the Western barons?"

"You could have said something. I would have come."

"You have better things to worry about, Ky."

"Oh, aye, so many things preferable. I have *so* many pleasant pastimes. And my audience of fieldhands and farmers and soldiers, who it seems now think I'm something from a children's skipping rhyme."

Yet another pause, quite different from those before it, and Kyali rose to escape that very direct green gaze. Taireasa followed, perfectly willing to press an advantage.

"It *does* bother you, then. I wondered."

"How can you ask me that? Why is *everyone* asking me that lately? Does it seem enjoyable? Would you enjoy being watched every hour of—"

The idiocy of complaining to the king's only child about audiences and stares caught her by the throat. She glared at the river and sighed. A leaf drifted serenely onto the water and floated, spinning, downstream. The birches rustled, dappling them with sunlight—all around, the forest went peaceably about its business. It was hardly a day made for brooding over dark and ancient prophecies that might or might not be true. And might or might not be anything more than stupid rhymes their grandparents' grandparents had sung as children.

"Gullible fools," she muttered to the water, which only burbled back.

Taireasa's arms came around her shoulders. Her sharp chin dug a hollow just above a collarbone. "I don't think you credit yourself for that expressionless face of yours. But for your eyes, Ky, I doubt I'd have the slightest idea how you feel about anything. Unlike me, with my hands, and my skin—"

"—and your eyes."

One arm came away from her shoulders. "*My* eyes? They stay green, at least."

"And your elbows."

"Now you're mocking me." Taireasa stepped to the side and buried her hands in her hair, sticking out the offending elbows. The locket at her breast, etched with the Marsadron hawk, winked silver in the sunlight. "You'd make a much better queen than I'm going to. Perhaps *I* should take up the sword and you can learn to enjoy ruffles and misdirection."

Gods, what a thought that was; it made her shoulders twitch. "You'll damn well make a better queen than I would."

"Don't curse, Ky."

Kyali glowered, irritated at having to state the obvious. "Imagine me dancing with Anders of Orin. Or trading barbs with your cousin Lainey?"

The corners of Taireasa's mouth twitched unwillingly upwards. "You *are* somewhat ill-suited to negotiation," she admitted.

"Mmmn. *Somewhat*. And what choice do we have, after all?" She struck a swooning, tragic pose, a thing she would only ever do when there was nobody but Taireasa to see. "I am Sword, you are Crown, and foredoomed both to our fates…"

"Gods bless, don't make light of this!" Taireasa snapped, utterly unamused. "Let be, Kyali."

Kyali sent a single frustrated glace at her friend and folded her arms. "It's a *children's rhyme*, Taireasa."

But it wasn't, not anymore. She'd been able to tell herself so until she'd heard her father speak it aloud yesterday; until she'd seen the worry in his eyes that he didn't quite manage to mask. Until she knew he believed it was a true foretelling, one of the old rhymes of legend, from so far back the burned library of the buried years was probably the only place that had ever held the truth of it... and that his children were tangled up in its verses.

Now it would never be that simple again. *Nothing* would, she suspected, even if by some miracle this turned out to be nothing more than a bad children's rhyme after all.

She'd just hoped for one more afternoon with Taireasa where she could pretend, but all along Taireasa had been ahead of her in this, as she so often was. Kyali pulled in a deep breath, let it out carefully, and made her face perfectly still. There was an ache sitting in her chest, one that felt too much like a farewell, and it probably lit her eyes like lanterns.

Taireasa took her hand, unfolding it and rubbing her fingers over the deep calluses made by the sword. "It's on the lips of barons and kings these days, Kyali Corwynall," she said softly. "Some think it's more than that."

Kyali tugged her fingers free. "And are you one of them?"

"I don't know, Ky. A year, even half a year ago—no. But it *is* passing strange that the only children of Houses Corwynall and Marsadron should happen be a Bard, a swordswoman, and the heir to the crown. When have we last seen a Bard?"

"I am not a swordswoman! And Devin's not a Bard."

Not yet, anyway. It was something of an event, the naming of a Bard, and it had not been done in living memory.

"Not yet," Taireasa retorted, echoing her unspoken thought a bit too closely. "We both know he will be one day, though, don't we?"

Gods, wouldn't her brother chortle over the notion of himself as a figure of prophecy? He'd preen like a swan. And tease
her endlessly... if, she thought in sudden dismay, he hadn't already drawn such conclusions himself. What might their father have told his eldest, on those occasional trips to the capital she did her best to dodge?

"Well, I'm not a swordswoman."

Taireasa had paused, knowing there was thought happening, doubtless knowing there was distress—how she always
saw such things was a source of constant consternation. Now
she took up the argument again, putting her hands on her hips.

"You are," she said simply, wielding that piercing stare of
hers like a blade. "Or you will be. You probably know as much
of martial strategy as my own father does. And you're more
skilled with a sword at fifteen than half the gentlemen at court.
It does occasion comment."

"And you wonder why I never come to court anymore," Kyali muttered.

"I never thought you cared."

"Well... I don't." This conversation had gotten far from
where she wanted. Her shoulders kept trying to hunch.

"You can't have it both ways, love."

Kyali looked away, feeling her face pull at itself. "Now you
sound like Father," she grumbled, and Taireasa snorted with
a decidedly unladylike lack of grace that Kyali loved to see.
Court had made her lifelong friend so careful as they got older;
it was good to see a glimpse of the waif she had skinned her
knees with.

"*Dark the wind that brings the storm...*" she muttered. "I suppose it is a rather morbid rhyme to skip to. Whose hands shall

I guide, if all are lost? If this Eairon person who's supposed to have written it foresaw the end of everything, why did he only write two damned lines of verse about it? It's stupid, Taireasa! I'm sure Alusyn of Arumilia had some business in my father's cellar besides scaring me half to death, but shall we go to our fate like sheep to a shearing?"

"I don't think the idea is that we go to it, rather that it comes to us."

"While we sit in our fields counting comets and the Western barons grow ever more bold. I think not, Highness."

In the heat of the argument, Taireasa barely flinched at the title, usually something to bring her to a blushing silence. That was nearly as alarming as this sudden fascination with the old rhyme. Kyali realized suddenly, in the length of her bones, in the spare beauty of her face, that her childhood friend was no longer exactly a child. She wondered what changes were being wrought in her own form, and what they spoke of to the prying eyes of soldiers and country folk.

Taireasa drew her attention with a hand on her sleeve. "Is that what your father told you? He spent hours with Mother and Father this last visit."

"I don't know. I think so. He never tells me very much of anything, you know that. Just 'you must be on your guard,' and 'discontent is not to discount'." Taireasa murmured the last adage with her and they grinned at one another in exasperated amusement; it was a favorite of both their fathers. Kyali pressed a finger to the bridge of her nose, trying to figure out how to steer the conversation elsewhere. The things her father had told her were still settling in her head, and thinking of them made her heart pound. "Nothing we haven't both heard a thousand times before," she finished.

Green eyes met hers for a long moment, penetrating.

"There was somewhat more than that, Kyali Elliana Cor-wynall. You're unsettled. What?"

Damn. So much for the benefits of a straight face. For all her claims to the contrary, Taireasa had an unerring talent for sniffing out the heart of a matter and pecking away at it until she got what she wanted. Keeping secrets from her was like trying to dam a river with bread.

"You'll make a very decent queen indeed," Kyali sighed.

"*Ky*."

"Oh, *all right*. We discussed the Gift, which I do seem to have now. The… prophecy, or whatever it is. The West. The man I killed, and what he was doing there. Father was a bit more foreboding than usual. I don't want to talk about it now. I'm still sorting it out."

Taireasa was silent, thinking.

Eairon's old rhyme, stripped of all the innocence of child-hood, sat between them like a third presence. Kyali looked to-ward the wide expanse of the river, unable to meet Taireasa's sharp gaze.

"Ah," Taireasa finally said, and stopped there.

"*Ah* yourself. What point is there in worrying? It will come or it won't. Father seems to think it will. So I'll keep studying. Shall I single-handedly hold off barbarian hordes from the lands over the mountains?"

"I don't think that's required. My father is aware, and, one supposes, taking precautions."

"I hope so. Gods. Why couldn't this century be as quiet as the last few? And when did you become so gloomy? I thought you'd be thrilled I'm wearing this wretched frilly dress."

Taireasa had dimples, which were very much in evidence at the moment. "It *is* becoming. Though I figured it would be better not to mention it, somewhat like salt in a wound?"

"Fie. My favorite is ruined, thanks to Lord Alusyn of Arumilia, who had not the courtesy to bleed decently on the floorboards. Prophesy or no, I'm not so ignorant of court fashion I'll go wandering about covered in the blood of my enemies."

There was that wide-eyed gaze she'd been hoping for. It was a bad day indeed when she couldn't shock Taireasa. "Ky, that's horrible."

"Isn't it?"

They wandered along the bank of the Sainey in silence, followed at a discreet distance by Taireasa's mounted escort. Kyali closed her eyes, letting the sounds of forest and river wash over her, and found some peace for the first time since a man had run himself onto her sword.

She said nothing when Taireasa linked arms with her, willing to be a child for this brief bright afternoon, sure in her heart that there were few opportunities left for doing so.

Dinner was unusually quiet that night.

Kyali kept her eyes on her plate and wondered if all the crops would be as dry: Cook had clearly struggled to make this palatable. She thought she tasted both butter and wine, not things one would normally expect to be in a barley stew. All the farmers were suffering for the lack of rain.

It would be different on the mountain, where there were

almost always clouds. Cooler, and windier, and probably rainier. Did they even grow crops on the mountains, or did they just hunt? Her father's first lieutenant had told her once that they did, that the mountain Clans cut great flat stretches like stairs into the very earth—but Deryn had also tried to convince her that they made magic with their swords, which was just mad, so he might have been having her on.

She supposed she'd find out soon enough.

She glanced up, mouth full of stew and sour unease, and was caught in her father's stare from across the table. His eyes narrowed. Kyali froze, feeling a chill twist up her spine. He gave a barely perceptible nod.

Devin's gaze darted between them. He frowned, and a spoon slid from the table to the floor. The general transferred the narrow-eyed look to his son.

"A little more control would be prudent, I think."

"I try."

"Try harder. The last time you played the flute, we lost another window. Do you think glass grows in the fields?"

"I haven't got anyone to teach me," Devin said reasonably. "The last tutor you sent me to made me eat flower petals and told me all I needed to do was *plant the magic in the earth*, for the gods' sakes. I think he was actually a confused farmer. If that's the best the kingdom can offer in the teaching of magic, we're in trouble." He took a bite, waving his fork lazily in his sister's direction. "Wait till Kyali comes into her own. Then you can blame us both for the broken glass."

"I doubt she'll break glass with her Gift."

"What, then, iron? Bones? The hearts of swooning noblemen from here to Madrassia?" Devin brightened, warming to this speculation. "Do you suppose she'll call lightning from the skies?"

Their father seemed to find this subject interesting in spite of Devin's gleeful foolishness. They both looked at her thoughtfully, in identical poses of contemplation, and Kyali rose and plucked the spoon off the floor, escaping to the kitchen.

Useless. Devin's voice, trained by years of singing, carried easily.

"I expect you'll have to bring some dried-up old wizard from the provinces here to keep her from bringing the house down around our ears. It will be a nice change of pace. I can offend him with bawdy lyrics and Kyali can frighten him into an attack of nerves hacking about with that chipped hunk of steel. Perhaps we can even invite some of the cousins in for some *real* sport. I haven't seen Bran and Conall and Bryce in years."

"There won't be a wizard, at least not one to come here. You're both well beyond the hedge-witches. And the last time that lot was here, you disarranged half a battalion."

Kyali shut their voices out, concentrating on her plans. It would be a long walk to the mountains, and horses were too precious to take one. Gods knew she wouldn't miss the hard-mouthed, spiteful gelding she'd been stuck with for the last year; walking seemed peaceful next to that gait. She wouldn't need much. A pack with bread and cheese, her practice sword and a few daggers. She would wear her leather armor under a peasant's dress and hide the sword in the skirts. It was a pretense she had managed more than once, couriering messages in secret in her father's service.

She debated leaving a note and decided against it. There was little she could think of to say, and her father clearly knew enough to tell where she had gone. And there was nothing at all she could say to Taireasa. Just thinking of that made her throat hurt, a hard lump of self-pity that she swallowed fiercely. She couldn't afford such things anymore: they belonged to children, and she was, after tonight, on her own path.

Whatever that was.

"What say you, sister mine?" Devin shouted from the dining room, conveniently interrupting a chain of thought that was beginning to tend toward panic. "Will you make the ground tremble or burn the forest down?"

"Leave me out of this," she hollered back.

Their father finally raised his own voice, sounding dryly annoyed. "Keep shouting, the both of you, and we will likely have one or the other."

Devin's generous laughter rang out, and in the kitchen Kyali felt that ache come back to her chest, a perilous slide toward sentimentality that she smothered in a reach after a wine bottle. Her father cast her a sardonic glance as she emerged and set it on the table.

"No goodbyes for your family? That seems cold."

Devin's laughter came to halt so abruptly she had to fight an unwilling smile, bowing her head to hide it. For a long, uncomfortable moment, nobody spoke. Their father calmly poured the wine for the three of them, the clink of glass the only sound in the house. Kyali looked up, feeling that dratted heat in her eyes undoing all her efforts at poise.

"There seems no use for them," she said. "You already know, and you would have guessed anyway."

Devin exploded, slapping both palms on the table edge. "I knew—I *knew* it! Where are you going this time, you secret-loving little wretch? I *hate* it when you two do this. Damn you both. Kyali, you're as bad as he is."

The general leaned and righted an empty water pitcher. "She's going to the mountains, a course you've suggested often enough yourself. Sit down."

"I will not sit down!"

"I sent to the Fraonir yester-eve." Her father turned a bland face to her as he collected several forks on their way to the floor. "You'll be meeting a party on the road, I expect."

Several comments sprang to mind. She bit them back with an effort. "Aye," Kyali said tensely, almost as outraged as Devin was now.

"Aye! Aye, she says!" Devin snapped. "How long have these plans been going on under my nose?"

"I imagine it's about two days, boy, roughly since a young man died on the point of your sister's chipped hunk of steel. I would have thought a Bard would be a bit more observant."

"Well, I'm not one yet, am I?"

"If you're waiting for the affirmation of the court before you learn to marry your mind to your mouth, it will be some few years. Do us all a grace and get an early start."

"*Enough*, you two. Father, don't make this worse, we're running out of cups again. Gods bless."

Devin made an inarticulate sound of frustration and wilted back into his chair. The general merely raised an eyebrow. Then the table itself shivered and they all eyed it warily. "Don't break a single cup, Devin," their father murmured.

Her brother sighed and rested his head in a hand with a look of intense concentration. Kyali sipped at the wine and watched him as he recovered. "The countryside will be remarkably free of bandits along your path, I imagine," he said mildly, which was Devin at his absolute worst, and the wise braced when they heard that tone from him. "When are you going?"

Kyali met his eyes, cautious.

Her brother blinked once. "Not tonight, then, is it? Gods, stay till morning, at least get a decent breakfast in you."

"Mmm, and leave under the fieldhands' watchful stares. Why don't I just have it proclaimed?"

"I could write a song about it."

Devin's eyes did not change color, announcing his state of mind to the world. *His* mother had been a quiet, un-magical baron's daughter, unlike her own. She glared across the table at him, and their father cleared his throat.

"It's settled. Enough bickering. Devin, you know perfectly well why she's going and if you'd use half the wit you were born with, you'd know why it has to be now. Don't throw anything, and if we lose so much as another cup, you'll muck stalls till dawn. Kyali. *Kyali.*"

She moved only her eyes, keeping her brother in her periphery. "Don't hit him," was all their father said, dry as a bone. "I'm going to see to the horses."

He left with admirable indifference. Devin watched him go and then blew a slow breath out, staring fire at her. Kyali held his gaze, feeling the heat in her eyes ruin all her effort at keeping her face schooled.

"I can be just as stubborn as you, sister."

"I don't doubt it. It's my practicality you're lacking, not pig-headedness."

"Oh, I can be practical enough when I want."

Crockery was in danger. Again. And she was having a difficult time keeping the smile off her face. "We should be past such things by now. Aren't you supposed to be the eldest? Act like it now and then. It would be far more shocking than any of your feeble pranks, I assure you."

"Ah, but this is so entertaining. And you shrieked like a banshee when you saw those spiders, don't deny it."

"Sad to be reliving past glories at seventeen, brother."

They leaned back at the same time, never looking away—one didn't, with Devin in this mood. Not twice, anyway.

"Changeling," her brother accused, unoriginally. "Síog child, with your hair and your sparking eyes and your sword, you belong in some bedtime faery tale... yes, I do think I could make a very *nice* ballad out of you. Ought I? Would you enjoy that?"

She blushed in spite of herself, and he smirked.

"And what does that make *you*, I wonder?" she retorted. "An ogre, perhaps."

"The storyteller, of course. Silly girl."

"Court jester, rather." The insult brought a matching flush to Devin's cheeks. She *did* smile this time. Devin grinned back at her, all teeth, and Kyali braced both feet under the table and eased the chair back as her brother toyed with his wineglass in an obvious parody of disinterest.

"A wandering mendicant," she suggested, to have it over with—and ducked under the table as Devin launched himself over it without warning. She heard glass break (mucking stalls it was, and never did a brother deserve it more) and scrambled on her knees for the other side as Devin tried to untangle himself from her chair, cursing and laughing. His hand closed over her ankle. She kicked. He pulled. She slid backwards, inadvertently gathering carpets. By now, she was laughing too hard to fight, and emerged breathless and sneezing in a rumpled mess of rugs and dust.

Devin leaned against the chair and wiped at his eyes, shoulders shaking with silent hilarity. "I ought to give you a sound thrashing for that," he declared, grinning at her outrage. "Alas, I'm not completely certain I'd win. Now that I have your undivided attention, dear sister: *what* is our father talking about?"

"As if you could!" Kyali struggled back to her knees, spitting grime and horsehair, her hair having escaped its braid to fly in her face as it always did when freed. "Devin," she said, trying not to struggle too obviously for breath. "What do you think that man was doing in our cellar? I killed *Alusyn of Arumilia*, brother mine, not some common thief. It's not going to go unnoticed."

"I just assumed he was looking for Father's maps, or the House heirlooms, or some such." His wry glance made a jest of the words. House Corwynall held lands and arms as old as the kingdom itself; it was rich in history and nobility, but little else. Their comfort was at Crown grant, as it had been for as far back as memory went. It was how the kingdom was run: Marsadrons ruled, Corwynalls held the borders. Except for the rare times when Corwynalls ruled, and Marsadrons lived on these lands and trained the soldiery—but the barons hadn't voted a Corwynall heir to the throne in so long nobody alive remembered it happening. Her House was made for war, and Lardan was not. She huffed at the humor and wiped the hair out of her eyes.

Then Devin frowned. "Wait. Alusyn? *Alusyn*? Isn't he—"

"Baron Walderan's lackwit nephew? Yes."

Her brother paled, his customary silliness giving way to horror and a shrewd, startling cleverness. Few had seen that, and fewer still suspected it existed—more fools they. He was a Corwynall, after all, raised by a man reputed to be the most brilliant strategist the kingdom had seen in centuries.

Devin's brow furrowed deeper. He stared at her, waiting.

"I'm too young to hold my own," Kyali said, unable now to meet her brother's gaze. She found a spot on her dress and rubbed at it, until the memory of Taireasa's hands twisting silk made her cringe. "I need training. The kind no one will question and few will dare try. And a few years in the hills will cool tempers here."

"What tempers? The barons can hardly *acknowledge* that he came here, sister... do you expect duels at sunrise? No one's going to be that straightforward about it."

That was the general's son, though still a bit naïve, which she was not, after nearly a decade of study with her father and his highest officers. The weight of her isolation from all others of an age with her struck her suddenly. When she thought about it—about couriering messages to troops dressed as a peasant, about learning the sword in a way none of the soldiers did—it didn't seem ordinary at all. But she had lived like this for as long as she could remember.

And now, would she would learn to live a different way, and put all this odd teaching into practice?

She stared at the floor until she could speak past the tightness in her throat. "Precisely," she said at last: there was a quiver in her voice. "They won't."

Devin's eyes widened. "You think they'd try—you think the barons would send an assassin? No, Kyali. They—" he stopped, frowning, and sighed suddenly. "They already did. It wasn't maps at all. He was here for *you.*"

"Or you."

Devin huffed, looking startled at the thought. Kyali shrugged. "But likeliest me, yes. Father thinks so. Unfortunately, so do I."

This conversation had gotten well past what she wanted to speak of. She stood, brushing at her clothes, and righted her chair. Devin made his way back to the other side of the table and sat, absentmindedly gathering the shards of his broken wineglass.

"But why now, when—"

He stopped again, cutting off the question. His eyes were suddenly intent on hers. The silence stretched out awkwardly between them and Kyali fought a flinch that seemed to start somewhere deep inside her. The old rhyme they had both heard and disregarded all their lives was suddenly weighing down the air between them, so plainly present she could almost hear it, and, in fact, Devin's lips shaped the first few words.

He did guess it.

She raised a hand, stopping his words.

"Let's not speak of... it. Let's just say I feel that instruction with the Fraonir would be useful." Devin closed his lips over his words and silently mouthed "useful." She could almost hear the doubt. "And see that you don't get caught alone with any Westerners," she added under her breath.

They were still sitting in silence when their father came back in, carrying a sword in a plain leather scabbard. He handed it to her without ceremony. If he noticed the state of the room, or the dust in his children's hair, he gave no sign. "You'll wear it belted until they've determined you've earned the baldric, mind," he said, looking at the sword instead of at her. "I don't think you'll grow much taller, but it ought to stand you in good stead for a few years even if you do." He set a pair of daggers, sheathed and bound in a belt, atop the sword. "You'll learn these before you learn the sword, I expect."

Kyali blinked up at her father wordlessly, arms full of weapons, and he looked impatiently about the room. "Right. Bread, cheese, water… and I suggest you get out of that silken target. Wear one of the roughspuns. And put a scarf over that hair of yours."

"Are you so eager to be rid of me?"

Gold flashed briefly in his eyes, then sank like a stone in a stream. *I must learn how to do that*, Kyali thought. His hand came up and smoothed briskly over her head, dislodging a drifting cloud of horsehair. Across the table, Devin's jaw had dropped.

"You've a lot of hard work ahead of you, girl," her father said. "Now's as good a time to start as any."

3

eaves had invaded the castle in large numbers and they skirled through the halls like frightened mice, rattling and crunching underfoot. Some crunched under his feet, and Devin grimaced as the noise drew the attention of Baron Cian, who was passing by with his lady on his arm in what looked to be the direction of the great hall. He leaned back against the tapestry-covered stone wall.

Then he smiled, with conscious charm, as Cian and Alys turned to face him, stately as ships, stalling the passage of servants and guards trying to pass by.

Master Emayn would be turning the corner any minute now, out of breath and furious, and it felt like half the people in the hall were looking at him. He thought briefly of just throwing the tapestry behind him over his head and holding very still, but he'd probably choke to death on the dust it hid.

"My lord Cian," he said, bowing. "Lady Alys."

She had a lovely smile. And she looked younger than Cian

by a decade. His bow in her direction was a little lower that he'd intended, and his smile got wider and crooked as she held her hand out for him like he was a lord, instead the wayward son of one. With Cian's gimlet gaze boring a hole in the top of his head, Devin only held her hand for a moment and bowed slightly over it, though she seemed as though she wouldn't mind if he kissed it.

Get caught leaving a lady's bedroom *once* and you were added to some list at the back of everyone's minds, like a reformed thief in a treasury.

At the other end of the hall rose a commotion of raised voices and footsteps. Lady Alys craned her neck to see, retrieving her hand. Devin cast a panicked glance that way and saw Master Emayn's wispy white hair flying like a flag in a high wind above a small cluster of servants bent over a spilled bowl of apples. He sucked in a chestful of air.

"Just come from lessons, then," Cian said, not missing that.

"Ah—yes, actually. My lord, Lady Alys, if I could—"

"Would serve you right if I held you here for him to catch up to, you young rascal. What did you do to him this time?"

"Nothing, my lord!" Cian had hold of his arm; he couldn't escape now without insulting a baron, which the man clearly knew and, by the flicker of humor in his eyes, enjoyed. He met Devin's best look of innocence with a stern frown.

Emayn was closing in, robes askew, his hair wafting up wildly with every stride forward. He could move amazingly fast for such an old man. *"Devin Corwynall!"* he shouted, his wrathful voice bouncing off every stone in the walls and the ceiling, and hells, now *everyone* was looking at him.

"He just found out about the Hedgewizard's Gavotte,"

Devin said, desperate.

Cian's grip grew tighter as he looked from Devin to Master Emayn and then back. Lady Alys made a surprised sort of noise, then put one hand over her lips and began to laugh, shoulders shaking. Cian sent her an irritated look, but a grin was spreading slowly over his craggy face.

"I *knew* that was your work," the baron of Maurynim said. "Your rhymes are hard to mistake. You're going to have to face him someday, Devin."

"Indeed, my lord. Some... other day, perhaps?"

Cian snorted, but let him go. "Good luck," he grunted.

"Thank you!" Devin said fervently, and bolted as Emayn came skidding to a halt in front of Cian and Alys. Two maids carrying linens leapt aside as he barreled past. Behind him, Devin could hear Cian asking his magic tutor something about the moon phase, bless him, followed by Emayn's slightly frantic reply. He threw himself around a corner, nearly collided with a footman, and raced down the next passage that offered itself without a thought except *away*.

It turned out to be a cul-de-sac, gods help him, and Cian wasn't going to hold Emayn much longer.

Desperate, he turned, and turned again, trying to tell just from the look of the shut doors if any of the rooms' occupants would welcome a general's son with trouble on his heels. Listening hard, he heard, with a certain despair, Baron Brisham's nasal voice behind one of the doors. The words were muffled, but the anger in his tone was enough to make Devin pause.

"We shall have to... if he does not accede... for her own sake."

"There are other options."

Curiosity held him in place. He didn't recognize the other

voice, though it was easier to make out. It didn't sound like a servant, or a soldier: Brisham, rumor had it, treated his staff like unwelcome houseguests, and they spoke to him softly. This person had the tone of an equal, or at least someone who thought he was.

Baron Brisham of Sevassis province had arrived only a mere month after Kyali had disappeared into the mountains, dragging a train of attendants and cooking staff with him and kicking up a storm of gossip and confusion. Western barons came East only for the great affairs of state—none of which, so far as *he* knew, were planned for some time.

It had made his father suspicious, which in turn made Devin wary. He stepped closer and tried to listen simultaneously for Brisham's words and Emayn's footsteps.

"And what of the other one?" the baron asked.

"No sign. But we know where she has run to, my lord."

"Not good enough!"

A shout from the main corridor had him leaning away from the door: Emayn had escaped Cian and Alys.

"What was that?" Brisham snapped from inside.

Devin spun and ran, even knowing it was pointless; there was nowhere to go. His heart was pounding so hard he could feel its beats in his temples, and it had nothing—well, little—to do with his magic tutor's wrath.

Had they been talking about his sister in that room? And if so, did that mean more of the West than Baron Walderan wanted Kyali dead?

Anger grew in him, grew so fast he didn't have time to swallow it down with reason or cool it with caution. And with it, inevitably, ever since the day he'd picked up a fiddle and shattered all the windows on the first floor of his father's house, came his unruly Gift. He flinched as the tallow candles in the sconce across from him flipped out of their holders to rattle on the floor. He pressed his back to the wall on the other side of a jutting lintel, then pressed his hands to his forehead.

"Not now," he hissed.

He was in more than enough trouble already.

Emayn's steps came to a halt. There was a scrape as the door that hid Baron Brisham first unlatched and then slid open, and Devin pressed further back, hopeless as it was. He didn't think he could look Brisham in the face right now and pretend all was well. He thought he might strike the man. He was actually shaking with fury.

"Devin," came a whisper from just beside him, startling him badly. He looked around, seeing nothing, and then the tapestry to his left twitched.

What in the *hells*?

"Get in here!" the tapestry whispered fiercely.

Not about to question the provenance of such a well-timed gift, Devin flung the tapestry over himself, received a face-ful of dust, and saw Taireasa looking up at him from a shadowed space in the stone wall. She got a fistful of his doublet and yanked with unexpected strength, pulling him utterly off balance. He fell forward into a darkness that smelled of dank stone and moldering linen and Taireasa's perfume, which had lilacs in it. His face was mashed into the soft wool covering her shoulder. The princess, apparently not as embarrassed as he was by this unintended familiarity, grunted, then got a better grip on him and hauled hard. His knee scraped over a sharp lip of stone as he came sliding all the way inside.

"Close the door!"

He turned around as best he could without outright sitting on her and pushed at what turned out to be a very heavy block of wood with a veneer of stone on the outside. It swung shut in total silence. Taireasa scrambled out from under him, elbowing him in the neck in the process, and stood. The brisk rustle of cloth suggested she was brushing herself off, but it was pitch black and he couldn't see even the faintest outline of her. He sat for another moment, hearing the distant rise and fall of voices outside the wall.

Gods, it sounded like they were a league away in a cave, not within arm's reach.

Her hand closed over his collar and tugged, then moved to his sleeve as he stood. He followed her silent direction through a series of turns, one hand out to feel the crumbly smoothness of very, very old stone.

"So this is where you two hare off to," he murmured. He felt Taireasa's fingers clench over his wrist and was sorry: she still went wet-eyed and hard-jawed whenever Kyali's name was mentioned.

"They go all over the castle," she said shortly, not bothering to keep her voice down now, and she let him go to fumble after something in the dark. A moment later there was a scrape and a rattle, then flame blossomed between them, casting their shadows hugely onto walls of pale, small, close-fitted stones and crumbling mortar. She shut the lantern's door and lifted it up between them, making Devin wince at the sudden light. "We'll be near the kitchens if we keep going this way."

She knew her way around these odd tunnels very well, it seemed.

Afraid to say anything else that might upset her, he brushed at his clothes, giving her a moment to collect herself. His anger was fading, though slowly. Taireasa swept something from his shoulder and then turned, arms folding and shoulders hunching, to stare at a wall.

"*Hared*," she said, her voice low and unhappy.

"She'll come back, Taireasa. It's not forever."

"It's years, though, isn't it?"

He'd been trying not to think of it that way. "Yes," he said, sighing. "It is. Can you say it's not necessary?"

One shoulder drew up in a shrug. She didn't turn to face him. "Of course it was necessary," she muttered. "That doesn't make it fair. Who were you running from this time?" she asked, just as he was opening his mouth to say something sympathetic and probably irritating.

"Oh, Emayn."

"He found out about the song?"

"He *heard* it," Devin said mournfully and Taireasa snorted, scrubbed at her face, and finally turned around. In the uneven light of the lantern, her face looked older, and tired, and... puffy, as though she had been weeping.

"Taireasa... why are you in here?"

"Baron Brisham proposed," she said, sounding more defeated than he'd ever heard her before. It hurt him, hearing that tone from Taireasa.

She had been in his life ever since she and Kyali had met, nearly a decade ago. They had been instantly inseparable, and Taireasa had become a familiar presence at the Corwynall estate: a jumble of thin limbs, messy curls, strong opinions, and mischief, her easy laugh and brash daring the complete opposite of (and perfect match for) his quiet, arrogant, serious little sister. The two of them had been his playmates, and opponents; the victims of his pranks, and his occasional tormentors. Taireasa was like a second sister to him, and seeing her like this made him want to go back to the cul-de-sac so he could, in fact, strike Brisham right in his pompous face.

"You're *sixteen*," Devin said, and cringed at the way his voice echoed in the closeness of the tunnel.

The look she sent him was part scorn, part rueful affection. "I'm a *princess*, Devin. We do tend to marry earlier. And he suggested the wedding might take place after I'm of age."

"How generous of him," Devin growled, and had to run his hands through his hair and take several deep breaths, lest he knock the lantern over with his anger and disgust and set the place afire. He thought about telling Taireasa what he'd overheard—but she was already so upset, and really, he'd no proof, only a handful of words and a suspicion. He leaned against the wall, then remembered how the mortar had been crumbling out of it and straightened, knowing his doublet was probably already ruined. "I hope you told him you're already spoken for."

The startled flicker of her eyes lifted his spirits a bit. "To whom, pray tell."

He linked arms with her, pulling her in the same direction she'd been pulling him just a moment ago. "Why, to *me*, of course. Dashing, handsome, melodic, charming... me. How could that old vulture hope to compete with such magnificence? Just think how he'd screech if he heard you were betrothed to one of the other two heirs he's supposed to choose among when they vote for you to be queen."

Taireasa laughed and let him lead her, though they both knew he had no idea where he was going. "I believe that violates at least a few laws, not to mention the fact that they may not vote for *me*, and you well know it."

"Of course they will," Devin scoffed. "Look what their other choices are. They're hardly going to choose me or Kyali to rule the kingdom. Can you imagine? You're the king's daughter, you're sensible and wise and, most importantly, you're not a sword-brandishing, war-mad Corwynall."

"You're not particularly war-mad, Devin," Taireasa said dryly.

"Well. By association. Which will be more than enough to put the barons off me."

"Fair point," she sighed, and freed her arm to go peer down a branch of passage that looked darker than night, but smelled faintly of bread. She set the lantern down. "This one."

"Does it lead straight into the kitchens?"

There was a flash of teeth in the dimness. "Closer to the wine cellars."

"Marry me *now*," Devin begged, and she giggled, sounding much more like herself, thank the gods. "I never knew you were carrying such useful secrets. Where else do they go?"

"Oh, everywhere. Perhaps I'll spend the next few years here, creeping out to steal food after night falls."

"Gods, Taireasa, surely you told him no."

"My father did."

"And?" He felt like he was missing something and pulled her around to look her in the face. "So?"

"This is the second time he's asked," Taireasa said in a small voice.

"Tell him no again! Say it until he hears it. If he's fool enough to think—"

"You don't *know*! You've no idea how—" She waved his

words away with an angry sweep, then paced off to glare at the floor, hands on her hips. The lanternlight threw her shadow over the tunnel in pieces. "We've gotten letters from all the other barons of the West and most of the lesser Western lords supporting it. Baron Cyrnic suggested that the vote would go more smoothly if I were *settled*, Walderan said that relations with the whole West would improve... they said that I would be a better... a better... *oh*."

Taireasa put her hands to her head and breathed carefully, every line of her shouting misery and hurt. "They said I would be a better queen if I had someone with experience in matters of state to guide me."

The anger he'd gotten mostly under control leapt out of his grasp and the lantern slid a full handspan sideways and tottered, but thankfully didn't tip over. Taireasa flung it a startled glance, then him a wary one. Devin barely noticed.

"Gods damn them, then! Taireasa, you aren't considering this. Tell me you're not. King Farrell would never stand for it—and your mother would burn Sevassis to the ground first."

"But what if they're *right*?"

There was no response to that she'd hear right now, so he gave her the only one he could: he pulled her into the circle of his arms and held tight. They didn't embrace often—he might think of her as a sister, but she was still the daughter of another House, and royal, and beautiful, and rumors bred like rabbits in these halls—and she stiffened in his hold before heaving a sigh and slumping to lean on him. They stood that way for a few moments, until they were both a little uncomfortable, and then separated. Taireasa wiped her face on her sleeve.

"They're not," Devin said firmly. "They're wrong and you

know it, just as you know they're only doing this to stir up trouble and get some concession or other. Why King Farrell doesn't just raise the trade tariffs on their wine, or levy some new 'contentious bastard' tax on anyone who holds a landed title, I don't know; it would shut them all up for years, I swear."

She put a hand to her face and leaned against the crumbling wall, her shoulders shaking. It took him a moment to realize it was laughter—prudently silent, but so hard she wheezed, and flapped her free hand at him.

"*Gods*, you are your father's son," she gasped.

"Oh, come now, he'd never suggest anything so silly."

"He'd suggest it and *mean* it," Taireasa contradicted him merrily. "I take it back. You *are* a war-mad Corwynall, to the very core. Oh, dear gods, that's wonderful. Thank you, Devin."

He was still stuck on the notion of his father making such a suggestion, whether in jest or seriousness. It was hard to picture. He followed her, content to be quiet now that she had composed herself, and held the lantern when she crouched to get her ear close to another of the odd little doors that led to the rest of the castle.

He was definitely going to remember about these tunnels. Escaping Emayn would be so much easier now.

Taireasa pressed on a clever iron latch hidden in a seam and the door cracked open in total silence. She peered out, ducked quickly back in, and then peeped out again after a long moment. She tugged the handle of the lantern out of his fingers and blew it out, then set it far to the side of the door.

"Come on," she whispered, and leapt out like a cat, letting in a flicker of daylight as the tapestry covering the door flapped around her. Devin threw himself after her, then quickly leaned out of the way as she pushed past him to pull the door shut with a grunt of effort. For a moment they stood together under the tapestry, stained by the sunlight shining through its colors, dust hovering thickly between them, both of them flush with success and the hilarity of a trick accomplished well and without consequence. Devin felt a fleeting envy for Kyali, who had done this so many more times, and who probably knew so many more secrets. He'd had their cousins, childhood friends and rivals and co-conspirators in a thousand mad plots, but what his little sister had with Taireasa was something else altogether, precious and uncompromising.

No wonder Taireasa was so wounded by Kyali's leaving.

He was getting maudlin. He flapped the tapestry up and ducked out from under it, then immediately started brushing himself off, because with the daylight shining on his clothes, he could see that he looked like a sculpture of himself, made of dust and old mortar.

Taireasa strode to the end of their little hall and looked around the corner. "Let's go, then," she sighed, tucking her hand in his elbow as he joined her. "We ought to cross the kitchens, but there'll be serving staff everywhere. Much as I'd rather not, we'll have to cross the main corridor."

"Just walk like you belong," Devin suggested. This should be interesting. Her eyes were still puffy, and he looked like he'd rolled in some strange pale dirt. He hoped Brisham heard about them walking the halls this way: that would give the old bastard something to worry over.

"I always do," Taireasa said, her voice cool and amused, her court smile fixed firmly in place as they entered the main corridor and met the first of many shocked stares. "I always do."

4

Mornings were the worst.

Kyali had never thought of herself as a slugabed—her father had the household up as soon as the sun rose, a habit that had taken root in her, if not in Devin—but the Clans were up well before dawn even during the long bright days of summer. She rolled off her mat with a sigh, having grown accustomed to this over the last year, if not accepting of it, and fumbled in the dark for a comb. Her hair seemed to have wrapped itself about her face in the night. Her arms were stiff and sore—a state they had been in since the first day she'd arrived in the mountains to learn the Fraonir way of the sword—but they weren't as bad as they had been a week ago. She stretched them carefully. Around her, at a small distance, she could hear Clansfolk rising: the soft murmur of greetings, a rattle of metal, the crackle of a fire being brought back to life.

An impatient scratch at the canvas wall of her tent.

Arlen had beaten her again; he did every morning. One day, she promised herself, she was going to wake earlier than her teacher, and perhaps on that day she might even get through her lessons without doing something that made her look like an idiot.

"I'm awake," she called, pulling on her boots, trying to make that statement true.

"Not so long as you're in there and I'm out here, you're not," Arlen said dourly, sounding as though he were standing right over her. Kyali finished securing lacings, pulled her hair hurriedly into a braid, straightened her trousers out, and pushed the flap of the tent back, trying not to scowl. It was hard not to believe, like some superstitious villager, that her sword teacher could see in the dark... among other things. Arlen always seemed to suspect what was in her head, no matter what she put on her face.

Which was still better than Saraid, her teacher in the Gift, who actually *did* know what was in her head.

It had been a long year.

"Yes, I can be awake even when you can't see me," she retorted, unable to keep the edge from her voice. There was a grunt from Arlen that might have been laughter. He was a tall, broad shadow in the faint pink light of a false dawn, arms folded, the long line of a sword arching over one shoulder. Kyali smothered a yawn and bowed, one hand in a fist over her heart, the other on the hilt of her sword, which was belted at her side.

"*Landanar*," she murmured, the title of respect for a Fraonir master of the sword.

"Student," her teacher replied. "Since you're so awake, girl, you can start with the Forms, I'm sure. All of the Forms."

Oh gods. She felt her shoulders trying to slump, and stopped that.

She followed him past the main common hearth of the Da-rachim Clan, where Mathin and Marya were putting the great kettle on for porridge, to the practice clearing, which was empty and calm and filled with that soft pink light. She set her feet carefully, drew the sword, and breathed in the pattern he had shown her. Arlen came to face her at a careful distance and unsheathed his own blade.

"Begin," he said softly, and Kyali brought her arms up, muscles protesting all down her back, to trace the first of the Fraonir Forms of Sword Combat against the glassy morning sky. The point of Arlen's sword mirrored hers, barely inches away. They circled one another in slow, endless revolutions, sketching patterns in the air as they made their way through the two hundred and twelve Forms. Sweat ran into her eyes and down her neck. Her breath, coming in the rhythmic pattern that matched these movements, burned in her throat. But her mind was as clear as the perfect bowl of the sky, filled with the flash of the sword and the feel of it extending her arms.

"Enough," her teacher finally declared, looking a bit worse for wear himself. Kyali staggered backward gasping, her head humming. It took her three tries to sheathe her sword; she was trembling with exhaustion. Arlen watched, expressionless.

"Well done," he said when she had finally managed it. She looked up, certain he was mocking her sudden inability to make her wrists work, but he actually seemed pleased. "Truly," he added, seeing her disbelief. "*Well done*, Kyali. Did you think these lessons were easy? For anyone? You've mastered a great deal in one year."

Mastered? She could barely stand. She looked at her hands, which were weathered by sun and wind, and so covered with calluses they looked like a farmer's. Like they belonged to somebody else.

Arlen tipped her chin up. "No part of it's easy," he said, sympathy plain in his voice for a rare moment. "Particularly not for you."

"I... " She shut her mouth again. She couldn't think of a thing to say to that.

"You're doing well," Arlen said then, almost too quickly, as though he didn't want this discussion to go... wherever he had thought it might go. It was one of his odder habits, completely unlike his usual methodical calm, and it always left her wondering what dread Clan secrets he feared she might learn. "We can move on to the Forms for mounted combat now, I think."

Whatever expression was on her face, it made him laugh outright. "Those lessons should go faster," her teacher added, apparently meaning it as reassurance.

For one horrible, overwhelmed moment, she was afraid she was going to either shout at him or weep. She drew a slow breath, fighting to make her face still. "How many more?" she asked carefully, after a brief pause to get a firm grip on her composure.

"Oh, just sixty more for swordcraft ahorse. Were you to learn the staff or the spear as well, we'd be at this for many more years."

"Oh," Kyali said faintly. "I don't have a horse, Arlen."

"Yes, you do—you just haven't been introduced. We brought her over from the Eanin Clan a fortnight past, and she's been waiting—impatiently, I might add; you two should be a match in temperament if nothing else—for you to finish your footwork."

This had a slightly grudging tone. The Eanin were the sister Clan to the Darachim, living on the western ridge, and while the Darachim were reputed better at fighting, nobody in the world bred horses like the Eanin did. Her father had one, long ago, and still spoke of it like it had fallen from the skies in a shaft of light.

"I..."

She was at a loss for words far too often today. She scowled, then nodded, because there was nothing else to do. She'd wondered about fighting astride, but a whole new *set* of Forms seemed excessive.

"Come on," Arlen said. "We're due a breakfast, and you're due a meeting with your horse. Rest yourself, if Saraid gives you the chance. I'm taking you out on patrol this afternoon."

He turned back toward the camp on this startling declaration, leaving her to follow, and to swallow a number of useless questions. She had learned in the first week here that Arlen would only answer the unasked ones, only comment when a subject was no longer in her thoughts, and in most cases, preferred to let her stew and come to her own mistaken conclusions.

The camp was empty when they returned, all the Clansfolk out hunting deer or on patrol, guarding against outlaws and the occasional incursion by the Allaida on the northwest border, who sometimes climbed the mountains to raid. Only Saraid remained by the common hearth, sitting on a bench and finishing off a bowl of porridge. Her gray hair was so long she was practically sitting on it. Kyali fetched herself a bowl, then fetched another for Arlen, who wandered off with it to whatever else a Clan leader might have to do for the day. When he was out of sight, Kyali folded herself stiffly onto the ground, trying not to groan.

"You look done in," her other teacher murmured.

"I'm well enough."

Saraid aimed a wry and somewhat exasperated look at her and Kyali felt her shoulders draw up and her face heat. Saraid could tell a lie from a hundred paces.

"Not always," the old woman said placidly. "It's harder than you imagine, and I'm certainly not listening *all* the time. Do you not think I have better things to occupy myself with?"

Her face only got hotter. Kyali ducked her head to the porridge and ended up with far too large a mouthful. "I hope... you do," she managed to choke out. "I'd hate to think this was your only source of amusement."

Saraid's lined face twitched into a smile. "No, I've several sources, never fear. But you're a challenge, child, with your sober face and all your thoughts hidden behind it. I never could resist a challenge. Finish your porridge, now. It's new lessons all around today. I've something to show you about breath..."

If she breathed any harder, she was going to faint. Wouldn't that be mortifying?

Kyali shifted, wishing she could have sat on a blanket, or one of the folding canvas chairs the Fraonir favored—or her own cloak, for that matter. The crackle of a small campfire teased her ears, but no warmth found her skin. There was snow on the air this morning, a cold bite that clouded her breath and stung her cheeks, and the cloak was a comfort. But there were small rocks on the ground here, and the harder she tried to concentrate, the more they made themselves known. The cloak would have served better under her, rather than on her.

Maybe this was Saraid's new tactic: discomfort. They had already managed confusion, frustration, and exhaustion.

Magic, she was perpetually discovering, was both easier and much harder than it was made to sound by the inept court wizards of her childhood, who had only their books of philosophy and history to offer. Easier, because among the Fraonir it was actually possible; harder because it was *work*. And harder because every tiny success was accompanied by a blinding headache. Though Saraid promised that would fade, with time and practice.

The wizards' lessons seemed even more pointless up here, where calling birds, or summoning gusts of wind, or hearing thoughts, or telling an arrow where to fly, or any of the other myriad little Gifts that cropped up among the Clans, seemed commonplace.

Memory dragged her mind from the task: sitting despondent at a table in Faestan castle, a book of theory open in front of her and Master Emayn droning on about the structure of the world. Taireasa making hideous, hilarious faces every time the old man turned his back—and finally flinging a handful of stolen goosefeathers into the hearth so that the flames flared high and the smell drove them all out of the room.

Gods. She was never going to get anywhere with this if she couldn't manage to concentrate.

"Kyali. Open your eyes."

She did, prepared to see that slight crinkle between Sara-id's brows that meant she was doing poorly. Instead she saw fire, red and gold and blurrily close, as though without moving she had somehow come nearer to the shallow pit. She squint-ed. Her eyes watered. A line of flame snaked toward her hand where it rested on her knee, and she watched it uncompre-hending; held her breath, foolishly, as though a bird had come to land on her. It touched her skin. There was no pain.

She hadn't come closer to the fire. It had come closer to *her*.

"Saraid..." Her voice was wobbly and rough. She bit it off.

"*Shhhh.*" Her magic tutor knelt close, her face soft in the glow of the fire. Her eyes were wide and wondering. "Oh, child," Saraid murmured. "No wonder this makes your head hurt so. What a thing."

"So this isn't—" She couldn't hold it. The pain in her head was making her queasy. The fire in her hand became smoke and blew away with the cold wind, and Kyali slumped forward to press at her temples. Saraid's cold hand landed on her neck, began to rub at the knotted muscles there.

"No, Kyali" she said. "It's not common. It's not even been heard of, what you just did—not for many long years. As you've guessed."

"What am I supposed to *do* with it?" Kyali asked, pain pitch-ing the words too high.

She could feel Saraid's shrug through the old woman's fin-gertips. "Whatever you have to. For now, we work at it, until doing this doesn't make you fall over. Do you think you can stand to try again?"

No answers, as usual. That, the Fraonir had in common

with the theory-mad wizards of Lardan. Kyali straightened.

"I guess we'll find out," she muttered.

She had thought, in those first few panic-filled weeks among the Fraonir, that walking on the edge of a mountain path was the most frightening thing she had ever done. The land seemed to leap away from one's feet. The tops of trees looked like shrubs. A pebble could fall for what must surely be hours before striking ground—and surely, so too might one muscle-sore, travel-weary general's daughter standing too close to the edge and trying to hide the fact that she was shivering.

Riding on a mountain path was far worse.

Riding a mountain path on a headstrong mare determined to test her rider's will was *terrifying*.

"I don't think..." Kyali swallowed a mortifying yelp and reined hard left as Ainhearag's hooves crumbled dirt at the edge. "I... damn it!" This as her horse bounced at a chipmunk in a tree and shied back toward the drop.

Kyali drew a breath that seemed at once too small and too large for her chest, then let it out slowly. Then she pressed a knee into Ainhearag's side and tugged once, sharply, on the reins. Her fractious Fraonir gift bucked gently—she *did* yelp this time, damn it all—then settled into the pretense of good behavior.

"I don't suppose," she finished, groping for her lost dignity, though it was probably halfway down the mountain by now, "that we might try her gait in the trees."

Her teacher said nothing. After a frowning moment, Kyali

turned back to where Arlen was riding behind her and found him laughing, silently but quite hard, into a hand.

She turned back around and kicked her horse into the trees.

She used too firm a heel. Ainhearag took the order with enthusiasm, bolting up the slope and into a thick copse of mountain pine before Kyali had a chance to choose a proper point of entry. In another second she was shielding her face from a hundred pine boughs, branches breaking all about her, as her horse forged a way through by main force. Between the two of them, they sounded like an army of sots lost in a forest.

After a brief struggle they came to a halt. Kyali sighed and stared at the pommel of the saddle.

"Interesting tactic," Arlen said, his cool, uninflected voice somehow compounding the disdain in his words. He and his own warhorse, Itairis, had come up on them almost silently. "I'm sure any outlaws camping in the vicinity are long gone now."

Was it possible to blush harder than this? She met Arlen's eyes with difficulty, hissing at Ainhearag when her horse made a reach after a branch. "I apologize," she said, bowing in the saddle.

"Words are well enough, girl. Words are easy. *Show* me you can do better."

Footwork began to seem pleasant compared to this.

Kyali bit her lip and turned her horse into deeper forest, sitting gingerly in the saddle, braced for Ainhearag's next disastrous attempt at mischief. She couldn't afford such foolishness out here, away from the safety of the Darachim borders, out where outlaws and raiders made their temporary homes. They rode forward, quieter, and she met every twitch of Ainhearag's reckless head with a twitch of the reins and a shifting of her seat. It was exhausting, particularly riding through dense woods—but after what felt like hours of struggle, her horse heaved a heartfelt sigh and began to obey without argument.

Kyali let out a sigh of her own and stretched muscles knotted tight. "What now?" she murmured.

There was no reply.

"Arlen?"

It was too quiet.

Turning in the saddle gave her a view of trees: endless, crowded trees... and no teacher.

Panic and annoyance shot through her in equal parts, banishing all her weariness. She opened her mouth to shout for him, but thought better of that and instead urged Ainhearag aside quickly, pointing them into deeper cover. There they came to a halt.

It was no doubt one of Arlen's lessons—he had ambushed her far too many times in the last year, until now her nerves twitched at every unexpected noise and shadow—but it was impossible to tell. She'd been too focused on her horse. She couldn't even remember when she'd stopped hearing Itairis's careful hooves behind them. And this was not a place to make assumptions of safety.

Ainhearag had gone still and tense in response to her own tension. They stood, listening to the wind whisper through the leaves. Far off, birds chattered at one another, but Kyali heard none around her.

She drew her sword.

She didn't question why. It was an act as necessary as breath, and every nerve in her was insisting on it. As soon as its comforting weight was balanced in her hands, Ainhearag shifted to a wider, more dangerous-feeling stance and turned one white-rimmed eye back toward her rider.

"Easy," Kyali murmured, listening hard. "Be easy."

Far off, a branch snapped. Closer, the bushes rustled.

She took a slow breath, willing herself calm, and pressed Ainhearag gently forward. Then the brush *behind* them spoke and she hissed a curse and kicked her horse into a run, not questioning that instinct either. Ainhearag bolted forward. Branches whipped into her face and eyes. Suddenly, a bow seemed like a very useful weapon.

Behind and all around them, the woods were coming alive.

Ainhearag launched into a full gallop and Kyali leaned forward, pressing her face to a neck wet with sweat and lively with straining, moving muscle. In their wake she could hear an increasing din of feet and hooves and shouts.

She'd sprung something, gods help her, and there was no telling even now if it was one of Arlen's surprises, but she was dreadfully afraid it wasn't. Arlen might, in fact, be caught in it.

Ainhearag made for the thinning edge of the deep woods, her powerful neck stretched completely out and her ears back. Kyali spared a single thought toward the possibility that they were about to run off a cliff, but it was impossible to turn or to stop: it sounded like at least fifteen men behind her, several of them mounted.

"Gods!" she gasped as the daylight hit her full in the face. Something whined past her ear; something else struck her leather-armored shoulder with numbing force, and she understood that whoever they were, *they* had bows, damn it all.

It wasn't a lesson. It was an ambush, and it was deadly.

She heard something else then, something worse—the rattle and ring of steel being pulled from sheaths—and she set her heels into Ainhearag's sides. Allaida: It had to be a party of Allaida that had gotten well inside the Fraonir's defenses. No band of outlaws, however well-organized, would be so armed.

"Raiders!" Kyali cried to any Fraonir who might be in earshot as they broke from the trees and Ainhearag's hooves struck rock.

The first man came alongside. She saw the horse first and then his short sword flashed in her vision and all she saw was sky: she had flattened herself backwards without even knowing that she was going to try such a mad move. Her horse's flanks roiled under her shoulders. Her arms came up, again without her conscious direction. A jolt like a thunderbolt rattled up to her shoulders and steel sang out as his blade went flying free from his grip. He shouted and went down, then she was past him and Ainhearag was shouldering another man aside.

Kyali sat up, saw a party ahorse breaking cover from the other side of the clearing, and felt an icy inevitability sink into her belly. She gripped her sword, thinking bleakly of Taireasa, of Devin, of everything she was to do that would, after today, have to be done by somebody else. She set her feet more firmly in the stirrups and kicked Ainhearag toward that advancing group, meaning to carve a path through them if she could— and then realized, as they grew closer and their dun-and-green tunics, the swords and bows over their shoulders, became clear, that she was looking at a Darachim patrol.

It was a *rescue.*

"Blessed gods," she whispered. She leaned down once more, pressing her face to Ainhearag's warm, wet coat. The Allaida were losing ground—nothing could be faster than this wonderful horse of hers, now that she had her head. The Darachim spread out, making room for her. Kyali got the reins in one hand and wheeled Ainhearag wide around as they met.

"Fine company you keep, sword student," one of the rangers shouted—it was hard to tell who, as they all wore mottled green cloth over their faces. Kyali nodded grimly, heart still pounding with terror... and with something else, something she'd only felt once before, struggling with an assassin in her father's cellar. A fierce, cold anger beat in her breast, urging her forward, her and her horse and her sword, to meet the enemy. She'd heard soldiers speak of such things happening in battle, but she'd never looked to know such a thing herself.

She wasn't sure she liked it.

She wasn't sure she didn't, either.

And it didn't matter right now. All that mattered was the messy charge of Allaida pelting toward them, their cavalry, such as they were, nearly running down the infantry as they rushed forward.

"This ought to be interesting," somebody muttered—it sounded like Donel—which was when Kyali realized there were only five rangers and herself to face this onslaught. She felt a breathless terror grip her insides, and then that cold, angry part of her mind noted how spread out the Allaida were, how weak their line was.

"Form up!" she blurted, and got several bewildered looks. The Allaida were almost on them, and she wasn't with her father's soldiers, who knew how to meet an enemy on open ground. The Fraonir fought in the trees, a quieter sort of warfare that tended toward ambush. *This* encounter was going to be far more like what her father's officers had taught her about.

Oh gods, this was not how she'd imagined her first battle happening.

"You—" Kyali pointed at the nearest ranger. "To my right and back a pace. You, on my left. You three, behind us, staggered like—yes, like that! We can break their line if we—"

No more time.

Kyali urged her horse forward, shuddering, trying to gain momentum before that scattered line hit. Behind her, she could hear the rangers following. Then she was in the midst of the enemy's line, horses and men screaming. She planted herself and swung her sword in a twisting arc, felt the impact of a spear rattle her all the way to the teeth, the ringing jolt of a blow on her arm. She ducked, swung, struck something that gave—and was suddenly through, with a small knot of Fraonir rangers crowding close around, their swords bloodied.

"Left, flank them left!" Kyali barked, seeing the weak point, not allowing herself to think about what she was doing, or the fact that she could keep riding east and maybe escape this madness. She wheeled her mare left instead, heading back into the Allaida, who were beginning to turn, having realized their line had broken.

Amazingly, the rangers came with her.

Kyali ducked under the sweep of a blade. Ahead, a man in mismatched plate armor shouted orders and she kicked Ainhearag into a run, breathing through clenched teeth. He turned and flung his sword up just as she reached him and the impact nearly threw her from the saddle. A streak of fire raced up her cheek. She shook her head, swung her sword. His weapon slid off the angle of her blade, a perfect demonstration of

Arlen's careful teaching.

Then he pulled a second, shorter sword from a saddle sheath, and suddenly she was parrying two blades. Ainhearag stumbled, driven sideways by another horse. The Allaida leader grinned. Blood was flowing down her face. Spinning her sword in wild loops, the pommel burning the skin of her palms and that cold, clear fury burning her eyes, Kyali kneed Ainhearag even closer.

Both his blades came down, right at her head, crossed like daggers. She yelled—she couldn't help it—and caught them where they crossed in the quillions of her crossguard.

For a second, his eyes met hers on the other side of that tangle of blades. Then she heaved and he went flying out of the saddle, looking almost comically startled. One of his own men trampled him. Kyali looked away with a grimace as his scream cut short. A ranger—was it Birgit?—came beside her, blood dripping from a nasty gash above her ear. The ranger shouted something. Ears ringing, Kyali shook her head, and the woman pulled her facecloth down.

"What now?" Birgit shouted. Kyali could only stare, appalled that anyone should be looking to *her* for direction. One desperate idea did not a commander make. Before she could voice her outrage, they were overrun by three more Allaida, and as she brought the sword up yet again—it had blood on it now—a plan formed in her head with all the imperative suddenness of a bolt of lightning.

"To the trees, run for it! And draw your bows!" Kyali bellowed, trying to make herself heard above the clamor. "I'll draw them behind!"

Birgit turned her horse and sped off in that direction with

never a word of question or protest. The rest of the rangers raced after her.

Kyali fended off a poorly wielded staff, unhorsed another wild-eyed raider. Probably she should take her own orders now. But she needed to be sure, first, that she would be followed. The enemy had taken losses, and looked to be losing enthusiasm for this argument. Squelching the panic that wanted to fly up out of her throat, Kyali turned her horse into the edge of the milling group of Allaida and whipped her sword out sideways, so the flat of the blade struck one man in the face.

"Cowards!" she shouted, and wheeled around toward the trees. *"Run,"* she whispered desperately in her horse's ear. Ainhearag replied instantly, her great hooves thundering against the ground.

The Allaida, what remained of them, came after her.

Kyali kept her head down as they broke through the treeline. She reined her horse sharply to the side as they hit deeper cover and clung on desperately as Ainhearag banked like a hawk, dodging trees by such a narrow margin that Kyali felt bark scrape her knees. She risked a glance up, saw a boot dangling from a branch at eye level, and put her head back down. Behind her there was a wild crunch and crackle as the remains of the Allaida band launched themselves headlong into the trees.

Then the sudden, deadly music of bowstrings.

It got very quiet after that.

Ainhearag slowed when she sat back in the saddle, but didn't stop. Kyali didn't argue. It didn't sound like anybody was following now—Fraonir were lethal archers—but she'd had enough of being chased for a lifetime. If her horse want-

ed to wander all the way down the mountain, she would ride
along gladly right now.

Ainhearag had no such plans, though, and slowed again,
breathing in anxious whuffs. Sweat foamed on her dark coat.
Kyali reined her to a stop and dismounted, then had to lean
against that great heaving side and hold onto the saddle: her
knees were wobbling so badly she was afraid she would fall.
Her sword was still stuck in one trembling fist. She pulled a
soft square of cloth out of her pocket and cleaned it standing
braced against Ainhearag, trying to slow her pulse. When she
felt like she could stand on her own, she sheathed the blade
and looked her horse in one white-rimmed eye.

"Thank you," she said. Ainhearag whuffed again and lipped
at her fingers hopefully. And then her big head rose, nostrils
flaring anxiously.

Kyali had the sword out in a heartbeat. She could see how badly she was shaking in how the blade threw sunlight everywhere.

"You did well," a familiar voice said, and Kyali lowered the
sword. A cry tried to claw its way out of her chest. She looked
away, breathing hard, and swallowed it.

"Did we lose anyone?" she asked instead, and was pleased
at how steady her voice sounded.

"Birgit took a hard knock on the head, Moiren has a gash
on one leg that will need stitching, and Evan will lose the use
of his arm for several weeks."

Arlen emerged from the cover of trees, and Kyali started
at the sight of his face: bruised and bloodied, with scrapes all
down one side. He smiled, seeing her shock. "Aye, girl, did you
think I'd left you to fend off the largest band of raiders we've
seen in months by yourself? No. I heard them before you—*well*

before you, I might add—and went to deal with them. I'd no notion there would be so many." He rubbed his head ruefully, then cast her a sharp, shrewd look. "There are none now."

She'd guessed that much. She only nodded, wordless, seeing once more the blood on her sword, the startled expression on the Allaida captain's face, the splintering line of them rushing at her. She started to shake again, and hid that shameful fact by folding her arms and staring at the toes of her boots.

"Well," Arlen said, after a long awkward moment in which he was clearly waiting for her to speak. "It's a relief. I can't teach you battle tactics for the field, as we don't fight that way, but your father seems to have that well in hand. Our way is saner, to my mind—this lining up and running at one another with weapons out looks like madness—and I can teach you that. It seems I ought to. You've a head for strategy. We'll put you on patrol in the evenings, student mine. You'll command a party of eight."

More lessons, always more lessons. These might get her killed.

She might get someone *else* killed.

Kyali bit her tongue, took another deep breath, and nodded.

O fae sword-wielding wanderer,

Orin festers in the hot season, who would have guessed it of a seahold? But the salt mists hang over everything like gloom: gloom made me think of you, and so here I sit, frustrating yet another useless court wizard. I trust whatever dread secrets you are learning, they hold more interest than the Nature of the Elements does for me. I am half asleep, and the old man knows it.

This is the third white-beard Her Imperious Duchessness Armelle has inflicted on me—she seems convinced persistence will prevail where wisdom has failed. Much like the other two, this man could not carry a tune had he a wagon and a team of horses. The last left weeping when I played "Pass the Cup." Whether his ears were more offended by the lyrics or the breaking of his glass (and every other in the room) remains a question for the ages.

I did write a song about you, by the by, which Orin's heirs find quite amusing. I look forward to your return, if only to see your face *when you find the Third Battalion singing it in three-part harmony to welcome you home.*

Father rides the border endlessly, and has taken to uttering cryptic grunts and stalking off whenever your name is spoken. Taireasa, I am told, pines and plays delicate court lady, a development that has kicked up suspicion throughout the city as we all wait for her to curse in formal hall, sneak sheep into the solarium, or shove Lainey down the nearest well. Wagers have been made, and King Farrell himself bet on the sheep, so I hear.

—I, of course, miss you not at all, you fire-haired, mad little wight.

mighty glass-breaking minstrel,

Where I stand, a pleasantly cool breeze is stirring the leaves. This mountain is so tall Caerwyssis is visible on the line of the sea in the distance, with an odd, dirty smudge on one edge...

Why, that must be you.

Shut your eyes and think of me looking down on you while I enjoy this lovely cool wind. I am certain that will help, as imagining you festering in the company of sullen old men has done wonders for my mood, brother.

The guard who delivered this has betrayed you: there is no song. I have never yet told of your midnight adventure with a certain well-born wife at the city towers, and surely you don't think I've forgotten. I feel fairly safe from your verse for the nonce, Devin Corwynall. And you have been sighted courting no less than half a dozen farmgirls this last year: shall I be aunt, I wonder, to any by-blows ere I return?

I look forward to hearing the list of offenses you have committed, by-blows or no. They are not a quiet folk I live with, but no one here has your bent for mayhem, and I find, oddly, that I was accustomed to a certain amount of turmoil.

Place a bet in my name on Her Highness cursing in hall. The sheep will be in summer pasturage, and Lainey is too wily to step near wells or I'd have drowned her long since.

—I don't miss you either, you cross-eyed village idiot.

Kyali flattened the parchment against a gust and looked up at the hazy clouds. It was possible, barely, to imagine the sea, but not the weathered stone of Caerwyssis castle, which she had only seen twice in her entire life.

Devin's face, his wry grin and the wicked light in his eye, came far easier. Taireasa she rarely allowed herself to picture; it hurt too much.

The soldier eyed her sidelong as she penned the letter, a half-rotted log serving for a writing desk and a crow's pinion for a quill—it had to look bizarre, but the man seemed not to notice. He was a regular, a face known to her, but his name escaped her. She searched for it in vain, wanting a warmer address for the courier who had brought her this gift. Every season or so, a man from the Third Battalion arrived; she had no doubt her father was well-informed on her progress. She wondered what they told him.

"Seal it when you reach the villages," she suggested finally, giving up on the name, and rolled the parchment. He took it with a bow, somber and watchful, not much older than she.

"Regards from your father, lady," he murmured.

"Give mine to him," she said dryly. "How stands the border? The capital? Is there other gossip of note that doesn't involve my brother?"

He gave a flicker of a smile—Devin was beloved by the troops, among whom his misadventures were legend—but his eyes were grave. "Quiet, lady," the guard (Ranan, his name was. Hah!) said after a pause. Under her stare, he blinked once and rubbed an amulet about his neck—a mother's gift to a soldier, a luck-piece. The gesture told her what he didn't and a sinking feeling filled her belly. "An odd quiet," he added then, seeing that she had seen. "But not so a man could put a finger on it. The countryside's uneasy. The border's well manned, m'lady, on both sides; nothing's come through but the barons, and they don't stop for nothing."

He meant it as reassurance. She took it otherwise, putting it with Devin's scant news of their father, and kept the worry from her face with effort. "Thank you, Ranan," Kyali said, and saw, out of the corner of her eye as she turned back to the cloud-hazed view, the look of the fieldhands in his sober blue eyes. "Stay a night if you wish—the Darachim will find you room, I am sure."

"I ought to get back, m'lady. The general, he wanted haste. He's hungry for news of you, if I could say."

It made her smile, and made her throat ache. "A meal at least, then."

"Aye, lady," he agreed, and bowed at the edge of her vision. She kept her face turned toward the sky, not wanting to see that look again. When he had gone, she turned toward the trees, to wait for Arlen and the next lesson in an endless progression.

The wood had never seemed more peaceful, the peace never more fragile.

Taireasa watched her hands. Fine-boned, they were perfect by court standards, but for the fact that they constantly wound themselves into any nearby cloth, wrinkling the tailor's masterpieces and drawing the avid attention of every lord, lady, pageboy, maid, and guard. All surely believed they could read the fortunes of the ruling House in the nervous twist of royal fingers.

With an effort of will, she transferred her attention to the couples on the floor. They danced in her honor: she was seventeen today, newly confirmed, consecrated, and anointed as the official heir of House Marsadron. *Implied* heir to the throne.

Never mind that it went so smoothly only because the two other candidates for succession were not present: one had taken a suspiciously well-timed holiday to Orin, and the other had hied herself off to the Fraonir in secret not two years past, and had not been heard from since.

She straightened her fingers, smiling at the twirling petticoats, the flushed faces. Though her hands were still beyond her governance, in the years since Ky's abrupt departure, she had at least learned to manage her expression.

More useful to carry a sword, she thought dourly.

The past two years had seen a steady swell in the ranks of the Western lords that visited the capital. They wandered the halls, complained about their residences, and drove the cooks to distraction with demands that never seemed to be satisfied. They spoke out of turn when her father held court and spread rumors in the town that panicked the markets. More than one had asked for her hand in marriage repeatedly, as though her politely phrased refusals were no real answer.

And they watched—mostly that. They watched and whispered among themselves.

Just dance endlessly with that prig Anders, Devin had written in his last note, when she had sent him a long, despondent letter. *He'll make you both looks fools* (true: Anders couldn't put a foot right under threat of death) *and all their ire will be aimed at him for a fortnight.*

Someone who knew less of Devin might miss the shrewdness of that advice. It was a pity she couldn't take it.

She missed him, missed his outrageous humor and his steady, if occasionally maddening, presence—missed feeling like she had a brother to watch her back, to laugh with her and at her, and see the things that escaped her.

Mostly, though, she missed hiding in the servants' secret passages with his sister, who Devin insisted sent her love by letter—but Kyali would never say such a thing, even if she did mean it. And if it hurt too much for her to write, surely it hurt Kyali too, who had been left with as little choice in the matter as she—and, if she knew Ky, had dodged a leave-taking because she hated to weep in front of people.

I am not angry, she would write, if she could only find the courage to. *I was. But you were right to leave the way you did. I would only have come with you had I known, and I have no Gift of my own, nor can wield a sword. Either would serve me better than this ridiculous dress does, or the careful words I hardly dare utter to these barons.*

But gods, Kyali, I miss you so.

Pointless to think of it; it only made her hands clench, drawing more of the attention she worked so hard, these days, to avoid.

What a wretched birthday.

The High Chancellor, robed in blue and carrying, as he always did, a handful of court documents rolled and tied with ribbons, leaned toward the king to whisper something—Taireasa caught the word *trade* and had to squash a grimace. People around the hall eyed this, too: Maldyn's whispers often produced decisions. But her father only waved a hand, indicating that the dancing should not stop. The Western lords watched, their eyes hungry, demanding. Taireasa turned her head, keeping her expression peaceful, trying to see every part of the room at once. She felt like she was missing something, but had no notion what.

Down in the kitchens, the serving staff would be well on their way to drunken oblivion by now, the meal served and only the court glasses to be filled by the haughtier maids and squires. They slipped among the tables, mute and unusually timid among such a tense gathering of nobility, topping glasses with wines from the Western vineyards. The kitchen staff drank better than the nobles of the kingdom tonight: Western wine was as dry and acrid as a wind off the Cruxi desert, and lodged unpleasantly in the back of the throat.

Much like Western demands did of late.

The heir to House Marsadron thought longingly of the celebration ensuing among the pots below and briefly wished to be a plate-washer, whispering gossip to spit-boys and undercooks. She wished to be two years younger and wide-eyed at Kyali's boldness, Devin's appallingly bawdy lyrics. She wished to be anywhere but where she was now, stiffly uncomfortable and increasingly worried, waiting for her father to produce a solution to an obvious and growing threat to the peace. A frown slipped past her carefully guarded expression, and a volley of glances sailed across the room like arrows.

"Balance. Breathe in. The blade is your mirror. It only reflects you. Breathe out. This is the beginning of real—stop twitching, girl. Breathe in. Follow—no. Breathe. Follow my hand with the point. Be the reflection. Be—gods, straighten up, you look like a felled tree. Better. Now. This is about *flow*. Be a still pool. Your movements must be smooth. Again. Follow—*no*, Kyali."

"I am not a *still pool!*"

"It's a thing to think about. It's supposed to help you concentrate."

"It's not bloody well working!"

"I see that." Arlen shrugged, expressive as a tree, and folded the little quartz ball, latest and by far the worst of the trials he had inflicted on her, inside a fist. Kyali clenched her hands, too flustered even to scowl. "So. We've found something you're not good at."

Her sullen slouch unbent itself in a hurry. Her teacher

matched her stare for stare, an uncommon amusement crinkling his dark eyes, which sparked gold with reflected light. The realization that it was her own eyes his mirrored cooled her temper.

I'm as transparent as Taireasa, she thought despairingly, and schooled her expression with fierce concentration, though she had to turn away to manage it.

A pebble soared past her ear. Sword came free of sheath without thought. She glowered, her blade far too close to Arlen's throat, fighting to keep her face smooth.

"Like that," Arlen remarked, as casually as if they were discussing last year's barley crops.

A tic began under her right eye. "Like what?" Kyali said, careful not to let her voice get to the volume it wanted to.

He might not have noticed. Except, of course, he had. Sometimes it seemed Arlen spent his days coming up with new ways to make her shout, or pitch something into the brush where she would be obliged to spend a prickly half hour trying to find it.

"You should move like *that,*" he explained, infuriatingly calm. "The ball won't stay on the blade unless it's either moving flawlessly or held perfectly still, girl—a concept worth more than a few thoughts from you, I might add. You do well enough when you're surprised into it, at least. I was starting to think I might have found your limits after all."

Words failed her. Again. Something like a growl crawled out of her throat. All she had was the sword in her hands, and that she could hardly throw.

Arlen tilted an eyebrow. "Not giving up, were we?"

Her anger cooled abruptly, as it always did when goaded

long enough, into a composed and hostile precision of thought. Eyes narrowed, she twisted the sword up and arranged her limbs. Arlen lobbed the ball in a gentle arc, reading her intention better than she would have liked him to. It landed on the flat of her blade and her hands tilted the steel in tiny, frantic increments until it caught in the center groove and held... held—

Stilled, sitting on her sword.

All the breath left her body. Her eyes met Arlen's over the flash of trapped sunlight in the crystal. Kyali clung fiercely to a startling upwelling of confidence and began breathing in pattern. Without allowing herself to think about it, she brought the sword up and around in the first of the Forms, listening in distant amazement to the soft grind of stone on metal.

The ball stayed, sliding smoothly in the groove of her sword, a strange new weight on her blade that nonetheless felt as though it should have been there all along. Her blood hummed in her veins. Her head began to ache and her eyes to burn, a sure sign that she was doing magic—though of what sort, she had no idea.

There was a strange shimmer in the air, and a stranger feeling in her middle, like something was pulling gently on her insides.

Second, third, and fourth Forms, done as carefully as she had ever done anything in her life. It went on. She lost count. Her muscles remembered what to do, her mind was occupied. She placed her feet exactly in the steps, feeling the weight of ball on blade, the weight of magic and of the strange pulling, as sensations suddenly and inexplicably familiar, utterly *right*, like a door she'd never seen before opening onto her own room.

The perception was alarming. She wobbled off balance and sent the ball sailing off into the brush. The warmth of confidence and of magic fled instantly, leaving behind only the desperate certainty that this was important, and she couldn't do it, and she had less time than she knew.

"Damn," Kyali murmured, and flushed hot when she heard the ragged edge of fear in her own voice. Her belly hurt. Her muscles were shuddering from the effort and the strange sensations. She sheathed her sword, unable to look Arlen in the face, and then didn't know what to do with her hands.

Her teacher walked off without a word and crouched in the brush where the ball had flown off. Kyali stared at the dirt, struggling with a sudden impulse to bolt into the trees like a spooked horse.

Arlen's worn leather boots appeared in her view, their toes scarred and scuffed. Kyali bit her tongue and tried to muster the courage to raise her chin, to meet that cool, scornful gaze. Courage seemed to have left her along with magic, though, and for a mortifying moment she couldn't make herself move.

Arlen's big hand closed over her shoulder, hard enough to make her wince.

"Damn?" he said. The frustration in that one word made her head snap up with a painful jerk. She met his eyes and the apology that was weltering up out of her froze in her throat at the intensity of his expression. "*Damn?*" he said again. "You young idiot, have you any idea how long it takes to learn what you just did? How few of us ever manage it?"

Kyali opened her mouth. Nothing but a sad little squeak fell out of it, and she shut her teeth over that sound before another one like it could emerge. Arlen's free hand fell on her other shoulder and she sucked in a harsh breath, feeling suddenly trapped.

"I... I don't..."

He shook her, not hard, but enough to make her teeth rattle. "One thing you've yet to achieve—one thing you'll need badly, soon enough—is a dispassionate judgment of your own skill. You'll have more than enough people underestimating you in your lifetime, Kyali Corwynall. You *cannot* afford to be one of them."

Kyali jerked away, wishing, for once, that her hair was free to hide her face. She had no idea what expression was on it, but she was sure it wasn't something she wanted there. "I don't know what you mean," she said, her voice quivering badly now.

"Stubborn child, do you not? You, who've spent more years studying the arts of war than many of the officers of your kingdom's court? Who knew the use of a blade and the feel of shed blood in a year when your agemates were all learning how to dance and ride? Who could—"

"I *don't know!*"

She turned full around on the tail of that outburst, lonely and shaken and furious with herself, fighting the desire to run away, all the way down the mountain if necessary, to get away from this discussion. A strange panic caught at her. Her heart was pounding in her chest like it wanted to get out. Her belly still hurt, that inexplicable pulling waxing and waning like a cruel tide. Arlen gave her no grace, though.

"I think you do know, general's daughter. A girl who could master all the Sword Forms in two years ought to know. A girl who could command a party of rangers in battle *must* know... and a girl who could do what you just did now, wielding your

magic and your blade together as one weapon—such a girl cannot help but know what it is to hold power."

Kyali gasped as though he'd knocked the wind from her;
it surely felt that way. She couldn't make herself turn around.
"I am not that girl," she said, and, hearing how stupid that
sounded, put her hands to her face and breathed through her
fingers.

Arlen was right behind her. She could feel him standing
too close. Her shoulders twitched. "You are."

"I don't *want* to be that girl," she whispered, the awful, humiliating truth.

His hand settled back on her shoulder, but it was kinder
now, too kind. Her burning eyes spilled over and it got harder
to breathe. She stood there like a fool, weeping and trying to
stop. "But you are," Arlen murmured, soothing and low, like he
was talking to a panicked horse. "There's no fighting that. You
were when you came here. You'll be more so when you leave
here to do—"

There he stopped.

Right where she most wanted him to go on. As always. He
had that in common with her father.

She turned, no longer caring that there were tears streak-
ing her face and her chin was quivering. "To do *what*? What
shall I do with this—this—" she waved a hand, lacking a word
to encompass everything this mountain held for her: all the
sweat, all the work, all the love, all the fierce satisfaction of
learning something so hard.

Arlen's expression grew even more intent. He opened his
mouth and Kyali held still, feeling like she was close to a real
answer for the first time in two years.

"Whatever you must do," her teacher said finally.

Kyali spun back around with a growl. For a long moment there was only the sound of them both breathing too hard. "You know far more than you say."

"It's the way of teachers," Arlen agreed. *His* voice was shaking now. Kyali straightened, still refusing to look at him, but thinking hard about that.

"*Sword shall guide the hands of men,*" she murmured. Behind her, Arlen was very still. "Whose hands? Guide to what? And when?"

"So you believe now."

"I believed two years ago," she shot back, and had to clench her fists and her teeth against the dreadful feeling of certainty that washed over her. Her guts ached with it. "I believed... I believed when I saw that my father did. When I saw he was *afraid*." The memory made her want to weep again, and she dug her nails into her palms and refused to let that happen. "But I still don't know what it means and you won't say, Arlen Ulin's-son."

There was a long silence.

"It's not so simple as saying or not saying," he murmured.

"It never is." Kyali folded her arms, trying not to shiver, and bit down on her tongue until the pain of that chased away the anger. "That leaves us... where, Landanar?"

"About where we were an hour ago, student mine."

A bitter laugh caught in her throat. She sighed. Around them the trees whispered peacefully and birds wheeled through branches in the mad way they had when summer was just beginning to stretch the days out. Kyali shut her eyes. "I want an hour to myself, if you've no immediate use for me. My head needs clearing."

"Take two." Arlen backed away, a soft sound of displaced dirt and pine needles. "It will come or it won't," he said softly. "Probably it will. Probably it will be hard. Much in life is. But don't *flinch*, Kyali. You've as fine a court face as could be wished for otherwise, but right now this is a hole in your armor anyone can see."

And he wouldn't tell her what he knew about it.

There was no use in saying anything else: she had her answer. What dread Clan secrets Eairon's prophecy might touch on, she had no idea, but she was tangled in it, trapped by it, and right now she couldn't find room in herself to forgive Arlen for holding back something so involved with her life, and Taireasa's and Devin's. Something that promised disaster.

Arlen left her standing alone, with her fists clenched and her belly still full of that odd tidal pulling. After looking around uselessly for something to hit, Kyali spun and stalked off into the trees, not caring which direction. She couldn't bear to be still another minute. Branches whipped into her face, only making her angrier; she elbowed her baldric back into place on her shoulder and flung an arm in front of her eyes, unwilling to slow her pace.

Damn this Clan and its secretive ways! Damn Arlen for teaching her everything in the world she wanted to learn except what to expect next, and damn her stupid self for trusting them all, for following blindly, for wanting so badly to be good at this, for wanting to be... to be...

Free.

The tears came back so suddenly she had no chance to swallow them. She pressed the heel of her hand to her mouth, stumbling to a halt, and gasped into her palm until she regained some measure of control.

Free was a lie. Free meant no Taireasa, no family, no House. No self.

At the thought, Taireasa's face, somehow older-looking, flickered on the backs of her eyelids. Her brother's followed it. There was a pressure in her chest, like grief, or fear. The pulling in her middle grew stronger, almost enough to make her sick.

What was she to do? Ride home wearing the Fraonir sword and daggers and wait to see what shape things took around her? Hope her father would tell her what was next? Training here had made her harder to kill, but also, she began to perceive, harder to place. And her presence would not make things easier for Taireasa, with the Western provinces pressing hard for advantage and Devin increasingly likely to be named a Bard, the first in some centuries, which would remove him from all other possible titles: *she* would be the only game-piece scheming barons could use against the Marsadron line.

In that thought she found a direction, and the glimmer of an idea.

There was no such thing as free. But maybe, just possibly, she could thread her way through the maze of court intrigues and keep Taireasa out of harm's way.

"Right," Kyali breathed, and shook herself, beginning to walk again. "Right."

But that answer took no account of prophecy, or fate. She saw no way to account for those things, because she had no warning of what to expect but *wind* and *storm* and *dark*. Whatever those meant.

The next branch took her unawares and caught her full in

the face. It stung, and she stopped. A hand to her nose came back bloodied. The realization that she was being a fool came to her somehow out of the sight of her own blood. Here she was, running from nothing, in the middle of—

Oh, *damn*.

In her preoccupation, she had been a very great fool indeed.

The trees parted just in front of her. Two men were gaping at her from where they sat on the ground near a smothered firepit.

Outlaws. And she was completely alone here.

For a brief instant, not even a whisper of wind marred the perfect silence, and then one man gave a wild shout, leaping to his feet. The other lunged at her from where he knelt, a flash of metal in his hands. She felt the shock of whatever it was as it grated off her vest.

Her sword came free of its sheath and cut his feet out from under him. His scream was terrible. The rest seemed to happen as if at some distance—the arc of blood following the sweep of steel, the bewildered agony on the man's face as she drove her sword through him. It was far too easy.

Her own ragged panting brought her back to herself.

Kyali backed up a step and then another, and moaned in what she first thought was horror and then realized was pain. At her side, her blood leaked out. A great deal of it was already soaking the leather armor.

A *very* great deal of it.

Not so easy after all, it seemed.

The second man held an old dagger, now stained brighter red. The pain, when she let fall her sword and tried to release the side buckle of her vest, loosened her knees. She dropped to the ground.

The locket around her neck leapt up and swung. She stared fixedly at the Corwynall dragon engraved on it as she worked at the armor's catches, hissing through clenched teeth, trying to ignore the pain, which was rising rapidly past endurance.

The buckle came undone. Her fingers found the wound at once, and she drew in a ragged gasp and shrieked at the feel of her hand against it. Unable to do anything else, Kyali pressed both hands against the outpouring of blood, rolling onto her back.

The peaceful trees grew shadowed, then faded altogether into a strangely gold-flecked dark.

There was something crawling on her nose. Devin must have found one of the barn spiders to disturb her sleep with, but she was tired enough to ignore it and disappoint him. Any moment now, Father would come in and make him remove it and leave her be. She burrowed deeper into the blankets, smiling at the thought of her brother's frustration. The bedclothes rustled oddly and smelled peculiarly of—

Dirt?

"Kyali. *Kyali.* Wake, child, can you hear me? Hells, I think this is all *her* blood—Arlen, help me lift her—good gods!"

She knew the voices, but her mind swung wildly back to the outlaws and the blood and the unbelievable pain of being stabbed, and she was suddenly on her knees in the dirt, her sword waving in her shaking hands as her vision came in flashes and gold flickered over everything. "No, *don't*—"

Saraid knelt in front of her, wide-eyed, hands spread out.

Her silver hair was crawling with gold flecks; her lined, gentle face was covered with them. Arlen, stepping into view and then halting as she lifted the sword, was in a similar state. Kyali squeezed her eyes shut, opened them to the same sight, and realized she was holding the edge of her sword to her teacher's throat.

"Sorry," she rasped, and lowered the blade carefully. "I'm sorry, Saraid."

"Child..." Saraid rose, leaning in to press a hand to her cheek. "You're bleeding."

"I'm not—I am? I was—I think I—"

"They're dead. You're safe. Let me see *now*, Kyali, there's too much blood."

She went still and dropped the sword, trusting, and tried to stay still as the old woman peeled back blood-soaked leather and pressed gentle fingers to her skin, first lightly, then harder. Saraid felt around for a long, uncomfortable moment while Arlen inspected the dead men and retrieved a blood-slick dagger. Kyali looked away.

"There's no wound," Saraid said, slowly, as though she didn't believe her own words.

Arlen knelt beside them, tossing the dagger into the brush, and shoved Kyali down on her side. She muttered half a curse, but didn't struggle as both her teachers pushed armor and tunic out of the way. The gold was beginning to retreat to the corners of her eyes. The sick pulling in her belly was tenfold worse than it had been.

"There *was* a wound," Arlen said, sounding both bewildered and frightened, as he had never before sounded. "It's... gone. But it's clear where the armor was pierced."

Kyali twitched under their fingers for another moment,

then rolled away and dragged herself to her knees, ignoring their objections. She felt her side, already knowing there was nothing there but unbroken skin sticky with drying blood. *Her* blood. Her hand came away covered in it. The flash of the dagger caught her memory, the awful draining pain. She hadn't dreamed it.

She should be dead.

She wished in sudden, aching homesickness that Devin *were* here, spiders or no—to mock her, to make her laugh in spite of herself, to chase away the dread that was making it impossible for her to think. He would say something to make her blush to the roots of her hair, but he would help her stay upright.

She felt her chin trying to quiver and bit fiercely into her own tongue.

"I've never heard of such a Gift," Saraid murmured.

Gift? A Gift that made mortal wounds disappear? "Starting fires isn't enough?" Kyali muttered, and knew she wasn't making sense.

Saraid smiled ruefully. "It seems not, child. Be grateful. This one saved your life. If only I could instruct you in it... but I wouldn't even know where to start, I'm afraid. We'll have to muddle through. Come now, can you walk? We can carry you, if not."

She'd had quite enough indignity for one day. Kyali rose, needing their steadying hands to do it, and stood on legs that threatened to buckle any moment. The pulling sensation in her gut grew with the effort, becoming so strong that for a moment she felt like she was going to fall off the mountain. Her knees *did* buckle, mortifyingly, and Arlen caught her in a strong grip. She tried to push away, but the world swung around her and the air was filled with a blurry shimmer that made everything immediately in front of her appear to be under water. Arlen grabbed her shoulders again and jerked back as though burned.

"What," she rasped, hardly able to get the word out, "*is* this?"

"Geas," Saraid murmured, a word Kyali had never heard, sounding both awed and grim. "That explains it. Oh, child—"

"I have to go."

The moment she spoke the words, the haze left her eyes and everything was clear. Too clear: oh gods, every fragment of news about the kingdom and the border coalesced in her mind in an instant, painting a landscape still shadowed with all the things she didn't know—but dark, so dark. The barons. The border. Her heart began to pound with panic.

She'd stayed away too long.

She had to see Devin. She had to see Taireasa. Thinking of their faces gave the pulling feeling in her middle a direction, and a strength that was agonizing. "I have to go *now*," she gasped, both hands pressed to her belly, and Saraid took her face in a gentle, firm grip, peering intently into Kyali's eyes. Her own, almost as pale a silver as her hair, held worry, thoughtfulness, and what looked, to Kyali's bewildered gaze, like fear.

"We'll get you back to camp and packed," the old woman declared. Behind her, Arlen made a small sound of protest. "*Now*, Arlen," Saraid scolded, and Kyali spared a thought for the tension between them, for all the things they weren't telling her.

Damned Clan secrets: she would have no chance to learn them now. She hoped that wouldn't be something she regretted later.

When they arrived, Saraid sat her at the common hearth

and sent Clansfolk into a flurry of activity. Kyali gripped the timeworn edges of the bench. When Arlen appeared next to her, looming like angry statuary, she looked at him only from the corners of her eyes. She was afraid she'd do something mortifying if she turned her head, like fall over, or throw up.

"You're not fit to ride," he grumbled.

"I will be."

There was a pained silence, then the bench creaked as Arlen sat next to her. "Kyali..." His voice trailed unhappily off, and she dared a glance his way that made her head spin. He was sitting hunched and he held something in his hands: a book. An ancient-looking, leather-bound book with lacings and parchment pages that crackled in brittle protest as he gripped it a little too hard. He set it in her hands. She squinted down at the worn binding, turned the first page to see the word written there, and felt the skin all over her body prickle.

Eairon.

She flattened her palm over the faded ink, as though she could pull all the secrets it held into her through her skin. "What is this?" she asked.

"A bad idea," her sword teacher muttered darkly. She darted another, sharper glance at him, and turned another page.

The earth is old, the first line read, and Kyali drew a shaky breath and shut the book. "This is what you won't tell me," she ventured, and Arlen heaved a sigh.

"No. Yes."

"Which?"

"Both," he snapped, not looking at her. "And neither. There aren't answers, girl. Not the kind you hope for. No clear ones. Just hints and suggestions. And I shouldn't be doing this:

you've a path of your own to find and this is—" he waved a hand. "Meddling. Dangerous."

This conversation was beginning to remind her far too much of her last few discussions with her father. "Dangerous *how?*"

"I don't *know*, girl. Had I given you answers over the last two years about this prophecy, about our own guesses—that's what you'd have heard most: I don't know. Nobody does."

Arlen looked tired. Arlen looked *afraid*. Kyali stared at her hands, spread possessively over the book, rather than at his face, because that sight made fear flutter in her belly, and she was already queasy enough.

"I can't take it with me, can I?" She didn't need the shake of his head to tell her that answer. Biting her lip, already regretting the choice, she slid the book back into his hands. "And I can't stay, Arlen Ulin's-son. I *can't*. So we're both spared, aren't we?"

"If you want to call it that," he murmured.

All her resentment fell away from her then, leaving only forlorn gratitude and a desperate desire to take it all back and stay here forever. She stood, still embarrassingly wobbly, and Arlen rose to face her. Mathin and Saraid arrived, Mathin leading her horse, outfitted with a set of saddlebags.

"Are you sure? We can—" Saraid eyed the book, and whatever she'd been about to offer disappeared in the white line of her pressed lips.

"I'm sure," Kyali said, already weary at the thought of journeying down the mountain once more, through the outer villages. She wouldn't have the luxury of pretending to be a villager this time. She'd be a girl in armor, an heir of Corwynall, wearing a Fraonir baldric.

A girl more skilled at the sword than any soldier in the Lardana army, now.

Dispassionate estimation of your own skill, Arlen said in her head, and she scowled and straightened her shoulders. Arlen gave her a crooked smile.

"Thank you," Kyali whispered, and fell mute, unable to get anything else out past the swelling in her throat. Saraid kissed her cheek, gripped her hand in a surprisingly fierce hold, and then turned away without another word. Kyali wilted a little in relief. She hated leavetakings.

"Arlen—" She got that far and then his arms were around her, lifting her half off her feet.

"You'll do fine," he said gruffly. Kyali pressed her face into his shoulder, feeling about five years old in his arms. "You carry a Fraonir sword now. You're a swordmistress of the Clans. I've provided a letter saying so. You'll likely need it—your court has no idea what's coming back to it, and many won't be pleased at how hard a mark you've become. But you're ready. Hear me: we could have dithered longer, but you were ready almost a season ago, to tell the truth. Don't forget it."

She clung fiercely, inarticulate with gratitude and terror. Arlen smiled again and set her back, his eyes suspiciously bright.

"Off you go then, general's daughter. You're ready. You're *good*. Don't ever believe different."

"Aye," Kyali said, the word half-strangled by the tears she was swallowing. She spun out of his embrace before cowardice could make her say more, beg him to come with her, beg him to let her stay.

There was no more room in her life for such childish wishes.

Ainhearag snorted at her as she pulled herself into the saddle, then pushed through the trees almost as though she knew they were headed home. They came to the wide grassy slope which would become the Maurynim path to the foothills and Kyali loosed the reins, letting the thunder of Ainhearag's hooves drown out the fear and the sorrow that clutched at her chest. Arlen and Saraid and all the Fraonir lay behind her; ahead lay the court, the House.

The Western barons.

Taireasa. Devin.

She wiped her face, gripped the reins in one white-knuckled fist, and didn't look back.

7

There was someone following them.

Devin shifted in the saddle, twisting to look behind him for the third time in the last hour. He turned back when his guard Hewet, a man who looked like he had been carved whole from dark oak but who moved with unnerving grace, hissed through his teeth. Amazing how much irritation such a small sound could hold. He scowled and faced the road ahead, which stretched on endlessly under patches of tree-shadow and the blistering blue arch of the sky.

"They're closer," he said sullenly, earning himself another hiss.

Orin's briny, moody winds were far behind them now and the rich fields of Syndimn province lay all around, shimmering under a heat haze. He missed the salt air and the fogs. He missed fish for breakfast, fish for lunch, and fish for dinner. He even missed Duchess Armelle, who had done what not one of the doddering theorists who claimed to be her court wizards had managed, and terrified him into taming his wayward Gift.

She was a frightening lady, Armelle Orin. He understood his Gift no more than he did when he'd arrived, but he could at least play a tune without a flicker of magic now. He was going to miss her.

He was going to miss her heir Ysmena more, though.

Devin sighed, stopped himself from casting another glance backwards just to see if the dust cloud in their wake had grown any larger, and brought out the bone flute in his pocket.

"Put it away, my lord," Hewet said, mournful as a foghorn and utterly unamused. "Now, please."

"Surely even *you* prefer a little music to lighten a long journey, Hewet."

That got him an actual glower. Hewet went back to contemplating the shadows ahead of them, or the sound of the Deepwash running in the distance, or the utter lack of birds in this part of Syndimn, or whatever it was that interested a man who could probably lift a whole horse by himself but instead chose to follow around irritable sons of generals, keeping them from trouble. For his part, Devin went back to contemplating the desultory flick of his horse's ears, but he kept the flute in his hand as a silent, petty protest.

Hewet was Armelle's man, not one of his father's soldiers, who would have put up with his humors. He hadn't given his father time to send one of his own guards for an escort. He'd woken three days ago with an inexplicable need to be *home*, and only Armelle's ferocious scowls had stopped him from leaping ahorse that very moment, his boots half-laced and all his belongings trailing behind him like lost children.

"There are six of them, they carry horse bows, and they appeared on our trail after we passed Savvys village, which is a known crossing point on the Western border," Hewet said, without sparing his charge another glance or even altering his tone to better match the grave nature of that statement. "They may be bandits, but they are more likely border guards from the other side, and here because you look like an opportunity, my lord. We can only hope they don't know what sort of opportunity."

Devin stared at him, gone loose and clumsy in the saddle. After a long, frozen moment, he put the flute away. "What do we do?" he asked in a small voice, when it was clear Hewet would volunteer no more information.

"Why, we keep riding, my lord. I am a hired guard and you a wealthy merchant's son, should we be asked, and we know nothing of Western affairs or border troubles."

That seemed wildly optimistic. "And if we did?"

"We'd still be outnumbered three to one, not counting the pair out by the bannerstone in the field, who are clearly prepared to drive us back to the road should we leave it."

"Oh."

He was going to think only good thoughts about Hewet from now on.

The sound of hoofbeats came to him faintly, a leisurely, insolent pace, and Devin swallowed down a throat gone dry. "Will they... I mean, they wouldn't *break* the king's peace. Would they?"

When he looked over, Hewet's expression was not reassuring.

He sat a little straighter, feeling the skin on his back prickle with the knowledge of eyes and possibly arrows aimed at it, and hoped the man riding next to him had a plan. Surely a man who looked like this, and who could put up with the sniping he'd been doing the whole journey so far, had something in mind.

"Should we leave the road?" Devin said finally, when the silence was strangling him, and received yet another annoyed hiss.

"They're driving us north, my lord, along the border road. They have scouts where they can prevent us from traveling across the fields. They have bows. We would have no chance."

Devin gripped the reins a little too hard, then sat back in the saddle when the gesture caused his horse to dance sideways. He flung a small, slightly desperate glance at Hewet, hoping this was some sort of terrible jest, but there was sweat on the man's brow and a grim look in his eye.

"But what *for*?" Devin bleated. "Who are they? There's been no breaking of the peace on the border, I'd have heard of it—it would be all over the kingdom!"

He said that, and then thought about his sister and Baron Walderan's nephew, and how few people knew the truth of *that*, and his hands went cold. He began to feel a bit sick.

But they wouldn't kill one of the heirs to the Great Houses out in broad daylight. Surely not. There was no way it had gotten so bad out here in the mere half a year he'd been holed up inside Caerwyssis's salt-pocked walls.

"What do we do?" Devin asked again, and Hewet sighed.

"We ride onward, young lord, and hope that these men are following opportunity and not orders, for they will not likely draw and break the peace if that is the case. We hope the Sarmin Mill, which is about an hour's ride ahead, is not occupied by more of them. We have a small chance of losing them if we move quickly, and if the old bridge is intact. We will pick up our pace when we reach the cover of the trees, just ahead, you see? You must do everything I say now, do you hear me?"

"I hear," Devin murmured, imagining the road ahead. He had never seen the old Sarmin Mill, reputed to be the first bridge built when the Western provinces were settled, who-knew-how-many hundreds of years back. He had never ridden the border road before. He was never going to do it again, if he got out of this. "I'll do as you say, Hewet. Lead the way."

His sword was wrapped and packed away in the saddle-bags. His bezaint vest was the only protection he had, and it wasn't much, but he swore he would never again complain about how it chafed. He eyed Hewet sidelong and tried to keep his heart from pounding too hard as he slid the flute carefully out of his pocket again to rub his thumb over the worn knobs and curves, an old habit and a comforting one.

They rode under a curving canopy of beech and ash. Hewet nudged his mount carefully, almost nonchalantly, into a faster gait, and Devin followed suit. He could, if he strained, hear the sound of hoofbeats behind them. His heart pounded harder.

Next to him, Hewet slipped the faded blue tie that held his sword in its sheath, the mark of a man bearing a blade in the service of the king's peace. "Young lord," he said, still serene as a man playing draughts over a cup of ale, "If you can find your blade in the saddlebags without sacrificing speed, you should do so now. Do not unwrap it yet."

Good *gods*.

This felt unreal, like a play put on for his benefit, or one of his longer, more dramatic ballads. Devin leaned back, fumbled clumsily at the saddlebags, and nearly lost his balance. Hewet was squinting ahead like a man facing down a high wind. The band behind them was fully audible now. He thought he could hear the two scouts that hid in the fields as well. It was a bit hard to breathe past the dread.

He caught the pommel of his sword in his fingers and slid the wrapped blade out, laying it across his lap. Hewet kicked his horse into a full gallop as the tree cover broke open and let the light back onto them in a blinding wash. Devin loosened his grip on the reins, leaned forward until he was breathing sweat and horse hair, making as small a target of himself as he could manage, and pressed his heel to his mount's side.

The burst of speed that called up startled him nearly out of the saddle.

They passed Hewet, who cast an astonished look after them. They flew down the road in a rising cloud of dust and a welter of hot sunlight, pelting toward the next stretch of trees and shade. Every strike of a hoof on the packed dirt rattled him right to his teeth. He had the sword pinned to his thighs with an elbow and the bone flute clenched desperately in the same hand that held the reins, and he was sliding in the saddle like a sack of turnips, all the muscles in his legs gone shivery and weak. When he and his mad horse crossed the line from sun back into shade, he heard a shout from Hewet. He didn't dare to turn and see; they were moving so fast now that any shift in his balance would send him flying, and he'd probably get a killing blow to the head from a hoof after he hit the ground, if the fall didn't break his neck first.

He brought the flute up.

One-handed and clumsy, he played the first few bars to "Lady Rose's Stables," a slightly filthy song that had been Ysmena's favorite to sing. And for the first time in half a year, he made no effort to curb the headlong rush of his Gift rising in the wake of the notes; instead, he welcomed it and squeezed his eyes shut as his head went light and strange.

Then he opened one eye to squint over the roiling withers of the horse and see what he'd wrought.

Not much, he thought, disappointed... and then realized the shadows under the trees were twisting in a way no tree branch ever could. He raised his head, blinking when wind struck him in the face. It certainly looked odd, but it was hardly going to deflect arrows or frighten off bandits.

It did produce a series of shouts from behind, and another series from *ahead*, bewilderingly—oh gods, had he tripped an ambush? Hewet was one of the shouters, coming up hard on his heels. There was a sound of steel meeting steel. Devin flung a desperate look over his shoulder, saw Hewet fending off two men behind him, and looked ahead in time to see ten men in light armor ride out of the trees up ahead and drive straight for him. He almost swallowed the flute.

He threw an arm over his face, too shocked to be terrified, and waited to die.

They thundered past, dividing around him like water around a rock, and met the two men Hewet was fending off. Those men flew out of their saddles and landed on the ground, and the four coming up behind *them* drew up hard. Devin wrenched his horse around, pulling at the reins when the damned animal went lightfooted and then tried to launch off in a different direction with another wild burst of speed—it had less sense than he did. He wrestled them to a halt a safe distance away. The sword tried to fall out of his lap. The flute was digging into his hand. He could feel the beat of his pulse in every part of him.

Everyone stopped.

"Lovely day for a ride," said one of the new arrivals. Half the air in Devin's body blew out of him in a furious gust as his father pulled off a wide-brimmed traveler's hat to survey the mess. "Where are you headed, sirs? Sarmin? Or is it perhaps points east?"

The Western band clustered together under the watchful eyes of the soldiers. The two who had fallen mounted carefully, moving as though it hurt.

"We spotted them at Savvys village," one of them said, defensive and angry. "We thought they were poachers."

A plausible claim, Devin thought—except nothing they'd done suggested they were chasing law-breakers, nor that they themselves were keepers of laws.

Hewet rode up, running a worried eye over Devin. Devin gave the look right back, and tore some of the wrapping from his sword to toss to his guard. "You're bleeding," he said, pointing to the man's temple.

The words earned a measure of quiet from the rest of the gathered men. Sixteen pairs of eyes locked on the slow trickle of blood making its way down Hewet's jaw. Devin realized what he'd said, and what it suggested, and he shut his mouth with a click of teeth.

"Just a rock thrown up during the ride, my lord," Hewet said, his voice soft and cool despite the sweat running down his skin.

"I should hope so," Devin's father said, just as soft, but ever so much colder. "I would hate to think the king's peace had been broken on so fine a day as this."

One of Westerners in the huddled group rode forward. He wore nothing to distinguish him from the rest, but he carried himself like he was accustomed to giving orders and having them followed. It was a look Devin was all too familiar with. This man didn't manage it nearly as well as his father did. "It was, as he said, only a rock. No one here has drawn." His eyes narrowed, raking over the general's face. "Who are you?"

"Niall Corwynall."

The name blew through the small band like a wind over a field: they all moved, and blinked.

"Far from your lands, great lord," the man said, venom and curiosity mingling in his voice. "Quite far." Devin held his breath, feeling the burning weight of that man's eyes when they fell on him. He was very glad the horse Duchess Armelle had lent him for this journey possessed such a bent for speed. He didn't want to think about how this might have turned out otherwise.

His father leaned back easily in the saddle, as though this were a discussion among friends, and waved a hand expansively. No one there could mistake it for anything but sarcasm.

"It is, as I said, a fine day for a ride," he said. "You seem to agree, sir, being out here as you are, enjoying the border road and the fine, eastern province of Syndimn. I've no wish to interrupt; I'll let you get back to it. I'm sure you have someplace to be. I suggest it is across the Deepwash. Good day."

They stared at one another. The man's gaze flicked to Devin, flicked away. Devin held very still, feeling like a mouse under a cat's eye. Then the Western leader made a curt gesture and the six of them marshaled into a tight formation and rode off without a word, looking almost indifferent, except for the stiffness of their backs.

Devin let the breath he'd been holding slide out of him

slowly, and slipped the flute back into his pocket.

"Padraik, Vanyel, see that they make it across safely," his father said, still perfectly cold and soft, which was the general about as angry as he ever got. Two men rode away without a word, keeping a careful distance from the Westerners. The rest of them turned in mutual agreement and began riding north.

"Sarmin Mill," Devin said, remembering.

"We took the bridge decking down," his father said calmly, putting the hat back on his head. "You weren't expected, son of mine."

"And yet, here you are."

"Armelle sent a courier when she couldn't talk you out of this notion. As I had no time to send you an escort, it seemed prudent to meet you on the road. I trust you've a good reason for this, boy."

"No, you don't," Devin muttered, and rolled his eyes when his father bent that *look* on him: the look stubborn soldiers and slow servants and misbehaving children received. It promised scathing politeness, delivered in the same tone that had worked so well on the Westerners, followed soon after by grim impatience, and eventually by a temper that never involved shouting but scattered people before it nonetheless, like a hard wind.

It felt oddly like home, and seemed far less terrifying that he remembered from just half a year ago, and he smiled fondly back. His father tipped his head curiously and raised an eyebrow.

"When did it get this bad?" Devin asked instead of trying to explain himself. He didn't really *have* an explanation, just an impulse, and now that the sheer fright of the past hour had begun to fade, he only had the same ache in his guts that he'd been living with for the past few days.

"Before your sister left, young fool," his father shot back, then frowned at the road ahead. Or at the very faint line of the mountains, little more than purplish shadows far in the distance. Kyali was somewhere in them, batting at things with that ridiculous sword of hers, shouting at whatever got in her way, scowling at whatever didn't immediately bend itself to her will, and writing the occasional pithy letter home.

He wasn't sure which of them missed her more, but he suspected it was his father.

"I think I'm keeping this horse," Devin said thoughtfully, a statement related to nothing in particular. He patted the sweaty, black-maned neck, and the contrary animal kicked out with a back leg and shook its head. He grinned. "He suits me."

"Twelve tempers for every moment and an amazing reliance on blind luck, you mean?" his father asked dryly, and one of the men at their backs snorted a hastily smothered laugh. "Perhaps he'll learn to sing and break the crockery, as well. What in hells were you doing, Devin?"

"Running," Devin said, unrepentant. "Somehow it seemed the thing to do."

"You might have asked yourself if there was a chance of ambush ahead."

"That occurred to me."

"Oh, *did* it."

"It occurred to me a bit late," Devin admitted; his father made an exasperated noise, which he hadn't known he'd missed hearing until just now, and shook his head. "Well," he added. "I *did* try to clear the way."

"With shadows and a breeze?"

He could feel a flush beginning to creep out of his collar. Gods damn it. "If you were hoping for a son who could call down lightning and crack trees, Father, you should probably have sent me north, not south. All I learned in Orin was how to make Armelle turn purple with fury."

The look his father sent him this time was both irritated and weary. "Nothing more."

"I can recite the name and course of every star in the heavens and brew you a transformative tea, if you like. And I do believe I've learned a new verse to 'Under the Haystack'." The soldiers behind them were definitely laughing now. "But that's not why you sent me there," Devin added, nearly sure of that. The laughter fell off into quiet as his father sighed and scanned the land ahead of them.

"It's certainly one reason why I sent you there," he said.

"But not all of it. Not nearly all. You wanted me out of the way. Is Taireasa all right?"

He'd worried over that many nights. She wrote—certainly more often and more honestly than his little sister ever would—but Taireasa never told anyone her great troubles, not unless she was caught in the middle of dealing with one. She was much like Kyali in that.

His father eyed him askance and Devin huffed, knowing the answer he had to give to get the news he'd asked for. Father hadn't changed at *all*.

"I have no idea why I left," he said curtly. It was more than a little embarrassing. "I just woke up with a head full of odd dreams and a belly full of odd aches, and I had to come home, and here I am."

Strangely, that didn't result in the annoyed look he was quite sure it deserved; instead, the general went expressionless and serious. "And that's done now, is it?"

"What's done?—Oh. No," Devin said. "Or, well... I don't know. Not very. It's better than it was. I can think. Don't say it," he sighed as his father opened his mouth, no doubt to issue some clever witticism about how seldom his son thought under the best of circumstances, and the general flashed half a smile. "Not yet, I suppose. Why are you asking me about this? It's not anything but—but vapors, or a bad kettle of stew."

"Your sister will be heading this way soon, I expect," his father murmured, and Devin felt his jaw drop. He shut it after a moment.

"So it's magic?" His father only looked at him. "I'd have bet on stew," Devin grumbled. A thought occurred to him, one worth almost as much fear as the mad chase of the last hour. "Kyali's coming, you say? Does that mean they'll be holding the vote soon?"

"Within the fortnight."

Gods. Poor Taireasa. He scowled at his horse's ears. "How many more Western barons have come to the capital?"

"All of them."

And between them, he and Kyali, they had left Taireasa alone to deal with this. She would spend the rest of her life dealing with it, in one way or another, and she did it far better than anyone else he knew, but still. Guilt crept over him, stealing some of the warmth from the day. He had no idea what to do to help her. He had no idea what to do, at all.

He wasn't sure his father did, either. Undecking the bridges suggested he was braced for something rather worse than a political ambush, but what, exactly, Devin didn't think any of them knew.

"What should I do?" he asked, and heard the echo to an hour ago and a very different set of circumstances that had the same cause, but a far simpler solution.

He got no answer, which was the answer he'd expected.

8

Crickets murmured to each other and hidden tree frogs sang to the faraway hazy stars. The barley rustled in the night breeze, standing out eerily in the dark against the distant trees and the sky. There was a scent of straw and earth in the cool air.

The nose knew it, as ears knew the creaking of the old oak—as bare feet remembered the feel of dew-wet grass and hard-packed dirt still holding the heat of the day. Nose and ears and feet informed heart, which beat harder, and knew itself home. Kyali pressed a hand to her lips, frozen in place for a breathless, glad moment. A guard turned the corner. She melted into the shadow of the house, suddenly feeling foolish with her boots in her hand. She dodged her way to the kitchen entrance, appalled at how easily she skirted the watch, and slipped inside.

Once in, she set down her boots and padded barefoot into

the dining room, meaning to creep to her bed and leave all homecomings and explanations for morning.

She met, instead, a faint silhouette sitting at the table in the dark. Her hands dropped to the daggers at her hips. She froze again, wishing she'd thought to duck under the window; the faint moonlight would mark her clearly.

The figure turned, became a profile that pushed the breath out of her lungs.

Her father stood quickly. The chair scraped over the floor with a clatter. In the next instant, his arms were hard around her, and that all-but-forgotten scent of leather and horse and ale was everywhere. She put her own arms around him, helpless to do anything else. The ache that had sat in her throat for days spilled into her eyes. She swallowed, refusing to let it get past that. They stood, pressing the air from one another, for a long moment. Then he set her back from him and looked her over in the dark.

"Well," he murmured. "Well. You've grown. You surprised me."

And that, she supposed wryly, was all the welcome she would get. But his fingers bit fiercely into her shoulders and his eyes glowed like candles in the gloom. Hers surely did the same. "The impulsiveness of youth," Kyali said, finding her voice. "Has it been quiet here, then?"

Her father gestured her to a chair, taking another as she sat. She could feel his gaze on her. There was no need for a light to tell her it was there.

"Quiet enough, though your brother has done his best to mend that state of affairs. He arrived a few days ago. Most of the commotion is at the capital these days. Farrell was kind enough to allow me to retire to the estate for the duration of negotiations."

The lightness in his voice was less irony than strain. The last courier hadn't overstated things, then—not if her father couldn't brush her off with his usual equanimity. She wondered what else had come apart in the careful dance of power and threat that was the East's relations with their Western cousins, and the dread coiled in the pit of her stomach put down roots.

With an effort, she matched his tone. "And the guard over the house?" she asked, fearing the worst.

His low chuckle shook the table. "Ah, now, I had need of more soldiers around, being such an important man. Though I fear you've missed most of them; I sent them off a few days ago."

She nodded as some of the tension left her shoulders. King Farrell still trusted him, then. And did *not* trust this incursion of Western barons. Taireasa's father was a cautious man who preferred negotiation to action. And her father was just the opposite. "To the border, I hope."

"It seemed prudent."

They sat in silence. Kyali stretched in defiance of the sense of threat all about, waiting to fall upon them.

"Well, it will be pleasant to rest at home in all this evident peace and quiet."

"You haven't lost your penchant for understatement, I see."

"You talk as little as I remember."

"And you seem to have learned a bit more about listening. That's good. Go to bed. We'll head to the capital tomorrow after breakfast."

A second's thought told her that sleep was the wisest course. There was no possible retort to this last statement, and the general never did dally once he decided a conversation was finished. She rose, and he did, and she gathered up the bundle on the floor.

"Good rest to you, Father."

His silhouette made a mocking bow in her direction.

She found her room by memory in the dark. She would rather save her brother for morning, when she hoped to be more settled. But Devin's door, at the other end of the hall from hers, stood open, a slightly darker darkness exuding a whiff of the oil he used on his gitars. Devin himself was no more than a glitter of eyes in that shadow. She paused, and heard him sigh.

"Is it well, then?" he mumbled, half-asleep.

"Is it ever?" she quipped, grateful for the dark.

A snort. Devin turned, knocked some part of himself on the door, hissed a drowsy curse. "I missed your pancakes," he said, and shuffled back into the dark, toward his bed. Kyali leaned a moment against the threshold of her own door before slipping inside.

Her rooms stood as they had on the night she had left, two years ago. Oddly touched, she removed armor and clothing, found an old and comfortable nightgown that no longer fit, and curled gratefully under the covers.

There *was* something crawling on her nose. She was sure of it.

A review of recent events informed her that she was indeed home, and that, being home, spiders were a reasonable assumption when one awoke from a sleep in this fashion. One of her hands flew up to flick away the crawling thing. The other, grown too independent in two years of training, had her sword drawn in an instant. There was a yelp from nearby, and Kyali came fully awake in horror and pulled back.

The sword fell to the floor with a clatter and her brother scrambled back from the bed, wide-eyed with alarm, tangling himself in the chair in his haste. He fell with a much greater clatter, and a breathlessly obscene exclamation. A large barn spider skittered up the wall.

She shuddered and turned to shout at her brother—but the sight of Devin's slipper-clad feet pointed skyward sent her into a helpless fit of laughter instead. He pulled himself to his knees and glared. She wheezed and flapped a hand at him, unable to speak.

His scowl trembled into a reluctant grin: Devin was nothing if not able to laugh at himself. He leaned against the mattress, snickering, and Kyali fell back into the pillows and threw an arm over her face, trying without success to stop laughing.

"Gods," her brother finally moaned. "I'd forgotten how quickly things take a turn for the absurd when you're in residence."

Kyali wiped her eyes. "I? It was you who ended up on the floor."

"Your memory always was uncertain. Two years have done nothing to improve it, I see. Pity."

"Oh, so that was deliberate! Was it a new dance step?"

"Hush, you starry-eyed Síog brat. What business had you defending yourself from a spider with a sword? Were you going to cut off your own nose? Though it's long enough, I'll grant you, to warrant trimming. Is that really what they taught you?"

She hugged a pillow, stung in spite of herself. Devin's look was amused and wondering, and she remembered with weary resignation the stares of the fieldhands—the expectations of strangers. She wanted none of that from Devin, who bore the same sort of weight, but (though she could never say it) with more grace.

He was taller. And broader. His skin was sun-darkened, and there were secrets in his eyes that hadn't been there before. She imagined he was seeing more or less the same thing, in a different form.

And between them the words of a dead prophet still hung, heavier than stone.

The locket at his throat winked sunlight from the window and she suffered a sudden chill, remembering how she had stared at her own as she felt for the wound that should have killed her. It was hard to believe that was only two days ago.

"Among other things," she muttered, trying to find her balance.

Devin leaned forward, clearly expecting more. "What?" her brother gibed. "Didn't we learn the secrets of creation? I've awaited revelations by letter. Your last was uninformative, to say the least. Though pithy." His tone gentled. "I thought I ought to give you a proper welcome before we expect you to conquer the world."

Kyali grinned. "Proper it was. I've been dreaming of your damned spiders ever since I left." Devin gave her a more sober smile and she frowned, remembering his letter. "Why are you here? You were in Orin, terrorizing harmless old men—"

"—And scores of farmgirls, yes, yes." He rubbed his brow, looking puzzled; the gesture was their father's, and it fit him so well it rendered her speechless. "I don't know, exactly. It just... seemed I should be here." He darted a shrewd look at her. "You returned a bit earlier than expected yourself."

"I grew bored." Devin gave her the disgusted stare that deserved. "Well. I thought *I* ought to be here."

That answer sounded silly even to her. She wondered if Devin had felt the same undeniable pull to come home, but that seemed impossible. They might be Gifted and of the same House, but Gifts didn't tie people together like that. And the pulling had faded as she had entered Faestan; it eased to almost nothing in her brother's presence. So perhaps it was just a—a warning.

She wished, wearily, that Saraid and Arlen could have come with her. She was already certain she was going to regret not reading that book.

"To do what?" her brother demanded and Kyali blinked, trying to gather up the thread of the conversation.

"Whatever needs doing?"

Devin's Corwynall-brown eyes narrowed, reading more of her than she liked. "Perhaps you can frighten the Western barons into an early move. Or was that your plan all along?" he asked. "No, then," he judged from whatever expression made it onto her face, folding his arms. "Don't you have a plan at all, sister swordmistress?"

"Don't call me that."

The chair on the floor flipped suddenly onto its side. Devin twitched away, wide-eyed.

Kyali drew a calming breath, and found nothing else to say. Two years of hard study, and her brother still found his way past her guard and under her skin in a matter of minutes.

At least she hadn't set the room on fire.

Devin cleared his throat after a moment. "Well—" He

cleared his throat again. "Well. One question answered. Is it my turn to tell you to be prudent? I hesitate to provoke you further, but I should point out *that* will in no way reassure the court that you are harmless."

"When have they ever thought so? I doubt I could manage to be well-mannered long enough to make them think so."

"Well, wight, at least you know it."

Her heart was pounding.

Down here, her choices seemed even more limited than among the Clans. She clung to the certainty she'd had not a day ago, to the decisions she'd made for herself, and hoped she'd lose nothing else of her time in the mountains. Already the Fraonir seemed like a dream. What she had now was the maneuverings and endless little betrayals of the court, and that seemed, still, like a nightmare.

But she also had her House, and—she hoped—Taireasa. She could keep Taireasa safe, and that was what mattered.

"I don't want them to think me harmless," Kyali said slowly.

Devin's eyes locked on hers. He opened his mouth, then shut it again with a considering look. "Good," he said finally. "As harmless is one thing you're not, sister. Neither are the Western barons, though I doubt you need reminding of that fact. They've been busy. You can hardly challenge them all to duels at sunrise."

It was an appealing notion. She tipped her head and contemplated it for a moment, smiling faintly, and her brother grinned. "All right, perhaps you can," he amended, and Kyali snorted.

"Wouldn't that be lovely. King Farrell would have my head."

"He'd just marry you off to some moon-eyed poet in revenge."

"I'd rather lose my head." She grimaced and plucked her

sword off the floor, gripping the leather-wrapped hilt, wondering if she'd still be holding it the same way and for the same reasons a decade from now. It was a lonely thought. "Perhaps I shall try to appear meek and harmless after all."

Devin confounded her expectations and declined to ask what looked to be a spate of questions darkening his eyes. "Fools aplenty there are in the court, little sister," he said instead; the words immediately made her feel childlike and small. "But few have made the mistake of believing *you* meek and mild. You've done too much to convince them otherwise." He got to his feet. "Hells, I learned better before you were eight."

Gods help her, that was almost a compliment.

Devin was worried. She couldn't remember seeing that pinched look around his eyes before. He had grown, and knew things she didn't, and thought things she hadn't. He had always been first, being older, if not necessarily wiser. But still: years passed, and they were more separate than they had been. Kyali curled under the blankets, feeling smaller than ever, and wondered in a quiet panic if the same had happened with Taireasa.

"I've done my morning duty, have I not? You're awake."

The level stare Devin aimed at her gave the words too much weight. She could only nod, and try to reckon where this older and cleverer brother fit in the pattern she was only beginning to perceive.

The morning hearings were done. Taireasa sat stiffly next to her lady mother on the dais, wishing for perhaps the thousandth time that there were some way to place a cushion on her throne without compromising royal dignity. Since she'd begun to take part in these judgments, she'd learned far more about the tensions within the city and also, to her dismay, about the precise contours of this wretched chair. She gripped its arms gently.

Her heart was in her throat, and the sharp angles of her throne had nothing to do with it.

In the hall, footmen swept the lesser earls and ladies out the doors. They lingered at the edges of the room in hope of catching some piece of gossip to take with them. Today was a day for barons and duchesses and lords, for great affairs of state, where her people would choose, once and for all, who would one day sit on the throne after her father.

She wasn't altogether sure she *wanted* it to be her. She was far surer that it wouldn't be Kyali or Devin. But it remained to be seen what the barons of the West had in mind.

For as long as there had been a kingdom, this had been the way of things: nine provinces, two royal Houses, and a single throne on which any one of the heirs might one day sit... as long as he or she was chosen by at least six of the nine provinces. There were whole books detailing the process. Taireasa had been required to read most of them. There were, so far as she could tell, no books that detailed *why* it must be so: it was so old a tradition nobody questioned it. Every generation a vote was held, a new heir was chosen, and the world continued on its slow, calm course.

Every generation for the last ten, a Marsadron had sat where her father did. It didn't seem likely that was going to change today—the Western barons had *something* planned, but voting one of House Corwynall's notorious children into the rule of the kingdom would hardly serve them well. Nevertheless, the way they had always eyed Kyali and Devin made her nervous. Unhappy with their more arid lands, their desert-covered coasts, and especially their taxes, the Western provinces had been a problem during her great-grandmother's rule, and to nobody's surprise, they were the biggest problem in her father's. It was an unlovely inheritance to look forward to.

A movement drew her out of her reverie. Baron Walderan stalked the corners of the room, his son by his side. His false smile made her want to fling something at him. Taireasa smiled back, watching his eyes narrow. He'd left his pompously large escort of guards outside the city walls this morning, as had his fellow barons. They'd done it with no objection at all. Her father took this as a sign of improving relations. Taireasa took it as a sign that they had something else planned.

She couldn't shake the feeling that something somewhere was badly out of joint.

The king stood, and all talk fell to silence. "Well," he said, loud enough to carry. "We have the matter of the succession before us. The heirs of House Corwynall are *both* present for this gathering. We will hold the vote this morning."

There was no shock at the announcement of the vote, but Kyali's presence today was not common knowledge. There was a rising murmur of interest from the lords. In the midst of it, before anyone had time to form a question, the doors opened and three figures strode through. The Lord General wore his armor, an appropriate choice. Devin, on his right, flashed her half a grin. And on the general's left swung that long red braid that was in her earliest memories.

Kyali walked with soft-footed, wary grace—and wore the trousers and tunic of the Fraonir Clans instead of a court dress.

The murmur grew into a roar of surprise. Kyali's face was as smooth and indifferent as stone, but Taireasa could see the pulse jumping in her throat and ached for her. Court had never been very kind to her strange friend. It would be far less kind today.

House Corwynall came to the foot of the dais. Kyali carried a bundle, which must be her sword—surely she had earned it. She couldn't imagine Kyali failing. Taireasa held herself utterly still. Kyali looked up, her face both familiar and changed—with time and sun and any number of events she knew nothing of—and a telltale fleck of gold flashed in that gaze as their eyes met.

Suddenly none of it mattered. Not the barons, not the prophecy, not the eyes on them, weighing and speculating. Not the years that separated them, or the dreadful tension of this moment. Only the growing pressure in her belly mattered, only the sparks of gold rising faster in Kyali's eyes, saying that she was just as glad, just as frightened.

Her hands were probably holding the arms of her chair too tightly, but she couldn't find room in herself to care for that. She could barely keep her seat. She felt an impossibly strong urge to descend the short steps of the dais, to take Kyali's hands. She wanted to learn what would happen when she did that.

Devin stumbled, recovering with a clumsy half-caught step that broke the spell. He had a hand pressed to his stomach.

What is this? What's happening to us?

"Welcome," her father said. "Devin and Kyali Corwynall. Do you stand for your House?"

"Yes, my Lord King," Kyali and Devin replied in unison.

"And do you stand before this court ready to accept the

path chosen for you?"

The pulling sensation grew stronger. Taireasa clutched at the chair arms.

"No, my Lord King," Kyali said, and the room filled with cries of shock.

In the rising din Taireasa saw clearly the path her childhood friend had chosen for herself, for them all... but most of all for her, heir to a kingdom split in two. There was a lump in her throat. Devin was wide-eyed. Kyali stood with her feet planted like tree roots, braced for storm.

King Farrell gestured for her to continue. Kyali bowed deeply. She had to wait another few moments before she could be heard above the noise. "Lord King," she said, then had to clear her throat and say it louder. "I wish to remove myself from candidacy for the throne."

"Explain," the king demanded. But before Kyali could do more than open her mouth, Devin stepped forward to match his sister.

"My Lord King," he said, "I too wish to remove myself from consideration."

The roar this time was enough to make the high windows rattle in their frames.

"Silence," her father bellowed. It was so rare to hear his voice raised that there was an immediate hush. "We will hear this! Heirs Corwynall," he continued, dropping back to a normal tone. "I trust you can explain yourselves. Do you mean to leave my daughter unopposed? Niall, did you arrange this madness?"

"No, my Lord King," the general said. "I did not. But I do agree. My daughter is now a swordmistress of the Clans. And my son is a Bard, which profession precludes any other title.

They are not suited to the throne. The Lady Taireasa, we have every confidence... is."

"We agree," King Farrell said.

The Lord General blinked once. The queen stared at her husband. Baron Cyrnic stood silent and furious, and Barons Brisham and Walderan were clustered together, whispering. The five Eastern barons ranged the room, murmuring to one another and to their lords. Taireasa met Kyali's eyes, then Devin's. The queasy pulling in her middle grew.

"Hear me!" her father said. "In order to preserve your right of choice, we shall postpone the vote until a fortnight from now. You may discuss possible candidates with House Corwynall, who will put two names forth for consideration. Obviously they must be of the blood." King Farrell sat, this time with a faint smile.

It was clear, now, what her father and the Lord General suspected the Western barons had intended for this day: a candidate of their own. It would never pass a vote, but it would gain them days of maneuvering room, and trade privileges as a sop when that candidate was voted down.

Or, a small, calculating part of Taireasa thought, *a candidate of their own who, when he is cast aside, will be put forth as a husband for the princess.*

She buried a shudder.

"And how are we to know the truth of House Corwynall's declarations?" Cyrnic shouted. "I would prefer to see some proof of their claim."

"Poorly said," the king observed, and waved a hand when Cyrnic tried to object. "But a valid question. Niall, how will you answer?"

"I believe my children can speak for themselves, my Lord King."

Devin, smiling grimly, slipped a hand into a pocket and produced his bone flute.

As he brought it to his lips, the guards, who had all drilled and served at the Corwynall estates, set their feet. Many of the lords retreated in alarm. Taireasa braced. But instead of the crack of glass, the sweet, mournful tune Devin played caused the sunlight streaming in from the colored-glass panes high above to shift in some indescribable way, and then to move in great, wheeling patterns on the floor. Taireasa stared. Kyali had turned to watch her brother. Devin let the melody fade into echoes and then, when no one spoke for several moments afterward, put the flute away and gave a foolishly extravagant bow.

"*Transformative teas,*" the Lord General snorted, just loud enough to hear from the dais.

The queen stood and gave the briefest of curtseys. "Young Devin Corwynall," she said quietly. "Young Bard. Well done."

"Yes," the king added, clearing his throat. "You've left us in no doubt. Unless anyone would like to argue it now?" He too stood and bowed, forcing everyone in the room to do the same, and then pushed on, so quickly Taireasa was left blinking. "We confer upon you the title of Bard, with all the rights and privileges thereof, including freedom of all the kingdom and the support of the royal treasury. No man shall harm or hinder you, no lord shall order you, and you shall be welcomed in every hall. We expect all here to abide by this."

Baron Walderan stepped forward, his face an unhealthy purple. "And what of the sister, Majesty? What proof *there*?

Shall we have a duel?"

"Are you offering, my lord?" Taireasa asked, and felt herself flush. Every face in the room turned her way. Her own father cast her a startled look.

"A fair question," her father said then, as though it had all been planned.

Walderan stood frozen. Kyali, Taireasa saw, had lost all her carefully maintained indifference: her chin was up, her eyes flashing as she stared down the man whose nephew she had killed two years ago.

"No, my lord," Walderan growled at last.

"Then you would like to suggest an opponent? Remote kin, perhaps?"

"I... had no suggestions, Majesty." Most of the court seemed confused by this exchange, but Taireasa could see comprehension on a few faces. It had not been the misguided plot of a single House, then. How far did it go? And what else would they be willing to do?

"Oh?" King Farrell said, his eyes hard. "Tharst? Sevassis? Canellys? You seem displeased. Have you thoughts on this matter?"

Silence.

"Don your sword, Kyali," King Farrell said then, ice in his voice. Kyali unwrapped the bundle and slid a tangle of dark leather straps over her shoulders, around her waist. She sheathed a set of large daggers at her hips and a long, shining sword over her shoulder. Then she knelt before the dais. Taireasa held her breath. The hush in the hall was profound.

When King Farrell drew the sword from over her shoulder, Maldyn came forward, holding a parchment in unsteady hands, and murmured the words for her to repeat.

"I, Kyali of House Corwynall, do swear my allegiance to the sovereign of the Kingdom of Lardan. I shall defend your life as my own and abide by your judgments in all things. To this I pledge my blade, my hand, and my heart."

For a moment the pressure in her middle was agonizing. Taireasa pressed a hand there, unable to help herself—and then, just as suddenly, it was gone. She met Devin's uneasy gaze.

Her father spoke the reply. Then he raised the blade, passing his hand over it in blessing. He pulled her to her feet. Kyali sheathed her sword, that faint frown still on her face, and went to stand with her family. The three of them looked very alone in the crowded hall.

A Bard and a Fraonir swordmistress.

Nobody said it. She was quite sure she wasn't the only one thinking it. Even Ky, with her impatience for all things fanciful, would have a difficult time calling the old rhyme nothing but a thing for children to skip to now. But the king made no mention of prophecy.

"The vote in a fortnight," King Farrell said then, before any in the hall had a chance to speak. Even the Eastern lords seemed affronted, and Taireasa could hardly blame them, but in the shock of the decisions and changes that had happened, nobody said a word. Her father stood.

"Good day, lords, ladies."

Good day, indeed.

The dining room was pleasantly cool this time of day. Taireasa leaned against the wall to look down at the bustle of the square, where merchants called their wares and market wives haggled over turnips and tapestries alike. The scent of pasty pies and roasting meat drifted up through the windowpanes. Her father came to stand near her, setting a hand on her shoulder as he pried the crown from his head.

"It gives me a headache," he said wryly, holding it up to the light so the single ruby embedded in the gold band glimmered. It was a favorite complaint of his. "You'll probably cushion it better with all that hair."

"It will probably fall off my head," Taireasa countered, trying for humor. But the look in his eyes gave the remark more weight than she had intended and a shiver twisted through her. Her father pulled her within the circle of his arm.

"Don't worry, Taireasa. We've weathered these storms before: every ruler must endure a few. We settled this one before it reached any height at all. They just lost the battle, and the cleverest among them know it."

Taireasa doubted it. For the first time she could remember, she believed her parents were truly wrong. She still struggled with the lingering sense that they had missed some vital moment in the hall... yet she could not for the life of her think of what it had been.

Perhaps it was just her mood.

The changes between her and Kyali and Devin had left her aching. She saw now what she had suspected long ago: the roles they were each raised to would set them at a distance from one another. They must. Her father must have seen it on her face, for he pressed a gentle kiss to her brow, as he hadn't done since she was much younger.

"I don't—" she began, before Kyali appeared in the doorway

and all the thoughts flew out of her head. Her father left her, moving forward to offer greetings and lead Devin and the Lord General to the table. In a moment, she and Kyali were standing opposite one another, staring.

Taireasa opened her mouth, but found her throat was closed too tight for speech.

Up close, Kyali was even less familiar. The planes of her face were more sharply defined, the line of her shoulders straighter and stronger. She was taller. Her eyes held a new wariness that darted toward every sound.

Kyali looked her over, seeming as curious and as disturbed as she at the changes they saw in one another. Mustering all her courage, Taireasa reached a hand out. Relief flooded through her when her hand was caught in a grip like a vise. At the contact, that faint connection she had perceived in the hall flared, becoming something bewildering and intense, as though Kyali had stepped into her head. She felt an uneasiness as strong as her own, and an aching gulf of loneliness and resolve.

They both snatched their hands back, wide-eyed.

Then they were hugging the breath from one another, and she had her face pressed to Kyali's shoulder, and her spirits rose in spite of the feeling of dread she couldn't rid herself of. She had her best friend back, and anything was possible now.

"Gods, I've missed you so much!" she gasped, fighting tears and laughter. "Couldn't you have taken me with you? It's been so *boring* here."

Kyali gave a little overwrought-sounding laugh. Her reply, when it came, was so muffled it was nearly inarticulate. "I wish I had. You'd have liked it."

"Did you miss me?"

"Do you really need to ask?"

Hardly a declaration of devotion, but that was Kyali. And she *didn't* need to ask: that brief, muddled glimpse into her friend's heart told her all she could ever have wanted to know. They pulled away, and Kyali allowed herself to be tugged toward the table.

"Come eat," Taireasa demanded, unwilling to let go. She couldn't stop herself from brushing at a wisp of blood-red hair, a gesture that made Kyali jerk away like she was dodging a blade. Taireasa ignored the flinch and ran the stray strand through her fingers, relief and joy making her thoughts fly out of her mouth far too fast.

"Your hair's darker! And so long. It must take forever to braid it. I want to hear everything! Those clothes look so strange. But they suit you." Another thought occurred to her and she seized Kyali's shoulder. "You can do magic now, can't you? I mean truly?"

Kyali blinked several times. Everyone was looking at them.

"I'm sorry, I'm just... here, sit." Taireasa sat herself, feeling a blush heat her face. Her mother's mouth was twitching. Kyali silently settled into her chair and reached for a glass of wine. She seemed to realize all eyes were on her and hid her face behind the cup.

The general leaned back in his chair. "She'll come around, your Highness," he promised, little flecks of gold flickering in his eyes, which were so much like Kyali's. "Some things need getting used to after a time in the hills."

"Walls," Kyali muttered into the wine. "Chairs. Conversation."

"Wit," Devin added, earning a glare from his sister. "Grace. *Baths.*"

"Manners," their father chided dryly.

"Ah, no, how can you lose what you never had?"

The Lord General fought a smile and aimed a resigned glance skyward. Kyali cast her brother a look of wide-eyed innocence. "Did I ever practice manners? I don't recall."

"You were a bit less inclined to perch on the furniture and hunch like a bird of ill omen, I think. But don't stop on our account. It suits you."

Devin coiled up in his chair with clawed hands, made a horrible face and uttered a strangled caw—half a year in Orin hadn't changed him at all—and Kyali finally laughed and lobbed a lump of cheese at him.

"Enough, you two," their father scolded. "I had forgotten the sound of the both of them in one room," he said to the king, who wiped an eye and set a hand on the general's shoulder.

"They *are* your children, Niall. I seem to recall you were no better once."

That was impossible to picture.

Kyali and Devin looked instantly to their father, faces incredulous. "Oh, aye," the general agreed blandly. "Far worse. As were you, Farrell." He aimed a cool glance at his son, who ducked his head in feigned remorse. "Though I believe we were both more subtle."

"Not *always*, Niall."

Whatever memory that recalled, it brought a genuine grin to the general's face, an expression Taireasa had only seen once, when one of Kyali's more elaborate pranks had left her brother mud-covered and running across the fields in a dressing gown. "All too true," he agreed. "And no, there's no use in asking," he added, gracing his children with a mock frown.

Kyali and Devin traded a look of determined intention, united by curiosity. Kyali darted a glance at Taireasa as well, invitation to enlist, and Taireasa raised a single eyebrow. The general surveyed the three of them. "Ah," he murmured. "They've made common cause, Farrell. Again. We'll not rest easy this season."

"Have we ever?" the queen asked wryly.

"Not in my memory, love," the king replied. "My own heir, who sits here so demurely now, managed this spring to incite more mayhem in the ladies' court than it has seen in a decade, and several chickens are now educated in the mysteries of embroidery as a result."

Her father aimed a reproving glance her way and Taireasa smiled, refusing to give even a hint of apology.

Devin snorted into his glass. "I was *sure* it would be the well," he murmured.

What that meant, Taireasa had no notion, but it made Kyali choke on her bread.

The past two years might never have happened. The past *ten* might not have happened when Kyali turned to her with a wicked light in her eyes, wearing that crooked grin that entirely transformed her face. She hadn't known how lost she had been without these two.

"My son and I will be riding back tonight, by your leave," the general announced when the meal was over. "We've things to see to. My daughter will stay a night and these two can reacquaint themselves, yes?"

The king stood and clapped a hand to his shoulder. "We'll deliver her back to you ourselves, old friend," he said. "It's been too long since we visited your estate. And you will come here again soon: we see too little of each other these days."

The general bowed to Taireasa and her mother as they stood, then laid hands on Kyali's shoulders. "You did well," he murmured low, meant only for his daughter's ears. Kyali nodded. Some of the tightness lining her eyes and her shoulders fell away. She caught Taireasa's gaze and flushed.

Devin followed his father, kissing first Taireasa's hand and then his sister's, the latter by ambush and with comic extravagance, as Kyali fought to free herself and finally kicked him in the leg.

The king patted Kyali's shoulder, then Taireasa's. "You did well today," he said simply, echoing the Lord General. "You *all* did. Now I need you to stay quiet and unseen—which, if memory serves, is not so hard a thing for you two. But no hiding in the old passages, and no pranks. There will be barons looking for trouble tonight, and I prefer they find none."

So her father *didn't* believe today's victory had settled the matter. That was a relief. Taireasa nodded, wondering what sort of trouble he expected.

"Aye," Kyali said. "Majesty—"

"I know. I *do* know, child. We set them back hard today, though. It will take them some time to come up with a new plot. They're a contentious lot, these barons. I've often thought they ought to have their own court—then they wouldn't plague ours. But we deal with what we have, no?" He pulled them both into a brief embrace. "Wait it out. It will blow over."

Kyali's frown was the mirror of her own worry. Taireasa felt some of the glow of pleasure leave her, and cold uncertainly steal in to take its place.

"Yes," Taireasa said, because there was nothing else to say.

She would wait to see, and stay on her guard.

With Kyali at her side. That was enough, and more than enough, to balance the rest.

Dinner was finished. They'd snuck a bottle of wine from the cellars (she hoped the king never learned of that small theft, or the passages in the walls would be barred for good) and had two glasses each, unwatered. Kyali's head still spun. They had gone to bed hoarse-voiced from talking and not a little silly.

Taireasa was still Taireasa, to her inexpressible relief: as kind, as clever, as perceptive. She was forgiven for leaving, and in spite of two years' distance, she still had a friend who knew her well enough to see all the things she couldn't say.

Kyali shifted gently in the bed. A single candle remained lit, bringing a flickering light to the tapestry-covered walls of Taireasa's bedroom. The darkness beyond the window seemed ominous, and all the triumphs of the day smaller than she had believed.

It wasn't over. She was sure of that.

She held onto the memory of her father's hands on her shoulders, the shock on the faces of certain lords in the hall this afternoon. She warded off the dark with them. She was still shaken from speaking, from choosing. Most of all from giving her oath, which had felt strange and strong in a way nothing in her life had until now... but also familiar, in the way that working magic was beginning to become familiar.

What that meant, she had no idea.

She had altered the course of things in some way she didn't

yet understand. Now things she'd been certain of for most of
her life were thrown into question, changing shape in the dark
on the other side of that decision.

Outside, the wind whispered and moaned to the old stones
of the castle.

It hurt to think of it: carrying a sword for the rest of her
life, Taireasa bound irrevocably to the throne, Devin to wander the land—welcome everywhere, but no longer with a true
home, and no longer able to bear the title of Head of House as
a firstborn should.

She was the heir to her House now. She felt entirely inadequate for that honor.

It was bitter. Tomorrow it would be better than it seemed
right now, with the dark pressing in on them all from the window and the wind keening secrets to the sky. Corwynalls and
Marsadrons had fulfilled such duties for generations. She told
herself this over and over. The lump in her throat did not grow
any smaller.

The warmth at her back shifted, leaned up on an arm. "Ky,"
Taireasa whispered.

"What?" The word came out more harshly than she had intended. She cleared her throat.

"Are you asleep?"

"Yes."

"Oh." Taireasa lay back in confusion, half-asleep herself,
and Kyali grinned into the darkness. "No, you're not!"

"Hush, you'll wake the guards outside."

"They don't sleep on duty, you fool."

"Care to wager on that? It's entirely possible to sleep standing up, I'll have you know."

Taireasa rose up again and looked at her, nothing more than a glimmer of eyes in the dark—and even half-awake and with no light to speak of, she still saw far too much.

"Fool, am I?" Kyali added, and prodded her fingers into a convenient ribcage, which was an instant distraction. They tussled for a moment on the bed like the children they had been. Fingers found her own sides and she had to stifle a shriek: Taireasa still remembered quite well how to win this sort of battle. She was challenged well past what she had counted on, but she was by far the stronger. She won by seizing two fine-boned wrists and bearing her full weight down on them, both of them breathless now with hushed laughter.

"All right, I yield!" Taireasa yelped. Kyali rolled to the side, panting. "Gods *bless*, you must weigh twelve stone."

"Lovely. They can use me to weigh down the canvas in windstorms."

Possibly they should both have outgrown such things by now. Probably so. But Kyali found she had no desire to do so, ever. The shadows still pressed too close, but the air was easier to breathe now, and Taireasa by her side after two years was comfort enough to balance all other wrongs, at least for tonight. She sighed, tired again, but Taireasa turned toward her, raising a tangle-haired head and resting it against hers.

"It's hard," she said simply, getting right to the raw center of the thing the way she always did.

"Yes," Kyali agreed. She heard the rough edge to her voice and didn't object when Taireasa twined long, chilled fingers with hers. She was grateful Taireasa found nothing else to say: the lump in her throat was back, an aching mix of gratitude and grief. They lay together in silence, listening to the wind rise from whispers to whistles, then to howls.

It sounded almost human. It brought the dark into the room with them.

Another sound came into the room then, a noise from *inside* the walls. A sound like a muffled scream.

Kyali froze, willing herself perfectly silent. A door slammed shut somewhere in the castle, hard enough that she felt the stones shiver. Every hair on her seemed to stand on end. That pulling in her middle returned with awful force and she drew her knees to her chest.

Taireasa's hand tightened painfully on hers.

Kyali rose to sit on the edge of the bed. Blood pounded in her ears.

Now, she thought, without knowing why or what it meant, but the dread that came with it was strong enough to make her stupid if she didn't push it down. The tugging grew almost unbearable. At her side, Taireasa made a small, hurt noise, and she knew that whatever was happening, Taireasa felt it too. She was suddenly certain that Devin was in danger, wherever he was. She wanted her father and her brother beside her with as fierce and desperate a desire as she had ever felt. She wanted Arlen and Saraid and all the rangers of the Darachim. She wanted an army.

She didn't have one.

The wind wailed like loss, and Kyali shuddered.

Beside her, Taireasa slid off the bed and stood. The small door to her handmaid's quarters opened and Marta emerged, her eyes shining and wide. They stood in the center of the room as footsteps and voices echoed through the halls. It did not sound like revelry. There was a muffled cry, a thump, and

Kyali could stand to be still no more.

She turned, scrambled in Taireasa's wardrobe for her trousers, her tunic, her leather armor, most of all for her sword. She flung off the borrowed nightgown without a thought for modesty and pulled her clothes on in desperate, clumsy haste as Taireasa yanked a dress free and began the laborious process of putting it on. None of them spoke. A panic that threatened to swallow rational thought was rising in her throat. Outside the wind howled, and inside came cries and screams, the unmistakable clash of arms.

She was beginning to understand, and she wanted badly to be wrong.

The Western barons. Their large entourages camped outside the city. They didn't intend to connive or marry their way to the throne; they had given that notion up in favor of another. They intended to take it by force.

And someone had opened the gates.

Their own door flew open suddenly, thrown wide by one of Taireasa's guards, his face stark and terrified in the torchlight, his sword bare in his hand.

"*Lady!*" he cried.

Kyali moved without thought, shoving a hand over his mouth. "Shush!" she hissed.

"The guards—the barons—the king and queen—" He stammered it out all in a rush, hanging a hand on her arm.

"Hold the door until you hear otherwise!" Kyali turned him about and shoved him back into the hall, barring the door behind him. She grasped in a single, ghastly instant what was required, what it would take, and was all but overcome by the horror of it.

But Taireasa's safety was all that mattered.

Screams filled the halls now. Taireasa's eyes were huge in the gloom, her face bloodless.

"My father, my mother, oh, Ky, the Western barons—oh, *gods...*"

Marta, bless her, was snatching after clothes, stuffing them into a bag in haste, filling her pockets with the bread rolls left over from dinner. She flung a cloak over Taireasa, not the royal blue of House Marsadron but a handmaid's plain wool. Taireasa clutched at the clasp and then at Kyali's wrist. Her grip was terror-tight.

"Taireasa." Kyali took her shoulders in a hard grasp, willing everything else, all the fear and anguish, away. She needed to think now more than ever in her life. The cold red clarity of battle-fury was waiting, and she hoped it would be enough to carry her through what had to come next. "You can't go down there. You have to get away. You have to go *now*; we are out of time."

"I can't! My *parents!*"

"Listen!" She gave her friend a shake. "Get yourself free and give us one less thing to defend! They are here for *you*, Taireasa—they mean to use you to give credit to their claim! Take the servants' passage and get *out!*" Kyali drew a breath, fighting tears of rage as much as grief. Thank the gods she'd renounced her candidacy today: she was no use to the barons alive. "Make your way to the guardhouse. You'll find men there who will protect you. *Ride to my father.* Marta—"

The older woman gave her a steady look and nodded, understanding perfectly what she didn't say aloud.

"Where will *you* be? You're coming with me! You can't fight,

Ky, you can't think of it!"

Good. Taireasa was thinking again. Though it left her nothing to do now but lie.

"I'll be riding after you." Taireasa's disbelief was evident even in the dark. Kyali embraced her quickly and fiercely, before her friend could see how the truth lit up her eyes. "I'm going to gather the guard here first. We'll need them. I love you. Believe in me, please, just *go*, now!"

Taireasa hugged her tight. "Go, go *now*," Kyali gasped, and shoved her away. She was choking on tears, on sorrow so great it was like a blade in her chest. Taireasa and Marta slipped behind a tapestry, where a door hid that led to the secret passages. As girls, they had done this a thousand times to hide from Taireasa's guards, as a game.

No game now: it was life, for Taireasa. All her hope was pinned on that.

Kyali didn't watch them leave. Instead she buckled her sword and daggers in place and breathed, trying to find her center, trying to drown the terror battering at her thoughts, hearing the approach of booted feet and the clash and whine of arms just outside the door. There was the fire, banked low; she could barely breathe at all, but if she calmed herself she might be able to kindle enough to burn whoever came in here.

But the tapestry would burn too. They would find the door behind it, and that could not be allowed to happen. A sob leapt out of her throat. Tears drew a hot line down her face.

Don't flinch, Kyali.

Her breathing fell effortlessly into pattern. She drew her sword.

They were at the door, demanding entrance and offering—

of all the stupid things—*safety*. There was no such thing, not anywhere, never again. Her heart thundered. The air burned her lungs. The bar splintered and the door burst open, flooding the room with the nightmarish light of torches reflected on steel, men standing stark-faced and bloody. They crowded in, blocking the entrance. Baron Cyrnic stepped out from among them, prudently remaining out of reach of her sword. Baron Walderan was behind him, and his expression promised revenge for his nephew.

"Where is the princess?"

Kyali raised her chin, swallowing past the tightness in her throat.

"You'll not have her," she said, and was astonished at how calm she sounded.

More tears spilled out. She couldn't help it. It didn't matter. *Taireasa, go,* she thought with all her desperate, terrified love, and for a second she was dizzy, seemed to hear panicked breathing, to smell the musty stone of the old passages.

She shut it out firmly. She was determined that Taireasa would not in any way experience these next few moments with her.

"Then we shall have to have you," Cyrnic said. "I think you will tell us eventually, general's daughter."

His meaning was plain.

Oh, gods, she thought—death, she had braced herself for. *This* possibility had never occurred to her.

She would just have to find a way to die, then. After she killed as many of these as came near her.

She set her feet as men fanned out on all sides. Her sword caught the torchlight and shone. She swept it up and around in a perfect, twisting arc, first of the Forms, the one from which all others grew. And all the fear left her as the blade cut first the air and then the face of the nearest.

Blood flew.

They fell on her.

9

The night was full of the cries of men and the screaming of horses. Devin crouched in the saddle, half-frozen with terror, as blood was shed all around him. His horse Savvys fought the rein and shied forward, sideways, back. Savvys didn't know what he wanted. Devin had some sympathy for that state of mind, but he dug his heels in anyway, wrenching the reins right, hoping he stayed ahorse.

Riders passed on his left, a thunder of hooves and a flash of steel. Savvys made to follow, knowing his place. Devin, utterly at a loss about where his own place might be, let his horse take him into the thick of the screaming and the ringing of steel. He set his hastily appropriated helm, hoping it would be enough.

An explosion came from behind, a blast of heat and sound so deafening that even the wails of wounded men and horses seemed small. Devin knew what that was, and grief and fury settled like a stone in his guts. The grief he ignored; the fury he welcomed. It made riding into the middle of battle easier, somehow.

Behind him, the house he had lived in all his life was afire, blazing into the night sky. Glass burst in the terrible heat of it. Smoke billowed out and mingled with looming thunderheads above.

They were outnumbered, losing rapidly. And he didn't know where his father was.

A sword flashed up at him. Devin ducked and swung his own with clumsy haste. He bit back a yelp as the jolt rattled up his arm. Blows rained on his back. He struck about with the sword and brought his shield up, yelling in sheer terror. Horses and men twisted past in struggling knots. Everything was glinting steel and black blood glistening in the firelit dark.

They had gone home to gather the battalions and head back to the capital in force, thinking they'd surprise the barons of the West. Instead, they'd met an ambush just outside the Corwynall estate by men bearing the colors of Canellys and Tharst. Betrayal, treason—every plot his father had suspected paled next to this unbelievable truth. This was no political maneuver, no attempt to wrest away the levies or gain control of the Sainey's trade ships.

They meant to take the kingdom.

Taireasa and Kyali were in deadly danger.

The thought gave him desperate strength and he kicked the next man that grabbed at his leg—kicked, then drove his sword through the gap in the man's armor at the shoulder. In the jostling madness of battle, the soldier's startled gaze locked with his—then his enemy slipped backward off the blade and was immediately lost in a deadly tangle of hooves. Devin shook his sword, struggling with a stupid but intense urge to reach after the man and pull him up before he was trampled.

He had just killed someone. Someone with a mother, a father, perhaps a sister of his own to worry over. And there wasn't even time to think on it: the battle was all around him now. Savvys stumbled, screamed, and bit a man. That man screamed, too, and Devin accounted for him with an awkward sweep of steel. Blood splashed him.

This was a day of many firsts, it seemed.

He fended off a lance, but took a blow to his head that made the helm ring. Through the ringing came a blessedly familiar voice, raised in a battlefield shout. Devin pointed Savvys toward that voice, using his heels.

Bodies were everywhere underfoot. Riderless horses wandered among them or lay screaming in the grass. It was chaos. He and Savvys bolted over the southern rise, dodging wildly.

On the other side of the hill was a knot of perhaps seventy men, grimly holding their own against a force twice that size. They raced right into the thick of that, too, and Devin tried to haul Savvys up short, thinking of pikes and arrows. Savvys cow-kicked and plunged onward with the bit in his teeth.

"Oh *gods*," Devin moaned, seeing the advancing line of the enemy rush toward him, and hunched over the saddle, holding the shield over his head. They knocked two horses over and trampled a man before anyone on the other side could lift a weapon.

As the enemy recovered, Devin struck blindly around himself with the sword. His grip was failing, his fingers grown slick with sweat or blood, he wasn't sure which. A streak of fiery pain ran up his calf; a spear blow dented the cuirass some soldier had lent him. It knocked the breath from him and he bent, gasping. Behind him, he heard his father's men shout as they took the opportunity—or perhaps they only felt obliged to rescue a fool—and charged. The air filled with the crash of metal and more screams.

A hand closed on his arm, wrenching him sideways. A sword crunched through the eyeslit of the man who had been trying to pull him down—a sword he knew well enough. Devin swallowed hard and pulled his own helm off to look into his father's soot-blackened face.

"Boy," his father said. Always *boy*—even when he had boys of his own and gray in his hair, he doubted he would ever be anything else to Niall Corwynall. Around them the battle was waning and waxing in fits, beginning to move past them. Savvys shied and shifted.

"Ride back to the capital," his father told him. "They will need you now."

Need me? Devin thought, dismissing that even as he heard it. They would need the army: *this* army, or what was left of it. They would need his father. Not him. What could a Bard possibly do for anyone at a time like this?

Their horses stumbled apart and came back together as the battle began to move past them. His father had a hand pressed to his middle.

Blood was on that hand. Blood was pouring, oh gods—*pouring* out around it.

Devin saw that and couldn't make himself believe it. It was *impossible*.

"Go!" his father shouted, and he felt blood spray over his face in warm drops. His father bent in the saddle and wiped his lips with the back of his hand. "Your sister needs you,

Devin, needs you *now*, there is no time. Fast as you can. Over the hill. Gather up the men when you pass and head back to the castle. You must rally the guard there, if you can."

If there are any left, his father didn't say, but Devin heard it all the same.

Shivers shook through him, making it hard to keep a grip on the sword. He felt like a child facing every imagined monster he'd ever feared might hide in the dark—he felt utterly lost. How could he follow such an order?

How could he *not*?

He was leaving his father here to—to—

His father stripped the Corwynall ring from his finger and tendered it in a shaking hand. Devin could only stare. His father snatched his hand, shoved the ring onto his finger—then, amazingly, pulled him close. They embraced, for the first time he could recall since childhood, the horses bumping under them. He could smell blood and sweat and, under that awfulness, ale, horse, pipe smoke: the scents he'd known all his life. Somehow that made it all real. The shivers turned into frantic words.

"Let me stay. Father, let me fight with you, please."

"No. *No*, Devin, this part is for me alone. You must go. Only you can, boy. You and Kyali and the princess. The kingdom needs you now. Farrell is dead. So is Marissa." They leaned back to look into each other's faces. There was something like pain in his father's eyes.

The king and queen were dead.

His father was dying.

"Gods," Devin said weakly. "Oh dear gods, no."

"No time, Devin, no time now: I wish there were. *Go!*" the general yelled, and wheeled his horse around. Savvys reared up. Devin kicked his heels in hard, reining about in the opposite direction. He was choking on sorrow, drowning in it. He'd had barely a day of a whole House, and now everything was ripped apart forever.

They topped the rise again and came thundering down the other side.

"Hyaaaaah!" he shouted—no, screamed, a ragged sound that was more grief than rage—and struck men down from a dead run. The sword was nearly wrenched from his hand. "To me!" he bellowed to his father's men as he passed them.

He had no idea if they followed. He hardly cared, but that was his father's last order, and he'd be damned before he'd disobey it. Tears blinded him, raked through him, making the night a prism of firelight and moving shadows. His breath came in shuddering gasps. He wanted to kill everything in sight, to make the whole world stop before he lost anything else.

But he had a direction and a mission, and a sister who was, like him, about to lose her father.

Will I have to tell her? Will she even be alive when we get there?

Oh gods, I can't bear this. I'm not strong enough.

He and Savvys pelted up the next hill and over it. Hoofbeats thundered behind them. Devin lifted the sword wearily, wheeling his mount around. But it was a ragged and diminished company of the Third Battalion facing him, perhaps three hundred men: they had come. He held aloft the hand that bore his father's ring, hating that he wore it. It felt like a theft, or a bitter jest.

"I'm going back to the castle!" he shouted—not the most inspirational of battle-speeches, but he was lucky he could put two words together right now, really. The hand he held up was shaking badly. He lowered it before anybody could see that. "Come with me!"

As they turned toward the main road, there came a burst of light and sound from behind them.

Lightning.

Devin slid halfway out of the saddle as the hillside tilted under him. A hole opened up in the world. A piece of him went away. The pain of it was stunning. He might have lost a limb.

Beside him, Peydan, his father's first lieutenant, cried out, and he understood.

His father had called down *lightning,* an ability he had never in his life suspected... and his father was dead.

There was silence now on the other side of that hill, a ghastly silence where better than two hundred men had fought only seconds ago. He was still breathing. Still thinking.

His father was dead.

Unable to reconcile these two things, Devin turned his horse wordlessly onto the capital road. There was nowhere else to go. Rain began to sheet down. His eyes still held the after-image of that terrible flash. The ring was heavy and warm on his finger. The Corwynall locket under his shirt was warm, too.

The rest of him was frozen and numb.

Taireasa staggered to a halt in the dark of the passageway, a dreadful wrenching in her chest stopping her breath. She leaned all her weight on the dusty stone wall, but her legs buckled and she dropped to her knees, gasping. Images pressed in on her mind. Her father—gone, *murdered*—a sharp sudden agony in her side and a sense of regret and surprise. For a moment she saw the outer walls of the castle as if from a great height, and then the wrenching came again, and she crumpled as her mother died on the northern wall.

She had no idea how she could know these things.

She hardly cared. The shock of it twisted through her, took all thought away. She clutched at the stones, trying to find herself in the middle of the terrible hurt.

"Lady, we 'ave to keep going!" Marta knelt over her, face panicked in the flickering light of their only candle.

Taireasa fended off Marta's hands and huddled over the center of the feeling, which was somewhere just below her heart, vast and awful as though a piece of her had been torn away. Her parents were both dead this very moment. She pressed her hands to her face as her lungs locked on a scream. Tears spilled from her eyes, over her fingers.

"Gods, oh *gods*, please no," she moaned.

The whole castle opened itself to her mind's eye. Men coursed through the rooms like rats, a deadly invasion killing wherever they found life not loyal to their cause. She saw it as though she were there.

Then something else intruded, something even worse. Her back arched. The agony was immediate, directionless, too great to think past. She was dimly aware of Marta fluttering over her as she curled up, trying to breathe, to move. The vision thundered over her, coming clear suddenly on a face, and then another face, and another—Cyrnic, Walderan, Brisham, Viam—

Her arms were tied. Her skin was bare. She could taste blood. There was rough stone against her back, and a pain that obliterated all else began. Kyali's ragged gasps filled her ears, and all at once Taireasa understood what was happening. She tried to rise, frantic to stop this final horror, but her legs only jerked senselessly. She heard her own anguished cry echo off stone as Kyali's consciousness swallowed her again, all of her torment and rage and terrible, resolute love completely overwhelming her.

Marta's palm covered her mouth, smothering her cries. Her lips tore as they met her teeth. It was nothing against this new pain, this awareness of wounds, of burns and bones broken, of her skin slick with blood, and this... this unspeakable violation of the heart of her. There were voices, chanting together, pulling at her thoughts. There were men crowded close.

Then the world in her mind shifted again, and the dark was suddenly rent by light too bright to look on. There was a crack like thunder. A horse shied under her. The Lord General was dead, too, and Devin was riding with desperate haste, armed men on all sides of him.

Devin was coming for them.

Picking this urgent notion out of the rest, Taireasa fought to be free, and was suddenly back in herself. She lay there, trying to remember how to breathe, how to live. The candle did nothing against the darkness. Around her, the whole world trembled.

There was no time for grieving now.

She got her arms under her, and Marta cautiously removed her hand. She managed to get to her feet and stood panting, pressed against the wall, shaken to the core.

"Lady..." Marta ventured, little more than a shadow in the gloom. Taireasa held a hand up for silence. She wanted to weep, or scream, and swallowed the impulse. Her friends were still alive. She had lost her family; she could not lose Kyali and Devin too. She *would* not.

Her feet moved her before she even knew the choice had been made, taking her back. She felt that pulling begin again in her middle and was relieved this time, because it was a direction, and it meant Kyali was still alive.

Marta rushed up beside her, even took her arm to tug it in the other direction. Taireasa turned, glaring. Her handmaid fell back gasping; from what, she had no idea.

"Marta," she said, as the woman flinched away and leaned into the wall. When their eyes met, Taireasa reached out and took her maid's hand, drawing her close. The air seemed to have a haze about it and her ears were ringing.

Is this magic? Gods, please, if there were ever a time to have it...

"The old passageways lead all over the keep," Taireasa said slowly, the thought taking shape as she spoke. "The hidden rooms. The servants don't talk about them, do they?"

Marta frowned and shook her head. "No, lady."

"Then we must go back."

Around them, that strange haze grew thick and shimmery and almost solid, then vanished as she shook her head. Kyali's presence was in the back of her mind. Voices hissed at her, urging her to speak, promising an end. The pain was rising and rising, unimaginable. A ghostly sheen of gold clung to everything.

I'm coming, she tried to say, to reassure Kyali, but she had no sense that the message went anywhere. The horror of it all but swallowed her and she bent, trying to find the courage to keep going, to salvage *something* from this.

She couldn't come for Kyali yet, not and live. But she would not waste the unthinkable sacrifice Kyali made. Nor would she leave her friend to face it alone. Pain—oh *gods*, there was pain—that, she could bear, now that she had the means to keep hold of Kyali.

"Find us one of the old rooms," she ordered, still curled over herself. "Deep underneath. We'll gather those that we can. The guard first, all we can reach."

"Lady," Marta whispered, and the fear in her handmaid's tone straightened her spine. Taireasa wiped tears from her face, hissing a curse.

Voices hissed back in her head: *Say it, stupid girl! Where is the princess?*

Taireasa swayed and caught herself on the wall again, tears smoldering on her skin and guilt and fury burning in her. Kyali would not say. And they would not kill her, not without that.

That anyone should endure such a thing for her... it was beyond bearing.

"The guards," she said, "then my bedroom. We are not leaving her behind."

"Yes," Marta said with toneless enthusiasm, never needing to ask who that was. She snatched the candle up, slipping past Taireasa to lead the way.

They couldn't keep this pace up for much longer. Savvys's bone-jarring gallop had dwindled to an exhausted, head-down trot and sweat foamed on his coat. Two horses had been left at the roadside already, blown and trembling. And yet they rode on, some three hundred worn-out men without home or hearth:

these were the men of the Third with him, who had spent most of their lives at the Corwynall estates. Tonight, they were as orphaned as he.

Devin knew it, and knew too that right now they would follow him unquestioning into death if he asked, but he had never felt more alone in his life.

Something was happening to Kyali—he had no idea how he could know that, but he was increasingly certain it was true. He'd felt her presence for the briefest of moments, as he had felt both hers and Taireasa's in the great hall today—a sense of bewildering newness and utter familiarity, like opening a strange door in his own home. That first time, anyway. This second glimpse had been a nightmare of confusion and terror, there and gone so fast he wasn't even certain it had truly been Kyali behind the experience. He got nothing from Taireasa, which filled him with both relief and fear.

They were still more than an hour away from Faestan even if the horses kept this speed. Which they wouldn't.

He was going to be too late. He was going to lose Kyali too. And there wasn't anything he could do to stop it; the distance was too great, and whatever Gift he had, it couldn't take him to Faestan in time.

The whole world had come unraveled so fast.

Grief choked him. Devin swallowed it back, determined to be strong for the night, fairly certain he wouldn't have to worry about such things after that. Here was Song riding east to the end of a kingdom: whatever plans prophecy might have had, they were nothing now. In bitter acknowledgment of all fate had laid on him, he drew out the bone flute, arbiter of all the useless magic he owned. He put it to his lips, meaning to play some marching tune—he had to earn his place in this company somehow, and it certainly wouldn't be with his fighting skills—but instead he chose, at the first faint peal of sound, to play his father's favorite song.

This was all the eulogy it was likely he would be able to give.

It was a mistake: the notes weren't made for anger. They broke the night open like an egg, let in all the awful truth the dark had hidden from him. He squeezed his eyes shut and played past the feeling that something in him was tearing apart, coming undone like everything else already had. All around him he could hear the stifled misery of men grieving. But he didn't stop playing; he was a Bard, after all, worthless in the kingdom as it had become tonight, and this simple noise was all he had to offer the world now. He forced his eyes open and stared at the unforgiving stars, swaying to Savvys's tired pace, and played until a hazy shimmer of effort was blurring his vision, till he was lightheaded and the grief he wouldn't give voice any other way sat in his guts like a stone.

Dizziness shuddered through him, a sickening lurch that hurt his bones. There was a dreadful pulling making it hard to draw the next breath. The air went away, returned in a rush. Then Savvys stumbled hard, making his last note jump an octave, and Devin looked up.

He felt the blood leave his face.

Where there had been fields stretched out on either side of them, there were thick trees now. Where the Sainey river had kept a quiet, distant counterpoint to his playing, there was now the hum and whisper of a sleeping forest. The ground under his mount's hooves had a marked tilt. It felt like something was pulling him down in one direction. Devin turned in the saddle, more disoriented than he had ever been in his life, and cried out when he saw the sharp slope of land outlined in moonlight, falling away from him in the starry dark.

They were in the mountains. *High* in them.

"Gods bless," Devin murmured, forgetting fury and even grief for one moment in favor of sheer terror. "What—?"

He looked at his old bone flute, friend of many years, still sitting in his hand, and blinked.

No. Surely not.

He stuck the flute in his pocket, hoping there was a better answer.

Around him, the men of the Third were riding in circles, moving their horses into the trees. He knew a scout pattern when he saw it and opened his mouth to call them back. He wanted to lose no one else tonight.

Peydan rode to his side. "We ought to scout out, m'lord."

"I—" Gods, he could barely find his voice. He cleared his throat and tried again. "Not just yet, Lieutenant. I don't want to spring any traps."

There, that almost sounded reasonable, didn't it? Devin passed a hand through his hair, looking at trees, trees, trees, and the faint outline of a game trail. How had they gotten here?

How would they get back?

Oh, gods, Kyali, Taireasa. He would never get to them now.

"An' where are we then, m'lord?" Peydan asked, breaking into his thoughts before the despair and panic that welled up in him could send him riding off a cliff in an attempt to get to Faestan.

It was a good question.

"I don't know," Devin muttered, too loudly. The sudden silence that fell around him felt like an accusation. "In the mountains, obviously, but gods, *how*—"

"Magic, Lord Corwynall, what else? Magic and *geas.*"

Swords leapt out of sheaths all around him.

The voice seemed to be coming from the woods ahead on the right. Devin urged Savvys carefully forward. Peydan followed close as a shadow, his sword naked and gleaming in the faint moonlight trickling through the leaves.

"Who are you?" Devin said to the darkness between the trees. "And don't call me that."

"It's what you are tonight."

Damn it, his hands had begun to shake again. He swallowed a hard lump of sorrow and hissed through clenched teeth: "Show yourself. Show yourself and *explain* yourself. How do you know that my father is dead?"

"Magic there too, Devin Corwynall. There are many things we know tonight that we wish we didn't."

There was a rustling. Devin gripped the reins, wondering if he were about to regret not having drawn his sword. Ahead, five men melted out of the treeshadow like ghosts to stand on the trail. A soldier shouted. There was a general jostling as men rode forward. But Devin, squinting in the dimness, raised a hand and Peydan immediately shouted over the din, ordering them to stand down.

He knew that style of dress, just as he knew the long shape over each man's right shoulder was a sword in a baldric. If it were daylight, he would see daggers belted on hips.

The Fraonir.

One of the shadows separated from the group and came to

his foot, looking up. In the dark, the lines of the man's face were deep and grim.

"I am Arlen Ulin's-son. Get down, Devin Corwynall. We have much to speak of."

10

Y ou know you are always welcome here."

Arlen's face wore an odd expression, both gentle and dreadfully sad. He brushed a strand of hair from her face, calluses rasping against her cheek. Something knotted tightly in her chest loosened.

It wasn't real. She was somewhere else, somewhere terrible and pain-filled and dark. She thought she might be dying.

Saraid knelt at her side and set one thin-skinned hand on hers, which rested on the leather-bound cover of a book she'd never read, one that might—no. She wasn't thinking of that. She drew her knees up, feeling like a child. She wanted only to forget: forget the book, forget the words it held, forget the rhyme that had changed the world, forget it all, even the feel of her father's hands on her shoulders, if it meant she could forget what had come after.

What was happening now.

But Taireasa's face intruded on her retreat, Taireasa's iron will and brilliant, passionate mind, like a hand clinging to hers. It made no sense, it wasn't real, but she was held by it nonetheless.

Taireasa wasn't safe yet.

Nothing was more important than that.

Flame touched the edges of the dream, searing first the blanket and then her skin. The pages of the book curled and blackened under her hand. Arlen's face vanished as she disappeared under the heat, became it, and cruel shadows pushed at the edges of her vision, man-shaped, blood-dark. Her limbs twisted as wounds blossomed on and inside her body. The pain was deep, all over, rising endlessly, too huge to breathe around. She couldn't even scream. Saraid's hand tightened on hers. Streaks of gold began to crawl over everything.

The fire swallowed her, leaving no room for love, scorching even sorrow from her as it raged through her bones and made them flame.

In the blinding gold-flecked light, there was an end to the pain; there was even something like peace.

Then the shadows faded, and all around was the quiet of old stone, the scent of blood. Someone was curled in sleep next to her. The stillness of night hung heavily in the air.

A man's voice laughed raucously somewhere else, and in the dark, flame opened its eyes.

Campfires made small bright points against the pitch black of a nighttime forest, throwing the shadows of men up against the trees. Devin huddled toward the flames, though the night was warm, and tried to swallow stew down a throat raw with smoke and shouting. Across from him, motionless as a statue, the lines etched deep in his face by the flickering light, Arlen Ulin's-son of the Darachim Clan watched his every movement like it were something fascinating.

This man spoke of the prophecy. He claimed that *his* people, not Devin, had brought their ragged company from a lonely Faestan road to the second highest peak of the Baar mountain range, a claim Devin was all too willing to believe. It was easier than thinking he might be capable of such things. Arlen also claimed that Kyali and Taireasa were alive, a thought Devin clung to even more desperately. He could no longer sense his sister's presence in any way.

The source of this astonishing knowledge, this unbelievable power, was apparently sitting next to the Clan leader, spooning stew into her mouth with trembling hands. Saraid's long silver hair was tangled as if from sleep, her eyes redrimmed and her face deathly pale. She looked like he felt.

Why she looked so was a question he had not yet found the courage to ask.

She left off eating and stared right at him. "You surely don't think you're the only one grieving tonight, Devin Corwynall? We were all surprised by this move—though I wish to the gods Niall and Farrell had done less to provoke it. Your part in this will be very different now, boy, than it would have been if things had gone as we planned."

Several things came clear, suddenly; several more were called into question. *"What?"*

"Easy on him, woman," Arlen muttered, darting a sharp

glower at the old woman, who scowled. "Ignore it," he suggested to Devin. "She does it to everyone."

Devin set his stew down with deliberate care; he wanted
so badly to pitch the bowl into this woman's face that he was
afraid he'd do it before he could stop himself. "I couldn't care
less about what she hears of my thoughts, sir," he said, trying
hard to sound calm. "I want to know what *plan* this is that was
set aside tonight."

Saraid raised her head abruptly, looking stricken. "Devin,
it was not—"

"And when, precisely, did it go awry, lady? Before or after the king and queen were murdered?" Even Arlen had paled
now, but Devin couldn't seem to stop, though he knew how
unlikely it was these folk had anything to do with the West's
treachery. "My home burned?" he spat. "The capital overrun
with the armies of the Western barons? My father... my... my...
before they... "

The soft murmur all around them had fallen to silence.

Devin clenched his teeth over the rest, words and grief and
rage rising like a scalding tide in his throat. He shoved himself up and away from the light and the presence of his father's
men. The shadows of the trees splintered into dim prisms. He
made it as far as a boulder and leaned heavily against its rough
side, shaking with sorrow, shattered by it. He couldn't breathe,
and for a moment he didn't want to: it would be easier, gentler, to die now, before he could get anyone else killed on his
behalf.

But Kyali, oh, Kyali. Taireasa.

A choking sound tore out of him. *Now* he could breathe,
and he gasped, air scraping into his throat. He pressed his face

against the unforgiving rock and wept, trying to be quiet, not wanting to give the men of the Third something else to worry about, or a witness to this moment. He wanted to be alone with this simple, merciless truth for a while.

"Devin."

The old woman. Of course.

"Go away," he said, but he pushed away from the stone, wiping his face.

"I can't."

"You can," he assured her. It would have sounded more impressive if his voice weren't still thick with tears. "Just turn around and head for firelight."

She knelt next to him. Devin fought the urge to fling an arm out and knock her over. "I can't," she said again. She sounded far too sure about that. "There isn't time enough to grieve right now, child, much as I am sorry for that. Things have gone badly, and we've so small a window in which to push events in our own direction. You must leave *now*."

"You're not speaking sense," Devin snarled—but unfortunately, her words were a familiar sort of nonsense: she sounded like the court wizards whose instructions he'd spent so much of his life ignoring. It caught his attention, even when he didn't want it to. "*What* events? What *plan*, lady?"

She made an impatient, wounded sort of noise and swiped a hand over her cheek, which was when he realized she was crying, too. Gods! Who *were* these people?

"Your sister's teachers," the old woman said, answering, as she had done before, his unspoken thought. It was thoroughly unnerving. "And *no* plan, Devin Corwynall: nothing that has survived this night. We spent many long years studying Eairon's rhyme, and it still caught us by surprise. And I cannot speak of it, boy: there is no time, do you hear me? Quiet," she snapped, before he could even get his mouth open to protest. "There is too much to do, and you have your part to play—in some ways the hardest part, but you are strong enough to bear it. You are *Song*, Devin Corwynall."

The words sent a shudder through him.

"Song," he echoed roughly. "A Bard, in a war. What exactly do you think I shall do, win battles with my voice?"

"Perhaps."

He glared at her, infuriated, but her face was solemn. "You *mean* that," Devin said, in wondering scorn.

"I don't know *what* you shall do. I know there is magic in you, boy, magic enough to bring you and a whole company of men to us. We could never have done it without your strength. I know that you carry the weight of *geas*, of fate, in you, and it's bending everything in your path, myself included. Devin Corwynall might not win peace with his words, but Song—*that* man might."

He wanted to laugh. It caught in his throat. "I am not that man."

"You will be."

Her certainty was *awful*. Devin looked away, but Saraid set her hand on his arm again, insistent. "Listen to me now. The other side of this ridge is the kingdom of Cassdall, and a company of foreigners near the size of your own. They are exiles, just as you are tonight, and they are in search of help and home, just as you are. They are your allies, though they don't know it yet. Ride tonight, Devin. Find them and bring them here."

"You want me to..." Gods, it was so outrageous he couldn't

even finish saying it. He gulped and tried again. "You want me to *leave*? To hare off into the kingdom next door in search of strangers? Are you *mad*? No!"

"*Yes*. You need them. Your *queen* needs them."

He realized, after a moment, that she meant Taireasa, and a fresh fit of shivers twisted through him. Taireasa was queen, good gods. He stared at the old woman, mute with horror.

"Devin, there is no time. You must decide."

That was Arlen, who had apparently decided to join this ridiculous discussion. Behind him, little more than a gleam of armor and a diffident posture in the dark, was Peydan, awaiting orders.

Damn it. He was not going to be pushed into something, tonight least of all.

"I can't leave Kyali and Taireasa," Devin said, finding, in that thought, a direction.

"You aren't, boy. They are coming *here*, I tell you. Everyone is. That will likely include your enemies, Devin Corwynall, and your numbers are not great. You need all the help you can get."

"Gods, how do you *know* all this?!" Devin cried, driving a fist into the soft dirt under his knees. He could feel his face crumpling with fury and confusion. "How? And if you see so much, how *not* what happened tonight? Where was our warning?"

There was a painful silence after that. He wiped at his face, and didn't even flinch when Arlen's heavy hand landed on his shoulder.

"We're not gods, boy. We have a better view from up here, and a few men in the lowlands, that's all."

"And magic my people can't even *imagine*. And years of studying a prophecy you didn't speak to *its subjects* about. And some way of knowing more about my sister than I do that has left the old lady haggard and exhausted, which does not bode well for what state Kyali is in. I am not a fool, sir. I'd prefer not to be lied to as if I were one."

Arlen ducked his head and heaved a sigh, then looked into his face with a wry expression. "No, you're clearly not. Neither are we—but we're only men, as you are, fighting off the dark with whatever tools we have to hand."

It wasn't truth, but it was such a vivid description of what his night had been like that he was rendered speechless. Arlen stood. Devin did, too—he could hardly sit on the ground and speak to this man.

"Kyali," he said stubbornly. "Taireasa."

"Safe," Arlen shot back. "My word on it, they escaped. They will be leaving the castle soon, coming to us. We'll be making ready for them."

"You don't know they'll come *here*, sir."

"Where else could they go?"

That was a point.

These were his father's allies. And Kyali had lived with these people for two years.

And there really would be nowhere else safe, not once the Western troops started crossing the border in numbers, which they had no way to prevent now.

"You're sure?" Devin said weakly.

"Yes. They won't be more than a few days before leaving. Your sister... has something to do first."

The wooden mask of the man's face thinned on that last statement, showing something far less hard and far more hurt underneath. Oddly, it did more toward convincing him to trust the Fraonir than any of their words. Devin knotted his hands into fists in helpless tension and nodded once.

Peydan turned toward the fires and the men without a word. They could hear his shouted orders echo back through the trees, and then the sound of weary soldiers making ready to travel.

"You'd better be right," Devin said quietly.

"I am. We *do* have scouts. Just head north by northeast and keep a watch out," Arlen said. "They are there. It shouldn't take you more than two days to find them if you ride hard."

Peydan returned, bringing torches and also Savvys, saddled and huffing at having his rest interrupted. Devin mounted, heart thudding, half panicked at the thought of riding farther away from Kyali and Taireasa—but there was something pulling in his guts again, and the direction was not down the mountain; it was north. He trusted it blindly, shaken and terrified that this would all go wrong.

Arlen laid a hand on his ankle and passed something heavy and awkward up to him. Devin had it in his hands before he realized he was holding a harp case. He pried it open, bewildered—it was odd timing, to put it mildly—and sucked in a startled gasp at the sight of the shining wood, the silver insets, the arc of the neck. The strings hummed softly as he shifted. He brushed one finger reverently over them and gasped again as the pulling feeling in his middle bloomed, for a flicker of an instant, into something potent and far too sure of itself.

"Dear gods," he whispered.

"Song you are," Arlen said, looking gravely up at him. "Song you shall be. Fare well, Devin Corwynall."

Devin closed the case before anything else could happen

and settled the thick leather strap carefully over his shoulder. The weight of the harp felt disturbingly right against his spine.

"What do I tell these foreigners to convince them to come back with me?" he asked, having little hope of an answer. Answers were not easily come by here, it seemed. But Arlen surprised him again.

"Tell them," he said, "that they are welcome to shelter in our mountains. Tell them the Fraonir Clans offer aid."

11

The stones were trembling.

Taireasa raised her head off an old cloak serving as a pillow and met High Chancellor—*former* High Chancellor Maldyn's worried gaze across the room. His tired eyes glittered in the dim candlelight. Beside her, Marta sat up, searching after a knife tucked in her skirts. All around, folk rose silently, guards straightening from a weary slump against the walls, servants and shopkeepers pulling themselves up from an exhausted sprawl on the dusty stones of the abandoned passageways.

Above their heads, shaking the very floors, was the sound of many booted feet.

"'At's another one, then," one of the villagers pronounced in a low, certain voice.

"Shh," a woman hissed. "Herself is thinking us a way out o' here. Be still."

Herself wasn't, though. Herself had spent nearly two days under the noses of the enemy, hiding in the very walls of the castle she'd grown up in, and Herself was no closer to a plan to take back her capital than she had been the night she'd lost it.

She wished her father were here. She wished the Lord General were here.

She wished most of all that Kyali were here.

But Kyali had vanished from what Taireasa had been sure was her deathbed almost two days ago. Vanished with her terrible wounds, her sword and her daggers, and not a word. And three Western barons had died since then, killed in their bedrooms. Only Cyrnic remained—guarded, it was said, by ten men who went with him everywhere.

They had deserved it. She remembered their faces out of a stolen nightmare of agony and clenched her fists in the rough wool of her makeshift pillow.

They had deserved far worse, for what they had done.

But cold, calculated killing was not a thing she had ever known Kyali was capable of.

"Be easy," she said, realizing she had worried her audience of soldiers and servants with her silence. "If they had found us, it would not be a company of Western guards we'd hear overhead. Our enemy would be in the passages, and far quieter."

That statement was considerably less comforting than she'd planned.

"Aric," Taireasa said, to forestall panic; he was one of the steadiest of her newer guards, young and shadow-eyed with a bandaged wound on his arm. He came to kneel by her. "How many of the guard do we have with us now?"

"Three hundred eighty at last count, Majesty."

Majesty.

They all called her that. It was her father's title.

Her father was dead. Her mother was dead. Devin was somewhere else.

And Kyali was… absent. By choice, it seemed. She was all that was left: one lonely, terrified new queen completely inadequate to the task of saving herself, let alone saving a kingdom.

"And the stables?" she asked, for they had been trying to gain a foothold in that place. She suspected they were going to need horses very soon.

Aric leaned closer, murmuring in her ear, "We've men there now, m'lady. The bastards—'scuse me, Majesty. They aren't well guarded, the stables. We might take them."

She couldn't imagine what they would do with the stables if they *did* take them. There was no way to take the castle, or the town. Their scant reports suggested thousands from the Western armies were camped about both, and without the now-scattered battalions that lived at House Corwynall, they had no hope. It was said that those barons of the East that survived had fled to their own holds, which meant that there was truly no help coming. They were alone, she and some five hundred refugees, hiding under the enemy's nose and stealing food from the kitchens like mice.

They had to leave this place. But where could they go?

Devin, Taireasa sent out into the dark, shutting her eyes and hoping her mad idea would work, and got back a sense of immense weariness and the uneven swaying of a horse. It made her dizzy. This new awareness of her longtime friend was bewildering, and she got the sense that Devin was just as confused by it. Their Gifts were both waking, in some strange new way no court wizard had ever warned her they might.

The thought frightened her.

Devin was doing something—she thought he was trying to tell her what, and she could almost get the sense of it. She received a baffling flicker of impressions, images of forest and mountain, the exhausted faces of soldiers. She probed at it like a sore tooth, sensing that Devin was doing the same with her. It was awkward being this close. But it was comfort, too, far past what Marta or Maldyn or any of the others here could offer. It told her that things were happening beyond the stone she was hidden in, things that might eventually allow her to take back her father's throne. *Her* throne. It told her that not all she loved had died.

But the bond she had briefly shared with Kyali was as absent as Kyali herself was.

"Do nothing tonight," Taireasa said, struggling to keep her mind in the present, for Devin's anguished resolve surged over her, making it hard to remember where she was for a moment. "But," she added, seeing Aric's disappointment, "I want more men stationed there. As many as we can keep secret. Tomorrow we move. We cannot stay here forever."

"Tomorrow," Aric echoed, looking thoughtful.

There was a murmur as the people around heard her and passed her words to their neighbors. She so hoped Kyali would arrive before then. The idea of leaving without her was unbearable. Taireasa fought down the swelling ache in her throat and set her jaw. They couldn't see her hesitate.

"Where shall we go, Majesty?" Maldyn asked, standing and coming close. Even in the faint light of their two candles, she could see the worry in his eyes. "We are many, and not easily moved in secret."

His words caused a hush. Taireasa sent an irritated look his way: he meant well, but she had enough to do, trying to hold five hundred refugees together, without her father's old chancellor questioning her judgment in front of them. "To the mountains," she said, and was startled at how certain she sounded. The idea was new, but she was as sure of its necessity as if she had spent days thinking it through. "To the Fraonir."

The hush around them grew deeper, and for a moment, she wanted to take the words back. She was proposing a journey that would take the wounded among them many days, on terrain that would leave them exposed and vulnerable until they made the treeline high up the slopes. If the last remaining baron of the West wished to find them, she was about to make it very easy for him.

They would need the horses badly now.

"Majesty..." Maldyn said. His tone was protest enough. She raised a hand to stop him from saying whatever else he was about to say.

"We cannot stay here, Maldyn. They will find this place eventually. There is no place in this city we could hide."

"But Majesty, surely we must fight! We cannot leave Faestan in their hands..."

"Fight?" Taireasa stood to face him. Her heart was pounding, but she managed to keep her voice level. She swept a hand around at the huddled refugees, the weary, wounded soldiers: the survivors. "There are *five battalions* occupying the city alone, sir. We are vastly outnumbered, poorly armed, and with many wounded. What would you suggest we do?"

"But..." The old man shrank into himself, then his jaw set

and he met her eyes stubbornly. Even as she cursed his timing, Taireasa couldn't help but admire his courage. "Majesty, I beg your pardon, but... you mean for us to flee? To leave the city to these traitors?"

Behind him there was a soft whisper of agreement, mainly from the soldiers, whom she had not expected to like this plan.

"I mean for us to *live*," Taireasa said in a fierce, low tone. "And one day we will come back many thousands strong, and then I mean for us to *win*." She drew a breath, intending to add to that, but cheers followed her words, stunning her. They were instantly shushed, and there were clearly still many unhappy men among the guard, but it was enough. Maldyn bowed, looking unhappy and ashamed.

"Your servant, in all things," he murmured. Taireasa set a hand on his arm and smiled at him. He *did* mean well.

"Difficult, Majesty, retaking this keep once we have left it," someone else said, and she turned, weary of the argument already, to meet a pair of Corwynall-brown eyes in an unshaven face. Feldan, cousin of Devin and Kyali, and a lieutenant of the guard. His cousins crowded around him, looking uneasy.

"Impossible to take it as we are now," Taireasa replied calmly. "Unless you have some suggestion to the contrary, sir?"

Feldan bowed, but did not seem convinced. "No, Majesty. I merely state that—"

Behind him, up the passageway, came a sudden commotion.

Feldan spun, a dagger in his hand in an instant. Taireasa gripped Maldyn's arm, felt the tremor go through him. All around them, villagers rose and stumbled toward the walls as the soldiers in the group came forward.

Then the commotion died into a shocked silence.

Kyali slipped through the line of armed men, her sword looming over one shoulder. Her face was as still as marble. There wasn't a single wound on her that Taireasa could see, though only a handful of days had passed since... since.

She'd been so sure Kyali would die.

Taireasa stared, frozen and flushed all at once.

"Kyali," she breathed at last, the name seeming to rise right out of her heart. Her eyes filled with tears and she dug her fingernails into her palms. She would *not* cry. She took a step forward. "Oh, Kyali, thank the gods."

And Kyali bowed—*bowed*, oh gods, like a courtier or a servant, a gesture as hurtful as a slap across the face. Taireasa straightened and halted, jagged splinters of grief twisting in her chest. "Where have you been?" she asked, catching the words she wanted to say behind her teeth, glad her voice trembled only a little. And then she winced, because of course they all knew quite well where Kyali had been, and what she had been doing.

"Gathering the guard, Majesty."

The irony stung almost as much as that title did coming from her best friend's lips. Taireasa drew an unsteady breath and forced herself to a cold calm. Kyali had never been one to speak her heart, and certainly not in front of several hundred witnesses. It might not be more than that. She tried to believe it, but the utter lack of expression in Kyali's amber eyes, that perfect calm in the face of absolute disaster, was frightening.

"I have done the same, as you see," she said. Kyali's gaze took in the soldiers and villagers crowded around. "We have nearly four hundred, here in the passageways and at the stables. How many are you?"

"Thirty within the castle. Close to four hundred have gathered from the surrounding towns, scattered from Corwynall's estate. Those men wait beyond the walls."

"We must take the horses."

"We shall, Majesty. We are. Two pastures are emptying now, and at your word we will empty the stables themselves. Many of the men there are yours."

Which was to say they were Kyali's: men trained by the Lord General, loyal to the crown, but who had called House Corwynall home all their lives. Kyali and Devin would be a great comfort to such men.

They had been working to the same purpose. It was almost heartening, but Kyali had done this without her, clearly knowing all the while where to find her, and that fact cut her to the quick. "We plan to leave tomorrow," Taireasa said. It was so hard not to grab Kyali by her broad, leather-armored shoulders and shake her until she became the girl Taireasa had known only a few days before—the girl who would have greeted her with an embrace instead of a bow and a *Majesty*. Tears welled in her eyes, but she clenched her teeth and refused to let them fall.

They were changed, both of them, forever. *Everything* was changed.

"Aye," Kyali said, not an agreement, nor approval—acknowledgment of an order received. "We should make haste, Majesty. Tonight would be better. They are left lordless above, and will have discovered it by now, but Cyrnic and Walderan's sons will be done squabbling over the throne and on our trail soon enough. We have the cover of dark. We should leave."

"Now it must be, then," Taireasa agreed. Her hands were starting to shake. If she had needed any proof that it was Kyali behind the killings of the Western barons, she certainly had it now.

She cleared her throat, willing herself as calm as she could. "Aric. Ready the back way out to the pastures. Take Ky—take the Lady Corwynall's orders in all things. The rest of you, gather what food you have stored and make ready for a long journey. We leave now."

Around them the murmur grew. She felt such a rush of relief at the thought of escaping these stone tunnels that she could almost forgive herself for abandoning Faestan.

She could not, however, forgive herself for what Kyali had done for her. And for what it had done to Kyali.

As the folk around them began to gather their meager collections of food and clothing, she and Kyali were left staring at one another in the faint light of the candles. Kyali's eyes held only calm. There was no hint of her heart there, or in Taireasa's seeking mind. She gazed back at Taireasa, serene and indifferent, a stranger wearing a sister's face. Taireasa wrapped her arms about herself as a shudder twisted through her.

"Kyali," she whispered, knowing she would get no answer.

Kyali was alive, but Taireasa had lost her all the same.

12

There was a menacing feeling in the air, like thunder, but the skies were clear. Kinsey wheeled his horse around, forcing several of his guards to rein their own mounts back, and glared upward. The cliffs above him were empty, as they had been all day. His men muttered.

Annan was looking at him again: he could feel that cool, sardonic stare piercing right through armor and cloth, boring into the tense spot between his shoulders.

He sighed. There was nothing on the cliffs and nothing in the trees, a heavy weight of nothing he could feel pressing down on him like hundreds of watching eyes, almost worse than being in his uncle's hostile court. At least at court he had *known* he was being watched. Here in the mountains, running into increasingly unfamiliar land, he had nothing but his growing suspicion and several thousand trees to blame.

He met his lieutenant's eyes completely by accident while

turning his horse back. Annan said nothing, only raised an eyebrow, which said everything Annan didn't.

"Tell me you don't feel it," Kinsey challenged.

Annan leaned back in the saddle, looking guilelessly at the sky like a farmer checking for rain. A young man with the sandy complexion of a marshlander and the dour look of a priest, wearing the dull black armor of the elite King's Sword regiment and *playing* farmer. He even held a palm up. It was a perfect act, and Kinsey felt his mouth turning up at one corner. He made himself frown instead.

"I do indeed, m'lord prince," Annan said simply. His glance bounced to the cliffs at their left and back to Kinsey, and he straightened. "I would, however, like to point out that actively searching for an ambush is an excellent way to trip one."

"A watched pot never boils," Kinsey countered, eyes narrowed. Annan's dark gaze flickered. Beside him, one of the men snickered, turning the sound into a hasty cough when Annan looked his way.

"Pots and kettles, m'lord prince. We are in a bad position here. I confess, I feel it, too—we're not alone on this mountain. But looking up at an occupied hill will only get you an arrow in your eye. We should ride quietly and keep to the cliff's side. You insisted on this road. Now we have no choice but to see where it ends."

Kinsey scowled. He *had* chosen this escape, arguing for it in the face of sea routes and the outlaw camps hidden in the marshes where his dead father's name still meant something—places where they might have been safer. The mountains had been a place of curiosity for him his whole life, but now that he was finally in them, with his uncle's troops on his heels and no way back, he couldn't say why he'd felt so sure about this particular direction.

"You could still ride back. My uncle would happily take your word of my death, and gods know he could use the soldiers. I'll go on alone."

Annan cast him a sharp look from under lowered eyebrows. "No," he said, apparently at the end of his patience with this topic.

"Truly," Kinsey pressed with false cheer. Most of his men had no family—Annan had chosen them with that in mind— but Annan himself had siblings, somewhere in the moors outside the capital. He felt guilty every time he remembered it. "That might be best. As things stand, my entry into foreign lands with an armed escort this size may be taken as something less than friendly. If I were to—"

"*No, my lord.*"

There was a wave of agreement from around them where men were in earshot.

Damn it.

He had never meant to have so many lives attached to him in this.

And now they were being driven like a herd of sheep up into the mountains, out of Cassdall altogether—into Lardan, home of every faery tale and whispered rumor of magic he had ever chased through a book as a boy.

He should probably worry more about that... but he wasn't precisely sorry to be where he was. He definitely wasn't going to miss the court. Now that both his father and mother were gone, there was nothing to hold him to Innisfell or even to Cassdall itself, and plenty of reason to leave before his uncle's assassins finally found a way past Annan.

Still, there were strange people living in the Baar mountains. There were ruins among the peaks, from a kingdom so long dead he had never found a written history that had more than a vague reference to it, though he had hunted eagerly, loving the mystery as a boy. He could see the dark stone of an ancient wall looming above them on the far ridge and he fought off a shudder. Childhood tales of the Síog, the fey folk that haunted the peaks and tricked travelers, came back to haunt him now.

A silly thing to worry about when they had assassins following them and a mountain to climb.

They made camp with the sun just beginning to set, its fiery light slanting through the branches of trees. Tents were pitched, and two of the men came back from the forest with enough game to feed them all. The air filled with the scent of roasting meat and burning wood. Kinsey sat on the ground next to the campfire, ignoring the looks his men gave him—a prince should probably have more dignity, but this particular prince was too tired to care—and accepted a mug of tea. Annan, being made of sterner, more suspicious stuff, did not sit, but strode around like a general, barking orders and pointing at tents. He was in a bad mood.

It had been a long few days. It promised to be another long span of them before they were out of range of the Cassdall army. And what happened then was anyone's guess. He had no idea what their reception would be once they crossed the mountains; they might be attacked on sight.

Kinsey sighed, worrying about the men who had, for reasons he couldn't fathom, followed him into exile, and huddled over the meager warmth of his tea.

Before he could settle into the hope of dinner, there was an outcry from within the trees, where the sentries were posted. Kinsey instantly came to his feet, his tea forgotten. There was no sound of fighting, so it probably wasn't his uncle's assassins. Somehow that thought wasn't very comforting.

Annan came to stand next to him. He had his sword out, and his eyes were narrow and hard. Many things were moving beyond the dark edge of the forest. It sounded like hooves, and the low voices of many men.

No way back now, Kinsey thought, and tried to keep his hands from clenching.

"A company from across the border, Highness!" one of the sentries yelled, invisible among the trees. "Claiming peaceful intentions! What shall we do?"

"Allow them!" Kinsey shouted back, before his lieutenant had the chance to do more than open his mouth. Annan sent him a look a little more readable than his looks generally were. Kinsey bit his lip. He'd had no idea he was going to speak until his words were already echoing through the night.

"My Lord Prince," Annan began quietly. Kinsey cast a glance at his lieutenant's tired face and felt a little bad for the man, who had given up a promising career to follow his lord into exile, and now had to deal with a scholar-prince's disregard for common sense in the face of mystery.

"We can hardly hide a hundred men," Kinsey said reasonably, his voice pitched just as low. "And this is what we came for, is it not?"

"You don't *know* that, m'lord."

"A good guess."

But it was a bit more than a guess, which he couldn't exactly say to Annan. He had never in his life felt so sure of something. The feeling worried him. It wasn't at all like him.

Gods, what was he getting them into?

Through the trees came a double line of soldiers, escorted by his own men. The strangers wore odd livery, and their armor was stained with dirt and what he was certain was old blood. Under the dirt many of them were pale, like Madrassians were, though not all of them. They looked beyond exhausted. Their lieutenant, a calm man with a bloodstained linen wrapped around his graying head and a strangely familiar shield, rode in front. He seemed oblivious to the bared swords of Kinsey's men.

Behind him, another horse shouldered its way forward. It bore a young man, perhaps his own age, dirt-smeared and haggard. He had a larger version of that odd red-and-black shield stitched on both shoulders: obviously the lord here.

Some of the enigma across the border had come to them.

Kinsey stepped forward, hearing and ignoring Annan's hissed objection. "Welcome," he said, but the word came out faint. He coughed and said it again, adding: "Your company seems in need of a rest."

There was total silence as they waited for the lord to reply. The man's face worked. Up close, he seemed even wearier than his soldiers, and far younger than most of them. His jaw was knotted as though only pride kept him in the saddle. He shut his eyes, and his throat moved.

"You're here," he said finally. "You're really *here*."

Kinsey couldn't think of anything to say to that. He tried anyway.

"I—yes. I am. We are. Here, that is. Wherever that is. Um. Perhaps we—"

Annan, having long experience with his prince's tendency to ramble like an idiot when he was thinking, strode right up to the young lord's horse. Kinsey hissed an objection of his own, and was ignored in turn.

"His Highness Prince Kinsey of Cassdall greets you, and invites you to dismount," Annan said, dry as a drought in a desert. The rebuke was actually more for Kinsey than for the strange lord. He swallowed his annoyance and set a hand on Annan's arm, trying to get a grip on the situation before the man could start a battle among tired soldiers.

"Excuse my lieutenant, please, sir. Rough living doesn't agree with him."

"Speaks the man who tried to wrap himself in a canvas last night," Annan muttered. The foreign lord didn't smile, but the quizzical expression on his face said he'd heard. Kinsey felt a flush trying to crawl up out of his collar.

"I am Kinsey, late of Innisfell, capital of Cassdall," he said simply, choosing to avoid the weight of his title, which probably didn't mean much now anyway.

"Devin," the lord said absently, and slid out of the saddle in a clumsy motion that had hands on both sides twitching. He shoved what seemed to be a harp case—odder and odder, this got—up on his shoulder, ignoring the sword that banged awkwardly at his hip. "Um. Corwynall, Devin of House Corwynall. Head of House Corwynall, actually. Late—late of—"

That expressive face crumpled, then smoothed out into a wooden mask. It looked like fresh grief. Kinsey sucked in a breath, astonished by the sudden force of his sympathy. He clenched his hands, resisting the urge to reach out and pull the other man to the fire where they could talk without this audience.

"Faestan," Devin Corwynall finished hoarsely. "Late of Faestan, capital of Lardan."

Kinsey looked the man over, thinking carefully. Corwynall was a name he knew, one of the two Great Houses of Lardan. And if this Devin was indeed Head, he was a very young Head. Kinsey wondered if the battle these men had clearly just come from had anything to do with that. Then he remembered where he had last seen that coat of arms, the black dragon on the red field, the daggers and sun... the symbol of the Corwynall direct, *royal* line. A chill went down his spine. If this Devin was who he claimed to be, he was a prince of the blood, or something very close.

Dear gods, who had died?

"Sit," Kinsey invited, not at all what he'd meant to say. He could feel Annan's eyes boring holes in his back. "Please. You clearly need rest. We haven't much, but we can share a fire and a meal, and you can tell us what brought you here. If—" He broke off as Devin Corwynall swayed on his feet, and gave up trying to be polite. Instead he got the man by the arms and pulled him over to a stump by the fire. "Sir, I don't know what has happened to you and your men, but we can surely spare enough tents to make you comfortable."

"We have tents. I think. I'm not sure. I haven't slept in a few days. We were sent to find you." Devin heaved a sigh and ran a hand through his dark hair. "I didn't really believe you'd *be* here."

After a moment, Kinsey realized his mouth was still open and shut it. "You were... sent."

Annan had come to hover over them, and so had the other lieutenant, the man with the bandage on his head. The soldiers went about rearranging the camp in a deathly silence. Devin Corwynall took a mug of tea and sipped, wincing. "Sent," he agreed. "By the Fraonir—uh—" He looked up, hesitating. "The people of the mountains. They said I would find you here."

"And how did these Fraonir know where to find us?" Kinsey asked, thinking of that feeling of being watched.

"I don't know."

"Well, *why* were you sent to find us, then?"

Devin looked at him mutely, grief naked on his face, and Kinsey felt again that wrenching pull of sympathy for the man. It frightened him. He'd never felt so drawn to someone in his life, nor so certain his life was about to change.

"We come over the mountain, m'lord," the foreign lieutenant said quietly. "Our lands is taken. The mountainfolk, they offered us help, and said we ought to seek you out."

Annan made a noise of utter disapproval and folded his arms. Kinsey sat, trying not to let his dismay show on his face. "Your kingdom is taken? By whom? And why did you seek us out? We are only a hundred men, Lord Corwynall. Exiles, yes, and looking for a place to settle... but we cannot take your kingdom back for you."

Annan made a less-disapproving noise and sat next to him, inviting himself to the meeting. At that, the foreign lieutenant did the same, and they huddled around their small fire.

"By the West," Devin said, taking up the thread again. The tea had put some color in his face. "The barons of the western provinces of Lardan, that is. Our own. We should have... I don't know. We were unprepared, and we shouldn't have been. Our capital is

taken, sirs. Our king and queen murdered. Our Lord General...
my father... also murdered. And I have *no* idea why we were sent
to you, except to say that the Fraonir offer you shelter."

It was not good news.

"The—ah." Kinsey took a plate of food and passed it without thinking to Devin. He'd read in some book somewhere of the
split baronies of Lardan, but he'd no idea it was such a contentious place. And these mountain folk... "Shelter. How do they plan
to accommodate that? And how did they know we would need it?
And are we to accompany you in—whatever you do next?"

"I truly don't know, sir. They knew things of me and mine
I would never have believed possible. I don't know what sort of
shelter or for how long, or at what price, if any. There wasn't
time to argue more answers out of them. But yes—you must
ride with us. And yes—we may need your help. The Fraonir
have offered *us* shelter as well. But we all have to live to find
it." Devin faltered, then wiped his face with a shaking hand.
"I'm sorry. I don't even know who you *are*. I can't promise I
even know where I'm going from moment to moment, and I'm
sure my company won't be safe for you."

It wasn't exactly a ringing endorsement for an alliance.

But he and his men were leaving Cassdall, seeking a life
elsewhere—and here was everything he had hoped for. Except,
of course, that it brought the threat of war with it.

Head reeling, Kinsey sipped his tea, giving himself a moment to sort through the information. Devin picked listlessly
at his food.

"Kinsey of Cassdall is who I am," Kinsey said, choosing to
answer the one easy question for now. "Formerly a prince of
Cassdall."

"*Still* a prince of Cassdall," Annan said forcefully. "You renounced *nothing*, my lord."

For Annan, it was a speech. And the sentiment behind it was touching, if it wasn't just Annan's way of tipping negotiations in his favor, but Kinsey only shrugged. "Leaving the kingdom rather does it for me, doesn't it? Forgive us, Lord Corwynall. It's a point of some contention. My own father died recently, and his brother claimed the throne by force. We've been dodging my uncle's assassins ever since. I rode into the mountains rather than face his troops."

"We seem to have common troubles, Highness."

"Don't call me that. Please. If my books on your House histories are correct, the same title could apply to you, and it's *your* kingdom we are riding into tomorrow."

Beside him, Annan went still. The silence after his words caught up to him and Kinsey went still, realizing what he'd said.

Who *was* this Devin, that he had such an effect on a prince of Cassdall?

Was this magic?

Devin's eyes had gone wide. "Then you—"

"My lord," Annan said, sounding genuinely worried now. "We should sleep on this decision."

"Yes, of course." He said it, but he was staring into Devin's red-rimmed eyes when he did, and the urge to agree with anything Devin said—to get on his horse and ride with him in any direction he chose—had become so strong it was almost painful. Kinsey shivered, genuinely afraid for the first time since he'd fled his kingdom toward freedom. He'd read more of magic than anybody in Cassdall, but he'd never in his life imagined he'd run headlong into it.

This wasn't like the faery tales. This was dangerous.

Across from him, Devin Corwynall shivered, too, and pressed a hand to his belly as though in pain. His weary face was a mirror of the alarm Kinsey felt.

"Yes, we should rest, and think on this," Kinsey said again, trying to make it true just by saying it out loud. He could feel Annan's stare radiating at him like unfriendly sunlight and he tried to put a less worried expression on his face. He stood, horrified to find his knees were wobbly, and pulled Devin to his feet. The lieutenant got Devin's other arm and held him steady.

"I'm asleep on my feet," Devin murmured. "I'm sorry."

"No need. Sleep a night; your men can rest in safety here, you have my word. Our sentries will keep watch. We'll talk again in the morning."

Kinsey watched Devin shuffle off, his head low, steps weaving with exhaustion. He didn't look at Annan. He didn't want to meet that accusing stare. He knew he hadn't done well or been clear.

But he'd already made up his mind, and he was fairly sure Annan knew that much.

13

The Cassdall prince was a man of many thoughts, not one of which had made it past his teeth.

They rose early and rode hard, exhausting the horses and themselves, and Prince Kinsey's faint, thoughtful frown never wavered. They had made the mountain's windy top at dawn and were now picking their way down the steep path on the western slope in a grim silence that Devin did nothing to break. He could feel Kinsey's gaze on him, those oddly clear gray eyes full of intelligence and worry. This was a scholar, a man who deliberated before rushing into a breakfast, let alone an alliance—and yet here he was, riding with a defeated company of complete strangers into what might become a war.

He should probably be wondering about that, but he didn't care.

His thoughts were all with Taireasa, with that sense of deep sorrow that flooded her brave, tired heart. Sensations and sights came to him in vivid flashes, along with the constant working of her remarkable mind, like a conversation he couldn't quite hear.

It was so very strange.

Her horse swayed out of time with his own. All around her were trees, an endless green that told him nothing of where she might be, except no longer in Faestan.

Next to her was Kyali, so empty of expression she might have been a statue.

His sister's face held no grief, no worry—no emotion at all, in fact. It terrified him. It terrified Taireasa, too. Kyali's face came to him in quick little sidelong flickers, as though Taireasa were afraid to look at her for very long. Every time he thought of his sister, Taireasa shied away from him. She was obviously more skilled than he at managing this odd new connection between them, and just as obviously avoiding his question.

What had happened to them? And what was wrong with Kyali? He was sure he should be able to sense her the way he could Taireasa: if this damned rhyme that had ruined so much of his life were true, then it should be all three of them dealing with this. Together.

Taireasa's grief came to him, too, a drowning heaviness she constantly struggled to push aside. In sympathy and mutual comfort, his heart reached for hers, bringing them into much closer contact. Taireasa was sore from riding, in places even someone well-versed in the mystery of women might blush at. Devin tried not to notice that, tried to offer what solace he could—and tried, with a maddening lack of success, to discover what was behind the chilling absence he got from Kyali whenever he searched for her. His sister was like a hole in the world.

The saddle slid under him as Taireasa pulled free of him again, hiding.

"Devin... are you well? Do you need to stop?"

Kinsey eyed him, eyebrows drawn together, and Devin blinked the world into place around himself. Everyone in this company probably thought he was a madman by now. He couldn't exactly argue the point.

"Well," he echoed, barely able to form the word. His father was dead, his kingdom taken by traitors, his friends in danger, and his sister was—was ill.

He had never been less well in his life.

"No." He swallowed, searching for words. "Thank you, no rest. We should keep riding."

"Is it this... sharing of thoughts with your queen?" Kinsey sounded as though he had to make an effort to believe that. Devin couldn't blame him. He'd tried to describe it this morning as they began their ascent, figuring these new allies, however temporary, deserved to know why he spent so much time staring off into the distance. He didn't think he'd managed to do it coherently, though. He hardly understood what was happening *himself*; how could he hope to explain it to others?

"Sometimes I can see out of her eyes," Devin said. "It's distracting."

The prince's forehead crumpled, but he didn't say anything else.

The land hit a sharper slope and the great prow of stone they had been riding alongside came to an abrupt end. Wind whipped into their faces. Suddenly, the whole mountain face was open to their gaze.

Savvys came to a halt, ears pricking. Eyes on the view,

Devin sat in the saddle like a lump, every muscle gone loose and numb. The wind snatched at the air, making it hard to keep his seat and even harder to breathe. He realized from the sudden cold on his cheeks that he was crying, and wiped his face.

Faestan was a distant darkness on the landscape, nestled in the great bend of the Sainey river. The tiny lines of the castle and the surrounding town were obscured by smoke.

"Damn them," Devin hissed. His hands clenched on the reins. Savvys half-reared. "Damn them, damn them, *damn them*! Oh gods, look what they've done."

He wasn't the only one weeping. The men of the Third were with him, bunching into a messy jumble of horses and soldiers as they came beyond the edge of the rock and saw Lardan spread out before them, burning.

"The barons are holdin'," Peydan muttered. "*Our* barons. Bless 'em."

That was true. No smoke hid the view of Maurynim Castle, closest to the mountains—close enough that he could see even from here that its gates were shut. Devin sucked in another breath, fumbling for sanity.

"My lord," the Cassdall lieutenant said sharply, and pointed down, toward a valley halfway up the mountain. Deep forest ringed it, and within the trees on the eastern rise, metal flashed back up at the sun.

Taireasa, Devin realized, hope flaring—but clear reason followed that. There were too many, and they were too well-armed. That was no group of refugees. He squinted, leaning forward in the saddle, and saw a banner at the edge of the treeline, yellow and green.

Sevassis.

"No," he said. "Oh, no."

"*Devin,*" Kinsey said, all the mildness gone from his voice. He truly sounded like a prince now. Devin followed Kinsey's gaze and saw, on the other side of the valley and deeper in the trees, more glints of metal moving between branches.

That was Taireasa and Kyali... heading for an ambush there was no way they could see coming.

"*No!*" Devin shouted, and reached back to where his helm was tied to his saddle, ready to *fly* down there if that was the only option. He couldn't lose any more. Not Taireasa, not Kyali. He'd rather die. If that was cowardice, fine.

Kinsey's horse bumped his, squashing his leg against Savvys's side. Kinsey's hand closed over his arm, a grip hard enough to hurt. "Tell her," the prince snapped. Devin scowled, not understanding, and the other man shook him hard. "*Tell your queen,* Devin—*use* this thing between you and tell her what you see."

"I *can't!*" he cried, wrenching his arm free of that iron grip. "We can't speak, it's only images, I don't know *how*—"

"Then *show* her!"

Oh.

Oh.

In the midst of his fright, Devin had to marvel at how quickly Kinsey had grasped the essentials of the situation. "Yes," he breathed. Kinsey let him go with a wary look.

Shutting his eyes, Devin reached for Taireasa again— reached this time without any hesitation, with all the desperate force of his fear. She was with him wholly in an instant, thundering over him, her startled concern for him so strong he could feel it speed his own pulse. He opened his eyes and felt her dizzy response to the view before him, then her joy at that glint of metal in the trees, the fact that they were within sight of one another.

He showed her the army on the other side of the valley then, the Sevassis banner flapping in its midst.

He was afraid his heart might stop altogether, her terror was so profound. Then the methodical intelligence that he was beginning to know her for overlaid that fear, and she left him in a welter of dread and determination. He came to with both hands braced on the pommel of his saddle and tears on his face once more, this time not from grief but in awe of Taireasa's defiant courage.

He had lived most of his life with her, and never known until now how brave she was.

"She knows," Devin coughed out, remembering that more than three hundred men were waiting on his word.

"Good," Kinsey said. "See to it, Annan."

Devin had no idea what that last was about. He needed to gather his wits, have Peydan muster the Third and get them ready. He didn't know what Kinsey would do—stay up here and watch a battle, probably—but he had to part from his new allies only a day after meeting them. He wasn't going to leave Taireasa and Kyali to face the Sevassis ambush alone, not when he had a chance to get there in time. Three hundred men could make a difference in a battle.

There was a deep, heartfelt sigh from near him. Devin raised his head as Annan spun his horse around, a look of grim resignation on his face.

"Arm and form up!" the Cassdall lieutenant shouted. The order echoed back, then was repeated by his own men as Peydan took charge.

Devin looked at Kinsey.

"Well," the Cassdall prince said, frowning at his horse's ears. He looked down at the valley below them, where two armies were on their way to a bloody meeting, and his gray eyes widened. "Magic, isn't it?" Kinsey asked, sounding just as young and just as terrified as Devin felt.

Four hundred men.

Speechless for once in his life, Devin got Kinsey's arm in a fierce grip and managed a smile. "My friend, your guess is as good as mine," he said.

Laughing and petrified, they rode down the mountain toward battle.

The sun had reached its zenith and was beginning a slow slide down the sky, heralding another night with only the hard ground for a bed. Taireasa cared nothing for the bedding, but she dreaded the nightmares: vivid and wrenching, full of the screams of friends, they left her curled up in frozen terror, sweat beading on her skin.

She didn't sleep alone, but she might as well have. Kyali, once woken by little more than a breath on her part, slept through all this without a twitch—slept so soundly Taireasa had begun to wonder if she were ignoring a friend's suffering.

That was a worse thought than many she'd had today... but she had to admit it wasn't impossible.

Kyali had cut herself off entirely. Someone far colder lived behind her eyes now: someone who could order soldiers and plan routes, who could set bones and bind wounds—but who didn't remember friendship, or love, or grief. Kyali moved through the days of their journey without a hint of expression, without anger or fear or any acknowledgment of what they had been to one another. What they had lost.

What she had given up, apparently, to survive the things the barons of the West had done to her.

Tell us, girl! Tell us where the princess is and it will end, you will live…

I will NOT!

Taireasa bit her lip until she could taste blood.

The memory haunted her, and not just when she slept. She refused to weep, because Kyali hadn't, and didn't, and perhaps couldn't—and what Kyali had done for her had made every hurt she lived with seem trivial.

She'd never before had someone give their life for hers. She didn't know how to live with herself now. She didn't know how to speak of it, even if Kyali were willing. What could she say? *I'm sorry? Thank you?*

I didn't leave you?

I stayed, I saw what you saw and felt what you felt, I used my Gift for this, and now I struggle to live with what you have chosen to forget?

It was a confession that had welled up in her more than once, not only because the memory of Kyali's torment haunted her so, but because her conscious use of her new Gift felt like an intrusion, like a betrayal of trust. And yet it had been necessary. She had held grimly onto Kyali's presence, unnoticed and half-mad with the echo of pain, waiting until the barons of the West left long enough for her and Marta to steal Kyali away.

And Kyali had a right to know this. The truth might even wake her from this frozen silence. But Taireasa was terrified of what it else it might do. If the memories gave *her* nightmares, what would they do to Kyali?

Did someone ever come back from such a thing?

"Kyali," Taireasa said, and clutched convulsively at the reins. Kyali didn't reply. She rode along as though dreaming.

"*Lady Corwynall*," she tried, and finally Kyali's gaze drifted to her, light and indifferent as glass. Taireasa opened her mouth to say it, say all of it, but couldn't get the words out. She swallowed, tasting bitter defeat. "What are you thinking?" she said, instead of everything that needed to be spoken. She shut her eyes, hating herself.

"Take my oath," Kyali said. "Tonight. So the army can witness."

Taireasa opened her eyes and glared. "No."

They had carried this argument with them all the way up the mountain. Kyali wouldn't let it go. And she was right, so far as it went. There had been no coronation. They were both of royal blood, and Kyali's renunciation of candidacy for the crown held far less weight now that the kingdom she'd given her allegiance to was overrun by traitors. They were *both* still eligible for the throne. There were Corwynalls in the army behind them, and their mutterings had grown over the last few days. Kyali barely spoke to her cousins, a tactic Taireasa doubted was quelling their ambition. And the Lord General's soldiers, who watched her friend with increasing reverence, listened to them.

If Kyali swore to her, it would settle this before it became an issue that demanded challenge.

But she had done enough. Enough for a lifetime. Just the thought of asking more, however willing Kyali was, made her stomach twist and bile come to the back of her throat.

"I won't have it, Ky."

"You are *asking* for a challenge, Majesty."

"*Let* them challenge. I don't care!"

She'd spoken too loud, and without thought. There was a listening hush all around them as villagers and soldiers strained to hear. Beside her, Kyali drew a measured breath, apparently still capable of frustration, if nothing else. "Majesty—"

She was so very sick of that title. "*I will not have it.* Leave me be."

"As you will," Kyali said coolly, and they fell back into a strained silence.

Taireasa put her fingers to her brow, trying to press the headache out of it—and nearly fell from the saddle when Devin's presence pushed into her thoughts with startling force, his heart full of panic. He was so bone-tired she felt her own shoulders slump.

"Devin," she gasped, and wrapped both her hands around the pommel of her saddle to keep from pitching out of it. He had never been so close, so strong. She could no longer see the trees that surrounded them or feel her horse under her. It was *his* horse she rode, his harp slung heavily across her shoulders, his terror beating in her veins. A dizzy height fell away from her, the Sainey river sparkling at the skies from a great distance, the stretch of the kingdom leveling out beyond an amazing drop. Taireasa made a shocked sound, felt hands close over her shoulders, weight pressing her back into her own saddle, her own bones.

But Devin pulled at her, wanting her attention, and she shut her eyes and gave in—saw, immediately, a stranger's face, brown like the men of Orin and noble, and beyond a crowd of similar-looking soldiers. They were not dressed like any soldiers she had seen before. The stranger looked alarmed. He said something she couldn't hear and the vision wheeled sickeningly to a forest-ringed valley nestled on the mountain's slope. A bright gleam of metal flashed in the trees. Taireasa gasped again, this time in joy, as she understood Devin was *looking at them* from that height. Soon she would have a friend by her side again.

Then the vision moved to the other side of the valley, where more metal sparked in sunlight. She strained to see through Devin's eyes, trying to understand that. There was a banner...

Taireasa frowned, feeling her weight slide in the saddle again. The colors on the banner came clear.

Yellow and green.

Sevassis.

"Oh no," Taireasa murmured as Devin let her go, leaving her with his lingering fear and his fierce love for her rolling through her head like some strange, wonderful perfume. Her heart began to pound so hard it was difficult to think. "Oh no, oh *no*." She pushed at the saddle, fighting for strength.

She opened her eyes and met two amber ones, very close. Kyali let her go immediately.

"What was that?" Kyali asked, all suspicion. She was rubbing her palms down her thighs, as though the contact had made her hands tingle.

"Is there a valley ahead of us?"

Kyali blinked once. "Aye. I'd intended for us to make camp

there tonight. How—"

"There's a company from Sevassis on the northeast side, hiding in the trees. A *large* company. We have to ride around the valley."

The quiet around them grew into something strained and awful. The officers nearest—younger, inexperienced soldiers Kyali had appointed in haste, as their wiser leaders were all lost in the raid on the Corwynall estates—stared at Taireasa as though she'd declared that their new home would be on the moon. Kyali blinked a second time, then nodded, accepting this announcement with perfect aplomb.

"How close?"

Taireasa closed her eyes, thinking. "Very. We're at the edge of it now, and Sevassis is on the other side."

"Then we won't be able to dodge them," Kyali said simply, sending a chill down Taireasa's spine. "We have villagers, and wounded. We're too large and noisy a force to sneak about in here. We'll either meet them in the valley or in the trees, and we've no chance if we meet them in the trees."

Taireasa stared at her, speechless.

Kyali turned to a man who had been riding by their side the whole way up the mountain. "Ciaran," she said. "Marshal the men into two lines with the villagers in between. Tell them to arm. I want the cavalry staggered down each side. Get the wounded together and leave them by the stream, with four guards. Take their horses." She caught the man's arm as he made to ride past. "And put my cousins on the right flank to the fore," she added. "If we're ambushed, they can meet it first."

Gods. Taireasa swallowed down a dry throat, as stunned by the ruthless practicality of that order as by the thought of riding into a battle. She allowed herself to be guided into the center, too shocked to argue. In another moment she was surrounded by soldiers on all sides. Kyali was an intermittent flicker of red braid far up ahead, riding faster, sword out and flashing in the sun. The whole line began to move quickly. Horses and men jostled around her. She tried only to breathe, to keep a calm expression. Her hands were white on the reins. She couldn't seem to fix that.

They broke through the trees suddenly and light struck her face like a slap, so bright after days in deep forest that it hurt her eyes.

There was a valley ahead, green and lush, sloping gently away from them. Taireasa squinted at it as soldiers began to spread out all around her. On the other side of the clearing, men in bright armor were pouring out of the trees, taking the low ground before their own company could hope to.

The first real battle in centuries would happen here.

I don't know what to do. Father, what do I do?

"Taireasa."

Someone had her by the shoulders. She blinked up into Kyali's grim face and bit her tongue when Kyali shook her. "Taireasa, *listen*. I am leaving you ten guards. Take the villagers into the trees on the northwest slope, as far from this as you can get. If we lose, you must head up the game trails to the ridge, to the Fraonir. Follow the river. They will protect you."

If we lose, Taireasa thought, eyes darting helplessly to the valley. Then she heard the rest, and terror turned to fury as she understood: Kyali didn't think they would win.

Kyali was about to do it all over again.

"*No!*" Taireasa cried. The word, ripping out of her, came

with an odd warping of the air that she recognized from some-where. *"Not again!* Not for me, Kyali Corwynall! Enough!"

And Kyali—flinched.

The blood drained from her face. Her eyes first went wide and then flared a bright, glaring gold like the heart of a fire. She stayed that way for a moment, frozen in place, and then bent in the saddle, shoulders hunched, curled over herself like she'd taken a sword in the belly.

"Gods," Taireasa blurted, horrified, feeling something terrible and dark pressing at her mind. Her Gift: she had done something like this to Marta when she had gotten angry. She reached a hand out and set it on Kyali's arm, felt the tension there. "Ky, I'm sorry—"

"No," Kyali whispered, and again, barely a breath, in pure desperation: *"No."* The muscles in her friend's arm shuddered, bunched. Kyali backed her horse away, trembling visibly.

Now there was an expression on her face.

Seeing it, seeing the awful struggle there, Taireasa knew Kyali *did* remember. For a second, it was all there between them—the blood, the questions, the agony and rage and help-lessness, all there. It blistered the air. It swallowed every good thing in the world. It took her breath, and all her words died unspoken.

Kyali bowed her head. Around them, soldiers looked on in justifiable panic as she clenched both hands over the hilt of her sword and fought for air, for sanity. Taireasa could only watch, mute and wretched, as Kyali put that cold mask of hers back together out of nothing but her iron will and the raw rage that was burning in her eyes.

And, guilt twisting sickly in her, knowing this might be the last glimpse she got of her truest friend, Taireasa let it happen. Their army was waiting. There was another army making its way across the valley toward them. There was a battle ahead. There was no fixing this now. There might never be.

It was like losing her all over again.

"Majesty," Maldyn murmured, close and worried, calling her away from this moment, this chance.

"We have no time for this," Kyali said finally, still trembling, but as cold as winter again. "You cannot fight. And we cannot guard you while *we* do. The villagers will follow you. Damn you, Taireasa, *get into the trees.*"

Something rose in Taireasa, past the terror that clamored at her thoughts and the mingled sorrow and guilt, something hard and determined and sure of itself. She brushed Maldyn's hand aside and urged her horse close, closer, until she was looking into Kyali's face from inches away and she could see the knots in her jaw.

"Then fight," Taireasa said. Her voice was shaking, but for once, she didn't care. "And *win*, Kyali Corwynall. I didn't come all this way to flee like a frightened sheep at the first sight of the enemy. I assume you didn't, either."

Kyali opened her mouth to retort. Taireasa held up a hand. She had heard all she could stand to hear. This was worse than anything she had ever felt, this breaking between them. She could feel tears pressing at the backs of her eyes and she couldn't, for all their sakes, allow them to fall. "Win," she said again, the word barely a hiss, and kicked her horse around.

To meet a crowd of terrified villagers waiting for orders.

"To the trees," Taireasa said, sliding from the saddle. She didn't look back, though the soldiers who were about to die in her name deserved that much.

She couldn't make herself watch Kyali riding away from her.

"Aye, la—cap... aye," Ciaran stuttered, flushing red.

None of them knew what to call her.

She didn't care one way or the other and only stared, waiting for him to sort it out. Finally giving up, Ciaran rode away to pass her orders down the line and Kyali shifted her gaze to the valley, where Sevassis was moving with slow, taunting deliberation toward them.

Fools. They would have to climb to reach the battle at this rate, but they appeared almost stupid enough to do it. She wondered idly who was commanding down there, if he was truly arrogant enough to try such a thing. An idea began to take shape in her mind, one born of two years of fighting with the Fraonir. She waved Ciaran back to her before he could make it to the right wing cavalry.

These new orders chased the pinched look of desperation from his face. He even smiled. The expression faded when she didn't return it, though, and he rode off again.

The effort of acting normally was wearing her to the bone, and she wasn't even doing a good job of it.

"Form up," she shouted, pitching it to carry over the din. She could hear the echo of her father's famous battle-shout in her own voice, and it was like a kick in the guts: she couldn't find her next breath. Every soldier's face turned toward her, like plants toward sunlight. They bunched together as instructed, presenting the sorriest possible appearance, making their numbers look even smaller than they were. Surprise was the only chance they had.

Jeers floated up to them, and a few arrows flew uselessly toward them, crashing down well out of range.

Still struggling for air, Kyali rode down the line of men, knocking the flat of her sword against their upraised blades in the old battle-blessing. She kept her eyes forward, because the hope she saw in her ragged, makeshift army made her want to strike every man who dared to look at her that way.

It was a bad jest, all of it. They were outnumbered, exhausted, poorly armed. There was little to hope for here. Many of these soldiers would die today, and probably she would with them.

And she didn't care, she didn't care, she didn't care at all.

If she kept telling herself that, maybe it would be true again.

Before this, there had been peace, a beautiful, cold distance from the world and everything in it. She had come to herself standing over Baron Cyrnic's corpse and not batted an eyelash, had dealt with all the things that needed to be done without a ripple of worry or confusion. Everything had been possible, and nothing mattered. But now—

Now she *remembered*.

The memory was a gaping wound in her mind, bleeding sick, black rage all over everything. Her hands shook. Her whole body shook. She lowered the sword before any of the soldiers could see and rode to the front line of the left wing, from which she planned to lead. Ciaran had the right wing. She had changed the battle order still further: Feldan Corwynall, cousin and would-be challenger for Taireasa's throne (as if she would ever let that happen) had the center now, where the heaviest fighting would be. He had understood that order clearly, by the pale, hurt fury on his face. She didn't need to explain to him whose claim she would be supporting, or how far she would go to keep Taireasa safe.

A cousin's life meant nothing next to that. Not even a cousin she'd known all her days.

One more thing she would have liked not to care about.

Damn Taireasa, who had done this to her.

Taireasa stood even now at the very edge of the forest, her dress blowing like a banner in the rising wind. At the sight of her, Kyali hissed a helpless curse, love and rage seeping out of her very bones, making thought almost impossible. Taireasa was there, but she was also *here* somehow, in all her stubborn, bright loyalty—far too close, a heart impossible to hide from forever.

Mystery solved. *This* was how Taireasa had known of the ambush, and that meant Devin wasn't far. She could almost sense her brother now too, pushing at her like Taireasa was, but thankfully without Taireasa's astounding strength. A treacherous part of her wanted it, whatever it was—wanted nothing more than to curl up in the headstrong, foolish comfort of their love and wail like a banshee until some of this unendurable darkness left her.

That could never happen.

They would see immediately what had happened, how she had fought and lost, what the price of that failure had been. They would see how the memory filled her and twisted her thoughts; they would see the dark and ugly stain of it all through her. They would learn about powerlessness, and cruelty. And then they, too, would have to live with it. The thought was more than she could bear.

Her heart clenched in her chest like a fist, one more misery on top of a thousand of them.

Kyali looked down the hill at the enemy, trembling and aching and wanting to kill everything in sight, to just lay around her with the sword until the death she dealt or the death she expected to meet in the valley below gave her back that cold, unfeeling peace.

Sevassis's forces came blithely into range and began their mad uphill charge, singing battle songs and shouting taunts, stupidly sure of themselves. Gods, what kind of fool was giving orders down there? They hadn't even raised their shields. Kyali lifted a single hand. A second later, the air filled with the deadly whine of arrows, as the archers she'd hidden behind the bunched infantry stood and loosed.

Screams filled the valley. The men in the front line went down and were trampled by their own cavalry, who were now moving too fast to stop. She felt a fierce, angry satisfaction kindle in her.

In that moment, Devin's presence came suddenly clear, a force like a gale, irresistible, breaking her open and making her *feel*, oh gods, not now—

"*Now!*" Kyali screamed, her voice cracking on the word. It brought the rage in an annihilating flood, sweeping all her hurt and horror along with it, and oh, dear gods, it was such a *relief* to let go.

Ainhearag leapt to life under her. They were racing down, down, the air filled with thunder. Her men were behind her, shouting and howling.

She set her arm, braced her feet into the stirrups.

Ahead, the Sevassis line loomed, and as she met the eyes

of a Western soldier holding a pike, she discovered there was still room in her for fear. But her hands knew their business. They swept the pike aside while her mind was still noticing the color of his eyes and opened a hole in his exposed throat. He went down, and she met the enemy line full-on. The impact was stunning. She kept her grip on the sword only out of habit.

Then there was no more time to think or feel, only a series of seconds streaming by in a welter of chaos: blood spraying, a gash opening in a man's head, horses screaming. Every man wore Cyrnic's face, or Brisham's, or Viam's, or Walderan's—she heard a strange, high sound of pure fury and realized she was making it.

A blow landed on her hip. Kyali shook her splintered shield off and got the sword in both hands, beginning the mounted Forms, making a space about herself that was filled with the wails of wounded men and horses. Ainhearag screamed and reared up, kicking a man, shouldering a horse aside. Kyali gripped the saddle with her knees, forced her blade through the arm-join of a chestplate with the Sevassis shield glaring bright on it, and spun to swing at the herald behind him. The blow took the man's head clean off, and the banner he was holding disappeared into the jostling mess as he fell.

A great cry went up from her men.

There should have been triumph, but she felt only the increasing pressure of Taireasa and Devin reaching for her. Her heart was cracking like a bowl, the pain and dark inside bleeding out—it was beyond bearing, she had nothing left to fight it with, and she screamed again, her throat going instantly raw with it. She swung the sword over and over without thought, until all around her there was a dreadful, perfect silence.

They had broken the enemy line.

No—they were *behind* it, all the left wing wrapped around it like a snake. Kyali let Ainhearag stumble to a halt and stilled herself with a ferocious effort, every limb trembling.

She was still alive.

There was no triumph in this either, only a vague, exhausted acceptance—that and the rage, the endless, angry wound. Killing didn't help. She suspected that nothing would.

Tears were leaking slowly from her eyes. She bowed her head, because the officers of her wing were struggling toward her and she'd given them more than enough cause to doubt her already. She swiped at her face with shaking hands, looked up, and was struck by the sight of the center and right wings of her cobbled-together army meeting the Sevassis line, turning the whole valley into a heaving sea of metal under the bright, indifferent sky. Her cousins were holding the center, but the bulk of the Western effort was indeed falling there. Men were dying by the dozens. The right wing was struggling to echo her sweep, snagging in the brush-ridden ground on that side of the valley, doomed to fall when Sevassis turned its attention to them.

They'd done better than she hoped, but they were still outnumbered, and numbers were going to tell. Her men were regrouping around her now, and there weren't many options left. Kyali tried to gather her scattered thoughts and wished hopelessly that Taireasa and her brother would stop *pulling* at her so.

"Captain!"

Gods, who was calling *her* that?

She looked around, frowning, but she couldn't tell who it had been. She felt Devin's presence grow into something fierce and close, and she held her hand up to silence any other remarks while she tried to simultaneously fight her brother off and figure out where he was.

Then she saw the metal flashing in the trees on the northern slope.

As she squinted, it became a company of soldiers, every one of them ahorse. They broke past the treeline onto bare ground, pounding toward the Sevassis line. It was Devin, dear gods, and what was left of the missing Third Battalion. She saw it all in an instant, how it would happen.

They were going to *win*.

The new company hit the slope at a wild gallop and drove down. Sevassis buckled instantly, and a sound like a whole hall full of pots rattling rolled over her. Men were running from the field, chased down by her center and right lines. Her officers were cheering.

Kyali sat numbly in the saddle, trying to feel something, trying to be glad. Even now there was only rage, and the futile, painful struggle to keep Taireasa and Devin from seeing it. Devin was fighting now, right in the thick of it: she could feel him more clearly than ever. His terror and his resolve not to lose her and Taireasa cracked her heart open further, a paralyzing, bittersweet sort of agony she'd never known. She doubled up, her hands pressed to her chest. Part of her was reaching for him, reaching for Taireasa. The pulling in her middle was agony. They were both so close that flashes of what they were seeing came to her—a tangle of men and swords, the faces of terrified villagers. She was lost in it, drowning under their love and their determination.

"No," Kyali gasped. "Please—no—"

Cyrnic's face. Walderan's. Pain, blood, failure, endless questions—fire—

Her heart shut itself like a door, locking tight around the memory.

Kyali straightened, dazed. Taireasa and Devin were gone. Only seconds had passed. Her officers were looking to her, worried, waiting. She stretched, trying to ignore the lonely, furious voice inside her crying out for her best friend and her brother. She could never have that, not without hurting them.

She was alone. As she would have to be from this moment onward. She thought she could live with this.

Somehow.

"We have help!" she cried, hearing and hating the rough edge of pain in her voice. "Let's finish this! *Ride for the center!*"

She kicked Ainhearag into a run and heard her men come racing behind her, their battle cries echoing off the watching mountain and empty dome of the sky. Her sword was in her hands. They were screaming her name, or her father's. It didn't matter which.

14

A harpy?"

"Yes."

"That's a bit extreme."

"It is *accurate*, my Lord Prince."

"She was fresh from battle. Nobody is at their best then. I'm sure her manners are perfect when she's in her element."

"She was in her element *then*," Annan said emphatically, his usual non-expression suffering a little. Kinsey smothered a smile. He'd known Annan for years, and he'd never seen his lieutenant so aggravated. To be fair, it wasn't exactly unjustified. The Lady Corwynall had practically frozen the blood in his veins when she'd appeared at the end of the battle, grim-faced and misted with blood, to address him in a voice more appropriate to sentencing a hanging than thanking him for his company's assistance in the fight.

But it was still funny to see how shocked Annan was, confronted with a commander both female and a year or two younger than Kinsey himself at the head of over a thousand men.

"Elaria of Fellisdown commanded a battalion, didn't she?" Kinsey murmured, avoiding the uneasy glances of the Lardana soldiers they passed. They were busy building cairns, retrieving armor and blades, burying the dead.

"That was a hundred years ago."

"I'm just saying. There *is* precedent."

"Probably much more of one here," Annan grumbled.

Kinsey bit the inside of his cheek against a grin.

They rode up the northern rise toward a great pavilion tent the Fraonir had provided. They were to meet both of the Fraonir Clan leaders and also Lady Taireasa Marsadron, the deposed queen of the Lardana. They had scraps of white cloth tied over the pommels of their swords. Kinsey looked back, over the ravaged valley and the yawning graves, the bodies, and shivered.

"So, second thoughts?" he asked, in this last moment for them, and Annan huffed in stifled outrage.

"Only a wagonload or three."

"Three, is that all? I must be on the right track, then."

Annan wasn't amused. "You trust too easily, my Lord Prince, and commit yourself too quickly to get the sense of a situation."

"Well, I hope to get that now."

"Too *late*, my lord; you are already committed." Frustration was written in the sullen hunch of Annan's shoulders. Kinsey felt bad about that, but not about the rest. He knew he should be worried at where his wild whim to trust a stranger had brought them, and more so still by the absence of any information about where they were headed now—but he found he was strangely cheerful about it all.

He should probably be worried about that, too.

"Maybe I'm bespelled?" Kinsey suggested, frowning mildly at the sky.

"I thought of that."

"*Did* you?" This was fascinating. "And am I?"

"This is unusually rash for you, but I see nothing that suggests it."

"Are there signs?"

"I don't *know*, my Lord Prince. I never took all this—*this*—for more than a child's tale. And now I've been dropped in the midst of singing fools and harpies at the head of armies, chasing over the countryside after a rhyme a dead man wrote." Annan rubbed the back of his neck and glared at the ground.

"It *is* rather extraordinary, when you put it that way. I think you can stop calling me 'my Lord Prince' now, by the way. I assure you no one else here is likely to."

That earned him a glower and, after a moment, a short grunt that might have been laughter. "What do you suggest I call you instead?"

"I'm sure you can think of a new title."

"Oh, several," Annan said, dry as bone, and Kinsey snickered.

"Just so you don't accuse me of—ah, Devin," he blurted, because the Bard had come to meet them at the edge of a great mass of encamped men. Meeting Devin's miserable gaze, Kinsey felt all the good humor flee him. Devin did not look as though winning a battle and being reunited with his sister and his queen had eased his mind at all.

Quite the opposite, in fact.

"You can leave your horses here," Devin said, and Kinsey dismounted without a thought to protocol. Annan eyed the army of foreigners they were now standing in the midst of and followed suit.

"What is it?" Kinsey asked, low enough to escape the listening ears of the soldiers all around them.

"It's not—it's nothing to do with you, Highness."

"Stop calling me that. I... Devin, are you all right?"

"*I* am," he replied, a note of bewildered despair edging his words.

Kinsey fell silent, because this was hardly the place for discussing whatever was wrong. There was a strange tension to the soldiers surrounding them, and a clear division in the camp itself, almost as though there were two separate armies taking up the same space. He slid a glance toward Annan, and his lieutenant jerked his chin very slightly in the direction of the pavilion.

"Lead the way, Lord Corwynall," Kinsey said, loud enough to carry. Devin nodded, not even seeming to notice the soldiers, and turned toward the tents.

This wasn't going well so far.

The pavilion was surrounded by tense soldiers, and also by men in odd long tunics and breeches mottled dark brown and green, most of whom had the same sand-shade of skin as Annan and his kin. Longbows arced over their backs on one side; swords in baldrics loomed over the other. The mysterious mountainfolk. Kinsey met the gaze of one inadvertently, realized it was actually a woman he was staring at, and slipped into the pavilion blinking. His eyes needed a moment to adjust to the dimness: all he could see were vague shapes. His pulse began to race.

"Your Highness of Cassdall, well met," someone said, sounding remarkably sincere, and a young woman came forward and took his hand. For a second, he could see nothing but the startling contrast of her hair and skin next to the dark cloth of her gown. A scent like clean rain and lilacs hit his nose.

"Thank you," Kinsey said. "...Your Majesty."

She must have heard the question in his voice. "Yes, Highness, I am Taireasa Marsadron." She let go of his hand and stepped back. Her face was coming clear. Kinsey wished suddenly that it wouldn't, because she was beautiful in a dazzling way he'd never encountered before, and he was already making an idiot of himself. He bowed, trying to gather his scattered wits.

"Thank you, Majesty, for the welcome."

"And I thank you, Highness, for your aid in the battle. It would have been a far harder fight without your arrival."

"You can credit the Lord Corwynall for that," Kinsey said. He slid a sideways glance at Devin, where he was standing next to a pair of tall Fraonir men in those mottled green outfits. Devin's eyes were only for his sister. The Lady Corwynall hovered at the edge of this gathering, a tall girl in simple armor with even less expression on her face than Annan, something Kinsey would not have believed possible. Her gaze flickered over him, and his shoulders twisted into an involuntary shudder. All the Lardana he'd met looked grief-stricken, but he'd never encountered anyone with such distance in their eyes.

He began to understand why Devin was so upset.

"And I believe the Lord Corwynall can credit the Clan leaders of the Fraonir," Annan said, so innocently it was almost possible to overlook the fact that he was fishing for answers.

His eyes had narrowed, taking in all the odd currents moving through the room, all the awkward silences.

Kinsey shifted and stepped on Annan's foot. "My lieutenant, Annan Adaron," he said, forcing Annan to be polite.

One of the Fraonir men approached, gripping his wrist in greeting. "Kinsey of Cassdall," the man said, which seemed like a fairly clear statement on where these mountainfolk stood on the matter of his title. "Welcome. I am Measail Sarn's-son, leader of the Eanin Clan."

The other man, tall and broad as though he had been carved from the mountain itself, came forward to take his wrist next. "Well met," he said simply. "You traveled hard to be here."

"We did, sir—"

"Arlen. Arlen Ulin's-son, leader of the Darachim Clan. Your arrival was timely."

As yours was not, Kinsey thought, for the Fraonir Clans had shown up only when the battle was done—they had provided aid afterward, yes, but it was a lapse he couldn't help but wonder about, given all Devin had said of them and their mysterious foreknowledge. Arlen Ulin's-son gave him a grim smile, as though he'd spoken that thought out loud. Kinsey gave the smile right back and was pleased to see a thoughtful look cross this Arlen's face.

"Sir," Kinsey said quietly. "Majesty," he added, turning to the Lady Taireasa, who set a hand on his sleeve and neatly blew every thought out of his head with that single, polite touch. What *had* he gotten himself into here? If every Lardana he met exerted this compelling pull, he was going to end up wandering around this wild country after them like a forlorn puppy.

"We have come from Cassdall because we've no place

there," he said at last, wrenching his brain back to the needs of the moment with a fierce effort that gave him an instant headache. "My uncle took the throne by force, and has made it clear that I am not a welcome member of his court. I know that your own affairs are anything but settled, but if it would be possible to reach some sort of understanding—"

Taireasa's fingers tightened over his wrist and the rest of the words dried up unsaid.

"Your Highness, for my part, you are most welcome," she said. "But I'm not in a position to make offers at the moment. We are refugees, too, and also in hope of aid from the Fraonir..."

"Which we are offering," Arlen Ulin's-son said smoothly. He eyed the point where Taireasa's fingers were resting on Kinsey's arm and she took her hand back, a faint stain of color blooming on her cheeks. Kinsey looked desperately away from that. "Prince of Cassdall, you will have seen some old stone-work on your way to meet us here."

"Yes..."

"Well. It is unoccupied, and more or less in good repair now. It will keep out the weather, at least. And it's large enough for both of your peoples, in whatever arrangement you choose to make."

Kinsey opened his mouth, but for a second he couldn't get anything out of it. This offer was both more and less solid than he'd been braced for: he had hoped, at most, for the freedom of the mountain, and permission to build a permanent camp. Instead they were offered a share of a *castle*, however old... and must make all arrangements beyond that with the Lardana, who apparently had first claim.

Interesting. And strange.

And, gods, how in the world had they known so far in advance that returning this castle to *good repair* would be necessary?

"More or less good repair *now*," the Lady Corwynall echoed while he was still trying to find his tongue, clearly thinking in the same direction.

"Aye, we have done what we could to make it ready," the Clan leader said, facing her.

Taireasa Marsadron frowned, her eyes narrowed in thought. "But if you..."

"We're not prophets, lowland queen—just men with a better view. We made the mountain keep ready in case it was needed. I am sorry to see that it is, but it is yours if you want it."

Ulin's-son's tone made it clear he considered this the end of the discussion, but judging by the line forming between Taireasa's eyebrows, Kinsey doubted that was the case. Taireasa looked ready to say more, but Kyali Corwynall pushed in.

"There is another thing that must be settled here," she said—and, as Taireasa's frown grew deeper, she bent at the knee, her eyes locked firmly on her queen's. Taireasa turned a strange color and stumbled a quick few steps backward. Devin caught her arm before she could fall.

"What is *this*?" he asked, obviously trying for humor, but his voice shook. "Sister, you've an odd sense of timing—" Horror dawned on his face. "Oh gods," he said. "Taireasa, she hasn't *sworn*? Are you mad?"

Taireasa wrenched away from him. "I won't," she said. "I will not do this. Get up," she snapped at Kyali, without looking at her.

"No," Kyali insisted. "We have *one* army, Majesty—do something to keep it that way while you still can!"

Devin blinked down at his sister. "What?"

"Feldan," Kyali said grimly. Some of the angry color in Devin's face fell away.

"Oh, far too ambitious, cousin," he murmured. He took hold of Taireasa's wrist again, carefully, as though he thought she might hit him. "Taireasa, Feldan's an idiot. But she *has* to swear," he said softly. "You know it. We can't afford to leave any question about who rules here. Take her oath."

"*I will not.*"

The effort of speaking the words left Taireasa visibly winded. She turned away from them all, her hands curling into fists. Kinsey took a diffident step back, not sure what he and Annan had come into, but positive it wasn't something he ought to witness. It seemed deeply private, and painful even to the Lady Corwynall, who was still kneeling where her queen had left her. Her eyes had a peculiar golden light in them.

Devin ran a hand through his dark hair, leaving it standing in all directions. "Taireasa, you *must*. You can't—how do you think—" He sputtered to a halt, flinging his hand out. "It was the vote that started all this!"

Aha. Kinsey searched his memories of Lardana histories, their strange customs. The schism in the army he'd noted earlier made sense now. *Two* royal houses. Devin was a Bard, a sacred profession that precluded all rank and title—but Kyali Corwynall was as eligible for the throne as Taireasa was, and the events of the uprising that had landed them all here had thrown the right of rule into question.

Gods, this could be messy if it weren't settled quickly.

"Leave me alone," Taireasa said, her voice bleak and exhausted. Her shoulders slumped. "Please, just leave it be."

"What *happened* to you two?" Devin cried. "You barely look at one another, you don't speak, you've left *this* of all things in question—"

Taireasa hunched over herself as though she were in pain. Kinsey felt a chill steal over his skin as Kyali sucked in a gasping breath, like a woman about to jump from a great height into deep water. She pulled a locket out from under her shirt.

Something like the heaviness before a thunderstorm filled the air in the tent.

Beside him, Annan stiffened, his hand hovering over the pommel of his sword as if the small space were filling up with enemies. Kinsey got his lieutenant's arm in a firm grasp and pulled them both backward on an impulse he didn't stop to question. *Something* was happening, something bewildering and a little bit horrible. The air was growing heavier, thicker. His hair began to stand on end.

Kyali Corwynall snapped the chain of the locket.

A guttural moan leapt out of her throat... and halfway across the tent, Taireasa cried out as though struck, while Devin crumpled to the dirt with a groan. Kyali fell forward with a strangled sound and caught herself on her hands. She was breathing in ragged gasps.

"What *is* this?" Annan hissed, his arm hard as stone under Kinsey's hand.

"Hush," Kinsey murmured. "Magic... I think it's magic."

The air snapped and sang, pushing at his skin, dragging at the air in his lungs. Taireasa had turned to face Kyali. "No," she choked out. "No, Kyali, *why?*"

Shuddering, Kyali pushed herself upright. Her eyes were on her brother. Devin rolled to his knees and crawled, head down and shameless, across the tent to his sister. "Don't," was all he said, in a tiny, sad voice.

Kyali's chin came up. She pressed the locket into his hands. "I have no House," she said into the silence.

Taireasa covered her face. Devin stared. After a moment, he swallowed audibly and looked down at the locket in their tangled fingers. "You have no House," he said to their hands.

"I ha... have no kin."

"You—oh gods, Kyali—you have no kin."

Tears spilled over Devin's face. Kinsey felt his own eyes sting in sympathy. Kyali herself was stone, only that small hesitation and the unhealthy pallor of her skin hinting at what this might cost.

"I have no allegiance but what I make hereafter," she finished. Devin drew a shuddering breath, his mouth twisting, and pulled the locket from her palm. He clutched it so hard a thin line of blood slid out of his closed fist.

"Kyali of House Corwynall is no more," he rasped. Then he shoved himself up to weave drunkenly to one of the tent posts and lean against it.

Kyali spared a single glance toward her brother's knotted form, then flexed her fingers. For a brief second, she had such a lost look that Kinsey bit his lip as the same sort of sympathy that had drawn him to Devin curled queasily in his guts. Her eyes caught his, and he watched her pull a mask of calmness over herself like a helm. When she turned to look at Taireasa, she was perfectly composed again.

"Bind me or cast me out, Your Majesty," she said.

"Damn you," Taireasa whispered.

"Yes."

The two girls looked at one another for a long moment, the air crackling between them. Kinsey waited, breath held, and nearly jumped into the low ceiling when a soldier pushed past the canvas door of the tent, letting in the burning light of the setting sun and the startlingly loud noise of the camp.

"Majesty," he said, kneeling. He sent a single, bewildered glance at Kyali, who was also kneeling at Taireasa's feet, and then bowed his head.

"Ranan," Taireasa said. "What is it?"

"The men... Majesty, Feldan Corwynall..." He couldn't seem to get the rest out.

"Such timing," Taireasa hissed, setting a hand on the man's shoulder. "All right. All right, then. I will meet him outside in a moment," she said quietly.

Devin turned. "Taireasa, no," he objected.

"What would you suggest? They have a right to challenge. I can hardly expect to carry this out in secret. Certainly not in a tent. I'm sure our army has heard an earful already. I want this done in the open."

Kyali heaved herself unsteadily to her feet. "Gods *damn* it, Taireasa! No more of this. *Take my oath.*"

"No, no, and no again." Taireasa turned to the soldier. "Leave us. We will be out in a moment."

"Majesty," the soldier murmured, wretched, and stood to slip out.

"So," Taireasa said, looking at her own hands. She met Kyali's furious gaze one more time. Her shoulders went back and she spun in a swirl of skirts to leave. Devin followed, casting an anguished glance back at Kyali, then at Kinsey. "Stay here," he said hurriedly, and vanished out into the dying daylight and the sound of a great many angry and desperate soldiers.

"Not likely," Annan muttered.

And it wasn't. This was a bad position to be in—and would be far worse if the Lady Marsadron didn't win this day. Kinsey had no idea what sort of welcome he would receive from another claimant.

Kyali strode past them to the entrance, but Arlen caught her by the arm before she could get there. She flinched away from him as though he had burned her, and the Clan leader let her arm go immediately.

"I have something for you," he said, his voice gone rough, and bent to retrieve a leather-wrapped bundle that clattered. "You might find it useful."

Kyali stared at his face, then at the bundle. Without taking it from him, she pulled a corner of the wrappings back gingerly, as though it might bite. Inside were a tunic and trousers of plain black leather, folded carefully, and armor: *beautiful* armor, shining silver and black, engravings running all over the steel. It was in the old style instead of a full, heavy suit: brigandine and segmented pieces buckled together, leaving far more of the wearer exposed—but leaving, also, far more freedom to move. Kyali stepped away from it. Her eyes had that disturbing light in them again.

"I have no time for this," she said, and indeed, they could hear Taireasa's voice echoing outside, speaking about loyalty and honor. A man's voice replied, not politely.

"You do if you want to answer that," Arlen said.

The look she gave him could have frozen water at a hundred paces. Kinsey squelched an impulse to step back, away from whatever was between these two. Beside him, Annan moved closer in silent curiosity.

"Do I have a choice?" Kyali asked.

"No more than I do, girl. I would have spared you this if I did."

Her hands knotted into fists. For a long moment, she stared at the ground, expressionless yet shuddering with tension, and then she set her jaw and drew the bundle of armor into her arms. She walked off without another word.

Kinsey eyed the Clan leader, getting as much information from that as he might have from staring at a tree. He wondered irritably if he would be spending the rest of his life trying to comprehend the currents between his new allies. Kyali reappeared several moments later clad in silver and black, looking like something out of a faery tale. A sword rose over her shoulder. Long daggers rode low on her hips. She spared none of them a single glance, only marched past them and out of the tent.

Annan grabbed his arm. Kinsey frowned at his lieutenant, then realized he'd turned to follow Kyali without a second thought. "You shouldn't go out there," Annan said, for once without a shred of irony or reproach coloring his voice.

"No, I shouldn't," Kinsey agreed. "But I'm going to."

"Of course you are," Annan said calmly, and drew his sword.

They emerged into a sunset like a brushfire. The army had left their tents and come to mass at the pavilion, more than a thousand men crowding close, craning to see. He could see his own, much smaller company at the edges, trying to get to him, but there was no hope of that in this crush. Taireasa stood at the edge of a space the soldiers had cleared away from, facing a stranger. The man wore a soldier's rough armor, but with the red-and-silver dragon shield of the House of Corwynall blazing on his shoulder.

That must be Feldan, the ambitious cousin.

"That she is unbound does not mean she is not eligible for the throne!" he was saying, evidently about Kyali. Devin had his sister's discarded locket in his fist, brandishing it high above his head. "You left us for your music, cousin. House Corwynall deserves a say in these matters! And do we not all deserve a queen strong enough to take our kingdom back?"

At his back stood two men with the same winged eyebrows and dark eyes as Devin and Kyali, clearly family. They were not rallying to Feldan, precisely, but they didn't leave him, either. And it was clear from the shouts behind him that Feldan had found some support in the army for this challenge.

"Cousin, you know nothing at all if you can doubt that of Taireasa," Devin shouted back.

"Then someone must teach me," Feldan declared, his face going red. "No more talking. Challenge, I say! I will fight whatever champion she chooses, and prove whose House is the stronger."

Taireasa's mouth made a hard line, but she didn't flinch. "So be it," she said, cutting off Devin's outraged objection.

Kyali pushed her way through to stand next to Taireasa. There was a sudden, shocked silence as the soldiers took in her shining armor, the sword over her shoulder.

"Are you quite done speaking for me?" she said coolly.

Feldan's chin lifted. "You know I'm right, little cousin."

"What I know is that you've put your ambition over your oaths, Feldan Corwynall." She stepped into the empty space in the center of the circle and reached up over her shoulder to draw her sword. "I know you've challenged," she said, and a rising wave of shock and worry echoed through the army. "And

I know I will answer. *Cousin.*"

Clearly this wasn't part of Feldan's plan. "I will not harm one of my own—"

"I'm not one of your own now, Feldan Corwynall. Her Majesty needs a champion: I am that. Or you can retract your challenge."

"Kyali, no," Taireasa murmured, but if she heard it, Kyali didn't bother acknowledging. It was, Kinsey had to admit, a neat solution: if she won, Taireasa's claim would be established, and if she lost, House Corwynall would have no one of the direct line on which to pin a claim of their own.

It was truly brutal, though. Kinsey didn't dare look at Devin just then.

"Then I suppose I must fight," Feldan said slowly, drawing his sword from the sheath at his side. *"Cousin."*

Taireasa reached blindly for Devin's hand, and he took it in a pale grip as Feldan backed farther into the circle and Kyali followed.

"I'll be sorry to kill you, little cousin," Feldan said. It had the sound of a taunt, but his face was grave as they began to circle one another.

Kyali said nothing.

She brought her sword up slanted across her face and placed her feet carefully. Kinsey felt some of the desperate tension around him begin to seep into his own bones. He hoped that this angry young woman was as good as she seemed to think she was. Feldan closed suddenly, feinted left and drove in with a quick, forceful stroke. But even as the crowd was gasping, Kyali had sidestepped it with fluid grace. She twisted her own sword in a complicated blur of movement and metal sang as their blades met.

Feldan staggered backward. He dove in at her again imme-diately, quick and vicious. This time it was she who stumbled away, a cut appearing on one cheek. Her eyes were a golden smolder. They circled again, both of them warier now.

"Yield or die," Feldan demanded, eyeing her over the edge of his blade.

"There will be no yielding today," Kyali hissed—and spun into a startling leap to avoid his sweep at her legs. The soldiers muttered: it was a coward's strike. But Kyali landed lightly and spun a second time, sword flashing up and around, quicker than Feldan by far. Feldan loosed a cry that seemed to be more frustration than anything else and battered her with a furious set of blows. Kyali staggered again, then seemed to find her footing. She parried each blow with one of her own, perfectly slanted so that her cousin's sword slid, time and again, from the angle of her blade.

And then she was done defending. She began to strike, faster and faster, until Feldan was backing away, trying to gain enough space to move. But Kyali gave him no quarter. Her sword flashed in patterns almost too quick to follow, leaving a streak of sunset-stained silver afterglow trailing through the twilight. She was faster than anyone Kinsey had ever seen. Be-side him, Annan muttered something, sounding uneasy. The air in the circle began to shiver eerily, like the trails of heat above a fire.

Feldan uttered a furious shout, raising his sword over-head for a killing blow, and Kyali's next, blindingly fast motion brought the point of her sword to his chest.

He turned right into it, and his mouth opened in a choked scream.

Kyali froze. Her gaze fell to the sword that connected them, the blood welling darkly out, and then rose to his face. For a moment, if Feldan had wished it, he could have split her head in two with his half-finished blow.

Instead the sword fell from his fingers. He wrapped a hand around the blade in his chest. He said something to her, too soft for Kinsey to hear, but whatever it was it bled the anger and all the flush of effort from her face. Feldan sank to his knees. Kyali followed, holding the sword in place carefully. He spoke again, blood bubbling from his lips to run down his chin. She nodded once, decisively, and set her hand over his, on the blade.

"Oh, gods, cousin," Devin murmured.

Kyali pulled the blade out in one quick movement and stood, cradling it in her bloody hands. Feldan sagged backward, hands fluttering helplessly over the wound. Blood pooled around him. He went still.

No one made a sound as Kyali pulled a small square of cloth out of a pocket and cleaned her sword, looking only at that.

"Is there question?" she finally said into the silence.

Clearly not. After a moment, someone shouted "Long live the queen!"—a cry that was taken up immediately, becoming a roar of approval that echoed off cliffs and filled the dusky sky.

Not seeming the least bit moved, Kyali turned to face Taireasa.

"Damn it," Taireasa muttered.

"*Now*, Taireasa," Devin said, never looking at her. "Take her oath. Please. No more bloodshed. It won't stop... you know it won't."

Taireasa sucked in a deep breath, nostrils flaring. "Not on these terms."

"Then damn it, *make your own terms*, Your Majesty!"

"Fine," Taireasa spat. "Fine. I *will* do that."

She shook Devin's hand from hers and strode out into the circle as the cheers rose and, all over the little valley, men knelt. The moon was rising in the east, piercing through leaves, and the last dying rays of the sun painted the western horizon. In the odd heat-shimmer still hovering over the clearing, thickening around the two young women meeting there, it looked like floating fire. Kinsey felt a shiver twist up his spine.

Kyali knelt, offering her sword up in both hands. She spoke her oath clearly. Taireasa set her hands on the sword, raised it, and spoke the reply as the air snapped and whined around them. Beside him, Devin made a small, surprised noise and went still. Kinsey sent him a worried glance. The Bard grinned at him fiercely.

"Watch *this*," he said. "Nobody gets the best of Taireasa for long."

Taireasa set a hand on Kyali's shoulder, still holding her sword in one hand.

"*Sword shall guide the hands of men,*" she said. It was so silent now it was possible to hear the tidal whisper of over a thousand men breathing. Taireasa smiled then, a grim, satisfied expression.

"This day has been one of sorrow and sacrifice," she said clearly. "We have lost as much as we are willing to lose. From this moment onward, we are *one people*, united in our determination to regain our kingdom, and *one army*, united in our defense of Lardan—and of each other. Kyali Corwynall. For your devotion to the rightful crown, for the skill you have acquired in hard years of study, and for the gift of command that we all witnessed when you fought and won our first battle, I name you captain of this army, the Exile's Army..."

She wasn't done speaking, but the cries of the soldiers drowned out her words. Men shouted and clapped and whistled like boys, rising to their feet almost as one. Kinsey swallowed a shout of his own. It was impossible not to be caught in the joy these soldiers gave voice to.

Taireasa waited until the noise had fallen. She handed Kyali her sword, pulling her to her feet. "Rise," she said. "*Captain Corwynall.*"

Kyali sheathed her sword in the gathering dark. For an instant, Kinsey was afraid she would refuse. But instead she clenched her hands into fists and squared her shoulders.

"My Lady Queen," she said, and saluted.

Then the soldiers began to chant, rhythmic and jubilant. They could probably hear it all the way down the mountain, where the enemies of these remarkable people sat.

"Lady Captain, Lady Captain, *Lady Captain!*"

BOOK 2

LADY CAPTAIN

15

"Excuse me, m'lord..."

"Yes, of course."

"Oh, m'lord! I'm so sorry—"

"No, it's fine, after you."

Devin ducked and dodged his way through a confusion of soldiers and servants and terrified villagers leading sheep and goats. Between the bleating and the shouting, it sounded like an invasion.

Another invasion.

A new party of refugees had arrived, bearing scant belongings, bad news, and sorely needed supplies from the Eastern barons—who, bless them, held strong in their keeps and sent what they could spare on the backs of newly homeless small-folk. The grain and livestock were much appreciated, but their band of refugees was rapidly becoming a city. The constant press of people rubbed his already short temper raw.

He made it to a doorway and all but fell over at the sudden cessation of noise. "Gods," he muttered, and wandered down the dark hall without a second thought, just because there was nobody in it but him.

It wasn't getting any easier.

Nearly two months they'd been here, clearing out rooms, building barracks, hunting mountain game, making this place as much a home as an ancient castle at the top of the world could ever hope to be to a horde of melancholy exiles... and every day was as much of a struggle as the first few had been.

He missed his father.

He missed his sister, who was still with him, but didn't behave as though she cared about anything anymore.

It takes time, Taireasa had said. *We all deal with grief in our own ways.*

But Taireasa couldn't meet his eye when she defended Kyali and he knew, through the thread of magic that bound them, that she hurt just as much as he did at that desertion. They had been joined at the hip their whole lives, and suddenly his little sister had nothing but coldness for Taireasa—and for him.

Did grief do *this*?

Devin leaned against the wall, probably getting dust all over his clothes in the process. His sorrow was a never-ending ambush, surprising him at odd moments—the sight of a child playing with a wooden sword, men singing war songs, Taireasa's strained, weary smile across a room—and he'd have to duck out of the company of others and bite his tongue until the pain chased away the threat of tears. Every time someone called him *Lord Corwynall*, it was salt in the wound.

He *couldn't* be Head of House—but his cousins, who were

the next logical choice, were now tainted by Feldan's treachery... and his sister, who should have been Head and had been groomed all her life for it, was by her own choice not even truly a Corwynall anymore. Though he would never stop thinking of her as one.

He let his head hang, since there was no one here to see him do it.

"Captain, the party on the eastern ridge sent word of an encounter with Western scouts."

"I've heard. We'll send out our own band this evening, and I want another ready to—"

Kyali.

Devin straightened, making something pop painfully in his spine. He was rubbing his neck and grimacing when his old friend from a wild trip over the mountain and his little sister came around a corner and stopped, seeing him.

"Begging your pardon, then, Captain, I'll see to the men." Peydan sidled past them with a muttered greeting and a look of sympathy Devin wasn't sure he was meant to see. Kyali, all silver and black in the armor she was never without these days, stared at him for a long moment and then began to move past him.

"It's going well, I see," Devin said, just to have something to say.

They both paused to listen to the echo of his words die against the stone walls.

"Well enough," Kyali said curtly, and moved around him in the dark little hallway, clearly wanting to get away. Devin's stomach knotted up into a queasy, homesick heartache.

"Kyali—" It came out sounding strangled and far too desperate for his pride. But it did make her stop. She halted with

her head bowed and her shoulders hunched as though she expected a blow. She didn't turn around.

"Where are you?" Devin asked, because he'd given up most
of his pride already, and what little was left didn't matter
much. He'd lost his father and his home. He didn't think he
could stand losing Kyali, too, but it felt like he already had.

"Here," his sister said grimly, never once looking at him.

"No. You're not. You're *really not*."

One of her hands clenched quickly, then relaxed. That was
the only sign that she'd heard him. "Then best I go on my way,"
she said, and left.

He stood there for a few minutes, listening to the noise wax
and wane outside this little hall, then wiped his face and turned
to follow the darkness to wherever it wanted to take him.

The hall ended in yet another hall. This one was lined with
high windows that let in the slanted afternoon light. The Baar
mountains loomed through the warped old glass like gods,
huge and indifferent and coldly beautiful. Devin followed corridor after corridor, blindly seeking the hint of fresh air in
the drafts blowing down the corridors, until at last he found
a door of dark ironwood barred by a metal beam so rusted he
doubted it would keep out anything but mice. He pried it open
with effort—not *that* rusted, apparently—and staggered when
the wind howled immediately in at him, snatching the air right
out of his lungs.

"Ah," he groaned, mostly in relief, and pushed his way out
into the merciless sunlight.

The view opened up before him, falling away in dizzy seg-
ments: first the lower wall of the castle, then the cliff's face,
then a series of increasingly distant hills and valleys tumbling

haphazardly toward the foothills. And after that came Lardan, green and brown and beloved. He couldn't see Faestan from here, and he was grateful for that. Everyone he loved that was left in the world was on this slowly freezing stack of rock.

Soldiers did drills in the courtyard below, the shouts and clangs rattling up to him. Devin shuffled forward, eyeing the drop warily, and leaned against the old black stone of the castle wall, listening. It sounded like home.

Home was gone.

He fumbled thoughtlessly at the strap of the case that held the Fraonir harp to his back, opening the catch. The harp fell into his hands like a favorite pet, and even though the air was cold with the promise of winter and snow, which he'd never seen, the shining wood of the neck and the pillar were as warm as skin. He set the instrument on his knee, leaned forward until his head rested on its carved shoulder, and let his fingers wander over the strings.

The notes, aimless as they were, soothed him. He sighed, heard it echo in the strings, and followed the sound until notes became melody. He'd never in his life been able to lay a hand on an instrument without thinking of song. It had driven his father and Kyali to distraction.

The memory of two exasperated pairs of eyes, both gold with that odd remnant of some other heritage, made his breath catch. When he pushed it out of his lungs, words rode on it. Devin let them come, finding solace where he always had.

> *Though our fields lie still and fallow*
> *And the sky is filled with cloud,*
> *Though our days seem darkly hallowed*

Yet these moments we're allowed.
Though the night is flame and shadow
And the stars veiled in a shroud,
Though our hearts are filled with sorrow
Still these moments we're allowed.
Give me strength to fight the heartless
And the grace to stand unbowed,
Give me love to light the darkness
In these moments I'm allowed.

A little dramatic, he decided, and snorted; he did feel better, at least. It was a good thing he'd come so far from the crowds to mope, or he'd have to explain this very audible fog of sentiment to half the castle. He waved his hand through the blurry shimmer of magic his playing had made in the air around him.

Then he realized the noise of the drills had vanished.

Devin leaned over the edge, a little panicked: the last time he'd played a flute, terrible magic had followed, and he still wasn't wholly convinced the Fraonir were the ones responsible. His wobbly look down to the courtyard showed him several hundred faces at a distance, soldiers all standing around holding their swords, gone still, staring up.

"Dear gods," he yelped, and fell off the wall—thankfully on the safe side of it—in his haste to get out of sight, just barely saving the harp.

"Sorry!" he yelled, and hissed in pain. This damned stone was *hard*.

"Play elsewhere!" came his sister's shouted retort. Laughter wafted up to him—laughter and a few approving whistles.

Well, *someone* appreciated him.

Clouds of dust traveled across the room like flocks of tiny birds, dimming the light from the high northern-facing windows. Kinsey sneezed once, then again, and knocked over a stack of books cracked and stiff with age. He dropped the dust-cloth and dove forward, catching them in his arms halfway under a table.

A carpet of dust shifted under his knees. Arms full of books, Kinsey sneezed again and banged the back of his head on the underside of the table.

"Ow!"

"This is an odd way to martyr yourself, my Lord Prince."

He cracked his head again as Annan's voice sent a jolt through his limbs. *"Ow! Damn."*

There was a slightly strangled cough from the general direction Annan was standing. Kinsey pulled himself up, sliding the pile of books carefully onto the table, and met his lieutenant's studiously blank gaze. Annan glanced once about the library, such as it was—at the broken shelves and the endless stacks of books coated in what might be *centuries* of dust—and edged one tiny step backward, as though he feared proximity might transfer all the mess onto his well-kept armor.

"You need servants in here, my lord," he said.

"I've a Fraonir assistant around here somewhere—"

"She's in the kitchens at the moment."

"Ah." Barely two months in, and Annan already seemed to know everything that went on in the fortress. He wasn't surprised. His lieutenant wasn't the sort to wait for a situation to sort itself out before getting his hands in it, pushing to see what would move, or break.

"How go the drills?" Kinsey asked, half in curiosity, half to change the subject.

"Well enough."

Annan folded his arms and stared out the window, not a particularly confidence-inspiring signal. Kinsey straightened, cradling a book gently in filthy hands, and stared at his lieutenant. Annan didn't meet his eyes.

It was a careful, tricky path, working with the Lardana forces without *becoming* the Lardana forces. Kinsey still wasn't sure what Taireasa Marsadron wished—or what the Lady Captain wanted, for that matter. He'd thought, right up until this moment, that Annan had navigated those issues on his own, but the set of the man's shoulders told him that wasn't the case.

It was probably something *he* should have done... and instead he'd been buried in ancient books and dust, paying no attention to anything else.

"How's the harpy?" Kinsey prodded, trying to lighten the mood a little, but Annan only shifted one shoulder in a shrug, still staring out the window.

"Competent," he replied.

And left a silence hanging that could have sunk a ship, it was so heavy.

Damn, Kinsey thought. He'd definitely failed to pick up on this problem in time. He chewed on his lip, trying to think of some way, any way, that his small company could work within the larger army of Lardana soldiers without taking authority away from Annan—but he knew little of the structure of com-

mand. And asking Annan would only get him more of that sto-
ic, uninformative stare.

Then something else struck him; he set the book carefully
down and picked up the cloth, sweeping the table. "It occurs to
me," he said, feeling his way through the idea, "that we have
things to offer our allies that they might not be aware of."

Annan still hadn't turned to face him, but he could see, out
of the corner of one eye, that the man's dark-haired head had
cocked slightly. Kinsey wiped the rest of the table down, letting the silence stretch out, and finally Annan spun on one
heel, that dreaded eyebrow raised.

"Yes?"

"They don't appear to have much in the way of intelligence
among their ranks."

"Unkind," Annan said dryly. Kinsey fought down a grin.

"No, not—stop it. You know what I mean. The Lardana men
are mostly cavalry and infantry, and all the lieutenants and
sergeants were promoted on the way here—they seem to have
lost most of their veteran officers in the uprising. We, on the
other hand, are spies and couriers. And one assumes that there
are folk somewhere in the kingdom below us that Her Majesty
and the Lady Captain might want to get word to. Or receive
word about."

Annan frowned, looking thoughtful. "Hm," he muttered.

"You don't think it's likely?"

"It might be, m'lord. They are woefully short on experienced agents." Annan hunched a bit more, like a dark gargoyle,
and bravely offered: "Shall I suggest it?"

To the Lady Captain, he meant—and rumor had it she and
Annan got along slightly better than a pair of roosters in a

single coop, likely part of why Annan hadn't arranged his own solutions long since. Which wasn't much of a surprise. The Lady Captain had not proven herself to be one for polite discussions, and Annan had a sarcastic bent that had prevented him from being promoted more than once before he became Kinsey's man. Being in the room with the two of them was like being stuck in a sandstorm: the space filled quickly with dry, stinging wit and very little usable air.

"Not necessarily," Kinsey said, picturing that conversation and thinking the fragile alliance might not survive it. "I can bring it to Her Majesty. I need to speak to her anyway."

And I probably would have come up with an excuse even if I didn't, he thought, and coughed to hide the heat crawling up his neck. Taireasa Marsadron was the wisest and kindest person he'd ever met—and she turned him into a babbling idiot just by looking his way. It was mortifying, and so far it seemed incurable.

He was going to have to do something about that, but he hadn't thought of anything useful yet.

"… about getting more housekeepers in here, at least until the dust is cleared out and it's possible to breathe," he finished, avoiding Annan's eyes. "I'll never get this library in order otherwise."

Annan cast a dubious glance around the room. The windows were coated with grime. The hearth probably had wildlife living in it. It looked like a few centuries had passed since anyone had cared to come in this place, and yet… there were books, more books than Kinsey had ever seen. Just *thinking* about them made him feel a bit giddy.

"What is it, exactly, you hope to find in here?" his lieutenant asked. Annan had been sitting on that particular question for a while now, Kinsey could tell.

Kinsey waved a hand at the books. "This isn't enough?"

There went that eyebrow again. It was a fairly good gauge for Annan's mood—often the *only* gauge, since the rest of his face moved so little. "You'd have rescued them one at a time and read them in your rooms if that's all you were after."

"A point." Kinsey abandoned the dirt-coated dustcloth and sat. "I'm looking for secrets. Or I will be, if I ever get this place to a state where I can sit in it for an hour without choking."

Annan's eyes lit at the word *secrets*. He brushed off another chair and sat down gently, as though he expected it to collapse under him. His armor scraped against the wood. "What sort?"

"History. History is *full* of secrets. And these books are older than any I've seen."

Annan still looked perfectly serious, but there was a shadowy quirk at one corner of his mouth, a sure sign he was trying not to laugh.

"...Right," Kinsey sighed. "The Fraonir are the only ones who have had any access to this library for centuries, as I understand it, so it stands to reason—"

"That any information they may have on this supposed prophecy they seem to know so much and say so little of, is in here." Annan folded his arms, leaning back in the chair.

"Exactly." Kinsey eyed the tumbled stacks and the scattered sheets of paper ruefully. "It may take one scholar-prince of Cassdall another century to find anything at all in this mess. But I have to try."

"Why?"

Kinsey shrugged. "Why not?"

The eyebrow rose a little higher. Annan could probably knock birds from the sky at short distances with that expression.

"Well, what else am I to do? Everyone here is busy making our new lives as livable as possible before the snows hit, but there isn't much use for a scholar. Except—" he waved a hand at the mess around them "—this. And our new allies need information badly, assuming this prophecy is what caused their misfortune."

"You *believe* that?"

Someone who didn't know Annan well might miss the genuine curiosity in that question. Kinsey held his lieutenant's gaze and shrugged. "A few months ago, no. And I'm sure the political tangle between the East and West was a deciding factor. It was never a stable arrangement, from what I know, and the late king seems to have let resentments stew. But it seems they are missing great pieces of their history, from some eight hundred years back when the royal library burned in some war or other: they call them the Buried Years. They are missing *explanations*. Why not magic? It seems to be a fact of life here, if not a particularly comfortable or well-understood one. Unless you're about to tell me you haven't seen the way the air blurs around our new allies when they are upset..."

Annan gave a tiny twitch of his shoulders. "No."

Kinsey didn't look away. After a moment, Annan grunted unhappily. "I saw it, my Lord Prince, yes. What it means, I wouldn't guess."

"Nor I, but it's clearly magic."

"I assume so; I'd hardly know."

"Me neither, but there are no other explanations. Hells, magic is rumored even in Cassdall, and every other land that has books I've managed to read... and all those faery tales and rumors must have come from *somewhere*. What if it was here? What if *that* is what they lost when they lost their earliest histories? And if magic exists, what rules does it follow? And why not prophecies? Perhaps they follow rules too. I don't know what I'll find in this disaster, but if the Fraonir are as old as they claim—and the age of these books alone might support that—then I have some hope that there is more to the stories. And the Fraonir themselves know more than they're saying."

"*That* I won't argue with."

"Well." Kinsey leaned back, folding his arms. "Maybe I can find something of it here."

Annan's face was as still as ever, but his eyes darted to the mess around them.

"Good luck."

Kinsey sighed. "Thank you."

Holding court ought to be one of those things that wasn't required when the kingdom had been taken by traitors, but somehow, four times a fortnight, Taireasa found herself sitting on a cobbled-together throne in a hall draftier than any room had a right to be, listening to cases. She had presided over two marriages (those had been lovely, actually), sentenced countless thieves to service, and mediated more property disputes than she wanted to think of.

It didn't seem fair, but fair, she was discovering, had no place in her life as it had become.

She rubbed her hands, trying to chafe some feeling back

into them, then gave the last judgment of the day, casting a
weary glance at her chancellor afterward to be sure he knew
she wished him to bring an end to the audience. But Maldyn
was staring past her, his face set in a complicated expression
that seemed part worry and part dismay. She looked back, and
the last man in the audience line stepped around a cluster of
shopkeepers.

Curran Maurynim, second son of the baron of Maurynim,
looked up at her, his face breaking into a broad smile. Before
Taireasa could do more than open her mouth, he strode forward and knelt in front of her throne. A slim girl by his side—
that would be Loessa, his new wife, she remembered—echoed
his movement and his shieldman Beagan knelt on his other
side. All sound in the hall stopped.

"My Lady Queen," Curran began, a thread of genuine pleasure warming his voice. Curran was an old friend, someone
she'd known nearly as long as Kyali and Devin, though they'd
seen little of one another since they both reached their major-
ity. "Maurynim swears fealty to the rightful queen of Lardan,"
he declared. "My father wanted to be here himself, but we are
preparing for siege and he had to stay to guard the fortress. He
sends me in his stead."

"We brought more supplies," the Lady Loessa added, and
blinked at the loud cheer that immediately met this news. She
would have said more, but Taireasa stood and left the dais, ignoring the way the guards at her back came to attention, taking Curran's hands and lifting him to his feet.

"Welcome," she said, and was dismayed to hear her voice
tremble a little bit.

It was so *good* to have a friend here who hadn't been with

her through the events of the rebellion. Someone who wouldn't look at her with pity, or the wounded, silent sorrow that Devin carried with him everywhere.

...Or not look at her at all, like his sister.

She shoved those thoughts aside, kissing Curran's cheek and trying to ignore the flicker of worry that crossed his face. She knew what he was seeing. The mirror gave her back a ghost these days, a shadow of a girl with dark smudges under her eyes. Her nights were haunted by Kyali's dreams. She'd discovered that no sleep was preferable to sleep punctuated by the sound of her own choked-back screams, and so she worked until she was too exhausted to stand.

Kyali herself seemed not to suffer this... but then, Kyali spoke so little, Taireasa had no real way to tell anymore.

She couldn't afford to think of this now.

She made herself smile again, so Curran wouldn't worry, and turned to greet his wife. Maldyn was herding the day's supplicants out the door at a turtle's pace, people craning for a last look. Earl Donal of Wyssin, a burly man with the voice of a herald and the tact of a drill sergeant, halted in front of the doors, damming the exodus like a boulder in a stream.

"Majesty," he bellowed, at what he probably thought was a perfectly reasonable volume. "If the lord of Maurynim is threatened in his fortress, should we not go to his aid?"

The flow of people leaving the hall came to an abrupt stop, leaving a crowd clogging the doorway and Maldyn and all the guards frozen in the act of trying to clear the room.

Burying a wince, Taireasa turned his way. "A matter for council, Earl Donal."

Which he knew perfectly well: this was just another attempt to get himself *on* the council. Not two months in and already the handful of nobles who had followed her into exile were jostling for power. It would have been funny, if it weren't so sad. She raised an eyebrow at her chancellor, who ought to be maneuvering the bluff earl of Wyssin out the door and instead was standing blank-faced and curious, as though he were actually considering the idea. The villagers around him had noticed and were listening avidly now.

Damn it.

"Maurynim stands firm, my lady," Curran declared, deliberately loud. "We ask no aid, nor require any."

Donal waved a hand in a wide gesture. "But surely, my lady, we ought to—"

"Surely, *my lord*, this is a military matter and not a thing to discuss in hall," Taireasa replied, trying—and failing, she suspected—to keep her voice from tipping into outright sarcasm. He wanted to be included in her innermost circles, but couldn't understand why blurting out an unconsidered opinion in the middle of a roomful of villagers was a poor notion. "We have hardly had news of Maurynim. Planning a counterattack this very moment does seem a bit premature."

Yes, the sarcasm definitely got through there.

She sighed and went to take Earl Donal's arm, speaking more quietly. "My lord, there are indeed things to be done, but we are not yet ready to face the army of the West on their terms. You realize this already, of course. I am only telling you what your experience has already told you, I know. I will hear your advice when our soldiers are called on. You will give it to me when I ask, yes?"

He puffed up like a bullfrog, letting himself be guided slowly out the door. "Oh, well, of course. Glad to, Your Majesty."

The size of him pushed the commoners out ahead like flotsam before the flood. Earl Donal had that to recommend him, at least. Taireasa had to bite back a real grin, and stood watching him stride through the lower hallway as the guards finally took possession of the doors.

"Well done," a low voice whispered in her ear. She turned without surprise, because these days she could feel Devin's presence from across the keep, and she'd sensed him coming up behind her. "He'll preen for days, and probably not realize until next week that he still hasn't been invited to your council table."

The grin got completely past her: for a precious second, she was just the princess, crowing to the general's son about another clever trick she'd pulled. But Devin's own smile was shadowed at the edges, by which she could be certain that he had seen Kyali at least once today.

It seemed they could do nothing but break each other's hearts, the three of them.

Or, well, the two of them. Kyali might have left her heart at the foot of the mountain, for all she could tell. Kyali had broken her *own* heart, had done it for the sake of a friend who would never, apparently, get the chance to repay her.

If Kyali wanted to leave it behind, Taireasa couldn't find the strength to argue. She could ask nothing else of the general's daughter, of the friend who had given so much. She was only grateful she still had Devin to lean on. She didn't think she could bear this exile from home and dearest friendship without him.

Thinking it brought Devin that much closer, until she could

sense his sorrow gnawing away at him, could feel the mingled pleasure and misery that seeing her called up in him. It wasn't a good time—there were plenty of witnesses left in this drafty room—but Taireasa *reached* in that way they were both learning to do, and let him see, for a second, that he wasn't alone in his grief.

He caught her hand in a drowning man's grip as the air between them shivered.

"You're so much better than we deserve, Taireasa," Devin murmured.

He turned then, and slipped away between Maldyn and Kinsey, who had appeared at some point in the proceedings and was looking around curiously, an owl out in the daylight. Maldyn, for his part, went to have a word with Curran and Loessa. Kinsey stared after Devin's retreating back with an expression of mild bemusement.

"I can't decide if he's avoiding me specifically or only people in general," the Cassdall prince mused.

"He's avoiding himself," Taireasa answered without thinking, startling him into meeting her eyes at close quarters. His were gray as old glass, and seemed to go on forever. His features, fine and strong, had the sheen of good bronze. She felt heat crawling up her neck and looked away, having been too honest for her comfort or Kinsey's.

But Kinsey nodded slowly. "Yes, that makes sense. I suppose I'll let him sort it out on his own, then."

"Oh, don't do that, my Lord Prince." Gods, she was nothing but impulse around him. She forced herself to finish. "Take him riding, or make him help you in the library. Pester him until he agrees. He needs a friend. And right now, I can only be a queen."

Kinsey's expressive face crinkled into a look that wasn't pity, but might have been sympathy. "I'll do that," he said. "The ride, not the library. I wouldn't wish that on my own uncle."

"Is it so bad?"

He sighed. "It's... messy. But I am making headway, of a slow sort. I hope to have it organized in another month."

"I'll assign you some servants. I can do that much. No, don't argue: there may be something important hidden in those stacks, and we know so little of—of—" Taireasa waved a hand vaguely, encompassing the hall, the mountain, the mess that was her new life.

"...present circumstances," Kinsey finished.

"Far more elegantly phrased than my description would have been," Taireasa said dryly.

He gave her a crooked smile. "I doubt that, my lady."

"You've no idea." She was getting flashes of feeling from him now: loneliness, worry for Devin, something complicated having to do with soldiers and command. Curse her intrusive, unruly Gift.

She exhaled, trying to make her shoulders relax through sheer will. It didn't work. Though he was already halfway to his rooms, Devin's sadness clung to her like dust, making her own that much harder to ignore.

"I think I need the company of friends myself, my Lord Prince. And Curran and Loessa deserve a proper greeting. Will you join us for wine in my apartments tonight? I've an appointment over dinner with a regiment of shopkeepers that I'll want to recover from afterward. Will you come? You and your lieutenant?"

"Honored to, your Majesty."

"Call me Taireasa, will you? I'm so everlastingly tired of that title."

"If you'll do the same."

"Call you Taireasa?" she asked, letting all the bone-dry sarcasm into her voice that Earl Dolan had been spared, and Kinsey laughed aloud.

"That may take more wine than we have in the kitchens," he remarked, then bowed as Maldyn moved closer to them. "You have duties. Annan and I will see you tonight, Ma—Taireasa."

He left on another bow.

Taireasa tried not to watch him go, but she didn't quite manage it.

16

The air had a distinct hint of snow on it today.

Having had two winters up here already, Kyali was accustomed to such things, but the soldiers with her sniffed and frowned, like they feared snow would appear by the wagonload and trap them forever in this forest of scrubby mountain pine.

Ainhearag was perky-eared, moving with a floating enthusiasm that was probably both pleasure at being back in her foaling ground and the anticipation of violence. They rode quietly, using hand signs when necessary. Kyali looked only ahead. She could feel the eyes of the men on her and it made her want to kick her horse into a run, enemy scouts be damned, and head for the first place absent of people and their damned endless expectations that she could find.

There probably wasn't any place like that left in the world.

Up ahead, the trees began to change to birch and poplar, a

lighter color of bare branches instead of the deep, spicy green of the pines. She raised a hand, making the sign for *stop*. They did, all six of them, in complete silence.

They were good men. Her father's men.

Her men now, thanks to Taireasa's little trick.

The trees sighed bleakly in the wind. Kyali and her patrol listened, frozen in place, even the horses making barely any movement. After several long and cold minutes, there came a faint crackling sound and then the low, faraway murmur of hushed voices. Ainhearag shivered under her, dark ears all the way up now, tension turning every big muscle to stone. Kyali ran a soothing hand down a cold neck and felt her horse's impatient twitch.

Another crackle sounded through the trees. Kyali drew her sword, heard the whisper of steel clearing sheaths all around her, and set her feet better in the stirrups. Her pulse began to pick up. Her fingers clenched on the grip of the sword.

Snow, she told herself. Ice.

One day, if she kept trying and stayed as far away from Devin and Taireasa as she could, she might learn to feel nothing but cold. It was a worthy goal. It would be so much better than the fire waiting for her every night when she finally let herself sleep.

The crackle came closer. Closer.

Then the brush exploded, disgorging a man on horseback, doubled up in the saddle, swaying ominously with every stride. Danyn Jerin's-son rode close enough that Kyali could see the arrow, the blood coming from where he had his arm wrapped around his middle. His eyes locked on hers, full of a dazed distance that told her just how bad the wound was. She wrapped her fingers tighter around her sword and looked past him, to where the trees were beginning to shudder and the sound of hoofbeats was rolling toward them.

Wedge formation, she signed, and took point without waiting for her men to move around her, just as the first of the Western band chasing her unlucky scout came rattling out of the woods.

They yelled, seeing her waiting for them, and raised their shields. They never slowed.

"No prisoners!" she shouted, and kicked Ainhearag forward, already swinging the sword.

The first man died at the edge of her blade, still trying to get his own sword into position. Ainhearag uttered a high squeal of rage as another soldier's horse snaked past to sink teeth into her shoulder. Kyali drew her dagger and sliced, and that horse went down kicking. Her own, much better horse executed a soaring leap over flailing legs, which landed them right in the thick of a Western band only a little bigger than she'd expected it to be. A sword flashed at her, hitting only the hard steel of her upper vambrace, numbing her arm all the way to the wrist. She slashed at her attacker's exposed face, barely noticing when his blood arced out, splashing her.

Blows rained over her side, striking the brigandine over her ribs. She leaned, turning the dagger into her sleeve, got a fistful of thick leather, and hauled. That man fell and Ainhearag accounted for him with a single heavy step as they turned to meet another pair of approaching soldiers, shields raised so high they must not be able to see anything but their own hands gripping the bars.

She surged forward again. She could hear the sound she was making, a feral, furious growl that hurt her throat. The

sword was just another piece of her, and she found exposed
knees, shoulders, necks, drew lines in scarlet on them, listening only to her own raw rage and the deafening thunder of her
heartbeat. Her lieutenant Ciaran appeared on her left, swinging his mace. He took out another man with the hateful Ar-
umilian green-and-black shield on his shoulder, delivering a
startlingly messy blow that sent the man flying out of the saddle and sprayed blood all over both of them.

Ciaran's face was slack with shock. He reined his horse to
a stop, made a gesture like he was going to reach for her, but
instead pulled back and said something she couldn't hear past
the wild thumping of her own pulse. Kyali sat back in the saddle and Ainhearag came immediately to a halt. She blinked,
breathing hard, and looked around.

Looked at her scattered troop, alive and bloody and staring
at her with wide eyes; looked at the dead strewn around the
tiny clearing.

The sounds of the woods began, slowly, to come back. One
of her men was muttering prayers. Another slipped off his
horse to stumble into the bracken and be sick. Ciaran, steadying himself visibly, dismounted and went to crouch next to
Danyn Jerin's-son where he lay curled on his side under a
lightning-blasted elm.

"Is that all of them?" Kyali asked, trying to winnow the rage
out of her voice as she spoke, to make her fingers unclench
from the sword. Out of habit, her hands found the oiled cloth
she always kept in a pocket and drew it out to clean the blade.
Her missing dagger was in the neck of a soldier halfway across
the clearing. She slid carefully from Ainhearag's back and retrieved it, breathing calm, breathing cold, breathing ice into

her burning veins, trying to push away the memory of someone's knife parting her own skin.

She would never be free of it.

Danyn was dead by the time she came to stand next to Ciaran. His face looked younger at rest. His hands were wrapped around the shaft of the arrow that had killed him, as though he had tried, in desperation, to pull it out of himself. Kyali looked at that, not at his face, and thought of snow until it seemed to be filling the space behind her eyes.

She moved away to bend over the body of the soldier bearing the shield of Arumilia on his shoulder and, grimacing, slipped her hands under his armor, seeking the purse most officers carried inside their shirts.

It was there, and it yielded a single folded scrap of rough paper.

Orders. From Tuan of Tharst, who had apparently succeeded his father Cyrnic and taken Faestan's throne.

Perfect.

"Udryn, Kemmel," she said, looking only at the paper. "Ride double. Danyn will have your horse. We should get back."

"Aye, Cap'n," one of them said quietly; it didn't matter which. They raised the body of their fallen comrade carefully and tied his arms to the pommel.

Kyali didn't look at that, either. It made it too hard to think of snow.

They met Devin and the Cassdall prince riding with a small entourage of guards down the steep path from the castle and had to stop and pull their horses to the side to let them pass. Trust her brother to pick the worst possible moment for a ride in the fresh air. She couldn't believe he was stupid enough to wander about on a mountain crawling with enemy bands. But that was Devin: risk was just a different sort of diversion to him.

He brought Savvys to a halt in front of them, his eyes gone wide and alarmed, taking in the blood on their armor, the silent passenger tied to the saddle on a chestnut mare.

The Cassdall prince reined in as well, blocking the path completely. Kyali let the air hiss slowly from her nose, refusing to speak, change expression, or move until they did so first.

Devin was pressing her again, gods damn it, in that way he had, with all his longing and sadness and that miserable, unbearable *pull* that he and Taireasa both exerted just by being nearby. It made her want to shout at him until her voice broke. It made her want to rip the second locket she knew he was wearing from around his neck and throw it as far down the mountain as she could.

It made her want to hear him sing that song again, to ask whether he was sleeping any better than she was, whether he had learned how to move beyond what he had lost into what he had to be, and could he show her how.

Ice, Kyali thought, miserable and furious. *Fire*.

And four dead barons. And the broken, jagged-edged pieces of herself she had to work with.

She stilled the tremor in her hands by gripping the hilts of the daggers on her hips. Her brother flattened his lips, carrying all his wounds right in his eyes where anyone could see them, and looked away.

"I take it we should not ride out today," the Cassdall prince said.

The understatement was bitterly funny. "No, my Lord Prince. Not today."

Kinsey's lieutenant, a tawny-complexioned, intensely irritating man with eyes like a basilisk, nodded calmly. "We'll precede you, then, Lady Captain, and clear the way through the hall. You have wounded?"

Did they? Yes, they probably did. "Nothing serious, but yes."

Kinsey's gray eyes darted from her to her men and, behind her, the still form on the mare that she was trying not to think about. She'd given orders that men died for before this. She was beginning to suspect it wasn't ever going to get easier.

It wasn't the sort of thing her father's officers had covered in her lessons.

"We'll make haste, then," Kinsey said, edging Annan out of the way and turning his horse.

As they followed the Cassdall prince and the Head of what was left of House Corwynall up to the great ironwood doors, the first few flakes of winter came falling out of the skies.

Being around people in a setting where he couldn't politely get away wasn't an experience Devin wanted to subject himself to, but it turned out that wine helped with that.

He held his glass up for the servants to fill again, breathing in the welcome scent of Orin's famous grapes, and ignored the worried look Taireasa was sending his way. She was sending more than a look, Her Majesty was—her heart had tangled insistently with his almost the moment he'd walked into her sitting room, and right now she was fishing impolitely for answers to his state of general misery.

"You had an uneventful trek here, then?" he said to Curran, dodging Taireasa's gaze and her seeking with effort. Curran's wife Loessa gave a small shudder.

"We had to hide in a cave," she said.

"It wasn't so bad," Curran retorted, grinning. "We thought we heard someone moving nearby, so we took shelter until we were sure we were safe."

"It turned out to be a deadly Sevassian boar," his shield-man Beagan added, perfectly deadpan.

Surprised into a snort of laughter, Devin covered his mouth with a sleeve. "Their most successful export," he said dryly. "No doubt there are many wandering the countryside these days. I take it you saw nothing else?"

"Not once we got past the foothills. We were careful."

And yet his sister, presumably far more experienced in moving about on this mountain, managed to run headlong into a band of the enemy large enough to bloody every man in her own patrol and kill a scout. Devin scowled.

She was obviously *trying* to draw them out.

Not a stupid notion, but hardly the job of the captain of the army. She seemed to seek out risk and violence now as actively as she avoided friendship and family. It made him want to shake her until her teeth fell out.

He had lost *enough*.

Kyali was, in fact, late. Taireasa had more or less ordered her to come to this gathering, refusing to hear objections or to acknowledge the indifference the captain of the Exile's Army had to being in the company of friends. Taireasa was getting very good at ignoring such things. She took every sign of Kyali's new and awful coldness with a quiet, sorrowful acceptance that drove Devin halfway mad.

Kyali had no right or reason to treat Taireasa like that.

She might have better reason to shut him out, if she knew their father had died while he was riding in the opposite direction, but Kyali didn't seem to know how to grieve anymore, so he doubted that was it.

He'd ruined what little appetite he had. Devin set down the apple he'd been about to bite into as Taireasa came up behind him, setting a hand on his arm and surrounding him, suddenly, with the steadfast warmth that was herself: her brave, sorrowing, brilliant self. She was extraordinary. Devin yielded, falling willingly now into the sense of her. She was just as sad and just as tired in her own uncomplaining way. Their hearts met in a knot of anguish and affection, possibly a bit too close for comfort.

Too close or not, it was all he had, and he was so very grateful for it.

"Ahem," someone said, and he opened his eyes to see Kinsey looking at them with intense interest. His lieutenant Annan hovered nearby, that serious face full of quiet estimation. Curran and Beagan had fallen silent.

The air was shimmering faintly all around them.

"Oh," Taireasa murmured, and withdrew heart and hand, looking up wide-eyed at the warping air near her head. "That keeps happening."

"Do you do that on purpose?" Kinsey asked curiously, not even a little unsettled at the evidence of magic happening in front of him.

"Not precisely," Devin said.

"It seems to have something to do with—" Taireasa faltered and looked away, obviously embarrassed. "That is, sometimes we can..."

"Share thoughts, yes? And impressions? It's *fascinating*. I uncovered a book in the library that seems to suggest it's hereditary, but I'm afraid most of the truly informative pages found their way into the mice's nests. Do you think—oh. Oh. I'm sorry. Devin told me, Majesty," Kinsey added, halting his monologue because Taireasa was staring at him in mortified disbelief. Curran and Loessa were listening with confused frowns.

"*Taireasa*," Taireasa said with odd emphasis. "And I would very much like to read that book."

This time it was Kinsey who looked embarrassed. Devin looked from one to the other, and felt his spirits rise just a little bit.

Interesting.

Hush, he heard distinctly, right inside his head. He almost dropped his glass.

Taireasa flashed an amused glance at him and tipped her head. **I'm learning,** she added with an echo of laughter and a warm flush of embarrassment—and with such startling force it was like being gently shoved off a cliff.

Devin blinked, tried to remember what he'd been about to say, and had to settle for sipping cautiously at his wine. Then the door opened, admitting his little sister. He tipped the glass all the way back and held it out again, insistently. This time even Annan gave him an uneasy glance.

Kyali shook her head at a servant as she entered, refusing wine of her own. She probably didn't want to risk even the possibility of enjoying herself. The unrelenting black of her trousers and tunic weren't exactly lightening the air of grim single-mindedness that followed her everywhere like a thundercloud.

She looked tired. And irritated, likely at the necessity of interrupting whatever else she did with herself to come here and be with people who cared about her.

He began to think it might be a very good idea to get drunk tonight.

"Lady Captain," Taireasa said, nothing but unruffled pleasure in her tone—Taireasa was disturbingly good at keeping that mask in place. Her heart was churning with grief and a truly appalling weight of guilt, and yet none of it made it to her face. She seemed to realize at that moment that Devin was aware of more than just her words: suddenly he was alone, left with the lingering impression of pain equal to his own and, oddly, alarm.

Hell with it. He *was* getting drunk tonight. Maybe that would help him sleep.

"I see you recovered from your encounter with the West in time to join us, Lady Captain," Devin said with only a little irony, as Kyali walked warily into the circle they had made standing by the hearth.

Taireasa went pale as parchment. Kyali's eyes flashed once, a rare thing these days, and one callused hand curled and flexed. He could see the muscles in her jaw tighten. "What?" Devin demanded, taken aback. It hadn't been particularly witty, but he didn't think it was worth *this* kind of reaction.

"Yes, Captain, were there any more casualties?" Annan asked, eyeing Kyali with a pointed interest that seemed to gather more from her non-expression than Devin was managing to. "And do you encounter enemy bands so close to the fortress often?"

"Annan," Kinsey said—mildly, but Devin could see that he'd pressed a foot on his lieutenant's booted toe. The Cassdall lieutenant was sharp as a blade, and about as diplomatically gifted as Kyali herself was. Watching them match stares was like watching two cats stalk the same mouse. At any other time, he'd have enjoyed the sight.

"What is this about?" Taireasa asked, gaze bouncing between them.

Kyali slid a glance at her and twitched a shoulder upward in a detached shrug. "A band from Sevassis was sniffing about today, Your Majesty," she said, her voice as low and calm as if they were discussing the weather instead of a skirmish that had taken the life of one of her men.

—and as though that *Your Majesty* wasn't the slap in the face that it really was. He could feel Taireasa gathering herself, holding that perfect mask of composure in place with effort. Devin couldn't help a huff of frustrated despair.

"But why were *you* out riding... yes. Of course." Taireasa cleared her throat delicately. "Did you learn anything of them?"

"It didn't appear that any survived, Majesty," Annan offered, still eyeing Kyali with that gimlet gaze, as though she were a particularly interesting book.

"None did," she shot back, not bothering to grace Annan with a glower this time. "But there was an officer among them, and he was carrying orders. I've a report for you later, my lady."

"Oh, give it now, we're all friends here," Taireasa said, her shoulders stiffening just a little as she turned to beckon a servant over for more wine.

Kyali hesitated a moment, then nodded, locking her hands behind her back, a soldier at attention. "Tuan has apparently succeeded his father," she said; Taireasa's head came up and her emerald eyes narrowed. "Unless he's commanding the Western battalions in Faestan without having taken the throne, but that seems unlikely. The officer had orders to seek out a means of entering this castle unnoticed, to cut off our route to Maurynim, and to halt the flow of supplies and refugees."

"Rather a lot to ask of one officer," Beagan murmured.

"Chances are he was in command of a far larger force that separated to circle the castle," Kyali replied. "I've sent out men to find them. What scant word I've had of doings in the lowlands suggests Master Tuan would very much like Her Majesty captured and brought to Faestan before the snow flies on this mountain."

"Small chance of that," Devin said angrily. Kyali's eyes flickered over and past him, and she pursed her lips in tacit agreement.

Taireasa, watching Kyali closely, took a sip of wine and then folded her arms. "There's something more that you're not saying, though, isn't there? What?"

"Mmm," Kyali muttered, then shrugged a second time before meeting Taireasa's eyes. "Nothing significant, Majesty."

"Ky."

"The orders also offered lands and title to any man who could bring back my head."

Devin inhaled a bit of wine and coughed into an appalled silence.

Curran gave a low, slow whistle. "Well," he said. "That's... extravagant."

Taireasa and Kyali were now locked in some sort of staring contest. Or perhaps they were both pretending to be
rocks. Mortally tired of the way the air fogged with secrets
when these two met gazes lately, Devin set his glass down and
pushed himself into the cold space between them.

"Have you done something in particular to provoke the man,
Lady Captain, or is this merely the usual response to your famous
charm?" he asked, and felt every eye in the room turn to him.

Every eye but the two in Kyali's hard, stubborn head, that is.

"I killed his father," she said with soft venom. Devin felt his
pulse leap in pure stunned horror. It became fury when Kyali finally turned and pinned that icy gaze on him deliberately.
"Apparently he didn't take it well."

"Some people don't, sister, when their fathers are killed.
Imagine that."

"*Enough*, you two!" Taireasa snapped, temper finally breaking through her self-possession. Before she got between them,
he had the satisfaction of seeing his little sister suck in a quick
breath, as though taking a blow to the stomach. "We've enough
to fight without bickering among ourselves."

When she set hands on each of them to push them apart,
there was a sudden shudder that seemed to come from both
the floor and the air—that seemed, nonsensically, to be as
much inside his bones as it was under his feet. Devin staggered, putting a hand out for balance, and caught Kyali's wrist
as *her* arm flailed outward. Something bleak and hurt flashed
through him, something lightless and searing and intolerable.
Taireasa made a strange whimpering noise, and then something else echoed it, and another thing—and all around them
grew a high, dissonant hum.

Kyali tore herself out of the circle they had inadvertently made with a faint grunt that sounded like pain.

Devin shook his head, trying to clear it of the odd humming. Taireasa pressed a hand to her breast, her face gone blank and startled. The shimmer was back, thick and blurry, pulling on his guts like a fishhook.

"Dear gods," Devin wheezed. "What was *that?*"

Curran, Beagan, Loessa, and Annan had all backed away, but Kinsey was leaning in, his sharp eyes taking in every twitch and gasp. He met Taireasa's eyes, flushed, and spun immediately to pluck up Devin's abandoned wineglass and examine it. The humming echoed from the bowl of it.

"Hm," the prince said, tapping the rim with a fingertip. "Something in the air that makes it—no. Oh! Perhaps." He glared at the glass, oblivious to the roomful of people watching (Annan had taken on a faint air of long-suffering amusement), and pressed his palm to it until it was silent.

Then he dipped a finger into the wine and ran it nimbly around the rim. Even as the sound began to fade from elsewhere in the room, it swelled from the glass in his hand.

"What does that mean?" Loessa came near, peering curiously at the glass.

"I haven't the slightest idea," Kinsey said happily.

"Oh," Loessa murmured.

"It must have something to do with the way the air warps when the three of them do magi—ah, sorry, Majesty, there I go again. I'm afraid I get a bit carried away sometimes—"

"*All* the time," Annan murmured.

"—when I have a puzzle in front of me," Kinsey finished, casting a sharp and rueful look at his lieutenant. "But this… I think I'd better make haste to get the library in order. There might be books that deal with this. I know nothing of magic."

"Evidently, neither do we," Taireasa said wryly, giving herself a small shake. "I'll have servants sent in there tomorrow morning. Anything you need, just ask."

"*You* do," Devin said, looking at his sister, who was several cautious feet away, as though she was afraid one of them would reach out and grab her again. She'd gone a bit pale.

Kyali gave him a cool stare. "I what?"

"You know about magic. At least I hope you do, after two years of studying it. Be a bit sad if you managed to learn nothing in all that time, Lady Captain."

Kyali's chin came up, which told him he was about to get a real reaction from her, possibly for the first time since the uprising. "Sort of like being shipped off to Orin to be tutored by court wizards and coming back empty-headed, would you say? That sort of sad?"

She might have changed, but the edge on her tongue hadn't dulled any. Beagan snickered, trying vainly to turn the noise into a cough. Curran didn't bother to try to hide his grin.

"Gods," Taireasa sighed. "Keeping you two from fighting is like trying to empty a lake with a bucket. Ky, I trust the Fraonir *did* teach you something more than the structure of the world?"

"They did," Kyali replied, folding her arms and looking uncomfortable. "Nothing that's going to help, I fear. Certainly nothing about—what just happened."

Taireasa's shoulders sagged. "They never *once* mentioned it?"

"Never," Kyali said flatly. "I'd say they went out of their way to avoid mentioning it, in fact."

"Yes," Devin murmured, thinking of a terrible night, an old

woman's words, the tears on her lined face. "I got the impression they were holding back rather a lot, actually."

"Interesting," Kinsey said, toying absently with the wineglass. "They teach the Lady Captain, yet tell her nothing; they draw Devin into the mountains to find me, which indicates they have some idea of what path this prophecy will take—"

"Or just an excellent system of spies in Cassdall," Annan threw in.

"No, I don't think so. We were climbing *their* mountain, Annan; I'm sure we were fairly visible. I'm also beginning to suspect they were expecting us."

"They know more than they say," Curran mused. "But why? *Why* won't they say, then?"

"Perhaps they can't," Kinsey murmured, more to himself than to Curran or anyone else, and got a surprised, considering look on his face.

"That sounds right," Kyali said quietly. She was rubbing her fingers over her thumb in slow, ceaseless circles, a habit she'd always had when worried or upset and trying to hide it. Devin bit the inside of his cheek, seeing that—it was a sharp reminder of the girl he'd grown up with.

"So what *did* they teach you, then, little sister? You knocked a chair over the day you came home, but I've seen no evidence other than that."

"You did?" Taireasa said, startled. "I didn't know. What else can you do?"

Kyali hunched a shoulder in a sullen shrug, looking down at her hands. She scowled, eyed the fire in the hearth balefully, and shut her eyes. Her breathing went odd, measured. Then Beagan yelped, stumbling back, as two thin skeins of flame wandered past the grate, into the air.

Loessa put both hands to her mouth.

"Dear gods," Curran said, and laughed, a little hysterically.

The fire wove past them, past Kinsey, who watched it like a man entranced; past Taireasa, who reached out to take Devin's hand in a tight, clammy grip. Devin could only stare. Flashes of cold darkness and fire far less tame than the flame sliding past him now were intruding on his thoughts. He had no idea where the impressions were coming from, but whatever they were, they nearly undid him: they *hurt*. They made him want to kill something. They made him feel every inch of the distance Kyali had put between herself and him, and every inch of the distance between where he stood and the home he'd watched burn to the ground.

He must have made a sound, because Taireasa reached for him and he could suddenly feel her shock and worry as strongly as though it were his—and then something shut off the darkness. He all but fell over at the relief of it.

The fire curled into Kyali's hands like a sleepy cat, then vanished as she clenched her fists.

"Well," Kinsey murmured. "Well."

Kyali heaved a short, tense sigh and went to stand by the one of the high windows, looking out at the night with her shoulders knotted and her hands still clenched.

"Can you do anything else?" Annan asked her, and she shot an irritated look over her shoulder at him.

"I seem to be able to heal," she said. Her voice had gone rough and next to him, Devin felt Taireasa stiffen. "From wounds that... might otherwise be mortal. It wasn't something the Fraonir had any experience dealing with."

"That's *useful*," Annan said, sounding, for once, a little bewildered. Probably at the notion that magic could be in any way practical.

"Isn't it." Kyali was doing that thing with her fingers again.

Wounds that might otherwise be mortal? How in hells had Kyali discovered *that*?

"Perhaps if we ask, the Clan Leaders will send someone who can teach us," Taireasa said, high and hurried. She rubbed at one arm, then,pulled a wayward strand of pale hair out of her eyes. "I had a message this morning that Arlen and Measail were on their way here with a handful of Clansfolk. They might even be planning to offer such a thing. One can hope."

"Yes," Devin said vaguely, still staring at his sister. "One can. Arlen gave me the harp, after all. I assume he meant for me to use it. Do you suppose they'll teach me to play the stones down around our ears?"

"It seems a short step from breaking glass," Beagan gibed.

Kinsey uttered a short laugh. "Could you really do that, Devin? Break glass?"

"I spent most of my childhood doing exactly that," Devin answered. "It didn't seem to matter what I played: something always broke. Sometimes I didn't even have to play anything. Until last year, actually. I started to get control of it then."

"Well enough to stun to silence the gathered high lords of the kingdom," Curran said.

"Not well enough to *stop* them," Devin snapped. He sighed into the hush that fell after that too-blunt reply and ran a hand through his hair. "Sorry. Illusion, glass-breaking, and a light breeze— these are all I can offer. Not much use. Fire and healing seem more helpful in a war."

"*My father* needed no stopping," Curran retorted, folding his arms across his chest.

"I know, Curran. Forgive me. Your father's no small part of why we survive up here."

"Fire was little enough use when the war started," Kyali muttered. Everyone looked at her, but she kept her eyes on the windows. It wasn't much of a peace offering, but it served to remind him he wasn't the only one suffering.

Devin took a sip of his wine and grimaced. Kinsey took the glass from him, flicked the bowl with his finger, and scowled thoughtfully.

"Does the harp…"

"Not really. No more than anything else, anyway."

"Maybe you should *try* to break something with it," Kinsey said.

"Inside the walls?"

"A point," the Cassdall prince admitted, but his expression said he was still trying to find some way to make it happen. "It would certainly make for a lively evening."

"Oh, gods," Annan muttered. "I'm not letting you two near the ale."

Kinsey looked much less like an owl rousted into daylight when he grinned like that. Devin couldn't help grinning back, and he felt Taireasa's faint envy coming through the bond they shared. "Good luck with that," he said to Annan, and then, taking the cue Taireasa silently sent him, bowed to her, and to the company in general. "I ought to find my own bed, begging your pardons—if glass-breaking seems like a good idea, it's probably time for sleep."

"Wisely said," Beagan agreed, and clapped him on the

shoulder hard enough to speed his steps toward the door. Curran echoed the movement on his other side, more gently: a silent acceptance of his apology, Devin hoped.

As they all began to file out the door, Devin glanced back. Kyali was still hunched by the window, avoiding the group, avoiding him, avoiding Taireasa. Taireasa had lost her distracted smile: she looked as unhappy as Devin felt most of the time.

For a painful second, the breach between them was perfectly visible on her face.

There was nothing he could do about it, nothing to fix it. And he couldn't stand to watch it happen.

17

She came across the first entrance to the secret passageways purely by accident, while trying to dodge her brother. The edge of stone under her hands as she pressed against the wall told her there was something more than ancient brickwork there: the memory of Faestan's hidden doors and passages was bright and sharp in her mind as she followed the seam. It was almost enough to drive her off—but she would be a fool to ignore such a thing, if it existed. Someone else would find it if she didn't. After three hard shoves, she fell into a darkness so clogged with dust that she thought she might put an end to the hopeless farce her life had become by choking to death.

That *almost* seemed preferable to speaking to Devin.

But if neither a Western army nor a cousin trained all his life for combat could manage to kill her, she supposed succumbing to dust in an abandoned passageway was a fairly pathetic and unlikely way to leave the world.

Shameful, hiding from her own brother like this.

But it was so much easier than seeing his face when she squashed yet another of his attempts to draw her out. She gave him nothing to hold on to—terrified, she had to admit, that one slip would be all it took to kick open the door of ice in her heart that kept him out. He pulled at her constantly, and his seeking heart held memories of the girl she had been once—before— memories she refused to acknowledge, memories that made her ache all over with longing and helpless fury. It was impossible to concentrate when he was in the room.

Taireasa let her be, amazingly, and wrapped her pain quietly around herself. Kyali was grateful beyond words for that.

Now if she could only find a way not to care how much she hurt them.

Ice.

The passageway wasn't meant for a tall person. With a fold of her sleeve stretched over her face to keep from breathing in dust by the bucketful, Kyali followed it anyway, feeling her way with one hand on the rough wall.

It branched out several times before landing her in one of the upper corridors, where she startled a Cassdall guard badly while shoving her way through the door in the wall. He watched her with wide eyes as she pulled herself out of the doorway and heaved it shut. When she began brushing herself off, trying not to make a face in pure disgust (no wonder she'd scared the man: she was so dust-covered she must look like a haunt), he got up the courage to ask her if he could help her find the guardroom.

Guardroom? On this floor?

"Please," Kyali said smoothly, and was led down a series of increasingly small corridors, each one less imposing than the last. At the end of one was a cul-de-sac with a shut door, the sound of laughter and good-natured shouts coming from behind it. The Cassdall guard, whose name she supposed she ought to learn, flung her a nervous sideways glance. In the sunlight from a narrow window, his face was the lovely color of new copper, and it was carefully free of expression, as though he knew before he even spoke what her reply would be.

"Begging your pardon, Captain Corwynall, but perhaps I ought to..."

"Thank you, I think I can handle it," Kyali said, so dry the dust might have been in her voice as well as all over her face. The soldier looked so uncomfortable she almost relented, but by then it was too late: he knocked in a complicated pattern she didn't bother to memorize, knowing it would probably change tomorrow, and the door swung wide. The laughter inside ceased and several strange faces peered out at her. They were no more alike than were the Fraonir, or her own people, but they were all quite plainly Cassdall. That fact was as evident in their features as it was in their dress: their light armor was different, making more use of mail, and their swords were shorter and broader than she was used to. They looked to be in the middle of some hilarious discussion, for smiles faded slowly from their faces but there was still merriment in their eyes as they gawked at her.

"Cap'n," one man said—it was one of Annan's officers, yet another name she should probably know—and stood. He looked at the glass of ale in his hand in dismay. The rest of them stood, too, like she was a great lady arriving to a dinner table, which was either bleakly comical or infuriating. She couldn't decide which.

"Lady Captain," Annan said, coming to his feet from behind the main bench, where he had apparently been stretching his legs out near a small hearth. "To what do we owe the pleasure?"

Amazing, how he could make the most basic courtesies sound like the opposite. And his *Lady Captain* always seemed to have the faintest edge of sarcasm.

"Coincidence," Kyali said, without bothering to add anything like politeness.

Annan raised an eyebrow, his dark eyes flickering over her dust-covered person. "We didn't wake the neighbors, I hope," he said softly, which she supposed was intended to be a jest. The soldiers at the bench were looking at her and Annan one after the other, like spectators at a jousting match.

"So far as I can see, you don't have any of those, Lieutenant," Kyali said. "I arrived here unexpectedly. Your man offered to take me to the guardroom. I figured I ought to know where that was. Now that I do, I'll leave you to your rest."

"She came out of the wall," the soldier who'd led her here blurted, then looked embarrassed when Kyali glowered at him. She'd rather not have these passages become common knowledge.

Annan's sharp gaze grew sharper still and he set his mug down decisively. "Not another word on that to anyone, Wendel," he murmured, striding to the door. "Lady Captain, perhaps I could accompany you back to the guard hall?"

Neither she nor the soldiers had time to object. Annan edged her out of the threshold, nudged the other soldier—*Wendel*, Kyali reminded herself—inside it, and shut the door firmly.

"There are passageways in the walls?" Annan asked, his

voice gone softer than ever, nothing but calm curiosity on his smooth-shaven face. Up close, which was something she'd managed to avoid being with this particular Cassdall until now, she could see that he was younger than she'd first guessed. Perhaps not much older than she herself was. How he'd ended up at the head of a prince's guard was a point of curiosity.

Then again, here she was at the head of considerably more than a lord's company of personal guard, so what was the bloody point in wondering?

"Apparently," Kyali said, just as soft, mimicking his tone perfectly.

She couldn't say what it was about him that provoked her, but it seemed like every time they were in the same room, they were digging at one another. She found she was tired of it today. She had far larger things to worry about.

"Will you show me?" Annan asked, dropping his barbed politeness for something far more annoyed-looking (it cheered her immensely, which was probably an unworthy response, but there it was), and Kyali shrugged and turned toward the open hallway. Her own dusty footprints marked the spot. She reminded herself to sweep that away, then shoved inward at the hidden door. Dust billowed out.

Annan coughed, waving a hand in front of his face.

"How far do they go?" he asked, following her in.

"I only just discovered them. I'll send someone in to map them out."

"Don't do that. My—" There was a shuffling and a thud, and he hissed. She should probably have warned him to duck. Too late now. The passage door hung open behind him, limning his hunched form in wavering shadows of torchlight. Ahead was darkness. "Damn it, it's blacker than night in here. I should have lit this."

In the faint light from the corridor, she could see the candle he'd pulled out of a pocket.

What sort of person carried a *candle* in his pocket? He probably had a sandwich in there, too, in case he got hungry. He was fumbling around again, and she realized he was looking for flint.

Annan was not only irritating, he was more than a little strange.

Kyali spent a handful of seconds arguing with herself, then sighed and glared at the barely visible wick. It was almost worth the headache to see his eyebrows rise in the flickering light, when it caught.

"...thank you," Annan said doubtfully, eyeing the flame.

"Don't mention it. Ever. You were saying?"

"Ah." He held the candle out, peering around, and pulled the heavy door shut. He began to edge carefully forward. "I was saying, let my men do it. They're bored. And this is their sort of work."

Kyali frowned, following behind him and not liking it much. "Their sort of work is crawling in ancient tunnels?"

"Now you're deliberately misunderstanding. I thought we were going to give up this battle of wits and snipe at one another openly? Captain?" He took the right branching, evidently following her earlier footsteps. He looked back, meeting her eye for a second, and the candle was close enough to his face that she could see the sharp slant of his smile.

"Fine," Kyali said, and coughed. "Their sort of work is spying and sneaking."

"Was that so hard?"

"I take it there's an actual purpose to this particular line of open sniping, Lieutenant. Maybe we could arrive at it before we arrive at the other end of this tunnel."

Up ahead, Annan came to a halt, turning to face her. The candle flickered between them, illuminating swathes of dust kicked up by their passage. He was taller than her, and broad enough to take up most of the passageway, and she could feel herself flinch deep inside where the memory of any man at close quarters would always equal pain. Her fingers itched for a blade.

She didn't let herself move, though. She stared up into his face, fighting a profound, encompassing rage that had nothing at all to do with him, annoying as he was. She hoped her eyes weren't sparking, but judging by her pulse, they must be.

"Oh, I think you've guessed it," he said. "I am offering our services as couriers and spies to your cause. Most of us look similar enough to your people. We can move around in your kingdom unrecognized. We've far more experience than you at such things. We're *good*. Surely you've thought of it already, Captain."

She had. And it made so much damned sense she'd been chewing on the disagreeable taste of it for weeks, unwilling to ask for that kind of help. It was dangerous work. Not everyone they sent into the lowlands would come back, and those that were caught wouldn't...

She wasn't thinking of that.

"I have," Kyali said, without any mockery this time.

"Well, now you don't need to ask, Captain. We are offering.

It was actually Prince Kinsey who suggested it."

"Generous of him," she murmured, and didn't miss the defensive flash of the man's eyes in the candlelight when he thought she wasn't sincere. It surprised her. But, she supposed, it would take a certain kind of loyalty to follow an exiled scholar-prince out of your kingdom and into someone else's war. "I did mean that, Lieutenant. And," she added, trying not to sigh—she'd probably choke on dust if she did—"I do accept your offer. We could use the help."

"Yes, you could," Annan said coolly, tension in every line of him.

Kyali huffed, acknowledging the point, and waved him forward. She was tired of standing in this ancient, fusty tunnel.

"Separate command," she said after a few moments, watching the silhouette of his shoulders, and snorted when they dropped noticeably with relief. So *that* was what he'd been worried about. "I assure you, Lieutenant, I have no desire to add any more men to my command than I already have, and while I spent the first five years of my studies acting as a courier, most of what I know about spying is how to apply the information it gains me."

"*You* were a courier?"

The unguarded astonishment in his voice was a little insulting. She made an effort not to bristle. It didn't work very well. "Nobody suspects a girl," she said.

Annan *hmm*'d, pausing at yet another branching of paths to run his hand along the wall. "I suppose not. Not a bad idea."

"Not unless you brought girls from Cassdall trained in combat. I'm not sending anyone down there who doesn't know how to kill as well as hide."

"Fair enough. We can meet tomorrow to work on locations, persons of interest, specific information you need. I'll want a handful of soldiers from various provinces who can mind their tongues, so my men can learn their speech and dress. Barring complications, they ought to be ready in a week."

Either they were indeed very good or he was just that arrogant. "As you say, Captain."

He nearly walked into the next wall, too busy looking back at her in shock. It almost made her want to smile and she bit her cheek, thinking of ice. "Her Majesty will agree," Kyali added. "You ought to be of equal rank. It will make things simpler."

And it would. And she had almost two thousand men where he had a hundred, so she didn't think she was giving away anything she might miss later. That was quite likely another unworthy thought, but she had her own men to think of, and Taireasa, and she didn't care.

Much.

"Never thought I'd get a promotion on *this* tour," Annan muttered. He stopped, looking down at her footprints ending at a blank wall. "Here we are. Where did you start from?"

"Just past the library."

"Ah." He brushed at himself, frowning. "Maybe I ought to go back the other way."

"Your choice," Kyali said, amused, and for once without that tang of bitter fury under it. That felt—odd.

Unexpectedly, Annan held out a hand. She shook it after only a moment's hesitation, feeling gritty dust, the rasp of calluses, warm strong fingers closing over her own—thinking of ice, of snow, of anything at all but the fact that he was too near, the space was too small, the memory of agony and failure too close to the surface of her mind. Her stomach did a lazy flip. She breathed carefully. "If your men could find some way to move some of this dust while they're exploring, I'd be grateful."

That word felt odd, too.

"I'll see to it," Annan said. "Captain."

"Now breathe," the old lady commanded.

Taireasa pulled in a large breath and held it until sparkles appeared at the corners of her eyes. She looked at Saraid.

"Dear gods, breathe *out*, too," Saraid said, laughing—it was always startling when she laughed, like hearing a tree speak—and Taireasa let the air in her lungs out with a faint whimper.

"I'm never going to get this right," she moaned. She was, after three days, already comfortable enough with this extraordinary woman to gripe in her presence. The fact of that kept surprising her: she couldn't remember the last time she'd trusted somebody this quickly. Certainly none of the court wizards who'd filled her head with dry theories of the workings of magic had inspired this kind of confidence.

"It's because we share a similar Gift, young queen, and because your court wizards were, at best, philosophers with vague dreams of magic—and yes, you will. In fact, you *are*."

That was so *very* unnerving.

"You'll be doing it yourself soon enough," Saraid said serenely, patting her hand.

"I think I'd rather not."

"Best get used to the notion, Taireasa Marsadron. Your Gift won't go away just because you fear it. Learn to wield it or it will wield you."

That was a familiar command—her father had told her the same thing about rulers and flaws. The memory was so clear that grief got her by the throat, clutching with swollen fingers, and she gulped air, pushing it out carefully. For whatever reason, that did it: the flame she'd been trying to picture turned, suddenly, to a pool of still water that held steady in her mind, and all around her the world went blessedly quiet as the never-ending hum of minds thinking, wishing, *wanting* that filled her head these days slid away.

A thing fell into place inside her, a thing that had been missing without her even knowing. She was suddenly aware of urgency and curiosity equal to her own, hovering just outside the precious bubble of silence she'd somehow created within herself.

"Oh," Taireasa said, astonished and grateful beyond words. "*Oh.*"

I should have guessed it would be water, came a voice, right inside her head. She swallowed back a yelp of pure surprise. ***Fire was never yours—***

The rest was drowned in a welter of regret and memory, and Taireasa raised her head so fast the movement echoed down her spine, because it was Kyali she was seeing, Kyali younger and scowling with effort, fire weaving around her fingers. Kyali before the world had made her grim and cold and distant. Kyali her other half, Kyali truest friend.

She didn't know she was crying until Saraid brushed a hand gently over her face.

Taireasa flung herself to her feet and went to look out the window, trying to get her breath back, to quiet the ache in her chest. The mountains looked back at her.

"The world is not kind, young queen," the old woman said softly. Taireasa could feel the heat coming from her thin frame when she came to stand by the window beside her. "We have to be that to one another."

She had no idea what that was supposed to mean.

"It means try again, Taireasa. This time, reach for me, and think of what you want."

What she *wanted* was to curl up on her bed and weep until sleep took her dreamless into the dark, but there was no such thing as dreamless sleep anymore, and never time for that these days in any case, and this was as good a distraction from her sorrow as any. Taireasa shut her eyes, fumbling around in herself for that sense of *otherness*, and found Saraid waiting for her. She was met with grief and iron resolve and patience like the sea, boundless and ever-changing, made strong by many long years of life. Those years echoed around her, rising up, framing the world in image and sentiment.

It was a mind to get lost in, more than the match of her own.

Taireasa thought of that sense of urgency she'd felt, that was surely Saraid's, and *wanted* with everything in her.

Saraid crumpled instantly, a puppet with cut strings, her hands flying up to her temples.

"Oh dear gods," Taireasa cried, and knelt to take Saraid's arms.

"No," the old woman gasped. "I'm... all right, Taireasa. I am. I'm sorry I frightened you." She pushed herself upright, shook her head. The lines on her face had turned to furrows. She kept her eyes shut. "Truly, you can let go now, you're still pushing at me—"

"I'm sorry. Saraid, I'm sorry! I don't know what I did. Please let me help you up."

Saraid laughed weakly and allowed herself to be pulled over to the chair by the hearth. "You did exactly what I asked of you, poor child. I just never imagined you'd be so *strong*, good gods! That, for my arrogance. You could blow my mind away like a leaf on a whirlwind."

That sounded like something she had already done once before. Taireasa caught her breath at the memory of Kyali's pale, stunned face on a hilltop over a valley filled with Western soldiers, the way expression had seemed to flow back into her features. She had done something like this to Kyali that day: her anger and love had opened a door between them.

Dear gods.

"Oh, Taireasa," Saraid said, sounding both tired and sad. "You may be able to make what you want from what you have, dear girl, but first you must *accept* what you have."

That made as much sense as the last piece of advice. Taireasa wondered wearily and a little irritably if she was going to spend her lessons with Saraid trying to decipher an endless series of cryptic utterances.

"There are worse ways to spend an afternoon," she said, because those were precisely the words Saraid was opening her mouth to say, and the old woman tipped her head back and laughed and laughed.

"Oh my, well done," Saraid said. "I haven't been surprised like that since I was—well, nearly your age. How refreshing. And yes, there are indeed worse ways. I believe you know a few, Taireasa Marsadron."

That called to mind things she never wanted to think of

again. Taireasa drew a breath, and another, and pulled that clear pool back to the center of her thoughts until silence surrounded her once more.

The slow clap of hands roused her from the stillness.

"Well done again, child," Saraid said as she got to her feet, grunting with effort. "Gods, but you learn fast. No, don't look so worried. You're not the first to test my boundaries, just— I admit—the only one to actually get *past* them. It's a hazard, teaching magic to the young. You *want* everything with so much urgency. Ah, but I ought to be going. You've appointments. And you ought to bid young Devin goodbye: I'll be taking him along when I go, so that Measail can teach him out where windows and walls aren't likely to suffer for it."

Devin had told her that. And packed a day ago, and begged her not to hold the farewell dinner she'd planned. It wounded her, but it wasn't unfair. Devin had suffered a great deal lately, first losing his father and then, in all the ways that mattered, his sister. She wished there were something she could say to help him understand, but there was still so much guilt in her, so much pain. And it would only hurt him worse to know.

Oh, she wished so badly that she had someone to talk to about these things.

Taireasa stared at the chair, trying to remember what the subject had been. She could feel Saraid's curious mind hovering at the edges of her thoughts. "Wanting is so important a part of it, then?" she asked, a little desperately.

"Magic is perception and intent, Taireasa," the old woman replied, winding a shawl about her shoulders. Her silver hair gleamed. "Wanting is a sort of intent, though one must be careful about it. You, especially, will have to learn to govern your heart as well as you do your head. Yours is a Gift very much of the heart, and the better you govern your own, the better you will govern others'."

"Why would I do *that*?" Taireasa asked, and shrank under Saraid's sardonic look.

"You are a queen, are you not?"

She didn't like the direction this discussion was taking at all.

Saraid shrugged and spread her hands: *There you are.* "You already do. Every ruler has some hold on her people's hearts. You can't argue it would have been useful a few months ago."

A point.

Crown shall harbor all their hope. Maybe her Gift would teach her how to do that. Gods knew she found little to hope for in this new, lonely life.

"Must you go?" Taireasa sighed, and the old woman grinned at her.

"I'll be back. I can't stay inside walls for more than a handful of days before I get restless. I need the mountain air. Meanwhile, remember the pool, and to breathe. Think of the structure of the world. Your court wizards weren't good for much, but they weren't wrong about that. Fire, earth, air, and..." she came forward, tapping a gnarled finger on Taireasa's breastbone, "—water. Less use than breathing, but not use*less*. I'll see you in a few days, Your Majesty."

"Please don't call me that, Saraid."

"It's what you are," she replied, not without pity.

"It's not *all* I am."

"No, Taireasa. You are much more than that." Saraid's face was as calm as ever, but compassion and sorrow flickered in her eyes and also in the mind behind them... which shuttered itself tightly. Taireasa carefully didn't let her face give away that she'd noticed that.

Yes, the Fraonir definitely knew more than they shared.

How *much* more was the question, but she'd gotten the impression, during the course of these lessons, that Saraid held herself apart from their efforts due to some great discipline, something that did, in fact, cause her pain.

Nothing was simple anymore. The days of hiding in Faestan's walls and sneaking sheep into the sewing solarium seemed so very far away.

"Safe travels," Taireasa said, and went to do the next thing, and the next, until there was a moment to rest.

Kinsey set the quill aside and blew gently on the page before leaning back in a newly repaired chair. Corin leaned over him, gawky as a colt in her Fraonir trousers (he was never going to get used to seeing a woman in those), and blew hard enough to send a stray drop of ink sailing across the paper, just to be contrary.

"I think that will do," Kinsey said, and she grinned at him, looking like a woodsprite with her long brown braid, her strange clothes, and her irrepressible good humor. Not exactly what he'd imagined in a library keeper, but the Fraonir were a strange people. And she *did* know this place, and these books.

These books were now cleaned, shelved, and guarded by a soldier standing outside the doors and one fourteen-year-old Fraonir girl from the Darachim Clan. And, Kinsey supposed, one wayward prince of Cassdall, because gods knew after all the work he'd done, he might very well kill someone who so much as sneezed in here.

"Go pester Annan, would you?" Kinsey said, on a sudden mischievous impulse that was probably the result of spending so much of his time with Devin. "I'm sure he could use cheering."

"Gladly," Corin said with a wicked grin, and slipped out.

Annan *could* use cheering, actually. He was far busier now, precisely what he'd been wanting, but for no reason Kinsey could see, his lieutenant had suddenly learned how to brood. Annan was mostly as inexpressive and sharp-witted as ever, but now he could occasionally be found frowning off into distances, a faint line of thought marring his forehead.

Twenty of their men were heading to the lowlands tomorrow; that was probably it. Kinsey was worried himself, but he always was when men whose lives he was responsible for risked them in his service.

"This is an improvement," came a voice from behind him.

Kinsey managed to bite back the undignified yelp that tried to leap out of him, but apparently couldn't wipe the stupid surprise from his face, because the Lady Captain's gaze flickered over him and one dark red eyebrow lifted just slightly. "Highness," she said, with the perfunctory half-bow that seemed to be her only form of courtesy. Her searching eyes took in the newly repaired furniture, the crackling fire in the hearth, the ordered shelves of books. She was wearing her armor: perhaps she expected ambush from every unoccupied room in the keep. She was nearly always wearing her armor when he saw her. Today, however, there was no sword over her shoulder, only the Fraonir daggers on her hips. One hand brushed a pommel, as though she would be happier holding the blade unsheathed. The eyebrow lifted a little higher.

"Credit to the housekeepers," Kinsey said. "And Corin. I mostly catalogued."

She didn't look as though she cared much either way. "Corin," she said, uninflected. He took it to be a question, since there wasn't any other reason to repeat the name.

"The Darachim Clan sent an assistant. She apparently knew the library already, something to do with her training. She's been a great help."

There was that flicker again. Kyali moved into the room and tipped her head, one hand hovering over the index on the table. Kinsey shrugged, trying not to look as uncomfortable as he felt. She turned the pages delicately. Her armor gleamed in the light from the windows—just standing there, she was, in and of herself, enough to make him believe in the old faery tales.

All three of them were, in their own ways.

Thinking that made him wonder how Devin was faring off with the Eanin Clan, and he'd blurted the question out before he knew he was going to. Kyali stopped turning pages to fix him with that *look* of hers that made sane people want to find other places to be.

"I have no idea, Your Highness," she said, and turned to look up at the first of the shelves.

Poor Devin, Kinsey thought. Whatever was wrong between them was still wrong, then. He hardly knew what sort of siblings they had been before, but judging from Devin's sadness, they had been far closer than this.

"Was there something you came here looking for, Lady Captain?" Kinsey asked wearily.

"*History of Lardan*, and a text by Hidarion on siegecraft, Highness. I don't recall the title."

He stared for a moment, finding it difficult to imagine her doing anything so mundane as reading—but then, she had the weight of duty on her shoulders, and probably much to study regarding this sort of war. It didn't seem likely her studies until now had prepared her for such a situation.

He scowled at the catalogue. "Hm. I think I've seen something by that person, but it was some time ago—one moment..."

Gods, but there was something wonderful about having so many books in one room.

He wandered into the shelves, running his fingers lightly over cracked leather, Kyali following behind. It was precisely where the index had said it would be, and Kinsey couldn't help but grin as he gently slid the book free and handed it to her.

His smile died as soon as he saw her face.

She was looking at the opposite shelf, and all the blood seemed to have fallen out of her skin, leaving behind a truly alarming pallor. Sparks of gold were rising in her eyes, swimming just under the yellowish-brown.

Now she *really* looked like something from a faery tale.

"Lady Captain? Are you all right?"

She blinked several times, still staring up at the shelf, and then frowned at him. "Yes," she said absently, and took the book he was holding.

She turned to leave, hardly seeming aware of the shelves around her now; by all he had seen of this girl, it was nothing like her. Kinsey followed her at a safe distance, eyes fixed on her shoulders, which had drawn up. She nearly walked into the table, swerving at the last moment, and turned at the door to meet his eyes. Kinsey stared, freezing in place, forgetting to be polite.

The sparks had grown, until there seemed to be light coming from her eyes. He'd only seen it happen once before, and she'd been quite upset at the time. It stood to reason...

"Thank you, Your Highness," Kyali said, and Kinsey knocked his hip on the corner of the table shuffling forward to keep her there a moment longer. He wasn't even sure why, except this was another puzzle, one that mattered a great deal to Devin and Taireasa, and he was looking at a new piece of it right now. He just had no idea where it fit.

"Wait—Lady Captain—"

Damn, he sounded like a fool.

Kyali turned again, her eyebrows falling together in a way that was hardly welcoming of questions. Her eyes were already fading back, but the wooden lack of expression she always wore was softened by a preoccupied distress that drew him as surely as Devin's presence had one night on the other side of this mountain. It made him remember that she was actually younger than he was by a year. It was also deeply unnerving, because he was fairly sure that in this moment, he'd do almost anything she needed of him without thinking twice about it.

Gods. The magic surrounding these three people was *terrifying*.

What had he been about to say?

"Did you want the other text, Lady? *History of Lardan?* It's in my rooms. I could have it sent to you."

She blinked. He could see her gathering herself, pushing whatever had put that look of startled unhappiness on her face far away. "If you're reading it, no."

"I'm not. I started an instructional text on magic that I'm afraid may take me far longer than I'd guessed, so you're welcome to *History*."

"*Tenets of Magic?*" she asked, wry sympathy threading through her usual coolness.

"Yes," Kinsey sighed. Just the thought of reading more of it made him want to sink into the floor. "It's... dry."

"Wretched," Kyali corrected firmly.

"Yes." His surprise at her familiarity with the accursed thing must have shown on his face.

"We all had to read it, Highness. Still, you could do worse, if you're looking for rules. I believe it's got an endless list."

This was easily the longest conversation he'd ever had with her. "It certainly does. I'll send you *History*, then, since I suspect *Tenets* will take some time."

Kyali nodded, then hesitated, staring at the book cradled in her hands with a faint frown. "There's a book in this library you should read first," she finally said.

"The one you were looking at."

Her eyes met his for just a moment. "Yes, Your Highness."

He went to retrieve it as soon as the door shut behind her; he'd noted the placement and the color of the binding while she was still staring at it. The leather was ancient, crumbling under his fingers, and he tapped it delicately, afraid it would fall apart in his hands before he even had a chance to open it. Corin would have looked over this one, since he had no memory of seeing it before this, and he spared an irritated thought for the Fraonir and their secrets. She had not mentioned it to him, nor set it down in the index. She'd simply shelved it without noting its existence anywhere.

The secrets these Clans held seemed ominous, suddenly. Why would she hide this book from him, yet leave it somewhere he might be able to find?

Oh. *Oh.*

"They *can't* interfere? Is that it?" Kinsey murmured aloud, then glanced around the library, making sure it was still empty. His fingers tingled where they rested against the book. There was a queasy, imperative pulling in his guts, like a command. He was beginning to recognize that feeling.

What an idiot he'd been. It had been in front of him all along.

The Fraonir had given them tents, food, medicines—were even now guarding the mountain from incursions by Western troops. They were teaching Taireasa and Devin to control their magic. They had offered more aid than anyone would have dared to ask for... but they had not fought in the valley with the Lardana against the West, and they would not answer questions. Where things touched on prophecy, they stood back every time, unwilling to mire themselves in events still unfolding.

Corin had not told him about this book—this book that Kyali Corwynall, who had studied with the Darachim, had clearly seen before, this book that had so surprised her he had gotten a glimpse, just for a moment, of something far more real and raw underneath the hard surface she showed the world. But Corin hadn't hidden it from him, either.

The Fraonir were *waiting* for something. What?

Kinsey sat, opening the cover with great care, his pulse beginning to pound.

There was no title, and the ink on the page was faded to little more than an impression, but he had long practice with old texts and he could make out the spidery hand if he squinted.

The earth is old, it read. *Many years has it seen, many more than I. Men have swallowed the world from the foot of this mountain to the far sea. Few come now to learn what I have to teach. I am the*

last of us, and I watch, from this last of our fortresses, this prison we
have been afforded—I stand guard.

The feeling of pulling became so strong he had to pause,
and breathe, palm flattened against the table next to the pages. On an impulse he didn't question, he turned to the very last
page, to see what was there.

> *Dark the wind that brings the storm*
> *and lost, all, to its breaking,*
> *Yet firm shall hold Sword, Song, and Crown*
> *A land of their own making.*

> *Sword shall guide the hands of men*
> *and Song shall ease their sorrow,*
> *Crown shall harbor all their hope*
> *And lead them to tomorrow.*

"*Oh,*" Kinsey said aloud and, turning back to the first page,
began to read.

18

Somehow she'd ended up agreeing to attend some kind of gathering of Cassdall officers: a tradition, she'd been told, after spies were sent out. Annan hadn't been specific—had, in fact, thrown the invitation out in the middle of a meeting about supply lines, and Kyali had agreed more out of the suspicion that he meant it as a challenge than from any real desire to go.

She wished now she hadn't.

She should meet his officers, she supposed. Commanders did that sort of thing. It wasn't all maps and numbers and planning things to surprise your enemy. They all ought to know one another from strangers in the halls, anyway.

Still, when the door to the Cassdall guardroom opened to her pattern of knocks and five faces looked out at her, Kyali decided she'd rather face a full-scale battle, and had to lock her knees to keep from spinning on a heel and heading back the way she'd come.

"Captain," Annan said, standing, managing by some miracle of politeness to keep the sarcasm in his voice to a low undertone. His men stood too, and Kyali moved warily into the room, taking in the small keg of recently brewed ale on the table, the mugs, the tray of savories someone had stolen from the kitchens. The door swung closed behind her and her fingers curled reflexively over the memory of a sword. Being shut up in a room with people made her heart pound, which inevitably made her angry.

Everything made her angry.

She woke up that way; she fell asleep that way, when she could manage to sleep, until her dreams woke her again, shuddering and gasping with dread and sick, helpless rage. Sometimes it was all she could do to rise, dress, think, plan. That she was also expected to speak to people, to say civil things and do civil things and pretend there was something else in her other than the darkness of memory and the useless, endless struggle not to let it swallow her whole seemed impossible much of the time.

She shut her eyes, then opened them and managed a short bow.

"Captain," Kyali echoed, not sure what to expect, or what was expected of her. She only hoped this would be over soon.

The Cassdall officers rattled off a series of names she did her best to commit to memory, grasping her wrist one after another in their style of greeting. It was clear they'd already had a bit of ale. Someone handed her a mug. She sipped cautiously.

The toasts began, almost before she could sit down. She had been braced for that—soldiers everywhere did this sort of thing, for luck—and she managed to say something short but hopefully not too stupid. After that came a comfortable quiet, as the savories slowly disappeared and the keg emptied. Kyali nursed her single mug down to dregs, noticed that Annan was doing the same, and wondered if this were a good moment for a graceful exit.

"To the Lady Captain," Annan's second, Jodin, said then, startling her, and there was a murmur of agreement all around the little table as they raised their mugs and knocked them together.

Kyali stared. She couldn't think of a single thing to say. She was fairly sure that fact was perfectly clear on her face right now. In her bewildered silence, one man—Martin? Yes, Martin—stood and slid a bottle off the mantel, clear glass filled with a cloudy white liquid she recognized from her days among the Clans.

"This calls for sommat stronger than ale, by yer leave, Cap'n," he said and, at Annan's curious look and waved permission, produced several smallish glasses and poured for them all. Kyali held a hand up, knowing full well this was a bad idea but wanting to do *something*—these men had welcomed her into their company, were trying to put her at ease, and she owed them more than an uncomfortable hour of toasts for that.

"This is a Fraonir drink," she said. "There is only one way to take this, sirs. Do we have a candle and a straw?"

Looking mystified, Jodin passed her what she needed. She lit the straw and touched it to the surface of the liquor. A cloud of bright blue flame appeared at the top of the glass like magic and Ellis laughed, incredulous and admiring.

"Now what?" Annan asked, eyeing her with a skeptical look. The flame cast sable shadows on his face, making him look older. "You're wasting good liquor there, Captain."

Kyali gave the look right back to him, and someone let loose a low, mocking whistle.

"Gods help us all, there's two o' them now," Martin groaned. Jodin snickered.

It *was* actually sort of funny, if she thought about it, or if she looked at Annan's slightly offended, slightly surprised expression. Damn it. She probably should not have had the whole mug of ale. She couldn't remember the last meal she'd eaten.

"To new homelands," Kyali said, raising the glass, and was horrified to hear her voice break on the last word. She tipped the glass all the way back as fast as she could, fighting a sudden pressure in her chest that felt like Devin's prying, but had no magical source that she could sense.

Flame curled warm hands around her face and went out; the liquor, on the other hand, burned like fire the whole way down. *Damn it*, she thought again, sighing inwardly, because she was definitely going to feel this in the morning.

Then the burning bloomed into a pleasant warmth in her belly, and the whole affair began to seem like a not-terrible way to spend an evening after all.

The Cassdalls followed her lead, lighting their glasses and downing the contents in one swift swallow. Jodin coughed after his, and blinked with such a look of alarm that she felt her face stretch oddly and realized after a moment that she was grinning. She made herself frown instead, but that wasn't quite right either. Across from her, Annan was looking at his empty glass with a faint air of distrust.

Glass clinked again, and she looked down in time to see Jodin empty the last of the bottle into her cup and Annan's.

"Captains g'down wi' the ship," he said, in a startlingly accurate Eanin brogue, earning snorts of laughter and scattered
applause from Martin and Ludor and Ellis. Kyali met Annan's
look from across the table. It held both dismay and challenge.
He lifted his glass and an eyebrow, waiting, a small smile hovering at the corners of his mouth.

"Bloody hell, that's a stupid rule," she said, unintentionally
out loud, and tossed the last glass back with a wince as laughter and cheers rose around her.

Getting to bed would be a good idea now.

Kyali leaned against the wall as the Cassdall officers took
their leave in an excess of friendliness, walking unsteadily,
singing some song together softly. She was suddenly very glad
they had chosen the far end of the keep for their guardroom:
no servants walked these halls yet, and none of the ever-grow-
ing list of escaped noble-born Lardana did either.

She was fairly sure the wall was doing more to hold her up
right now than she wanted anyone to see.

"Thank you for coming," Annan said from behind her, and
she had her daggers out and aimed at him before she could
stop herself. He rocked back on his heels, seeming only a little
alarmed, and kindly didn't acknowledge her confused flush or
the curse she hissed as she put the blades back.

"Thank you for inviting me," she said, furious with herself,
and went to find the nearest entrance to the passageways without bothering to shake his hand, or bow, or do anything else
polite people were supposed to do in these circumstances. It
took her a moment to realize he was still next to her, apparently
heading the same way and as uninterested in being seen in this
state as she was. His steps weren't much steadier than hers.

"Your rooms are in His Highness's apartments," Kyali said, having just figured that out. She wasn't sure why it surprised her.

"As yours are in Her Majesty's," Annan agreed. "It's what bodyguards generally do, isn't it?"

"You're a captain."

"So I am. So are you. And yet."

She didn't at all like this discussion. "Glad we cleared that up, Captain Adaron," she said, stalking over to where the door should be, hiding under a tapestry that looked very out of place in this empty corridor.

"Happy to be of service, Captain Corwynall," Annan shot back pithily, then put his hand out and leaned against the wall for a moment. Kyali paused, watching, not really sure why, except that it was reassuring to know he seemed to be having as hard a time with the drink as she was.

"Another unworthy thought," she muttered to herself: she had too many of those around him. She felt her whole face heat when Annan shot her a puzzled look.

"We all have those," he said, sounding so gravely concerned she actually *laughed*, dear gods, for the first time since—

She wasn't thinking of that.

The sound stopped as suddenly as if someone had cut her throat, and they both listened to the echoes die. Annan looked...

Actually, she wasn't sure what that look on his face meant.

"Come on," Kyali sighed, then cursed again, far louder this time, when the hidden door opened much more easily than she'd expected and dumped her on the floor of the tunnel.

At least it had been cleaned.

There was a strangled cough from behind her that she was fairly certain was smothered laughter. She pushed herself upright. Annan's grip closed helpfully over her arm. The complete, unreasoning panic that chased that touch didn't have more than a split second to freeze the breath in her chest and the blood in her veins, before he'd hauled her upright with such speed the dimly lit tunnel swung wildly around her. She threw her hands out to keep from tumbling back to the floor like a broken doll and met the smooth, faintly scarred armor of his steel spaulders.

This time *he* moved too fast, jerking back and hitting the lip of stone at the entrance. Kyali had to pull at his shoulders to keep him from going down, and nearly fell with him when she discovered he was far heavier than she was. Instead, they ended up pressed together against the wall just inside the door, illuminated by the flickering light from the lantern Annan had dropped.

Even the floor was spinning now. And gods damn it, it was more than funny, it was *hilarious* when they pulled away from one another only to find that the tiny metal plates of their brigandine had caught, and they were stuck.

"I'll bet *this* never happened on a battlefield," Annan muttered.

Kyali lost the battle before she even realized there was one to fight. She laughed silently, helplessly, her knuckles pressed to her mouth, swaying with the effort to stay upright against the dark and the drink coursing through her, the shocking feeling of *feeling* something that wasn't pain or fury or exhaustion. Her elbow was digging into Annan's shoulder and through it she could feel him shaking with soundless mirth, too.

"I'm glad we don't have an audience for this," he finally wheezed, and gods help her, *that* was funny, too.

"It would cer... certainly make tomorrow's drills interesting."

"Oh gods," Annan managed to say while snickering, and he reached out to pull the door shut, throwing them into darkness leavened only by chancy light from the lantern at their feet. "No more of that drink. Ever again. What *was* that stuff? I can barely stand."

"Fraonir. Something Fraonir. I can't remember the name for it. I don't even know how they make it."

"We ought to send some to our enemies."

She knew she was drunk when that seemed like a brilliant idea.

"Sound strategy," she declared, and then they were laughing again, leaning on one another, winded and very, very stupid.

"I should never have had that last glass," Kyali moaned, then clapped a hand over her mouth when she heard how pathetic she sounded. By now Annan was picking delicately at the point where their armor had gotten tangled. She could feel the faint pressure of his hands even through the steel. A strange, crooked little smile twisted his mouth up on one side.

"I should never have had the *first* glass," he muttered, his breath ghosting over her neck, and then he uttered a low growl of frustration and tugged too hard. Her forehead knocked into his nose and they both grunted.

"Brilliant," Kyali said, wobbly-kneed and trying without success to find a place to put her hands that wasn't on him— and then without any warning his lips were against hers, warm and surprisingly soft. She froze. Annan leaned back just a fraction, enough that the panic she knew should follow this strange moment, this closeness, didn't happen. He tilted his head a little. She didn't hit him. She wasn't sure why.

He was kissing her again before she had realized that was his intention. She was kissing him back before she had any idea that was hers. The new angle pressed their mouths all the way together this time: it was far better, far more... more... something she had no word for. His hand slid up to trace the line of her jaw. The calluses on his fingers were sending little rills of shivers over her skin.

She thought she'd better give him a minute to remember who he was and who she was, and that they didn't do this. They—they argued and jabbed and sniped and fought—

Annan scraped the edge of her lip gently with his teeth, and Kyali heard the breath whistle out of her throat as if from very far away. Her hands braced on his hips. His were slipping over her neck, calling up more shivers and a wild, weak sensation that made her knees want to buckle and her eyes want to flutter shut.

The lantern clattered over in their stumbling press toward one another and the sound brought them both back to their senses.

Kyali jerked backwards, hit the opposite wall hard enough to knock the wind from her lungs, and heard several small *plinks* as tiny steel plates went flying every which way. Annan spun away, throwing one hand against the wall to keep himself upright. She was panting like she'd just run up a flight of stairs. It didn't sound like Annan was doing much better, which she supposed meant she hadn't been too bad at—that possibly she wasn't—

Gods, she couldn't believe what she was *thinking*.

"This is idiocy," she said, staring at the ceiling and trying to pretend she didn't notice how her voice shook. She was so shocked at herself she was halfway to sober now.

"Yes," Annan replied, low and rueful.

"We ought—we shouldn't—"

"It was the drink. We should never touch that stuff again."

"Yes," Kyali said, hearing the desperate gratitude in her voice and hating it. Her skin was so hot the stuffy air in the tunnel seemed cold by comparison.

"So this never happened."

"Never. It's already forgotten."

After another few moments of mortified looking-else-where, Annan turned to face her, which meant she had to be brave enough to do the same, and she only hoped the lantern-light wasn't enough to show him how flushed she still was. He didn't show it as clearly, being darker than she, but it seemed like she wasn't the only one.

She wasn't thinking of that.

"Agreed," Annan said then, and offered his hand on it. They shook like merchants over a cow. Kyali let go as fast as she could and began to walk, trying to forget how that hand had felt on the bare skin of her neck, how the muscles under his hips had moved against her palms. She could feel the faint current of air from the door moving over her neck. Her pulse wouldn't take a slower pace.

Dear gods, what was *wrong* with her?

Annan left her at the last branching before the one that would take her to the hall outside the royal apartments, mumbling a hurried goodnight. For a moment, she let herself lean against the crumbling brick wall in the dark. Her head was swimming. Her hands were clenched. She didn't know if she was angry or something else, hardly knew how to tell.

She *wished,* so badly her guts ached with it, that she could ask Taireasa.

Taireasa was sleeping. She'd wake when the mattress sank under a friend's weight; she'd mumble sleepily, and then her voice would rise with shock at the whole stupid story. She'd see more, because she always did, and she'd say something to make one achingly confused captain of the guard simultaneously curl up with embarrassment and laugh out loud, and see the whole thing in a new and far more forgiving light. She'd—

—wake hours later to a bedmate swallowing screams of terror and rage, fighting shadows, losing the battle over and over and over again. Learn something new and terrible about the world: how cruel it could be. Live with that forever, because there would be no other choice.

"Oh," Kyali said, and wrapped her arms about herself in the perfect darkness, breathing, only breathing, looking for *ice* in her heart and finding it scarce at the moment.

19

The wind snatched notes out of the air and flung them off the edge of the world, carried them far up into the unrelenting blue sky, scattered them through the bared branches of trees. Devin gave the wind all the music in him, his fingers flying over the strings of the harp, a grin of effort baring his teeth to the brutal cold. Next to him, Fortyn of the Eanin Clan played a flute with such speed it was like having a flock of birds sing with him, and his twin sister Aileana pounded a complicated rhythm on a set of skin drums. The sound the three of them made together was wild, haunting.

He'd never played with people who could keep up with him. It was *wonderful*.

He caught the eye of Measail, Clan leader of the Eanin and father to Fortyn and Aileana, and remembered what they were doing here, and breathed, and *wished*.

The air around him blurred into a mad shimmer, turning

Aileana and Fortyn into vague shapes. Devin sent his voice out
to join wind and sky, and watched that shimmer travel away
from him in spreading ripples. He was supposed to bend it
to his wishing now, but that was far harder, and he could feel
sweat break out on his brow and freeze in the winter wind. He
began to sing an old lullaby.

Night, he decided, and dreamed stars into his imagining.
They shaped themselves out of nothing, blooming over the
blue, taking the sunlight away.

The vision found memory, wrenching his raw and sorrowing heart right into the last place he wanted it to go—but that
was the price of magic, he was discovering: there was no way
to be anything but brutally honest when it was the workings of
your heart that made it happen. The sky filled with a thousand
pinpricks of faraway light, filled with the constellations of his
childhood, the ones he and Kyali had learned together at their
father's knee, sitting on the porch steps late one summer night.

He could feel her beside him suddenly, staring up, her eyes
full of light and simple contentment—felt her sharp elbow in
his ribs when he poked fun at her. A hand landed on his shoulder, heavy, callused, restraining and affectionate all at once.

His father's voice in his ear, pointing out the Carter and
the Mare, Old Grandmother, Point of North.

"*No*," Devin gasped, and stilled the strings with his palm,
suddenly choked with grief.

The illusion fell away, blue bleeding through the false night
sky he'd built around them. He rested his head in his hands,
fighting tears and fury, trying to make the muscles of his face
obey him and be still. A hand landed on his shoulder—a real one
this time—and he jerked away. "Give me a moment, Measail."

"Devin," the man said. The rough edge of sorrow in his voice brought Devin's head up.

All three of them had tears on their cheeks, too.

Fortyn swiped his face into the crook of his elbow and shoved himself unsteadily to his feet. "That's enough for to-day," he said, his voice thick. "I can't do any more. Bloody Bards, it's like being mauled by a—"

His voice vanished into the whistle of the wind as he stomped off.

"We'll come back to this tomorrow," Measail said simply, squeezing Devin's shoulder, and went to follow his muttering son back in the direction of the Eanin camp.

Aileana stayed, watching her brother's retreat with a wry expression, her dark braids blown into tangles and her cheeks stung pink by cold. She wiped her face, frowned at the tears on her hand, and rubbed her fingers.

"What in *hell* was that?" Devin finally managed, and she gave him a smile full of sympathy.

"You miss your father," she said, taking his breath away all over again with the simple, awful truth of it. "We could feel it. It was like—gods, like losing my own—"

"Thank you," Devin said curtly, and stood.

It was mostly worthwhile, this training, but there times when it bared far more of him than he'd ever want anyone to see. It was the nature of his Gift, he'd been told, and he supposed it made sense, but oh gods, it was *appalling*.

"Come on," Aileana said comfortably, hooking her arm through his, pulling him into the warmth of her. She'd found his tent two nights ago in the dark, surprising him. He was hardly going to turn her down, of course, even knowing what poor company he was these days: she was clever and strong, and unapologetically frank about her wishes—and besides, the bed was so much warmer with her in it. She didn't seem to expect more from him than his nights and his friendship, and he was grateful for that, since he didn't have more to give. Some days, it was all he could do to hold civil conversations.

"Is Fortyn all right?" Devin asked, because her brother was now shoving his way through branches like he was fighting a war all by himself, and his irritable shouts could be heard even over the wind. His father, Clan Leader of the Eanin or not, was giving him a wide berth.

"He gets sullen when he's sad," Aileana said, no sign of either of those things in her own tone. She was as unlike her brother as... as he was from Kyali, not at all what he would have expected of twins.

The comparison was like shining a light on some hidden corner of his mind, and he stopped in his tracks.

"Sad," Devin murmured, trying that concept out, finding it fit much better than he'd ever have guessed. His little sister's actions since the uprising couldn't *all* be explained by that— he could almost feel the anger she carried around baking off her when he was nearby—but it made more sense of her than any other foolish, frustrated thought he'd had where Kyali was concerned.

Sad.

Maybe there was hope?

That was such a dangerous thought he actually took a step backwards, as though he could get away from the idea that way, and Aileana tugged harder on his arm, pulling him off balance. Devin tripped into her and she chuckled, pressing her face into his.

Her lips were cold, but they warmed fast. His pulse picked up.

"Come on," she said again, a little breathless. "*I don't get sullen.*"

Devin tipped his head back and laughed. "I see that."

Measail was waiting for them at his tent, looking grim.

Devin let go of Aileana's hand immediately, going cold, pulse fluttering up into his throat. Another man was standing next to the Eanin Clan leader, a thin, young Cassdall with fading bruises on his cheekbone and angry red scars criss-crossing the rest of his face. He held himself like he was in pain, and he saluted in the Cassdall fashion, hand over heart, when he saw Devin.

"Lord Corwynall," he said. Devin halted, blinking. He *hated* that title.

"Waylen," Measail said by way of introduction. "A Cassdall—"

"—spy," Devin finished, understanding all of it in a single flash of comprehension.

Of *course* they had sent men down to the lowlands. And of course those men were Cassdalls, who looked like Orin-men or Fraonir but were strangers to everyone, with years of experience saving Kinsey from his uncle's deadly attentions. Kyali was their father all over again in these things: brilliant and quiet and ruthless... but dear gods, it was such a risk for those who chose to go.

"Aye, my lord," the man said. "I can only hope the others made it farther than I did."

"What happened?"

"I was to take a position in the royal armory, to..." Waylen waved a hand, then grimaced; the movement made muscles in his too-worn face jump and shudder. Devin could only guess what sort of wounds the man carried under his clothes. "You understand, my lord."

"I think I do," Devin said bleakly. "What *happened?*"

"I left," Waylen answered, then bent over and coughed. Blood slid from an open cut on his neck.

"Gods, *inside,*" Devin snapped, and bustled Measail, Aileana, and Waylen into the tent without ceremony, pushing until they all fit; it was close, but at least the warmth the four of them created under the heavy canvas would chase away the chill of the wind. Aileana immediately shrugged her coat off and lit the brazier in the middle of the floor, and things became bearable.

"I didn't make it to the armory," Waylen was saying, his voice faint and growing fainter. "It takes time to work into such a position. I joined the house staff of the castle as a footman, intending to work my way in from there, but I overheard something just a day later that made it necessary to abandon the effort and head back. I must make it to the fortress as quickly as possible and report. Lord, there's a traitor somewhere in Her Majesty's inner circle."

Taireasa.

All the air seemed to have left the tent. Devin tilted, and then slid slowly to his knees, because his legs weren't going to hold him for much longer.

"Who?" he whispered.

"I don't *know.* There were no names, my lord, forgive me.

It was a conversation, one I'd have lost my head for overhearing if I'd been caught. I tried, I swear to you, but I could learn no more and I was afraid to stay longer, knowing what I knew. I'm sorry. I must ride back today, *now*, and see my captain. The Clan Leader insisted I see you first."

"Dear gods," Devin said, and then shoved all the horror and outrage aside, because he had to think. "You're in no shape to ride, Waylen. I need you to tell me the rest right now, all of it."

Waylen wrapped his long arms about his middle, looking miserable and cold and worn to the bone. "My lord, I wish there were more to tell. I heard two men speaking: I was certain one was Tuan's master of the guard, and the other might have been Tuan himself, or possibly an advisor. They spoke of the fighting on the mountain, the witch and her troops—and then their man inside, who had sent word with the numbers of the army here, the placement of the Lady Captain's bands around the mountain." Waylen met his eyes and the fierce worry in the man's gaze made Devin's hands curl into fists. "The numbers were *accurate*, Lord Corwynall," the spy said. "Accurate from when I left. Someone among us who knows a great deal is Tuan's man, and is sending messages. Time is crucial in such things. I can ride if I have to. I need to report.»

«You already have,» Devin said, and shut his eyes, ignoring everything and everyone.

Taireasa, he sent, reaching for the sense of her with all the strength in him. In an instant she was with him, a moil of surprise, pleasure, loneliness, and an exhaustion so great it wore at the edges of her presence like sand on stone.

"Gods!" he gasped aloud, because she was so strong it was like stepping into what he'd expected to be a lake and finding it was a river in full flood. He was almost swept away by the force of her. All the guards he'd ever set against her keen perception were demolished, and for a terrifying second he was completely exposed, every impulse and resentment and silly, sad wish bared.

She pulled back, horrified at what she'd done to him, and he felt her mute apology as he tried to catch his breath.

Devin, I'm so sorry, I've been learning—Saraid taught me—

Not now, Taireasa. Listen.

He gave her everything he knew, spilling it out without any attempt to organize it. Taireasa's presence grew stronger and then weaker as she understood, and he could feel her distress at the thought that anyone she had trusted with so much—anyone who had lost the same kingdom she had, who had struggled and suffered as she had—would be willing to betray them all in this way.

I have the spy with me. We'll leave tomorrow. I'm coming home.

You should stay, Devin, you have things to learn still.

Don't argue with me now. You want me there and I can stand to be nowhere else.

She was both irritated and grateful almost to the point of tears. She was so *lonely*. It scraped at the scabs over his own wounds.

You're in danger, Taireasa, Devin had to add, as if she hadn't already gotten there on her own. In intrigue and politics, as in magic, she could run rings around him. But he couldn't help it. *Tell Annan, and tell my sister. Kyali will keep you safe.*

What that got him was another kind of loneliness entirely, something shadowy and wounded and full of secretive guilt. Devin opened his eyes on three staring faces, not knowing what to do with that or how to take it.

Yes, Taireasa said briskly, and vanished, shutting him out as thoroughly as she ever had.

"She knows," Devin said, because Waylen and Aileana and Measail were still staring at him, looking increasingly confused. "Taireasa knows. I told her. She'll tell Annan, and... and everyone else that needs to know."

In that moment, he couldn't even make himself say Kyali's name.

What had she and Taireasa done to one another? What were they hiding? Because it was very clear now that they were both hiding *something*, something Taireasa was terrified he'd discover.

"That's... amazing," the spy was saying, his voice beginning to roughen with weariness and relief. "You can *speak* to her? You just spoke to her now?"

"Surely you've heard the rumors," Devin said, not at all comfortable with the way Waylen was staring at him. "We can—ever since the night the kingdom was taken, we've been able to—"

Gods, there was no explaining it. He just shook his head, going mute.

"I didn't believe it," Waylen said frankly. "People make up all sorts of strange things about noble-borns, and about you three in particular. But this... this is..."

"Magic," Devin sighed. "And prophecy."

Stupid, blind, vicious prophecy.

"Can you tell the Lady Captain, too?" Waylen asked, having no idea how many wounds he rubbed salt into with that simple question. Devin bit his lip as the Cassdall spy went silent and chagrined, which meant there was far too much of his heart on his face just now.

"Not so far," Devin said, trying for a light tone and failing miserably. "I don't think she—"

He stopped. He didn't need to see the frown on Waylen's scarred face to know that made no sense at all. The prophecy named *three*, and three of them had felt the pull of it. *Geas*, Arlen and Saraid had called it—fate at work, reshaping the world. It had drawn Kyali down from this mountain as surely as it had drawn him home from Caerwyssis, as surely as it had pushed both of them to renounce the throne that day.

And he *had* felt his sister's presence, hadn't he? That terrible night when the whole world had come crashing down around their ears, he had *known* Kyali wasn't well. And then days later, riding into a messy and unequal battle between Sevassis and the newly formed Exile's Army, he had been sure he felt her nearby, and just as sure something was very, very wrong with her.

Your sister needs you now, boy.

Their father had known it, too.

Taireasa knew more—that was very clear. Taireasa, being so much stronger than he was in matters of their hearts, probably knew a great deal more. And whatever it was she knew, it hurt and haunted her, and she was hiding it from him. She was even, he suspected, hiding it from Kyali.

For Kyali's sake, or for his?

Or for her own?

What happened to my sister? he sent, angry and increasingly panicked, and got back only that sense of a door shut and bolted between them. It was enough to make him want to scream.

But the edges of the mystery were in his grasp now. He had a feeling they were sharp enough to draw blood, but by the gods, he wasn't about to let go of them.

"I don't think she's *willing,*" Devin said, finishing the thought several minutes after he'd started it. Beside him, Measail made a soft, satisfied sound.

Gods *damn* these Clans and their secrets! And gods damn *him* for not pushing harder for answers. He'd known the night of the uprising that Arlen and Saraid had more information than he did about Kyali, and he'd let that go in favor of more urgent things. And he'd let Kyali push him away; let Taireasa shield him from.... from whatever it was; let himself sink into his grief and his hurt and forget that he had responsibilities, whether or not anyone wanted him prying.

Your sister needs you now.

Did she? Did Taireasa?

Every word spoken between them lately said not, but perhaps it was time to stop listening to what those two said, and start listening to what they *didn't* say instead.

They didn't say how his little sister had found it in herself to slay four barons in their sleep—or why Taireasa, who could barely countenance the killing of rats, had deemed what amounted to four executions without trial—four *assassinations,* hard as it was for him to believe that word applied to his little sister, or to Lardan—justice. They didn't say why they could barely stand the sight of one another lately, but still protected each other fiercely from challenge, harm, and even the curiosity of friends. They didn't say why Kyali hid her heart and smothered her Gift; most of all, they didn't say why Taireasa was allowing that to happen.

"I'm going home," Devin said abruptly, mind on the problem, barely hearing himself, feeling *awake* for the first time since his father had died. "Tomorrow morning."

There were people there who had been in Faestan the night the barons of the West had taken the castle, and it was time to start asking questions.

20

The war council had become a stifled, miserable affair full of awkward silences and distrust. There was no one who didn't feel it, no one who didn't resent it. Taireasa walked back to her apartments in slump-shouldered exhaustion, trying not to be irritated by the endless grating of armor that now followed her everywhere. The six bodyguards Kyali had assigned to her didn't deserve the glare she wanted to aim at them. They were just tired and worried men doing the job they knew how to do, willing to lay down their lives to keep her safe.

That was the problem, right there.

She was so everlastingly sick of people risking themselves for her.

Kyali paced soft-footed behind her, several steps back—presumably so as not to get in the way of the bodyguard, but Taireasa suspected it had more to do with not wanting to be within speaking range. Neither of them was in good temper tonight. She thought she had far more reason to be angry than her Lady Captain did, though—mainly because she was angry *at* her Lady Captain.

The guards left them at the door, and Taireasa shut her eyes and massaged her temples. Exhaustion left her wide open to the thoughts and feelings of everyone else in the castle. Saraid had taught her how to shield herself, but lack of sleep made even simple things impossible, and blocking out the endless cacophony of thoughts was... not simple.

Taireasa sank wordlessly into the chair by the fire, leaving Kyali to stew, or stare out the window, or think about ways to escape the people who loved her, or whatever it was she did with herself. She thought of walls, high and impenetrable: walls that swallowed *wish* and *want* and *will*. Walls that shielded her from the minds around her, that wrapped her in merciful peace.

After several long moments, Taireasa was able to breathe evenly, to know she was alone in her own head. That head was throbbing, but it was no longer ringing with the silent voices of several thousand others.

There was a mug of tea steaming next to her hand.

She looked up, but Kyali was standing by the windows, reading some report or another. And it didn't change anything between them.

She could forgive a great deal. But finding out in the middle of a council of war that the captain of her army had sent bands of soldiers to take contested ground more than a fortnight ago—that was not something she could take quietly. It touched her pride. It woke something in her she'd begun to doubt she owned, truth be told: some silent but fierce queen hiding in the far reaches of herself.

"When were you going to tell me?" Taireasa asked. She could hear her anger in the words and she drew one breath, then another as Kyali turned to face her, as calm as always, because Kyali had never backed down from confrontations even *before* she stopped caring who she hurt.

"When it bore fruit, Your Majesty," she said.

"Ah, of course. And I take it you don't consider the loss of some fifteen soldiers or the battleground the Maurynim foothills have now become to be fruit worth mentioning. I suppose I can understand that, Ky, as it's fruit only our enemies would find safe to eat."

She could see the flicker of gold that rose in Kyali's eyes, and gods help them both, she wasn't sorry to have caused it.

What have we come to? some part of her mourned, but it wasn't a voice Taireasa was willing to listen to at the moment.

"You'd rather we let the West take our supply lines?" Kyali asked, dry as bone. "Or perhaps you think we've enough mouths to feed, Majesty, and holding the paths open for refugees is no longer in our interest?"

Taireasa was on her feet before she knew she was going to stand, fury singing in her veins. She could hear the high hum her mug was making and didn't care at all. She took three quick steps, bringing her within inches of Kyali's clenched fists and set face.

So *that* was what it took to get a reaction out of her.

"Am I queen?" she hissed, and watched Kyali's chin come up and her eyebrows knit together. "Is this not where you think I ought to be?"

"It is *exactly* where you ought to be," Kyali replied, low and fierce.

"Then I'd be much obliged, Lady Captain, if you'd credit me with some measure of intelligence and bloody well *consult me* before you hare off risking men's lives and provoking a war! Do you plan to inform me when you've decided to take back Faestan, or shall I learn it only after the first charge?"

Kyali's eyes flared bright gold. Taireasa wanted so badly to stop everything, shut them both up, and simply enjoy the sight, regardless of how it had been achieved.

"Should I come to you with every decision I make?" Kyali asked. "Every rumor? Is that what you intended when you named me captain—a mascot for your troops? If so, please tell me now, Majesty, before I make any more choices."

"That's not what I mean and you *know* it," Taireasa snarled.

"Maybe you ought to stop assuming what I do and don't *know*. Your Majesty."

"I stopped assuming *anything* about you some time ago, Kyali Corwynall. Everything I thought I knew has turned out to be wrong."

Oh gods.

All her anger vanished. Taireasa spun before the anguished horror she felt could spread across her face—but not before she saw a flash of genuine shock and then bleak acceptance on Kyali's. Dear gods, what were they *doing* to one other?

"I didn't mean that," she whispered.

"Yes, you did," Kyali said, almost as quietly.

"I didn't—I didn't mean it *like* that."

"Yes," Kyali said again, her voice growing cooler, firmer. "You did."

Gods damn it, was Kyali *trying* to make her angry? Taireasa flung her a furious look, met a pair of eyes like candles in a desolate face.

"Ky," she said. "Don't."

"You *should*. Mean that." Kyali seemed to be having trouble speaking. She frowned, coughed once. Her face lost the desolate look—lost *all* expression, turned wooden and serene. "Stop," she finished. "Assuming. Waiting. You should stop now, Taireasa. My Lady Queen."

And while Taireasa was still trying to form a reply, to get her mind around the fact that Kyali was throwing off the long-held pretense that there was nothing between them only to end what little was left, the Lady Captain bowed deeply and walked out of the room.

Outside, the snow fell, swallowing the world in white. Inside, Taireasa curled as close to the fire as she could get without risking her skirts or the stuffed chair, and still it felt like she was encased in ice, slowing everything to a crawl, muffling thought and feeling and sense.

She should probably be grateful for that.

She leaned closer to the lantern by her chair to read Kyali's cramped scrawl. The handwriting was so poor it might almost have been some kind of cipher, but she had long experience with this particular code and she picked out the words one by one, piecing together a list of spies, incursions, defenses, places her Lady Captain wished taken, or yielded and taken back later.

It was the strategy of a brilliant, methodical mind, something meant to wear down a larger enemy over time, to claim supply lines and eventually the whole mountain all the way to the foothills. It was a long game, and Taireasa suspected she wasn't seeing half of it.

The report had appeared half an hour ago, carried by a young lieutenant. At the bottom, squashed into the margin in nearly indecipherable writing, was a postscript.

You were right in what you said, Majesty. I should have consulted.

So.

It didn't take away the ache in her chest. That *Majesty* wasn't a temporary thing, she began to understand: it was Kyali's insistence on separation. On a new order in the world, one where they might as well never have been friends. She had never in her life felt so alone.

Was this what it meant, being a queen? It was a fate harsh beyond belief. But it might be a fair penalty for letting her best friend sacrifice her life for the life of a queen.

Taireasa leaned closer still, slid the paper and all the secrets it held into the hearth, watched flame flare and ash drift down. She had an appointment with Curran in an hour, and she needed to find in herself the will to deal with that. But it felt like half the stone of this keep had landed on her shoulders.

"Ah," said Saraid from behind her, and she started. "I'd about lost the use of my fingers."

Taireasa twisted around, took the cloak Saraid shed, and gave up her chair for the old woman, who was indeed blue-lipped. "Gods," she muttered, finding she did still have enough room in her heart for worry. "Sit, Saraid, you're frozen through."

"I am and I will," the old woman groaned, reaching out to snag a cushion and set it on the floor. "Now *you* sit, young queen. Right here. Pretend you're a hound and lean your head on my knee."

Taireasa stared, then uttered a short, sharp laugh. Why not?
It wasn't like there was anyone to witness, and she didn't really want to leave the meager comfort of the fire's heat. Saraid's
knobby fingers settled, gentle and comfortable, in her braids.

"You're in a state," she remarked after several minutes had
passed.

Taireasa watched a stick collapse into coals. The walls in
her mind held firm, but she could feel her teacher just outside
them, curious and patient.

"I'm all right," she said finally.

The fingers in her hair shifted. "Does it ever work?"
Saraid asked.

"Does what work?"

"Telling yourself that. Being ancient and unable, at this
late point in my life, to remember precisely what it felt like to
present the world with the thing I *wished* to be true instead of
the thing that *is* true, I confess I have no idea. Do you *feel* all
right, Taireasa Marsadron, just because you say so?"

"No," Taireasa replied. The word leapt out of her throat all
wobbly. She bit her lip and dug her nails into the palms of her
hands.

"I could never teach my other student this, either. I think it
must be youth, curable only by time. Either that, or I am a far
poorer tutor than I hoped to be."

"Your *other*—?" Oh.

Kyali.

"She always insisted she was all right, too," Saraid murmured. "She'd have remade the whole world before she'd let go
of that. She *has*, in fact. Will you let her do it forever, Taireasa?"

Clumsy with shock, Taireasa met a pair of forthright eyes

filled with sorrow.

"You're not the only one who stayed with her," Saraid said softly, and Taireasa flung herself to her feet, understanding in an instant. Her heart was trying to fly out of her chest. She couldn't seem to fill her lungs and she staggered away, fighting the air, the carpet, the unendurable twist of shame and guilt and grief clawing at the center of her. Her feet tangled and she dropped to her knees. The pain made her eyes fill. She felt around for a chair to help her stand, tears like liquid coals sliding down her face.

Two thin but surprisingly strong arms hooked under her own and she was pulled first up and then forward, into an embrace like being wrapped in living branches.

"You can let go now, Taireasa," Saraid said.

All the walls came down at once. She was remembering pain, pain like nothing she'd ever imagined, pain and fury and determination, a love like scalding sunlight and an icy iron resolve: Kyali's terrible gift to her.

"I can't—I couldn't—"

"It's not all right, child. *It's not.* You're not and neither is she, and you're both very young, and you *need* one another. It wasn't your fault. It wasn't your choice. Stop *carrying* it, Taireasa. Let it go."

Taireasa gave up, put her forehead on a bony shoulder and sobbed, a shuddering release that wrung first the breath and then all the strength from her. Saraid bore her back down to the cold stones and the crumpled carpets, held her like her own mother hadn't since she was very, very young. She had no idea how long they remained that way, but eventually she realized she wasn't the only one weeping, and that was enough to let her get a grip on herself.

"What do I do?" Taireasa rasped, hating the trembling hoarseness of those words, the way they sounded anything but queenly. "I don't know what to do."

Saraid stroked her head. "Stop trying to make the world what it was," she said simply.

That made no sense. Taireasa was about to say so, but suddenly it did—suddenly it made *perfect* sense, falling together neatly and inexorably. She could see the line that drew her to Kyali, that held them together. That held her to Devin, to Kinsey, Annan, Maldyn, Curran. Saraid. It was all there, a set of currents flowing and shifting around one another, shaping the world that was hers.

Not the world she wished, but the one she had to work with.

"Oh," Taireasa whispered, stunned. "*Oh, oh gods.*"

"*Finally,*" her teacher murmured and let her go, standing with a faint grunt. She swept up her cloak while Taireasa was still blinking and shrugged it onto her shoulders.

"Saraid, wait! You can't go *now!*"

"Of course I can," she said, laughing. "I have a bed, and it's calling my name. And I've set you straight, haven't I? Well then. What more can an old lady be expected to do?"

"But—but I have—I need—"

"You need to *think*. And to sleep, my dear, perhaps that most of all."

"I have her nightmares," Taireasa said miserably, because there wasn't really anything left to hide now, was there?

Saraid sighed. "You don't have to, though. Surely you know that? Stop punishing yourself, Taireasa."

It brought her up short. She stood mute and stunned while

Saraid let herself out. Then she sat by the fire, staring at nothing, thinking as hard as she had ever done in her life.

You're both so young, and you need one another.

None of that was wrong, none of that was even *difficult*, so why had she needed Saraid to tell it to her before she could see it?

Kyali wasn't thinking any more clearly than she was. Kyali had not been, all along. She was stubborn, and she was insisting that she was all right: it was what Ky had *always* done when she was wounded. She refused to acknowledge friendship because she would have no choice but to acknowledge—and admit—the terrible things she had suffered in the name of that friendship. She only tried to make her way forward in whatever desperate mending of herself she could manage alone. And Taireasa had let her do it, wrapped up in guilt and just as confused.

It was obvious, and so desperately, sadly, courageously wrongheaded of both of them that it brought tears back to her eyes. Taireasa sniffed, refusing to cry again, and reached for a quill and paper to write a reply to a report.

Thank you for the report. As to the rest, you have no less of my love, nor ever shall.

That was enough, for now.

What Kyali did with it was up to Kyali.

Taireasa rolled the paper and sealed it, then went to find a page, who would give it to a lieutenant, who would deliver it to the Lady Captain.

She'd aimed for the drill hall and from there the stables, where Ainhearag was probably tormenting the horse boys: she was not a patient creature, and often said so with her teeth.

A ride in the freezing wind was exactly what Kyali needed.

But the lower hall appeared to be full of the latest new arrivals, echoing with weeping and shouted orders and what she could swear was the outraged screeching of chickens. She'd like to know who had managed to bring a flock up the mountain. Peasants were stubborn, resourceful people.

Taireasa's words still rang in her ears.

"Damn," Kyali hissed, rubbing her chest, which felt like it was full of air and glass, and ducked behind a tapestry into the hidden passageways before anyone could see her and want something from her.

They'd discovered Faestan's secrets much like this, pushing through a hidden door they had found into a maze of dusty tunnels. Taireasa had hooted like a mad little owl, fingers wrapping around her wrist, and dragged them unhesitatingly into the darkness. Taireasa had always been blazing trails into the unknown, pulling one awkward, reticent general's daughter along for the ride—

"Stop," Kyali said, and shoved the heels of her hands into her forehead.

Everything I thought I knew has turned out to be wrong—

"*Stop*," Kyali growled. Ice. Snow. A bloody blizzard of it, swallowing everything she'd known and done before...

Before.

Her feet weren't carrying her to the stables. She frowned, looking around—she should have brought a light—and pushed open the nearest doorway just to see where she'd ended up. It cracked, and she listened for voices or footsteps, but it was quiet and bitter cold: one of the wings on the northern wall, where nobody wanted to live yet.

Hearing nothing, she let herself out, then hung her head when she recognized the tapestry and realized she'd brought herself to the Cassdall section.

Why in hell had she come *here*?

Scowling darkly, Kyali turned to find somewhere else to be... but of course Annan chose that moment to appear around a corner just as she was heading back in. "Captain," he said, his face doing that thing she couldn't interpret and didn't want to, by the gods, no, because she absolutely wasn't thinking of... of... that. "Something you wanted to discuss?"

"No," she said with total certainty, and was most of the way back into the passage before she remembered there actually *was* something she needed to discuss with him, damn it. She halted, half in and half out, fighting with herself. "Yes," she finally sighed. She swung back out, trying to ignore the tiny, amused look that flickered across Annan's face and vanished into the non-expression she was much more comfortable with.

"The guardroom's empty," he said, and went that way before she could form an objection. But that was stupid. It wasn't as though just walking back in there would get her drunk and make her—make them—

Stop it right now, she snarled into her own head, beginning to wish she'd never crossed Taireasa's path today, or ever.

The Cassdall guardroom was empty, as Annan had promised, and there was, thankfully, no evidence of bottles of any sort on the shelves. There was a stuffed couch by the fire with a blanket, a bucket of water, a kettle on a hook. If he hadn't told her he had rooms in Kinsey's apartments, she'd have guessed he slept here. Then again, she had spent more than one night at her desk in the lower hall.

Annan waved a hand at the table, where several maps were spread out, marked with ink in his precise hand. A pot of ink and several quills sat at one corner. The quills looked slightly chewed at the feathery ends.

"You should have an office," she said, apropos of nothing, and Annan shrugged.

"This works well enough. It's quiet, it locks. I've certainly had worse."

"Mmm." Kyali folded her arms and squinted at the paths marked on paper. "Is that—?"

"Waylen's route, yes. He followed the river. I'll speak to him when he arrives, which ought to be tomorrow if the Lord Corwynall did indeed head out this morning. I want to know what the lay of the land is there." Annan leaned forward over the map. Kyali stared stupidly at the top of his dark-haired head, then caught herself and bent over the map too, trying to ignore that this brought them far closer than she wanted to be.

"I can give you something with far more detail," Kyali said, and tipped her head when he shot her an irritated look. "You could have asked," she added, because sniping at him was the only distraction there was, and the air-and-glass sensation in her chest was beginning to feel too much like an ache.

Annan's eyes were nearly black up this close. He didn't scowl at her, only stared, holding her gaze steadily and perhaps a little too long before raising that eyebrow again. "I suppose I could have," he said, which wasn't exactly the pithy retort she'd been braced for. "What was it you needed to speak to me about, Captain?"

Right.

"I wanted to know if you'd had any word of Tuan's plans for Maurynim."

Annan eyed her thoughtfully. "I'd have told you. No. Have you heard something new?"

"No," Kyali grumbled, and slid one of the maps closer to her just to have something to do with her hands. "I have not."

It had been a stupid question, hardly even a question at all. But Annan didn't point that out. Instead he braced his hands on the table's edge and gave her a look that seemed to see too much, then frowned.

"You're thinking of going to their defense."

He didn't sound incredulous, or scornful, or even particularly startled by the notion, so Kyali looked up from the maps and nodded. "It would need to be completely unexpected," he murmured, chewing his lip, plans beginning to flicker in his eyes. "They'll send far more troops if they know we're coming. Hard to accomplish such a thing in secret, on a mountain in winter."

"Yes," Kyali said, trying not to be annoyed by this statement of the obvious. She'd already thought of all of this. She wanted *ideas*. None of her officers had any to offer.

"You'll think of something," Annan said mildly. She huffed in irritation, fighting air and glass and memory, and the complicated logistics of a war where they were forever outnumbered.

"I should go," she said, and pushed herself upright.

"You should," Annan agreed soberly, which made both no sense and entirely too much sense.

They'd agreed to forget the—that, but being in a room with him made her palms itch, and Taireasa's damned words were circling in her head like lost birds, and she just wanted to hit something until her knuckles bled. Annan got to the door first and pulled it open for her, a gracious, courtly gesture that had just enough irony in it to sting.

Kyali hesitated, stuck between wanting to throw that gesture back in his face and wanting to get out of the room and away from him—and then, gods *damn* it, out of nowhere they were pressed up against the threshold, breathing into one another's mouths. She was going to shove him off. This couldn't possibly have been her idea.

—Why *else* had she come here?

I stopped assuming anything about you some time ago, Kyali Corwynall—

She'd bitten into his lip. He made a sound that said he didn't mind that nearly as much as she would have in his place and ducked, sliding his face under her jaw, scraping with the edge of teeth and the faint stubble on his skin—oh *gods.* Her spine arched; she went right up on her toes, air leaping out of her throat, telling him more than he needed to know about how that felt. He wasn't wearing armor, and his chest rose and fell swiftly under her palms, which didn't itch anymore sliding over the moving warmth of him under cloth. He smelled of leather, mint, snow, sweat. He licked a line down her neck and her knees went wobbly.

Then his fingers found the laces at her hips and she was reaching for her daggers, shoving him away, her lungs locked on a scream. She hit the wall so hard she knocked most of the breath out of herself, and Annan staggered back, blinking.

She couldn't get enough air. She couldn't see him. She could only see Cyrnic's face—Brisham's—Viam's—Walderan's—

"Captain," Annan said. His voice was shaking just slightly. It brought her back to herself, to the absolute, stupid, humiliating discomfort of this moment. Kyali dropped the daggers before her hands could do anything else she wasn't planning on. They clanged to the floor and she pressed her fingers into her temples.

—*Everything I thought I knew has turned out to be wrong*—

She couldn't breathe for another reason now, and she dropped her hands, made herself meet his eyes. She wasn't expecting him to have come closer. She wasn't expecting the hand that curled warm and solid over the side of her face, and she certainly wasn't expecting the air-and-glass ache in her chest to expand into something hurtful and strangely, horrifyingly sweet.

"I'm sorry," Kyali growled, and kissed him again before he could say something that would make it worse. She didn't want to talk. She didn't want to think. She couldn't stand to feel. She just had to stop all of it, *now*, stop being afraid, and this was the only way forward.

Annan froze for a long moment and then took her mouth with his—gentler, more carefully this time, probably because he knew she still had a sword and another dagger in her boot, and she was clearly a little mad.

She undid the laces herself this time. She was shaking so badly she almost couldn't, and his fingers had a faint tremor in them too, so it was several minutes before they stood before one another with far less by way of defense than either of them was used to. She couldn't look him in the face. She couldn't look anywhere else. She only wanted it over with. But the blood was racing in her veins, her nerves were afire, and her heart was thumping so loudly he could probably hear it.

Annan did that thing with his teeth again and she wobbled into him, appalled and fascinated, her fingernails scraping down his sides. He was warm. He twitched and shuddered, and then he was bolting the door shut and turning them both around. Her knees hit the edge of the couch and she toppled, surprised, very glad the sword was on the other side of the room because she was so close to hurting them both right now, wracked with shivering, fighting the darkness in herself. Panic twisted sickly through her.

He leaned over her, eyes serious and unreadable, pressing in the last place she wanted him to be. But she had invited this, had wished it, it meant she wouldn't have to think for a little while, she was so tired of being afraid, and besides she was hardly going to back down now—

Oh.

Kyali went still, her eyes going wide.

Memory rose, knotted every muscle, and was chased away by the—by what Annan was—dear *gods.*

He began to move, and every thought in her head vanished, along with her breath and what little control she still had over her expression. Kyali arched up with him, needing to move, needing to choose, and together they found a rhythm like a horse's sway, or a tide scraping the shore. Annan made a soft sound and buried his face in her neck. It went on, and on, stripping away the last of her self-restraint, smoothing out the edges of her anger and her fear, washing it all away in a flood of mindless sensation. She dug her fingers into his shoulders, forgetting everything, all of it, hating herself, hating how grateful she was for the sudden, perfect silence in her own head.

It got very much better then, or perhaps it was very much

worse. She didn't know anymore. She couldn't swallow the sound that tore out of her as the world flashed white. Annan's breath hitched once, then again, and he shuddered, holding her without holding her, his eyes shut tight.

They lay still then, tangled together on a couch far too small to hold them both. The fire popped and crackled. Kyali tilted her face away, still trying to get her expression back under control, still not having any luck with that.

It had been such a stupid thing to do. She'd never thought—

Gods help her, it hadn't occurred to her she might like it. It had never occurred to her she *could*.

A callused finger traced her collarbone. She scowled. Another joined it, moving lower, drawing slow, simmering circles, making nerves still recovering shudder and sing. She glared over at Annan, found him watching her with that narrow-eyed look of challenge that had started this whole stupid mess in the first place.

A third finger, moving yet lower. It was wildly distracting. She bit the inside of her cheek, started using her own hands, taking a certain satisfaction in the way his own breath halted and his eyes lidded.

"I was thinking we could sail men down the river on rafts," Kyali said, and almost grinned at the offended look that crossed Annan's face. "To Maurynim," she clarified. Then she shut up, because the noise she'd make if she kept talking wasn't going to have any dignity in it at all.

"Mmph," her opposite number said, breathless but not beaten. She knew this game, though the pieces were unfamiliar. She wasn't playing fair, but neither was he. And she was certain he had more experience to draw on than—no. No. She wasn't thinking of that.

She didn't need to think of anything at all right now.

Annan was going to win, she knew that much when he moved his hands lower still, did something that pulled a startled moan out of her, and kept right on doing it while her heels thudded against the couch arm and her fingers got too clumsy to be useful.

Oh.

They could talk about Maurynim later.

21

The air was so cold it hurt his throat; he wrapped a fold of his heavy wool cloak over his face, leaning on ice-slicked stone, and looked out over a landscape glittering with snow under the cold, bright sun.

Cassdall's winters had been *nothing* like this.

He guessed, from the groaning complaints of soldiers coming back from patrols, that Lardana winters were also mild. The heart of the lowlands wasn't visible from here, but the land stretching past the distant roll of the foothills was brown rather than white.

Kinsey frowned into the wind, trying to hold several pieces of a story in his head, trying to make them fit with the story he found himself in now. It was like building puzzles, a pastime one of his nurses had taught him when he was very young. It was a game most of his cousins had laughed at him for, but the exercise had become a way of thinking that let him set aside all other attachments and work at a problem until he had a full picture before him, complete, yielding up its secrets.

Who would have guessed that silly hobby would serve him so well so far from home?

The Book—gods, it had already acquired capitals in his mind—was the most confusing thing he'd ever read, which was something of a sweeping statement coming from a scholar-prince. He'd been through it twice. It wasn't long, just bewildering, full of natural philosophy melded with magical theory, predictions of disaster and salvation—some of which had, alarmingly, already come to pass—and all of it woven through a tale of invasion, war, a land occupied, a people exiled to this very mountain and doomed to watch their kingdom overrun by their conquerors.

The parallels gave him chills that had nothing to do with the frigid wind.

Behind him, his bodyguards, newly assigned since Devin had passed on his grim news, shifted and coughed. They didn't want to be out here and Kinsey felt bad for that, but he couldn't *think* inside walls today. The fortress was filling with refugees; all the empty rooms were being swept out in a commotion of talking and weeping and orders. He needed quiet and today, that could only be found outside.

Devin ought to be on his way back, speaking of Devin: Taireasa had said he was riding up the ridge with Waylen, who was in poor health after his ordeal and needed rest.

"But if they knew what was coming, why didn't they act to *prevent* it?" Kinsey muttered, running a hand through his hair, which was tangled from sleep. He'd been coming back to this question over and over.

"Certain events have a weight in the world, Cassdall prince. They cannot be moved without terrible consequences. Surely you know that; you've witnessed a few of these already."

The old lady: Taireasa's teacher, the Lady Captain's former teacher. She'd slipped past his bodyguards like a ghost. Now poor Ludor and Jerin were hovering, daggers in hand, wide-eyed as though she really *was* one.

Gods, she *looked* like a ghost, with her silver hair and pale eyes and creased, graying skin.

"I've been trying to meet with you for some time," Kinsey said coolly.

"I know. Here I am." She came forward, a heavy fur cloak wrapped about her shoulders, and rested her elbows casually against the battlements. The wind didn't seem to bother her. Kinsey waved his bodyguards back, trying not to scowl. A fortnight past, he'd have given a great deal to speak with this woman, but right now, with all the pieces tumbling around in his thoughts, he wasn't sure what to say, what to ask.

To be honest, he wasn't sure he wanted to know.

"Which is precisely the state I've been waiting for, young prince," Saraid said, making him go even colder, if that were possible. Dear gods, he'd forgotten she could—

Read every thought in his head.

That was *horrifying.*

"It's less interesting than you think," she said placidly. "Also less invasive, at least on my end. I'm afraid that much of the time, I have little choice."

Kinsey stared at her. "You... can't help but hear me?"

"Can you shut out every voice in a crowded room? Can you shut out even one?"

He glared down at his hands, wrapped in wool and pressed onto dark stone. "No, lady," he replied, thinking of Taireasa and her headaches. Gods, if he found magic frightening from where he stood, how much worse must it be for those who had such a Gift?

"It gets easier," Saraid said, smiling. "The more organized the mind, the more force behind the sending. You've a very organized mind, young Kinsey of Cassdall. They need you here."

"Do they?"

It wasn't an idle question.

Had he chosen the mountain path because it was the quickest and safest route, or because he was drawn here? Had his uncle objected so strongly to his presence because his advisors thought a shy scholar was a threat to a new ruler's reign, or because this particular scholar had to leave Cassdall? Could any amateur historian have filled this requirement—or, like Devin, Taireasa, and Kyali, did *he* have to be here?

And if so, how much of his life had bent itself around that necessity?

He was shaking. He didn't think it was from the cold. He felt like he stood on the battlements instead of leaning on them—like there was only the wind between him and a very long drop.

"*Geas*," Saraid said, a word he'd seen more than once in the Book.

"Fate."

"*Necessity*, young prince: fate is far too mild a word for it. Fate gets confused with romance and power and other things men concern themselves with. *Necessity*. A thing that must be in order for the world to continue. A linchpin for all time. Your three friends, they must be here. They must be together. Many hundreds of years ago, events were set in motion that made that necessary, and all the world is remaking itself around us now to achieve it. I believe you've read enough to understand me."

Oh gods, he'd been right, he *didn't* want to hear this.

Kinsey huddled in his cloak, teeth chattering, more afraid than he'd been in... in more years than he could remember right now. He'd faced assassins with less distress. And here, there wasn't even anything to point to, except one iron-willed but otherwise benevolent old woman watching him with a disturbing blend of amusement and sympathy in her eyes.

"I'm a long way from understanding," Kinsey admitted.

"You're closer than you were, Cassdall prince. Closer by far."

"So *now* you come to speak to me. You could have saved me several months of dithering, lady Saraid, if you'd just *handed* me the Book when we got here."

"I think you know why I couldn't, Kinsey prince."

He turned to face her. From fear he'd moved to anger, still shaking, not wanting her to see that—though it was probably a singularly moot point when you were dealing with a woman who read thoughts. He had little he could complain of in his exile, but he had seen how Devin and Taireasa suffered, and he ached for them.

"Yes," he said, hearing the edge in his own voice. "No interfering with—with geas, if that's what you want to call it. We had to find our way to one another, and to here. We had to win the battle with the Sevassis army, we had to make peace between ourselves. And I had to find the Book on my own. That's a fairly broad definition of *alone*, though, Lady Saraid: Corin hid it in plain sight. And your people have provided shelter, food, protection, teaching in the use of magic, Devin's harp, the Lady Captain's armor, and then these..." He waved a hand. "These odd little nudges in the right direction. Excuse me if I'm a bit slow in understanding, but how are these things *not* interference? And how, if they are, do you justify not offering all the help you can give?"

Her eyes had gotten darker: he could see the iron under the gentleness now, and he was glad of it. Kinsey sucked in a frozen chestful of air, trying to slow his pulse, to unclench his fists.

"My, you do have a sharp tongue on you," Saraid finally said, which was so infuriatingly patronizing Kinsey made a noise of pure scorn and spun, unable to look her in the face. He leaned on the dark stone, trying to remember the last time he'd been this angry about something.

Her hand pressed on his shoulder, not at all welcome. "You'll need that edge, prince of Cassdall," she said easily.

"I'm hardly a prince of anything. Why do you keep calling me that?"

"It's what you are. Or did you really think the only role you had to play here was as librarian to a crowd of exiles?"

Gods.

"It is, granted, the role that's important right now," she allowed in her dry, meditative way and Kinsey glared at her, feeling a flush crawl up out of his collar in spite of the freezing wind.

"How do you *know* that?!" he cried. Ludor and Jerin looked over from the door, alarmed. Kinsey flung a hand out before they could come over and settle what must look like a fight from there, never mind that one of the participants had to be at least seventy years old. *"That*, Lady Saraid, is nowhere in the Book I just read. *Nowhere."*

Then he shut up, feeling the blood leave his hands, his face, because dear gods, it *was*.

"A hart as swift in thought as fleet of foot," Saraid quoted softly; Kinsey could see the rest of the passage in his mind. A stag courant with two crossed rolls of parchment was the arms of his father's house. But he'd read it as *heart*, the spelling being less clear that far back, and Taireasa's description of her connection with Devin being very much a thing of hearts.

"But—but that makes no *sense*," Kinsey murmured, leaning most of his weight against the wall. "How would I—I'm not—"

"Evidently you are."

"But it didn't say what I have to do!"

"That's the trouble with prophecies: they're so dreadfully vague. It didn't mention what *I* have to do either, young prince. Only what Her Majesty and the Corwynall siblings *must* do. Our duty is to see to it they have the chance to figure out for themselves how to achieve it." Saraid twisted, coming to lean next to him, staring up at the great blocks of weathered stone that made up the western wall. "I've had many more years than you to study this, Kinsey prince, and I'm afraid that's the most solid of my conclusions. Eairon saw much, being halfling and far more Gifted than those of us with blood diluted by the centuries. But the Sight isn't such a clear tool: one gets things in snatches, scattered images, and has to piece them together as well as one can."

Kinsey dared a sidelong glance at her, found her smiling wryly, like she knew what he was about to ask, and he supposed she probably did. "You... have the Sight, Lady Saraid?"

"My sister did," she said simply. "She's been dead for many years now."

"I'm sorry," Kinsey murmured.

"Me too."

There was an audible ache in the words and he scowled, because he didn't want to feel sympathy for this unapologetically blunt, maddening old woman who had turned his whole life upside-down in fifteen minutes of conversation. She pulled her cloak closer around her neck and sighed, looking like she was preparing to leave. Kinsey blurted out the rest of his questions in a desperate rush, not knowing if he'd ever get another chance.

"Why did your Clans hold onto your magic? Why didn't the Lardana? Or did they ever have any? Did Eairon charge your people to be—some kind of guardians? What else are you waiting for?"

Saraid stood blinking in the onslaught, her pale eyebrows rising slowly into her hairline. She set a hand on his sleeve, tipped her head back, and let out a great shout of laughter.

"Dear gods, boy, *swift in thought* indeed. Slow down."

"Lady—"

"Kinsey, you're going to have to get used to the notion that we don't know much more than you do. We had the Book to read over many long centuries, and we're more Gifted, as a people, than either the Lardana or the Cassdalls could hope to be. But that's where it ends. We're guessing nearly as much as you are now: we just had a head start. Surely you know better by now than to believe we know all."

"But—"

Saraid sighed. She reached out, making him flinch back

slightly—years of bracing for assassins made it hard to let any-one, even an old woman, get this close. But Kinsey held him-self still, one hand lifted to stay his bodyguards, who definite-ly wouldn't like this, and let her set her palms gently over the sides of his face.

He couldn't remember the last time someone had done that. He coughed away an unaccustomed tightness in his throat and stared into her pale, knowing eyes.

"We are the last," she said, sounding so tired, suddenly, that he gave in to impulse, brought his hands up to cover hers, and kissed her cheek.

"Good lad," Saraid said. She patted his cheek once and left him standing in the wind, shivering, trying to parse that last statement. He didn't get anywhere and he blew on his fingers, trying to make his mind work.

Saraid's words circled in his head, trying to fit them-selves somewhere in the piecemeal picture he was building for Taireasa, for Devin, for himself. Kinsey shut his eyes, ignoring the wind, the piercing sunlight, the faint grumbling from his frozen bodyguards. He was seeing fragile parchment pages, seeing the words on them, re-creating the Book out of mem-ory. It was a good thing he'd read it twice. Even so, the effort brought beads of sweat to his forehead, which froze immedi-ately. Something... something Saraid had said echoed...

It was right on the first page.

I am the last of us, and I watch, from this last of our fortresses.

We are the last...

And: *Eairon being halfling and far more Gifted than those of us with blood diluted...*

"Faery tales," Kinsey breathed. "Halfling Síog...oh dear

gods, I'm an idiot."

He pressed his hands to his aching head, concentrating fiercely, trying to remember a single passage in *Tenets* he had passed over more than once. It was far harder: his tired mind wanted to forget *Tenets* and its endless list of rules, begats, and lineages. But he had thought this particular phrase important somehow, though he'd had no notion why at the time, so he ought to be able to...

And certain of Men made their Way to the great Fortress of the last of the mighty Síog to learn of them; and some Men returned with great Skills.

"Yes."

Shaken, Kinsey collapsed against the wall. The Clans weren't men who had served the fae folk, nor men who had learned from them, or they weren't *just* that. They were also the *remnants* of the Síog. And Taireasa, Devin, Kyali—their Houses had bloodlines that mingled, long ago, with the old occupants of this fortress. All those dreadfully boring *begats* led *here*.

"But what does it *mean*?" he murmured.

Nothing simple, he thought, and frowned down at the distant treeline, where four figures on horseback were struggling through the deep snow, so muffled by their cloaks they looked like strange bears.

It was Devin, he realized, and felt a weight he hadn't even known was there lift from his heart. He'd missed his strange, impulsive, musical friend. He wanted to know how Devin was, if the Eanin's teaching had helped, if he was perhaps willing to try playing the harp indoors. Taireasa was someone he thought he might be able to call a friend (*though you might want to call her much more,* his treacherous mind whispered) and Curran and his wife were more than pleasant company, but by and large he was alone in this society, an item of curiosity and gossip, a foreigner.

It wasn't a new experience. But having learned Devin's loud, intrusive, and entirely whimsical notion of friendship, Kinsey had, for the first time in a lifetime of hovering unaffected at the edges of everything, discovered loneliness in its absence. He raised a hand, knowing he was barely visible from here, but it felt good to do it.

Then he saw the movement on either side of that small party, the gleam of armor in between bare branches, and he began to shout, hands curling into fists against the cold stone.

"Devin! *Devin*, look out—ah, *gods*—"

"M'lord!"

Armed men burst out of the trees. The four cloaked figures turned, far too late, then turned again as the party to the other side of them broke cover. Kinsey spun, seeing Ludor's shocked face, Jerin's glance over the wall, the hard look of dismay that followed.

"Alert the guard. And the Lady Captain!" he snapped, and flung himself through the door into the hall already running.

They had no paper large enough to copy whole maps. Kyali had two scribes and the aide she had finally admitted she needed filling the available sheets with pieces of maps instead, because it was damned impossible to plot the movement of troops without writing something down.

Ink stained her fingers black. She avoided wiping them on

her armor and scowled as Slade set a cup of tea on her desk, moving carefully, as though he was facing an angry bear.

"Thank you," Kyali said, tired of being offered tea by a boy who acted as though she was going to draw her sword on the spot. But that was, she supposed, her own fault.

Carrying her sword bare everywhere would be comforting, actually.

She preferred to deal with enemies she could *see*. Trying to flush out a skulking traitor was far harder—someone spying for a self-proclaimed king who wanted them all dead—someone who could be standing next to Taireasa *right now*—

The quill snapped in her hand.

Now there was even more ink on her fingers. She breathed *ice*, shut her eyes, and sipped at the tea, ignoring the stain she smeared all over the cup. It was no wonder Slade looked like he was ready to bolt out of the room at any moment. He kept hovering by the door.

"The Cassdall captain to see you, Capt—er, Lady Captain," the boy announced. Kyali nodded, turning to the map cabinet, more to hide the expression on her face than because she wished to smudge anything in there with ink. Slade let Annan in and ducked out, and Kyali snatched up a cloth and scrubbed furiously at her hands, glowering at ink stains and not-quite-steady fingers.

Ice.

Nerves. Damn.

She was so short on sleep it took constant effort to keep her face still, to stop her Gift from flaring out and setting fire to half the things she touched. To keep her mind clear enough for decisions. Annan's presence wouldn't help with any of that.

"Captain," she said, looking at him only from the corner of her eye.

"Captain," Annan replied, coming to sit, uninvited, on a stool at the map table. He had been outdoors: there was frost melting on his spaulders, snow clinging to his boots, glistening in his hair. His gaze was mild and unreadable when she finally gave up on the ink stains and made herself meet it, and Kyali felt a few muscles in her shoulders unknot.

"Do you have any regulars who have served in the Western provinces in their careers?" he asked.

She blinked, then frowned. "One hundred and twenty-eight," she said, not bothering to soften the edge of sarcasm in her voice. "At last count." Surely he didn't think she'd have missed something so obvious.

That eyebrow went up. She wished she knew what it meant.

She didn't care. She folded her arms, remembered the ink too late, and sank her teeth into her tongue in annoyance. Her armor was in need of cleaning anyway.

"Can you spare a few?"

"Were you planning to question their loyalties or ask them for a description of the latest dance steps over there?"

Annan cast her a sidelong look. One foot began tapping a slow, irritated rhythm against the floor. "The latter."

Her weary, battered mind gave her only the image of Annan dancing a gavotte in Tharst's great hall and nothing came out of her mouth, which had apparently opened on its own. Then his meaning came clear and Kyali sat across from him, forgetting ink stains and not enough paper, forgetting that this was the first time they'd been in a room together since she'd stumbled to her bed already regretting—

Not thinking. *Definitely* not thinking. There was nothing safe left in her head.

"You want to send your spies West," she said, stuck between dismay and admiration, because the idea was brilliant— and more than a little mad.

Annan shrugged. Something flickered in his gaze and was gone, which was just as well because she didn't care what it was, nor did she care that his mouth had turned up at one corner in a satisfied not-quite smile. "Only a handful," he said. "Three at most. We ought to know what's going on there, don't you think?"

"Of *course* I think. I've thought it for months. But the Eanin have a poorer view than they used to, the borders are shut, and the Sevassis foothills are guarded."

"It wouldn't be the first time someone's crossed the *Allaida* border."

Kyali leaned forward, considering. "You mean them to take the river down?"

"Perhaps."

He left an uninformative silence after that and she glared at him. Annan met it with his usual unflappable stare. Kyali let the silence spread, holding his eyes, not willing to give ground here—or anywhere else, for that matter. Finally Annan let out a small huff, twitching one hand briefly palm-up in a tiny surrender. "The Brysan Map suggests there's a river trail through the Sevassis foothills, Captain. I've a man who knows woodcraft, and two others raised on the Allaida border with Cassdall. They can pass fair enough, if folk on your borders and folk on ours are similar, which they seem to be. A handful of days learning Western speech and customs might be enough."

"Why?"

That got out before she could shut her teeth over it, and Annan finally looked her in the eye without the mask. What was under it was sharp as a new blade, and surprisingly fierce.

"Because I don't *know*," he said, voice full of the cool, dry certainty that seemed to be him at his most irritated. "They took your capital in a single night, Captain: they prepared so well it was nearly invisible. How did they move so many troops across your borders? How did they have so many to spare? And who rules those provinces now, if all their barons came East with their sons and then—"

Annan hesitated, his gaze dropping to her hands. Kyali realized she'd dug her fingers so far into her forearms that the leather tunic under her vambraces was straining and looked away.

"You killed them," he said, in an entirely different tone. Not quite a question. And it wouldn't be; that much, Kyali knew, was common knowledge. It made her remember blood soaking into a bedspread, a dead man's face frozen in fear.

Her brother's horrified look when she'd thrown a tiny piece of truth in his face like a slap.

It wasn't possible to meet Annan's eyes now. She could barely stand to be in the room with him. The walls were too close. She stood and crossed to the fireplace, knowing the gesture revealed far too much, but she couldn't help that. She had no idea what was on her face, but it certainly wasn't anything she wanted him seeing.

"I did," she acknowledged, fighting to keep her tone level, thinking of ice and snow, then of blood and dark. She could feel her eyes flaring. She willed herself still, refusing to shiver.

"Good," Annan said, surprising her into a glance over her shoulder.

He had stretched his long legs out, one heavy boot resting on the other, dripping snowmelt on her floor. He wore his armor like a second skin, easy in it. She wasn't thinking. She didn't-think her way back across the room, where she stood over him, studying his hair, his steady hands, the rise and fall of his chest, which got subtly faster as she watched. Her pulse picked up. The door was shut; it could be locked. And there was no better way not to think.

Oh, she was so hopelessly stupid.

And what was *he*? Just as stupid? Did he have something to forget, too?

Did it even matter?

He looked up at her.

"I'll send some of the soldiers who served in the West to your office tomorrow," she said. "Captain."

"Thank you," Annan said, and stood, slow and careful. It wasn't the same sort of careful that Slade was. That most were, around her. Not fear, not worry. Something very different. She had no idea what to do with it. She scowled—scowled harder when that corner of his mouth curled again. Kyali put a hand out and met the still-frozen metal of his armor with her bare palm, pursed her lips in satisfaction when Annan blinked.

His hand was cold, too, she discovered a second later, when it landed on the side of her neck. She jumped and he gave another ghost of a laugh, and all the thoughts flew out of her head into blessed silence, and there was no couch in her office but the floor would probably do just as well if they were quiet.

Then an unbelievably loud thump came at the door. They

jumped apart in a desperate rattle of armor as one of the Cassdall guards flung it open, Slade hovering nervously behind him.

"Enemy," the man gasped, winded and hanging on the doorjamb. It was a bad word to stop for breath on. "Outside, Captain—Captain. The Lord Corwynall's party is—"

She didn't stay to listen to the rest. She shoved the man and then Slade aside and sprinted for the guard hall, Annan right on her heels.

The cold in the air was so deep it drove a spike of icy pain into his chest, so Devin had the hood of his cloak wrapped around his mouth like a lady's scarf. He was well beyond caring what he looked like. He never wanted to spend another winter on this mountain. He had no idea how the Fraonir weathered it in tents, how Kyali had managed in the two years she'd spent among them.

"Not much farther!" Aileana shouted from up ahead.

She sounded far too cheerful.

"It's still *too damned far*," Devin muttered into his fur-lined cloak.

"We're nearly there," Waylen said, being close enough to have heard that last statement. The Cassdall spy was huddled in his own cloak, looking grimly determined. The healing scars on his coppery face were washed pale by the cold. "I can see the wall, which means they can see us. Someone should be out to meet us soon."

"I hope so. No, by the gods, I know so, hold on—"

Devin reached for Taireasa, found her sitting on a throne

that looked much more comfortable than it actually was, listening to cases. She was sore from the chair. ***Put some cushions on it,*** he suggested, surprising and then embarrassing her. She shut him away in indignant outrage and he snickered, feeling like a little boy pulling braids.

"She'll send someone," he said, since Waylen was watching him sidelong.

"Useful, that," the spy grunted. "One wonders why we even need couriers with you two."

"I'm fairly sure I'd be noticed in the lowlands. Unless you're proposing to turn me into a spy, in which case I'm fairly sure you've lost your mind."

Waylen snorted. "No, my lord, I don't think you'd have much success living a subtle life. But even in the land as it is under Tuan's boot, there are still minstrels in the taverns."

Good *gods*, that was actually...

Perfect.

"You don't have to call me that," Devin said, instead of *when can I go?* He set the thought aside to mull over later, when they had found this miserable traitor and Taireasa was safe. He wasn't going anywhere until then.

And until he'd had it out with Kyali, however impossible that looked from here.

"What, 'my lord'? I don't mind. It's what you are. I'm plainborn myself, and not sorry for it. You nobles seem like such a harried lot."

"Ah, yes, well. It's the titles that do it: who can keep them all straight?"

His wit earned him a bark of laughter, muffled in wool, that turned into a cough. Waylen hunched in the saddle, shak-

ing, one hand pressed to his mouth. Devin was about to knee
Savvys closer to make sure the spy wasn't choking, but Waylen
looked up with a grin.

"I always knew you lot had it hard," he wheezed.

"You should see the clothes. Horrid."

"How *do* you sort out all that silverware at the table?"

"Easier than keeping the list of illustrious ancestors
straight in your head, I promise you."

They were giggling like children now. Aileana cast a confused look back at them.

"All that bowing and scraping must be so *tiresome...*"

"...And then you're betrothed to some total stranger and
you have to romance her into not hating you..."

Waylen snickered, "Actually, my lo—Devin, that last one
sounds a bit dreadful."

"I'm sure it is," Devin said feelingly.

"You could probably just write her a song. Isn't that what
you do?"

"Clearly you haven't heard my songs," Devin replied, and
Waylen let loose that shout of mirth again, making both
Aileana and Fortyn look back and wave their hands for silence,
no doubt wondering why they'd been saddled with two mad-
men for this trip.

They rode in a companionable silence after that, and Devin
decided this was someone he could share a pint of ale with.
He wondered if the other Cassdalls were so easy to be around.
Kinsey was just... Kinsey, shy and quiet and sharp as a honed
blade, full of curiosity and wonderfully dry, subtle wit. He
wasn't sure yet what to think of Annan, who saw much but said
little, had a sense of humor as edged as his sword, and avoided

discussions of everything but politics or war.

Waylen rode a little easier now, as though laughing had made other things hurt less. His bright gaze took in everything around them. Devin pushed his hood back, more willing to suffer the cold now that he knew he was nearly out of it. He could hear faint shouts coming from somewhere and squinted up to see a distant figure on the battlement walls waving frantically.

Then Savvys went tense under him, a hitching motion of fright.

Up ahead, Aileana and Fortyn wheeled their mounts around in perfect unison, pounding back toward them in great sprays of snow. Fortyn already had his staff untangled from the saddle ties. Aileana was stringing her bow as she rode.

"*Draw, Devin!*" Waylen snapped, all the humor gone from his voice, and ripped his sword free.

Devin was retrieving his sword when they burst from the trees to both sides, a motley band of men in armor that looked as piecemeal as it did hard-used—but for all that, there were at least ten to their four. They came in yelling and Devin was in the thick of them before he had time to turn Savvys around.

Then there was another volley of shouts from the trees to the west, and a band of their own soldiers came out riding hard. Devin reined Savvys up, trying to get out of the way. A sword flashed out at him and he ducked, raised his own, yelped when a line of fire streaked over his arm and a blow at his shoulder knocked the breath from him. The cloak made it hard to move.

Waylen ran a man through. Devin yelled, swinging the sword, trying to keep the harp case at his back from pulling him off balance. Aileana was trading shots with a bowman in a

dented helm and a ragged leather vest, and Devin kicked Savvys around, ducked when the archer swung his way, struck the
man in the chin with the flat of his sword, and knocked him
from his horse.

Someone was screaming.

He looked up, desperately out of breath, and saw yet more
soldiers ahorse racing out of the great fortress doors. The enemy saw it, too, and all the sound of fighting fell away into a
shocking, ringing silence as they scattered.

It was very hard to breathe. It didn't seem to be the cold.

"Devin, you should have—oh, gods. Oh, no."

Waylen's face was streaked with blood on one side, all his
scars flaming with exertion. Around them he had gone gray-
ish-pale. He put a hand out, got Devin's arm in a painful grip,
and then turned and shouted for Aileana and Fortyn.

"I'm all right," Devin said—or tried: the words came with
a terrible flare of agony in his chest. He coughed, which made
it so much worse he felt himself slide sideways into Waylen's
arms. The party from the fortress came down to meet them.
Aileana drew close, made a sound somewhere between a gasp
and a moan, and dropped her bow to fumble in her saddlebags.

"What in he—"

Kyali. Who reined her horse to a stop and just stared at him
open-mouthed, her eyes wide and gold, bright as twin suns.

"Finally," Devin said, or thought he did. He went altogether
sideways, the world upended itself, and then he was staring at
the sky and a crowd of faces and horse legs, and the pressure
in his chest was so bad everything began to seem faraway. His
sister bent over him, wooden-faced, breathing hard.

"We have to get the arrow out quickly," someone said.

Arrow? Devin wondered.

The sun went out without warning.

They came back inside in a knot of armor and cloaks and frightened faces. Taireasa flung herself forward, clumsy for the first time Kinsey could remember ever seeing. She nearly tripped. He caught her by the elbows and kept her upright, pulling her forward with him in a stumbling rush, ignoring the suspicious attention from her bodyguards.

"Thank you," she choked out before falling to her knees on the packed dirt where Devin was stretched out.

Blood, gods, so much blood.

A Fraonir girl was cutting Devin's shirt away. A boy who looked so much like her he had to be her twin was sawing with great delicacy at the shaft of the arrow jutting from under Devin's shoulder, and the Lady Captain was holding her brother down, pushing against his shoulders.

"Ky," Taireasa said, and those two met gazes in a soundless shock of warping air. It blew outward from them like an invisible brushfire, blurring everything, frightening the gathered crowd back several steps.

"We're taking it out now, Majesty."

"How bad?"

Devin groaned, arching underneath his sister's iron grip, and they looked down at him.

"I don't know yet," Kyali said.

Kinsey knelt, not caring that there was no room for him, that he was no help here, that he was caught in a bubble of

shuddering, rippling air that was snapping against his skin
and making his hair stand on end. He caught Devin's hand,
felt the faint pressure of fingers, and had to swallow a sob. He
couldn't even remember the last time he'd wept, but he was
suddenly very close to doing just that.

"Annan," he said, trusting that his captain had found this
little disaster.

"My Lord Prince."

"A stretcher. An herb-woman. Have them build up the fire
in Devin's room."

"Done, my Lord Prince."

Shouted orders ricocheted away from them while the Fraonir girl did something with a knife and her bare fingers and
Kyali pressed her brother into the dirt, and Devin's grip grew
crushing. His groan rose higher, became a scream, drowned in
a dreadful choking cough. The arrow came out blessedly whole,
and a rush of blood came after.

"Bad," Kyali said grimly, and Kinsey looked up at her, remembering something she'd said, the hunch of her shoulders
against a dark window, firelight, magic, gods what *was* it...

*I seem to be able to heal from wounds that might otherwise be
mortal...*

"Geas," he said.

"What?"

"*Geas*, Lady Captain. Binding you three. *He* can't, but your
Gift—you may be able to—"

"*Yes*," Kyali breathed, hope breaking through that stony
mask for a second. She shut her eyes, going still and calm, and
put her hands to her brother's chest, against the place where
blood was pulsing out. The Fraonir girl growled something

and tried to push her away, but Taireasa shot a hand out, getting the girl's arm in a white-knuckled grip.

"Let her," Taireasa commanded.

Kyali's face, already pale, went white and then crumpled. She took a sudden, shuddering gasp. The air snapped and sang, pulling at hair, clothes, thoughts. Kinsey held onto Devin's hand, listening to Taireasa's fervent, mumbled praying, to the sound of footsteps running toward them.

Kyali's hands were... blurring, like the air. Golden light shivered down the backs of them, seeming to slip right out of her pores. It fell into Devin, who took a ragged gasp and twitched. Brother and sister breathed together for a long moment, the sound of it the only thing in the hall.

The air got very still. Devin's grip slackened.

Then Taireasa's voice rose into a cry of joy. She bent and pressed her head into Devin's unwounded shoulder, and Devin's hand rose to smooth over her hair.

Devin blinked up at Kinsey. "What in hell was *that?*" he asked.

Kinsey leaned back, certain for a horrifying second that he *was* going to cry, but instead he began to laugh out of sheer, stunned relief. He pressed Devin's hand, swallowing both tears and laughter, and heaved a sigh. "That was you getting arrow-shot and your sister saving your life," he said, and Kyali staggered to her feet.

She nearly fell; she seemed to be having trouble making her legs hold her weight. She held her hands out in front of her curled, like they hurt her, and took a few clumsy steps back.

"Ky?" Taireasa said, her voice muffled by Devin's shoulder.

"Get him on the stretcher," Kyali said, looking mostly at the ground between her feet.

"Oi, I can *walk*..."

"You were shot, Devin," Taireasa said, sitting up. Her hair had come partially free of the crown of braids she always wore. Kinsey tried not to stare: he'd never realized it curled so much. She darted a glance at him, felt at her head, winced. "*Shot.* In the chest. You're not walking anywhere. Don't argue. We'll follow you up. You're going to sleep."

"Fine," Devin groaned—mostly, Kinsey suspected, because soldiers were already lifting him, and the blood drained out of his face as soon as he sat upright. He pressed his fingertips to his temples, face twisting. "Dear gods, my head hurts."

Looking up at Kyali, Kinsey suspected he wasn't the only one.

As two men bore Devin past a growing crowd of the curious, Taireasa made to rise and winced again. Kinsey got to her before the nearest of her bodyguards could and pulled her up. She wobbled, flung a hand out to stay upright, clutched at his shoulder. He tried very hard not to pay attention to her touch, remembering that she had the same Gift as Saraid, only stronger. He felt himself flush.

"Oh, my head," she murmured.

"Lady—"

"*Taireasa.*"

Her green eyes were filmed with tears, but she wasn't going to allow them to fall, that much was clear. A line had formed between her eyebrows. She had been through rather a lot in the last few minutes. Kinsey squeezed her hand gently and let it go. "Taireasa."

"Better," Taireasa said softly. "I'm going to sit with Devin.

On him, if that's what it takes to keep him in bed, and it very well may. Ky, will you—"

She looked around, but Kyali had vanished while they were helping one another stand. Her shoulders slumped. "That shouldn't surprise me anymore," she said, mostly to herself.

"I'll find her," Kinsey promised, partially out of curiosity, mostly to see Taireasa's faint smile. "Go, Majesty. Taireasa. I hope I'll be able to see him later, when he's awake and—"

"—Driving us all mad out of boredom," Taireasa finished, sighing. "I'll send word, Kinsey, when the herb-woman is done with him."

She took the stairs in a clatter of armor, her bodyguard all around her.

Feeling eyes all over the room on him, Kinsey turned and crossed the hall, following his curiosity. He wound his way through knots of people to the corridor where the army's offices were, following a guess.

It turned out to be a correct one. The Lady Captain was in her office, not quite having managed to close the door before falling into the uncomfortable-looking chair behind her desk. Her head was in her hands. The look she gave him when he slipped carefully inside was unwelcoming, to put it mildly, and also bleary with pain.

"Highness," Kyali said, making an effort to straighten. Kinsey grimaced in sympathy.

"Don't stand, Lady Captain. I just came to make tea."

She stared, hollow-eyed. A muscle next to her right eye twitched. One hand curled into a loose fist on the plain wood of her desk. There were rolls of paper and parchment all around her, two newer-looking codices, a cabinet overflowing with maps. Several pots of ink, a pile of used quills. Ink stains on her hands. A stack of books. *History of Lardan* was perched on top of the cabinet. He wondered if she ever slept.

"Tea," she echoed vaguely.

"You look as if you could use some," Kinsey said. Checking to see there was water in it first, he swung the kettle out over the tiny hearth. Kyali scowled down at her fist.

"I suppose I could."

"They both have headaches, too," Kinsey remarked, ignoring the glower this earned him, and picked through a few canisters on the mantle until he found what smelled like tea leaves. "I imagine yours is worse, Lady Captain, considering. Perhaps the tea will help."

"Willowbark," she murmured, which was probably as much of a concession as he was going to get, and more than he'd expected. "Second jar."

"Excellent." The kettle was steaming; he found a pot and poured, spooned in tea leaves and a generous helping of willowbark, and set it on the desk in front of her. "I'll leave you to it, then."

Some of the tension went out of the line of her shoulders. She nodded down at the mug of tea in her hands. Kinsey raked the room with one more curious glance, thinking of the expression on her face just before she'd healed her brother, the strange play of tension between her and Taireasa, wondering what it was he was missing. She looked utterly exhausted.

"Thank you," Kyali said, barely a whisper, as he let himself out.

He didn't think she meant the tea.

22

Corwynalls all had the exact same expression when they were fighting something.

Taireasa had learned this simple fact many years ago, when the boys standing before her now had come to stay at the House estate for a summer and had caused such gleeful mayhem that even the Lord General himself had been reduced seven times to shouting, and twice to helpless laughter.

Bran Corwynall, third cousin to Kyali and Devin, first cousin to Feldan, lost that fierce, determined look and sank to his knees under the force of her seeking. His gasp was echoed by his brother Bryce's, and another pair of knees struck stone. Taireasa felt the echo of that in her own knees and winced, hurting for them, hurting *with* them, cause and fellow-sufferer and so miserably confused she could barely keep her own feet.

She was trying to be gentle. She didn't know *how*.

I'm sorry, she said—but that only seemed to hurt them

more. The pain echoed through her own mind, a ripping, rippling invasion that tore memories out of their heads and hearts, sifted through them, leaving nothing hidden, nothing private. Her temples throbbed. She didn't know if it was worse to feel what they felt or to know that she was the cause of such suffering.

—*Fields under a sunrise, Devin running from farmer Angus's bull, mother, red-haired and laughing*—

—*Riding to the border, carrying a sword, feeling like a grown man for the first time in his life*—

—*Riding up a mountain, miserable and grieving: broken House, broken kingdom, broken world*—

Both of them were wheezing, air whistling past clenched teeth, muscles trembling.

She couldn't do this much longer. The pain it caused her was nothing to the pain it was causing them. She'd never dreamed that her Gift, so undramatic next to Devin's illusions, Kyali's command of flame, could do so much harm. It struck her to the core. It wounded her in a way nothing had.

Nothing but Kyali's desertion.

Kyali was here with her now, still and staring, a perfect blank spot in the cacophony of minds, like the eye of a storm. Three soldiers held the door, blades out, ready for anything— horrified and grimly determined, and hoping Her Majesty never felt the need to do such a thing to them. Curran was next to her, thinking about one of his brothers, someone lost, a grief. Maldyn and Beagan flanked her protectively, a jumble of sorrow and shame, fear, and unwavering determination.

Feldan. Whispers in a tent. Swords meeting in the firelight.

"There," Taireasa gasped, and let go of Bran and Bryce with

a relief so great it was another kind of pain. They both collapsed immediately and Taireasa bent to catch them, snarled an objection when someone's hand closed over her arm and tried to yank her away from the two suspected traitors.

"It's not them," she snapped. She put one hand on Bran's sweating forehead. "I'm sorry," she murmured, then swallowed the rest of what she wished to say, because queens didn't beg for anything, certainly not forgiveness. She tried to still the trembling in her hands, to stop thinking of Kyali held down, her fingers broken one by one, a knife parting her skin. Pain beyond comprehension. She had suffered it with Kyali by choice; she had caused something like it now, also by choice.

Oh, she wanted so badly to be a child again. What kind of world was she making if this sort of cruelty was necessary—was an acceptable answer to a threat to her safety?

She had to do better than this.

"Majesty," Bran said, and curled up in a futile attempt to hide the tears streaming down his face. He gave up and wept, one fist shoved against his mouth.

Beside him, Bryce was trying to sit up, hunched around himself like he'd taken a blow to the belly, his eyes wide and lost. "Lady queen, thank you," he managed to say. Taireasa sucked in a burning lungful of air, wanting so badly to weep it felt like her eyes were on fire.

"What could you possibly have to thank me for, Bryce Corwynall?"

He swallowed, his eyes squeezing shut. "For giving us a chance to prove our innocence," he said, as if it were obvious, and Taireasa had to stand, had to walk to the window and look outside at the frozen world while she fought her tears.

"Majesty…" Maldyn looked like he'd aged ten years in the last day. He set a hand gently on her shoulder. "They should swear."

For a moment, Taireasa couldn't speak.

He was right. And yet it was horribly unfair, to ask men she'd just—that she'd just… dear gods, they were still unable to stand, both of them sprawled trembling and winded on the floor, and she was going to demand they *swear fealty* to her? They were going to have nightmares of their own now.

Her Gift had done this, was capable of this.

She had done this. Was capable of this.

Bran was speaking from where he lay, still curled like a worm in the sun, still leaking tears and so out of breath it was hard to make out the words. She knew what he was saying because part of her was still threaded around his heart. The oath of fealty to a sovereign. Bryce began it, too, and Taireasa drove her nails into the palms of her hands until she could feel them break the skin, hating herself, hating the awful weight of responsibility that had left her no option but this.

She turned, because nobody should have to make this kind of oath to someone's back. She couldn't make herself smile, but she knelt again, taking their hands.

"I will never do this to you again," she said, instead of the ritual acceptance of fealty. "Hear me. *I will never harm you this way again.* Nor will I doubt you. What faith you've given to me, I give back to you."

There was a faint shimmer to the air at the edge of her vision. Maldyn made a sound that might have been protest. It was far more than any king or queen before her had ever sworn, she was sure. The whole room had gone silent, astonished.

"My lady," Bryce said, hushed and very moved. The thin

thread of his heart still tangled with hers bloomed into something broader, fixed and full of certainty. She didn't deserve it. He bowed over her hands, a clumsy motion that put everyone in the room on edge and had Kyali up on her toes next to them, hands hovering over her daggers. Taireasa cast a look up at the captain of her guard, ready to snap out an impatient rebuke— renunciation of House notwithstanding, these were her own *cousins*—but the haunted look hiding at the back of Kyali's eyes strangled the words in her throat.

For a second she stared, as she had rarely let herself do, directly into her old friend's face, set the terrible weight of guilt aside and just took in everything. There were great shadowed hollows under Kyali's eyes, little color to her skin, strain wound tightly into every one of her muscles. She looked like she was braced against an invisible wind, fighting just to stay upright. She looked like she was at the last of her strength.

"It's all right," Taireasa said, holding that bleak, fractured gaze, refusing to flinch. She wasn't completely sure what she was talking about. She was painfully aware that it wasn't *all right*, though: that it hadn't been *all right* for some time, and she bit her lip. Presenting the world with the truth she wanted instead of the truth that was.

"It *will* be all right," she amended.

Kyali's mouth made a flat, unhappy line and she looked away. Kyali had, she supposed, no reason to believe that.

"You ought to see the herb-woman," Taireasa said to Bran and Bryce.

"I'd rather a glass of wine and my bed, Your Majesty," Bran said, trying to smile, not quite managing it. He pushed himself off the floor with a grunt of effort and Taireasa let Curran help her to her feet as the two brothers pulled one another up.

"So would I," Taireasa said wearily as they stumbled out.

"It was... effective?" Maldyn asked, when it was only him and herself, Curran, and Kyali left in the room. Taireasa thought she had never needed sleep so badly in her life. But she leaned against the windowsill, studying her trembling hands, and tried to muster the wit for yet another discussion of tactics.

"Yes," she said.

"Perhaps Your Majesty should consider applying the same—that is, consider speaking so to all of us on the inner council," her chancellor said. His gaze flicked over Kyali, then Curran.

Applying the same method of interrogation, he'd been about to say. A shudder twisted queasily through her.

"No," Taireasa said. "Never again."

Maldyn shifted, chafing at his hands, which were blue with cold. "My lady, your safety is paramount. If it would uncover this person..."

"Not at such cost to Her Majesty, surely," Curran murmured. He took her arm gently.

"Your thoughts, Lady Captain?" Maldyn said, and Taireasa bit her tongue, hardly daring to look at Kyali right now. Maldyn must be desperate indeed to look for support there: Kyali unsettled him deeply. Not many of the nobles and house staff of his age knew what to do with a woman in armor. For that matter, not many of the others did, either.

"I think you should sleep," Kyali said, not acknowledging Maldyn's question.

Taireasa hissed out a bitter little laugh. "I will if you will,

Kyali Corwynall," she retorted, and left the room before she
had to see what sort of non-expression that backhanded challenge put on Kyali's face.

Devin set the harp down gently, shaking the tingle from his
fingers. Around him, birds bled out of the air and the Sainey
grew faded and then blew apart. After a moment, so too did
the weathered oak and stone, the horn-paned windows and
broad-boarded porch, the iron-barred doors and light-filled
rooms of House Corwynall.

Kinsey sat among shelves and tables and the drifting remnants of a dream of childhood, his gray eyes round and de-
lighted. He was still as stone, and Devin let him be that way for
another moment. He seriously doubted he was going to be able
to get any words past the aching lump in his throat anyway.

The library actually *looked* like a library now. He pulled
the Book closer, almost afraid to touch its fragile parchment
pages, the heavy cracked cover, leather cord lacing that looked
very close to coming to bits. The ink was barely visible. He pic-
tured Kinsey bent over it in lantern-light, squinting, all elbows
and weariness and fierce concentration.

"So… the Síog were real. Were here, in this fortress. And we
drove them here a thousand years ago? I confess I'm having a
hard time with this."

Kinsey pulled in a huge breath, still wide-eyed and star-
tled-looking. "That was amazing," he said. "I don't understand
why you were afraid to do this indoors before, though."

Devin hummed the first few bars of "Pass the Cup" and

grinned when Kinsey's tea mug jolted sideways several feet. Kinsey let out a yelp and snatched up a messy sheaf of notes before the tea could slosh over them, then shot him an accusing look.

"I broke every window on the lower floor of the house the first time I picked up a fiddle," Devin admitted.

Kinsey might be clutching the notes a bit now.

"This doesn't surprise any of us who know you, Lord Corwynall," Annan said, appearing in the library door. Kinsey uttered another yelp, muffled this time, and twisted to glare at the Cassdall captain.

"Spies," he sighed, and Annan flashed half a grin, one that vanished almost before Devin could see it.

Devin flipped a page delicately. The feeling of it was almost like the feeling of the harp in his hands: a weight beyond the object itself, a faint, hidden spark flaring through the fingertips. Distant pulling in the belly.

"You honestly *believe* they were real?" he asked, though he knew the answer. Kinsey could jest, was actually quite funny when he wanted to be—but he wouldn't ever jest about research.

"I *know* they were," Kinsey said simply. "You do too, if you think about it. There are tales of them in every province of Lardan, of Cassdall, of Allaida and Madrassia and every other kingdom nearby. If you haven't read them, I assure you, I have. And the old histories always spoke of a people before us. It just never occurred to me the faery tales and the histories were talking about the same thing."

"I can see why," Devin grumbled.

"I'm sure it's a little unsettling, learning you've the blood of faeries in your veins," Kinsey said with false sympathy, a hint of wicked humor hiding in his gaze. He yawned, rubbing an eye, and then ran a hand through his hair. It always looked like a barley field after a hard wind: now it looked like a barley field after a hard wind had knocked a few trees onto it. Devin coughed to hide a laugh and saw, out of the corner of his eye, Annan cast a long-suffering look up at the ceiling.

"Oh, it's not such a surprise," Devin sighed. "I grew up with Kyali, remember. Fire-haired, spark-eyed, even-tempered as a bear in spring, always batting at things with that damned sword. You should have seen her when she was ten. She *looked* like a faery. Just not the nice kind."

Annan and Kinsey had the strangest expressions on their faces, like they were trying to picture Captain Corwynall of the Exile's Army as a knobby-kneed ten-year-old carrying a grown man's sword, and finding it impossible. It almost made him smile. It also put the lump back in his throat.

Getting shot with an arrow had made him stupidly sentimental.

It had also, apparently, knocked some disturbing new magic loose in him. There was a constant sense of darkness hovering at the edges of everything now, a feeling like walls pressing around him—cold, high walls that hid something important, something he both needed and dreaded. He had dreamed of them every night for five days, dreamed of following the smooth icy shape of them blindly with his hands, of searching for a door he was certain existed but that he never found. Ever since he'd woken in his own bed with a blurred memory of pain and gold light, and Taireasa sitting beside him.

It meant *something*, he just didn't know what. And it made for very poor sleep.

"What brings you to the library?" Kinsey asked, eyeing his captain. "You didn't come here just to scare the daylights out of me and mock Devin."

"Either one would have been worth the trip, my lord," Annan said smoothly, and Kinsey hurled a crumpled knot of paper at him, grinning. "I came to find the Lord Corwynall, however. Your cousins are no longer under suspicion, my lord."

Devin sagged in his chair. "Thank the gods," he murmured. And then straightened. "Wait. How did we discover this?"

Annan's look was wary. "Her Majesty... asked them."

Asked them? What was that supposed to mean, that Taireasa had brought them in for tea and a polite discussion of...

Oh. *Oh*, dear gods.

He must have blanched. Kinsey stood abruptly, poured tea into another mug, and set it before him with a firm look. "Drink," he said.

"Are they all right? Is *she*?"

Taireasa?

No answer but a sense of great weariness and sadness— and then, as she became aware of him, of walls of warm stone rising between them, shielding her mind from his. It didn't feel like a rejection, more like the self-protective effort of an exhausted heart.

"Her Majesty complained of headache, but is otherwise well," Annan was saying. "Your cousins are sleeping, I believe. They came through it with no injury."

Devin was only half-listening now, probing the shuttered sense of Taireasa, the guard she held against not just him, but everything. It was a trick he hadn't learned yet. It felt strangely familiar, and then he understood why.

Walls of warm stone.

Walls of dark ice.

Hearts bound to his own behind each of them.

He might have fallen out of the chair. The world seemed to have moved under him, showing him something from a new angle, undoing and remaking itself around his bewildered gaze.

Was it Kyali he was dreaming of? Was *that* what she had become, that cold darkness shut in on itself? Oh gods, what had done *that* to her?

That wasn't his sister. That *couldn't* be his sister. She could indeed be cold, practical in a way that let her move men around like chess pieces, let her risk and lose their lives for a greater goal and still find a way to sleep afterwards. She had a temper that, when loosed, sent seasoned soldiers running for cover, and her will was hard enough to break stone—but past that was a heart irrevocably loyal, vast and stubborn and silently, boundlessly generous. *That* was the sister he knew, who trusted seldom but without reservation, who never sang but knew the words to every song he'd written, who preferred little notice of her cleverness and none at all of her compassion. Who would give her life without a second's hesitation for him or for Taireasa.

That sister would *never* desert her best friend, her brother, her House. That sister would have torn herself apart before letting that happen. And yet she had. And did. Assuming the rest was still true, which he had to believe—that Kyali was somewhere under that immense and awful cold—what would make her *choose* such a thing?

Taireasa, who never slept. Who curled around a guilt so great it was a wound.

Kyali, with shadows just as heavy under her eyes, and fury

in them. Who was, under all that, *sad*.

Warm stone, dark ice.

"Annan," Devin said faintly. He became aware that both Annan and Kinsey were watching him with more than a little concern. He didn't know how long he'd sat there thinking. He took a sip of the tea, mostly to take that look of growing alarm out of Kinsey's eyes, and found it was already cooling.

"Lord Corwynall?"

"Gods—don't call me that. I *hate* that. And it's not even true: I can't be Head of House. I'm a Bard. We'll just have to find someone else once we've taken the kingdom back." Never mind that he was wearing his father's ring, or that he was the only Corwynall now wearing a dragon locket.

Two lockets, actually, because he hadn't been able to make himself let go of Kyali's.

"You must have asked anyone who would talk about that night what happened in Faestan castle during the Western uprising," Devin said, and received a cautious, considering nod.

Of course Annan had. He was a spy, an information collector, and since Kinsey had chosen to ally himself with Taireasa, he had a new enemy. He would want to know everything about that enemy.

"What happened?" he asked.

Kinsey shifted in his chair, frowning. "Devin—what are you chasing?

"I don't know yet. Humor me."

"It's a piecemeal story, my lord," Annan said, settling himself gingerly in a chair, evidently wary of the damage his armor might do to the wood. "I've reports from servants, soldiers, throne room guards, cooks, and townsfolk. The Western force that accompanied the barons into Faestan was camped outside the town walls: late that night, someone let them in the town gate and then into the castle. It was not, by all accounts, one of the barons themselves."

"Yes," Devin said, waving impatiently. That much was obvious. "And?"

Annan shrugged, eyes lighting with the challenge. "And I'd bet my blade the person or persons who let the Western force in is the same one passing messages to Tuan now."

Kinsey's head snapped around. "Ah," he said, an admiring sound. "Now *that's* a thought. And it would rule out the Corwynall cousins, except that Taire—that Her Majesty has already done so. Anyone not in the castle at the time would be cleared of suspicion."

"*Was* it the same person?" Devin said, momentarily distracted from his aim. "Who let them into the town, and into the castle. The same, or more than one?"

Annan's face showed a flash of surprise, then intense thought. "Good question," he said.

A disturbing question, actually.

"What about Taireasa? What do they say of her? Where she was, how she escaped?"

She'd hidden, he knew that. Hidden in the same passages she had once pulled him into to save him from his old magic tutor's wrath; hidden and waited until a large enough force had gathered, then taken the stables and the northern gate and fled to the mountains. But she never spoke of it. *Wouldn't* speak of it, and since she'd lost both her parents that night, along with her throne, Devin had never wanted to press her. He knew too well how grief could cut.

Annan worried his lip, slid Kinsey's abandoned mug of tea over and sipped it, then made a face, presumably at the temperature. "Her Majesty was in her rooms at the moment the attack began. She escaped through some servants' passage in the walls, I am told, and remained hidden under the fortress for three days, gathering refugees and supplies before leaving for the Fraonir lands."

"Where was my sister?" Devin asked, and Annan met his eyes uneasily.

"My lord..."

"She killed the Western barons, Captain. You've no need to spare my feelings. I've heard enough from servants to know what my sister did, and that it was what allowed them to escape. But where was she *before* that?"

"In Her Majesty's rooms. They had dinner brought there, anyway."

Annan had pieced the night together just as thoroughly as Devin had hoped. "But she was not with Taireasa in the chambers under the castle," he said.

"No, lord. She appeared just before they left for the mountains."

"Then she didn't take the servants' passageway with Taireasa."

It came clear, then: so brutally, appallingly clear he could see it happening.

Two girls in a royal bedroom, listening to fighting outside the door. One the heir to the throne, one just returned from two years of sword study. Both loyal to the last breath to one another. Kyali had grown up under a general's tutelage. Kyali knew the Western barons would never stop looking for Taireasa if they met the mystery of a locked and empty room. They would have found the hidden doorway soon enough. Kyali had renounced the throne just that day, to keep Taireasa safe from the West's machinations.

Kyali wouldn't have hesitated.

"She stayed," Devin murmured, horror making his skin prickle. "She stayed behind."

Dread was weighing his bones down into the chair, blooming into a sick knot in his stomach. Taireasa's Gift, which had woken that night. Her terrible, silent guilt. And Kyali, who was twisted around herself, burning up with anger, pulling away, always away from the closeness he and Taireasa shared, the space in their hearts where there could be no secrets. Who had learned that she could heal from wounds that might otherwise be mortal.

Oh yes, the edges of this secret were sharp. They were going to carve him in two.

Devin drew a burning breath as Kinsey's hand closed over his. He realized only then that he was weeping. Kinsey's eyes held dawning comprehension, and more compassion than he could stand to see right now. Annan sat back, gone wooden and unreadable, but his hand on the stolen mug of tea had closed into a hard fist.

Devin shut his eyes, retrieved his hand, wiped at his cheeks. Stood, needing to lean on the table to find his feet. The whole world was changing into something else around him. The sick dread in his belly had a direction.

Oh, Kyali, gods.

"I think I need some air," he said, which wasn't much of an excuse, but he was barely able to think, let alone speak.

He didn't make it more than a few steps before a terrible pressure filled his head. Pain and fear spilled through him, pain and fear and a sense of betrayal. **HELP,** he heard—and then she was gone, gone as completely as though she had never been there at all.

"*Taireasa,*" he gasped, and flung himself at the library doors, fear greater than he had ever known roaring over him. Annan and Kinsey were right behind him.

There were too many damned doors into the castle.

Kyali had set guards on them all, had men walking the halls in pairs, but the sense that it wasn't enough, that she was missing something that would cost her everything, followed her everywhere. It hovered over her meetings with her officers, it soured her tea, it swallowed her thoughts and stole the little sleep she got, until she was wandering the halls in a haze of exhaustion and worry.

They still hadn't found the traitor, and Taireasa had paid such a terrible price.

Bryce and Bran were asleep now. She had made herself meet with them after—*after.* Had told them of her mad idea to send three hundred men down the Maurynim river on rafts, because at least there were two men, now, that she knew beyond a doubt she could trust.

Had asked, nearly choking on her own hypocrisy, if they'd be willing to lead such a force.

It was days away, maybe weeks. Which was good, because her cousins were not at all recovered from the ordeal she and

Taireasa had put them through.

They had accepted—sounding, gods help her, *grateful* for the chance.

Kyali shoved her way through the hidden door in her office and leaned on the wall, breathing, only breathing. The sandwich she'd eaten gods only knew when was trying to come back up. Her heart was fluttering in her chest. *Ice* was no longer a wall stretching up to the skies, it was slick and treacherous under her feet. She didn't know anymore what to do, how to keep moving forward, how to save Taireasa, how to avoid Devin, how to go on living the way she had. How to stop sensing them both just outside that thin, failing barrier.

She had laid her hands on her brother's bleeding chest and opened the door between them herself. It wouldn't shut again now.

The sandwich did come up. She staggered away from the mess, wiping her lips, breathing in pattern, but breathing didn't help. Nothing helped. Inside her it was all rage and burning, the terror and fury of being helpless, the knowledge of finding and then sweeping past her own limits. Watching Bran and Bryce learn their own the same way, through pain, had been almost more than she could bear. Watching Taireasa pull herself apart to achieve it, and then to fix it, had been even worse. And it hadn't accomplished a single thing. They *still* didn't know who among them was Tuan's man.

Someone could be with Taireasa now.

Her feet were taking her back into the passages and toward the royal apartments before she could process that thought fully. Kyali stopped, turned, then turned again, unable to decide. As she was hovering there like an idiot, unable to muster the wit for even so simple a decision as which way to go, a faint whisper of sound told her she wasn't alone in here anymore. She pressed herself against the wall instinctively, though the rational part of her said it had to be a Cassdall officer. Aside from her, they were still the only ones who knew about these passageways.

The footsteps were soft, careful. They shouldn't be.

They were coming her way.

She drew her daggers, because the sword was too big to be useful in here, and waited. It took forever: whoever it was, he wasn't a fool. Kyali wished she could shut her eyes. The gleam would give her away if the man had a light.

A figure materialized out of the deep shadow where the passage branched off toward the kitchens, moving slowly, looking around every few steps. There was something familiar about the shape of him, which wasn't what one would expect of a soldier: tall and broad but rounded, softened, not a man who spent much time using his muscles. Kyali folded her daggers up into her sleeves and crouched, feeling something prickle at the edges of her awareness.

The man drew closer, became the faintly outlined figure and dimly lit features of Earl Donal.

Kyali stood.

He started, one hand flying up to his broad chest, and breathed a curse. "Who... ah! Lady Captain," he said, his voice horrifyingly loud in the tunnel, like he was hoping to bellow up an armed guard to get him out of this. "Just the ma—ah, woma... just the officer I was planning to find."

"Keep your voice down, sir. What are you doing?"

An expansive wave. He had something in his hand: paper,

by the sound of it. "I found a *door*, Lady Captain, a door hidden under a wretched old wallhanging by the dining hall. It's remarkable! It led me here. I deemed it best if I—"

"*Shhhh.*"

"Sorry," he said, and went on in a hoarse whisper that would wake the dead. "I was saying, I took it upon myself to discover where the door led. But this place is vast. I thought perhaps I'd better warn you about it." He stopped, gaze on her. "I see you already have some awareness of this. You are an attentive officer, Lady Captain."

She still had her daggers in her grip, but they stayed in her sleeves. Gods knew she'd been waiting for just this to happen, though almost anyone else would have been better: the man was as subtle as a wild boar.

"What's in your hand, Earl Donal?" Kyali said—or started to say. He was on her in a second, much faster than she'd ever guessed he could move, shoving her back into the cold, dirty wall, one hand coming up, and what was in it now was definitely not paper.

The panic was instant, overwhelming. It brought something else with it, something that wasn't her, was firelit and frightened, was startled and so tired she knew it had to be Taireasa. The double vision was badly disorienting. Kyali yelled into the arm Donal shoved up against her face, brought her knee up, unfolded the daggers from her sleeves. One scraped over his ribs and he shouted; the other clattered to the floor when he struck her arm so hard it went instantly numb.

Kyali ducked without thinking about it, felt his blade pass just over her head. Taireasa was in danger, Taireasa was furious and *terrified*, was seeing something, someone, someone wrong and twisted and sorry and she couldn't tell who—

A blow struck her face, knocking her off her feet. Donal threw himself on top of her, hand scrabbling after the dagger in hers, his considerable weight knocking the breath out of her.

The panic swallowed her whole, left no room for anything else. She was back in Taireasa's bedroom and the pain was huge and awful but not as bad as the shame of being helpless, the shaking rage, the sick comprehension that she was going to die and that it was going to take a very long time. She screamed and heard it echo, which wasn't right.

She was in the tunnels. On the mountain. Not in Faestan.

This time she had a blade, this time she wasn't tied. This time there was only one of them.

She arched up and slammed her head into his chin, wrenched the dagger free and drove it deep. Then again, and again. Again. He stopped moving after the third blow, but she kept going. She couldn't stop until she was sure, very sure, and dead men weren't dead till they stopped bleeding.

Oh gods, Father!

HELP, Kyali heard, right in her head, blowing down all the walls, opening all the doors.

She left Earl Donal dying or dead, drew her sword, and ran as fast as she had ever run in her life.

23

The wine tasted heavy and bitter, like it had gone bad. Taireasa grimaced and, looking around to make sure no servant was nearby to see, spat it back into her glass. It had made her tongue strangely numb. She stared at it for a moment, frozen, then snatched up her tea mug. The water was scalding, but she rinsed and spat into the fire four times anyway, until the numbness went away.

Then she sat, shaking like a leaf in a storm, and tried to decide if lack of sleep was a reasonable explanation for such paranoia, or if she was going mad.

It had been a very hard day.

"My lady?" Camwyn, her day maid, said, peering into the sitting room with a look like she expected to get a shoe or a glass of wine in the face. "Is the wine not to your taste?"

For no reason at all that made her laugh, and then she couldn't get it stopped. Taireasa put her hands over her face, giggling madly, a little frightened by the shrill sound of it. When she finally got herself under control and wiped her eyes, Camwyn seemed horrified. Behind her stood Maldyn, looking grave and worried, and almost as tired as she felt.

"Her Majesty should have supper now," he said calmly, and Camwyn left with plain relief to go order a plate from the kitchens. "You should at least *try* to eat, my lady," he added, seeing Taireasa's face.

"I suppose," she mumbled, and tried to breathe herself back to some kind of equilibrium. Her chancellor sat in the other fireside chair, glancing once at the abandoned glass of wine, steepling his fingers and frowning at the flames. Taireasa leaned back, letting him think. He'd get to what he wished to say in his own time. Maldyn was the most unhurried man she'd ever known.

Finally he shifted in the chair. "The Maurynim plan," he said, sounding hesitant, perhaps a little offended. It had barely had time to become a plan: Kyali had mentioned it only yesterday, the notion of rafts and soldiers and a far swifter, quieter route to the lowlands. A small force, not meant to overwhelm an enemy, only to help repel an attack.

"Yes," Taireasa said.

"I have doubts, Majesty. It is rash. But... I know very little. Could you explain?"

He glanced at the wine again.

Taireasa shrugged. "There is, at the moment, very little to know," she said. "I never had any intention of sitting by while traitors attack our allies, Maldyn. The Lady Captain's notion is an unusual one, but that might be why it works."

"Granted," Maldyn murmured. "Still..." A third time, his

gaze flickered to the wine.

He met her eyes, saw that she was watching.

"Oh, Maldyn," Taireasa said, not angry, or even all that frightened—only sad, so sad.

His face, so clear and calm under the lines of his age, crumpled. "I'm so sorry," he whispered. "My lady, I'm so sorry. They have my wife."

The truth of that was evident in his miserable gaze, and in the horror and sorrow and helpless, doomed determination in his heart. She had never read it, never thought to. He had invited it only today. Had that been a way of pointing suspicion elsewhere, or a genuine desire to be done with the long charade? She could hear Camwyn coming back to the door, hovering, waiting for the right moment to present a tray. She could shout for help, could order him imprisoned, killed...

She couldn't imagine what she would be willing to do, who she would be willing to hurt, if it were Kyali or Devin the barons were holding.

"Tell me everything," she said simply. "And we'll see if we can fix this."

Maldyn's lips made a firm line. Tears followed the folds of skin down his cheeks. "I'm so sorry," he whispered again, and she understood.

It wasn't Camwyn at the door.

She turned her head, met the eyes of Aric, one of Kyali's lieutenants, one of her own bodyguard. Aric who had been in the tunnels under Faestan with her, who had come up the mountain by her side.

Aric, who was holding a drawn sword in her sitting room.

Taireasa stood, putting the chair between herself and

the two of them. Sadness was filling her up, sinking into her bones, making it hard to move, to think. Fear and anger were there too, but distant, unreal. She slid farther back, knowing there was no way out of her apartments but the door he was standing in. Her bedroom was behind her.

Then Aric stepped all the way into the room, filling it with his armed presence, and she was ducking, reading his intention in his heart, and fear was everything.

HELP, Taireasa sent, with no aim, no thought who to ask for help *from*. The rest of her bodyguard was outside the door. They would never get here in time. There *was* no time, because Aric was coming at her, his sword easily long enough to make up the distance the chair put between them. Maldyn stood up.

The sword passed close, a flash of firelit steel. Taireasa flinched back, tripped on the damned carpets, fell hard enough to knock the wind from her. She scrambled up as Aric got a fistful of her skirt and flung herself toward her bedroom door. Fabric tore, and the door fell open, and suddenly, from somewhere behind her, there was a great deal of yelling. She could feel Devin's terror and fury, hear his voice.

He was going to be too late. Aric was full of grim, desperate conviction, moving very fast. Devin would arrive just in time to watch her die, and then probably die himself.

No. That *couldn't* happen.

Taireasa spun, just barely missed being skewered by another flash of the sword—and let all the walls keeping her wrapped in silence fall down at once.

It was, for a terrifying second, overwhelming. Thoughts rushed at her, battered her senseless, filled her ears and her head and her consciousness. She could see the whole mountain, every soul on it. She was going to come apart in it, she couldn't hold on—

There was a noise behind her like two stones grinding together. A shout.

A blade at her throat, pressing against the delicate skin under her jaw.

"*Let her go*," Kyali hissed, trembling and barely recognizable she was so hoarse, so breathless.

"Get away," Aric said. He sounded far less sure.

"Taireasa—"

Oh gods, *everyone* was here. Devin skidded into the room, Kinsey and Annan on his heels, and came to a halt when he saw the sword poised just under her chin. Taireasa made an abortive twitch toward him, toward Kyali—where had Kyali come from?—and jerked up short with a small, smothered moan when the steel pressed in.

I can't die in front of them. I can't do this to them. Oh gods.

"She dies if anyone moves!" Aric sounded truly desperate now.

"*You* die one way or the other," Devin promised him.

"Let. Her. Go," Kyali snarled.

Kyali was here with her. Kyali was right here—and not just in body. There was another presence where before there had only been Devin. This one was small, curled tightly in on itself, black and bloodied and wounded. But it was—it *had* to be—Kyali.

Taireasa turned her head carefully and met a gaze gold as coins, bright as lanterns. Kyali was bleeding from a cut on her cheek. There was a bruise blooming there. There was more blood on her armor, on her hands. She was trembling in visible waves, rising up on her toes, her sword held steady in spite

of her quivering muscles. She looked stunned, wretched, terrified, furious. She looked *awake*.

"It will be all right," Taireasa said, for the second time
that day... and she shut her eyes, shut out the voices, shut out
the shouting and the terror, and fell backward into Aric's unfriendly embrace. The sword followed her, biting into her skin,
but it didn't matter. Her mind found Aric's—found it and held
it hard.

He froze against her, making a high and horrified sound
like a rabbit in a trap. Taireasa dropped to the floor as Kyali
drove forward and ended his life in one blurrily fast thrust.

Aric fell sideways, sword toppling out of his hands.

Taireasa knelt, looking at that, at the thin film of her blood
on its edge, and heaved out a long sigh. Then Devin's arms
were around her, pulling her up, and he was murmuring nonsense into her ear while he rocked her like a man holding a
small child.

"I'm all right," she said, because if he kept doing that she
was going to cry. "Maldyn."

"Dead," Devin said. "In your sitting room, with wine all
over him."

"It *was* poisoned." She laughed into his shoulder, only it
turned into something else halfway through and she had to
bite her lip hard until she dared to raise her head and let the
world see her face.

Annan had already dragged Aric from her bedroom, bless
him. Kinsey had taken command of the sitting room and was
ordering servants, telling his bodyguard to find more Cassdall
men to guard the queen, which was a wise idea, considering.

"Don't look," Devin murmured when two servants carried

Maldyn's twisted, crumpled form past the bedroom door. She was only too happy not to see that. She could still hear the despair in his voice, see the misery in his face. "Just stay here. You don't need to see. Where'd you come from?" he said then, and Taireasa blinked slowly.

"Secret passageways," she heard, and understood he'd been talking to Kyali. "Like in Faestan."

"Excellent timing. You're bleeding. What happened?"

"I met Earl Donal on my way here."

Donal.

"Oh gods, that *bastard*," Devin hissed.

"All that time I spent placating him," Taireasa muttered. "What a waste of effort."

Devin went still against her in sheer surprise. From behind her, she heard a strangled sound that might be laughter, or possibly something else, and she turned to see Kyali wipe her sword on her sleeve and sheathe it.

"I'll go, then, and speak to the guard," the Lady Captain said, and if she hadn't the faint thread of presence in her heart to tell her otherwise, even Taireasa might have believed Kyali was all right. It was that good a performance.

"Stay," Taireasa said. Kyali darted a glance at her, looked away.

"Stay," Devin echoed.

There was something new in him, a sadness, an understanding. Kyali began to look a little desperate. She was bleeding rather a lot, Taireasa saw, and she went into her small bathroom, found a cloth by candlelight, and soaked it in water from the washing bowl. Her hands were shaking badly. Nothing felt quite real.

When she came back, Annan and Kinsey were hovering by the fire, and Devin and Kyali were facing one another. Kyali looked like she was close to bolting, all blood and bunched muscles and desperation. Taireasa handed her the cloth, ignoring that desperation because acknowledging it *would* make Kyali bolt, she was sure. She peered into the darkness beyond the little door of stone in her bedroom wall. The door was just big enough for a tall person to step through, if she bent her head. She'd never had the slightest suspicion it was there.

"Just like Faestan," she said, and heard Kyali draw an unsteady breath behind her.

"I suppose, Majesty."

"Much of tonight is just like Faestan, Ky," Taireasa observed, ignoring that *Majesty*. The symmetry of it was horrible, and strangely comforting. Kyali had kept her safe again. It was what Kyali did.

Devin reached out and caught Kyali's hand in his. She flinched, rose up on her toes again like she was preparing to leap away, and then, surprisingly, held herself still.

"You've carried it long enough, don't you think, sister? Far enough? Aren't you tired? "

Oh—gods.

"Speak sense. I don't know what you're talking about. Let go, Devin."

"I am, you do, and never, sister mine. *Never*. You're stuck with me for good. I think you're beginning to understand now just how stuck, aren't you?"

Or don't you hear me? he said, in that other way that they could. The air around their joined hands was beginning to shimmer. Kyali stared at the floor, trembling with the desire to flee, the desire to stay—the two urges shivered through her, through all three of them. She didn't take her hand away, though. The shimmer grew pronounced.

Taireasa, I think this will take the three of us.

I don't want to hurt her. I've hurt her so much already.

She hadn't even realized she believed that until now. Taireasa put her hands to her face, too late to catch the tears.

Taireasa, it was never you! It was them, and they're dead, and good riddance. But she's hurting herself. *Enough. I know the truth now, and you always did, didn't you? My stubborn, courageous, blind little sister is the only one who believes she's still hiding something to spare us pain.*

Dear gods, that was *exactly it*. And of course, Kyali would.

"We're not going to be able to do this without you," Devin said aloud, strong and steady and sure, looking at Kyali, talking to both of them. He reached out with his other hand and set it on his sister's face, cupping it gently. She flinched, but she didn't bolt: she seemed frozen in place, her jaw knotting and her breath coming faster. "I don't know what it is we're supposed to do, or how we fix this, but I know it can't happen without you. We need you. And you need *us*, Kyali, like it or not."

The air was snapping now, making the drapes and the bed-skirts flap. There was a faint hum coming from the abandoned glasses in the sitting room. Eyes grave, Kinsey got Annan by the arm and pulled them both back toward the wall, out of the way.

"I don't know what you're talking about," Kyali finally whispered. The faint thread of her presence was full of hope and terror and total despair.

"You stayed in my room that night," Taireasa heard someone say. In the stark silence that followed, she realized it had been her.

Kyali's eyes locked on hers. Taireasa swallowed, stepped closer, and made herself go on, because Devin was right. "You stayed to make sure they wouldn't find the doorway, that they wouldn't think to look for it. Didn't you? You were never going to gather the guard. You told me that so I would leave you there. And gods help me, I did, I should have known but I didn't, and I'm so—ah gods, Kyali, I'm so *sorry*—"

She caught the first sob, but she had to cover her mouth to stifle the rest. She squeezed her eyes shut, looking for the calm center of herself. "But I stayed too," she said. It was obvious that was not clear, so she fumbled for the words. "My Gift." It was so hard to breathe. It felt like the tears were burning into her skin, leaving scars. "That's when it woke. There. With you. I didn't leave. You stayed in my room... and I stayed with you."

"No," Kyali said in a small, shocked voice.

"I never left you," Taireasa said, the words coming faster now, rushing out. "How could I? I haven't since. I'm not going to. I'm sorry, I'm so sorry, Kyali, I never meant for that, I would never have asked it of you, and I don't want you to hurt any more. *I* don't want to hurt any more. I miss you."

"*Stop!*" Kyali cried, and stumbled a step back. She tangled her foot on the edge of the rug and thudded to her knees before Devin could catch her. He went down with her instead, pulled both her hands gently into both of his. He was crying now too, his presence alive with sorrow and horror and pity. Kyali curled into herself, breathing in great panicked gasps.

"I can't. I can't. Let me go. There's nothing left, it's all ashes, just let me go."

"Not true," Devin said. "Breathe, sister." **You never backed down from anything, little sister, not once in your life.**

I can't!

Taireasa knelt by Kyali and Devin, put her hands over theirs and lent her force to Devin's. They didn't press—she only knew now that they *had* been pressing, she saw that in Kyali's frustrated memory—only waited, open, hoping. Kyali shut her eyes, made a noise somewhere between a moan and a growl. And oh, there she was, wounded and despairing and stuck in that moment, that awful moment when she had known there was only a long, agonizing death in front of her and all hope was gone. There was the dark fury of her dreams, that Taireasa knew inside and out, knew by heart. Knew by her own choice.

We skinned our knees on the same stones, Kyali Corwynall. We laughed and wept together, we shared all our secrets. We grew from children to where we stand now, side by side. Whatever you think they took from you, I have long since held. Take it back from me.

Kyali opened her eyes. All her careful indifference was gone: her face was stark and bloodless and ravaged with sorrow and rage. They were at the center of a silent storm of warping air. Annan and Kinsey were no more than vague shapes outside it.

...I don't know how.

Like this, Devin said, impatient, full of grief and a love so hard and unyielding it was like a blade. He tore one of his hands free, pulling a locket from under his shirt. "House Corwynall takes you back," he said grimly.

"No," Kyali said.

"Yes."

"You can't do that."

"I'm Head of House. For now, anyway. I can do anything I want."

"You can't—"

Devin leaned closer, and dropped the locket over Kyali's head, stopping her words. She shuddered as the shock went through her, into Devin and Taireasa; not the pain of that long-ago separation, but something warm and solid and enveloping. Devin shook his head. "We'll only follow you wherever it is you go, you bloody-minded, hard-headed, fire-haired wight. You'll never get rid of us. You'd do the same for one of us, and you know it."

"Shut up," Kyali rasped, head bowed, trembling with the effort it took to hold herself apart from them. Her presence was coming alive with memory, with pain, with a thousand things too complicated and sweet and hurtful for words. She was fighting that with everything in her. "Just shut up."

"Not likely."

Taireasa thought of Kyali swinging a wooden sword bigger than she was, Kyali flinging herself fully clothed into the Sainey because she hated the dress her mother had made her wear, Kyali standing at her mother's grave, pale and silent. Kyali laughing, Kyali shouting, Kyali with that ferocious scowl that everyone else thought meant she was furious, and Taireasa knew only meant she was thinking.

"When you were seven, you rode farmer Angus's prize milk cow halfway to Faiche Ford on a dare," Devin said, catching her tactic. "The same year, you rolled in a whole bag of flour and snuck into my room and scared me so badly I ran into the pig's trough trying to get away from you. I put eight crow-spiders in your bedroom the summer you were thirteen and you shrieked like a banshee, but you killed them all and put one in my pancakes the next morning. You thought I didn't know. I did. I ate them anyway."

It surprised Kyali into a choked laugh, which became something else. She pulled her hands free, and then simply knelt there, fighting and losing, yearning toward them and then away, her hands curled into fists on her knees and her eyes full of tears.

"There is no part of yourself you could ever lose," Devin said steadily. "Between us, I promise you, we have them all."

Kyali shook her head, fumbling for that cold distance, because moving forward was so frightening it made everything in her shake. Taireasa breathed with her, feeling that fear with her, that futile search. She reached out and put her hands over Kyali's as more tears spilled down her own face, no longer burning but clean, a cessation of pain.

"Did I thank you, Kyali Corwynall?" Taireasa asked. "I should have long since. Thank you for saving my life. Thank you for keeping me safe."

"Oh *enough*, I'm sorry, I'm so tired I can't think—oh *Father*, I'm sorry—"

Kyali rocked forward, pressed her forehead to Taireasa's. It hurt in so many ways, that gesture, and it was quite possibly the best thing she'd ever known. Kyali was shaking with sobs, coming apart under their hands, but it was exactly right. Devin wrapped an arm around his sister's heaving shoulders. Kyali let them hold onto her. After a moment, she let herself hug them back, a panic-tight grip, her heart a moil of gratitude and fury and drowning, terrible sorrow.

Taireasa didn't even hear Kinsey and Annan leave.

24

Kinsey stood in his own bedroom, swaying with weariness. Annan was shooing the servants out, poking the fire back to life—stomping around like an angry general, snapping orders at retreating maids, stabbing at the hearth like there was an enemy hiding in the coals.

Kinsey stared at the high, lonely moon through the window. Tears kept stinging his eyes and he put a hand out and gripped the edge of his bed until the pain cleared his head a little. He leaned against the glass, trying to catch his breath, find his balance, *think*.

Gods, he'd never hurt so much for someone else. For all three of them. Tonight had broken his heart more than a little. He wiped at his face, cleared his throat, and wished he had a bottle of wine.

"Bed, my Lord Prince?" Annan said, coming up behind him, short-tempered and obviously hoping for his own. He turned, snapped something at a lingering servant who certainly didn't deserve it, and Kinsey met his eyes in surprise and curiosity.

Annan looked away first, which was interesting. He supposed even his unflappable master of spies was entitled to a twinge of sympathy now and then. A rock couldn't have remained unmoved, witnessing that.

"Bed," Kinsey agreed, wiping at his face again, because damn it, he couldn't seem to stop leaking tears. It was embarrassing, or it would have been if he had the energy to care. Annan hunched a shoulder, folded his arms, and heaved a gusty sigh. The man looked about as unsettled as he ever had, actually.

"But first..." Kinsey said, and turned to pull out a bottle of the Fraonir liquor Devin had given him, a dusty thing full of clear and somehow bright liquid. Annan looked at it with something approaching horror, which was a rather odd reaction, and then his broad shoulders slumped.

"Aye," he said, and went to retrieve a glass.

Two glasses.

"You're drinking with me, are you?"

"I am tonight."

Which was as much as he needed to know, Kinsey decided. It didn't look like Annan was in a talkative mood. He never was, when it came to himself. Kinsey poured generously, peering at the liquor curiously. Annan's dour look was telling.

"You've had it before?"

"Once, my Lord Prince," Annan said flatly, lifting his glass. "To new homelands," he proclaimed, and raised one defiant eyebrow when Kinsey stared at him.

"To new homelands," Kinsey agreed hastily, trying not to grin.

They drank, wincing.

Dawn was breaking in the east. The cold sunrise wind whistled around the tops of the fortress, kicked up sprays of snow from the rooftops, carried it spinning and glittering off the edges of the world. The trees began to have definition, shaping themselves out of the dark as the sky paled.

Kyali leaned against the battlement wall, watching, discovering that she was hungry for the sight of the faint pink light of the sun's first push toward the world, for the way the land drew itself in grays, then whites, then golds as morning broke over the mountains.

Her eyes were puffy and sore, and when they teared up again at the sight, they were also frozen. She rubbed at them, weary beyond words... but better, so much better.

She had gotten so lost. She was so lucky to have friends who loved her enough to bring her home.

An arm, heavily cloaked, leaned on the stone wall at the edge of her vision. Devin's presence, tired and sad and satisfied, settled against hers. It took her breath away. She wondered if she'd ever get used to that.

"I haven't yet," her brother said, eyes on the sunrise.

"Well, I may before you do," Kyali said soberly, but she couldn't keep the smile from pulling her lips up when he sent her a look of offended challenge. Her face wouldn't stay still this morning. Devin snorted, then shut his eyes and breathed carefully, face working.

"Gods, I missed that," he finally said, his voice gone a little watery. "I can't tell you how much I missed that."

"I can do it more often," she promised, and Devin barked

out a strained laugh.

"You can *try*, wight."

She looked at the sunrise, trying to bite her lip hard enough to make it stop trembling. She was very tired of crying. "Minstrel," she shot back, and lost the battle as Devin pulled her into a ferocious, cloak-muffled hug like being mauled by an affectionate bear. He'd gotten bigger somewhere along the way: he was half a hand taller than she was now. That was going to be annoying. "I missed it too," Kyali said into his shoulder, spitting fur. "You've no idea."

"I love you."

"I had that much figured out, actually."

He didn't rise to the bait this time. Just held on, while the wind got colder and the light got brighter, and that was all right. He knew what she couldn't say, and she knew that, and it was all right.

"You two are going to freeze out here, and you would make particularly poor statues," Taireasa said, appearing more or less soundlessly. They jumped apart like thieves caught in a shop after dark. Devin swiped a sleeve over his face. Kyali sniffed hard, which gave her away completely—but there was nothing she could hope to hide from these two anyway. Taireasa was a blaze in her mind, like another sunrise.

"We'd make *lovely* statues," Devin assured her earnestly. "Dignified. Imposing."

"...Dripping."

"Just Kyali," Devin said. "Such a dramatic one, that girl, always weeping all over everything. Should have been a poet. Can't turn a phrase to save her life, though, it's very sad."

"Oh *shut up*, you—"

She couldn't finish; she was laughing too hard. Kyali leaned
back against the wall, stuck between mirth and grief, and put
her hands over her face, breathless, bewildered, hurting and
healing at the same time. "I don't know what to do," she said
through her fingers.

Taireasa leaned on the wall on her other side. Taireasa
leaned in that other way, too, a heart as broad as the sky folding around hers, holding memory and certainty, pain and love,
a faith as unshakeable as the rock this fortress was built on.
Friend, confessor, fellow troublemaker, queen. Other half.
Kyali lowered her hands, put one on Taireasa's shoulder. She
would have to learn these gestures again. They didn't come
easily. But they were worth the effort. Anything was worth the
effort, to see the way Taireasa's face lit from the inside.

"Come inside now," Taireasa urged, leaving so much unsaid. And not. It was alive in her brave, perfect heart, flowing
between them: the way home. "We can figure the rest out later."

The sun climbed over the edge of the world in a wash of
fiery winter light, falling on the three of them, bringing every
stone and branch into sharp relief. Taireasa turned her head
to watch it. For a moment, she was a girl by a river, features
alight with wonder. For a moment, the whole world might have
been as still and peaceful as this tiny corner of it seemed.

"Yes," Kyali said, throat too full for more, and followed
them in.

Sword,
Song,
and
Crown

Kyali Corwynall

Devin Corwynall

Taireasa Marsadron

If Wishes
Were Stones

a story of Lardan

by Amy Bai

he fields were full of swinging scythes and slow-moving carts, and the breeze smelled sweetly of turned earth. Devin Corwynall sat on the remains of the old western wall, which he had claimed just this past summer as his very own thinking spot, and breathed long and deep, his knees hugged to his chest, his eyes on the horizon. Ink stained his fingers. A small pot sat beside him on the crumbling stone, a chewed quill jutting out of it. He had been out here for most of the morning, having evaded the head maid's watchful eye with unusual ease, for she was worried and preoccupied. *Everyone* was worried and preoccupied.

Inside the house, his stepmother was dying.

The breeze snatched a crumpled and much-marked sheet of paper from his hand, sending it tumbling down the steep, grass-matted slope of the ditch that shadowed the low wall. Devin leapt after it in a wild jumble of limbs. He lost his balance when he landed awry on the slope, rolled hard onto his shoulder, and kept rolling. Stinging fire spread over his bare wrist as he crushed a nettle plant. He hissed, caught the paper in one hand, and with the other dragged at the earth until a half-grown merrybush brought him to a halt.

The bottom of the ditch was muddy from recent rain. He glowered at it and pulled himself to his feet. One knee was soaked through with mud; the rest of him had been spared that indignity—but grass stains and dirt were smeared all over his doublet and breeches. He doubted his father was going to congratulate him on having dodged a total drenching. He clutched his nettle-stung, throbbing wrist and counted ten careful breaths.

His father wasn't going to care about his stupid clothes, anyway. Nobody was.

They all had better things to worry about.

Where the rain and the wind shall come mourn, said the bottom of the paper in streaked, blotchy ink now smeared with mud spatter—one of a hundred tries that fell maddeningly short of what he wanted to say. And it wasn't even true. The sun shone and the wind was gentle: it was a beautiful day. Nothing about the world said *mourning.* The weather in his head was darker. In his head, the world was slowly coming to a standstill as Lady Elliana Corwynall, who had treated him like her son for all the life he could remember, fought for breath and slowly (but still too fast, oh, far too fast) came to a standstill of her own.

Every time he thought of it his mind shied away, like a horse from a snake.

"It should be raining," Devin muttered, and took his hand away to inspect the raised welts from the nettle.

"You ruined your clothes."

He nearly fell back down. He spun, his heart thudding in his chest like a drum, and there was Kyali on the wall behind him, looking down. Her dress was in disarray and so was her hair, and she had slipped her nurse's watch, which she was constantly doing and getting into trouble for. But nobody would yell at her for those things, though she was nearly eight and she should know better.

It was hardly fair. *He'd* had to behave better when he was eight.

"I thought I'd try to match you for a change," Devin snapped. Shame flushed through him when her face crumpled into a frown. Her hair looked like a bonfire with the sun behind it, if bonfires had burdocks stuck in them. The head maid would have a fit, if she had any time for cleaning up the lord's children, which she hadn't, not for weeks.

Kyali got away with everything now, because it was her mother who was ill. But then again, he himself had spent the morning on the old wall, with no one to tell him to come inside and do his lessons, so he supposed he was getting away with things, too.

That wasn't particularly fair either. Not much was lately.

"Father's going to be angry with you," his little sister sniffed.

"Father's not going to care." Devin stuffed the paper in a pocket, next to the flute given to him last month by a minstrel who had begged shelter and then stayed for six marvelous days, singing songs and eating cook's pasty pies. Lady Elliana had even come down from her bedroom once to hear. She had sat near the great hearth, propped up on cushions and speaking softly to the maids, while Father paced the room like a restless hound and guardsmen ringed the walls, listening. In the firelight she had been very pale and thin, like something out of a faery tale, one of the dark ones. Devin had lingered, desperate to hear the new songs, but so filled with sadness and fear that he had finally fled to the kitchen storeroom and wept into a pile of linens, because she was the only mother he had ever known and the bones showing through her skin told him that she would not get well again.

He wondered if Kyali had figured it out yet. He hoped so and not, all at once, and scowled at the grass under his feet. The flute was smooth and strange against his fingers. He was almost sure it was made of bone, and he tried not to wonder what sort of bone it had been before it became a flute.

"He *might* care," Kyali said, but she didn't sound like she thought that was likely either. She kicked at a loose stone, which sent old mortar rolling down toward him. Devin glared up at her.

The wall was not difficult to climb, being only as high as his head, but the easiest way up was *forever* away from where he stood. He contemplated the walk with a frown and kicked one foot farther into its boot before setting off. He could get back up right here if he wanted to, but it would be hard and he might fall, and there was no way he was doing that in front of Kyali.

She followed along the top of the wall while he walked, her arms out, keeping just ahead. Devin frowned deeper and tried to keep his balance on the slope without looking like he was trying very hard.

"Did you fall all the way to the bottom?" Kyali asked.

Devin squashed the urge to throw a clod of dirt at her. She'd only throw things back: his sister *liked* to fight. And she had the advantage of height, something he was learning about from Father's officers. Archers liked that. It would probably work just as well with rocks and dirt, and Kyali would know it because she was learning the same things he was about war and battle, which was silly, but she had wheedled and begged until she was allowed in those lessons.

She did much more shouting than wheedling, lately.

"Did they make you leave because you were being a pest?" Devin shot back, picking his way carefully over a pile of broken stone.

A shower of dirt and pebbles hit his head and fell down the back of his collar. He bent and swept up a stone without thinking, then dropped it in favor of a clod. Even though she deserved it ten times over, he didn't want to hit his little sister with a rock.

The dirt struck her ear and burst apart all over her dress. Kyali, who always noticed things like his choosing dirt over stone yet never seemed to appreciate the courtesy, launched herself off the wall in a silent fury, landing on him hard enough to knock the breath from him. They rolled down the ditch in a tangle of knees, Devin knotting his fingers in his sister's hair, Kyali's small but very hard teeth buried in his arm.

The mud at the bottom was more like a pond than a puddle, it turned out: they struck it sideways, still thrashing, and sank up to their noses. Kyali's eyes, already flickering golden in that eerie way they had when she was upset, went wide and startled. Devin sucked in a breath to shout, got an unexpected noseful of watery mud, and immediately sneezed in his sister's face. Kyali shrieked and batted at him, driving one of her bony elbows right into his eye as she scrambled away.

Soaked, truly filthy, and aching in too many places to count, Devin rolled over in the mud and shouted laughter at the too-blue sky.

"Shut up! Ugh!" Kyali flung herself upright, then caught her foot on something and fell back into the mess. Laughing too hard to speak now, Devin splashed her and crawled out, slipping in the mud, clinging to bramble and grass to pull himself up. He sprawled backward against the slope and giggled until the sky in his head was a nicer color. By the time he caught his breath, Kyali had clawed her way out and was wiping her face and eyes with her ruined dress. The bracelet she wore, which Lady Elliana had made from old thread and bits of cloth, was sodden and dangling from her wrist. Devin's was gone, and he spent a frantic minute scrabbling around the mud before he saw it caught on a bramble on the slope. He retrieved it with a sigh and put it in his pocket with the flute. Kyali wrung a puddle out of her skirt.

Father was probably going to notice them when they came back to the house today.

"I thought you liked being covered in dirt," Devin gibed, and his sister kicked some at him.

"I *don't* like it, it just *happens*. You aren't any better. At least my dress isn't new." She was really mad now, her eyes bright like candles and her mouth a long thin line. The mud made her look like a creature from a tale told to scare children.

"I *am* better, *you're* the one who knocked us both into the mud. Why'd you do that, anyway?"

"Because I'm not a pest!"

"Oh, yes you are," Devin said, with the assurance of years of experience, and shielded his face with an arm when Kyali kicked more dirt at him. "Stop it, pest! You know you are."

"I am not!" She picked up a clod and threw it, with unusually bad aim, and then she was on him again so fast he didn't see her coming. He brought both hands up, catching her wrists. She twisted. Devin pushed back and Kyali kicked his shin hard enough to really hurt.

"Brat!" Devin snapped, and rolled until he could pin her with his greater weight, which was the only way to win when she was really fighting. "They made you leave the house because you're a pest to *everyone*," he said furiously. One of Kyali's hands struck him just under the eye. "*Nobody* wants you around."

When he had her fixed in place he froze: her face was streaked with tears. Kyali *never* cried where anybody could see. Immediately Devin sat up, his belly roiling with an awful tangle of sadness and confusion. It was worse than the night he'd hid in the storeroom. He let his sister go, ready to bolt away to someplace quiet where he could sit still until the misery stopped trying to find a way out.

But as soon as Kyali was free she hit him, hard enough to drive the air from his lungs, then scrambled to her feet and up over the wall in a flash.

Devin launched himself after her with a growl, scraping his hands on the rocks and falling over the other side almost as soon as he reached the top. A flock of starlings burst out of a bush as he landed and began to run. The carts were almost to the barn. Kyali was a muddy, flapping streak crossing the yard, already hidden in the shadow of the barracks buildings. He was not, and had to race for that shadow, trailing mud, in full view of a hundred fieldhands and most of the House Guard. His face flamed with the indignity of it, but that only made him run faster.

The barracks were empty, all the soldiers out helping with
first harvest or on guard duty or patrol. It smelled of sweat and
ale, and it was cooler inside, though the walls were wood and
not stone, so it wasn't nearly as cool as the house. Light fell
from small windows high up and spread patches of sunlight on
the cots along the walls. There were pegs on the nearest wall
hung with cloaks and soft helms, and a long table in the middle beside a fire pit with a kettle and tripod.

His sister was nowhere to be seen.

"Wight," Devin called softly, and heard a hiss from a far corner. She hated that one. "Come out, come out, wherever you be."

"Don't *call* me that, Devin."

"It's what you are," Devin said reasonably.

"Leave me alone! Just go away."

She was still crying; he could hear it in her voice. He hovered by a cot, wanting to leave, wanting to stay—wanting to
tell her he was sorry, actually, but that stuck in his throat,
and what came out instead was a strangled coughing sound.
A shadow moved all the way on the other side of the barracks,
below a cot, and suddenly the shape of her was clear, huddled
underneath. Devin sat on the cot he was leaning against and
sighed, trying to ignore the stinging behind his nose. One of
them sniveling was quite enough.

"I didn't mean it," he said finally, sullenly, when Kyali had
let a long time go by without any noise at all.

"Yes you did."

She wasn't in the same place now. Her voice came from the
other corner. He sat up straight, peering into the dim places
where the sunlight wasn't touching. He felt a prickly sort of listening feeling come over him when he realized she had moved yet

again, amazingly silent in her wet shoes. It was the kind of feel-ing Gedric had told him to pay attention to, an animal-feeling, a warning. Gedric spent more time looking at maps and talking to rough-dressed men that came to the estate at odd hours than he did riding patrol, for all that Father called him a captain, but he was the most fun of Devin's tutors, full of sly tricks.

So Devin paid attention. Kyali was now several cots clos-er. She moved like a fox in a field, on her tiptoes, staying to shadows. He held very still and watched as she made her way toward the southern door, learning something new about his pest of a little sister, which was that she was possibly better than he was at what Gedric called *sneaking about*.

Well. Maybe not *quite* better. She was still little.

Devin reached for the pillow at the top of his cot and slid it closer, careful to look only at the shadows near the kettle, like he didn't know where Kyali actually was. When she darted at the door, he stood and flung the pillow with all his strength. It sailed across the sunlit space and struck her in her back, knocking her into a cot. He crowed a pleased laugh. Kyali ut-tered a wrathful shout and shoved, and the cot slid, and some-thing fell out of it all over the floor, rattling softly in the dirt.

"Now look what you did," Devin sighed.

Kyali snarled, hurling the pillow at him, and crawled un-der the cot to retrieve whatever it was she'd spilled. Devin knelt and followed, feeling along the packed dirt. His fingers met smooth, flat shapes that felt like stone, each with a single rough edge. He gathered seven before his hands were too full to work properly and knelt to set them carefully on the cot they had fallen from. Kyali was on the other side, leaning against the thin pallet mattress, turning several things over in her fin-

gers. They were stones, but carefully polished stones of wonderful sorts: he saw dark gray river rocks and the creamy clear-
ness of witchglass, and other colors he'd never guessed stone
could hold. Each had a symbol scratched into it.

"Wishstones," Kyali said softly, rubbing a finger over a
blotchy blue one.

Most of the soldiers from the Eastern provinces carried them
around their necks in little pouches when they did things that
were dangerous. They were supposed to grant one wish each, but
not just any wish: you had to find the right wish, the one that the
stone would grant. Father called it country superstition... but Father carried one sometimes when he led the men. Which might be
a way of making the men want to follow him, or might be something else: Father was clever, and never one to say.

He'd never wondered how the stones were made, or who
did the making. The soldier that slept in this cot must be a
maker of them.

A sudden, desperate conviction filled him.

Devin grabbed two fistfuls and stood. Kyali looked up at
him, her expression darkening. He backed up a step, his heart
beginning to pound. He could see himself walking into the
house, walking in with a handful of shining stones that each
granted a wish. He and Kyali and Father could make them, one
after the other, until they found the right stone for the wish in
his heart. In *all* their hearts.

Kyali stood and pointed. "Those are Ellan's," she said. "You
can't take them."

Trust Kyali to know the name of the one who made them.
She followed the soldiers around everywhere, when they
would let her.

"He wouldn't mind," Devin said, already edging toward the door. The picture in his head was so strong it was a little hard to breathe. "You know he wouldn't."

"No, I don't. You can't just take his things, Devin!"

"I'll bring them back, Kyali. Shush. Don't be a baby."

He wanted to run out the door, to get to the house as fast as he could, but he knew if he turned around Kyali would jump on him from behind. She was following him already, never knowing how plain it was, what she planned to do. She always thought she was slyer than she actually was. She slipped out into the aisle, moving in that sneaky way.

"You *can't*," she said again, and Devin felt his face twist into something angry and ugly. He turned and ran.

"Stop!" Kyali shouted, hard on his heels.

He dodged a cluster of soldiers talking with a housemaid in the yard and ran for the watchtower on the north side of the gate. Behind him there was shout from one of the soldiers, and an answering shout from Kyali. He looked back to find her tearing free of the maid's grip—it was Meryn, the head maid, and she was a true terror. Devin tripped, skidded to his knees (the breeches tore outright this time), yelped, and rolled into the shadow of the house just as the soldiers began to come toward him. He scrambled up as best he could with his hands full and ran up the wide stone steps to the porch breathless, his knees trailing blood in fat drops all the way.

"I'm to see my father," he gasped as the soldiers came up the steps after him and the guards at the great doors came forward, everyone looking alarmed, like he was an outlaw come to rob the house. "He's inside."

He hoped not: the idea of facing Father right now was

dreadful. Father was usually riding the fields at this time of day, looking at fences and guard stations. He could only hope the door guards would forget this long enough to let him in.

"Lad, what's *happened* to you?" Faryn, the headman of the house, caught him by a shoulder and peered into his face. Kyali arrived from around Faryn's broad belly, out of breath and pink-faced with fury. "To *both* of you, good gods, you look as though you spent the morning in the midden!"

"He—"

"Kyali fell into the ditch," Devin declared, before his brat of a sister could tell tales, which she clearly meant to do. It was sort of true, after all. "I went after her."

"*Liar!*"

"Changeling," Devin retorted, knowing it would make her so mad she would lose all of Faryn's goodwill when she shouted back, and she might even forget why she had followed him here. Faryn got his sister by the shoulders as she charged forward. Devin slid, slowly and carefully, for the doors. He was nearly there, just about to slip into the shadows in the entrance, when Meryn came up behind him like a ghost, her baleful eyes glaring. She startled him so badly that he dropped all the stones, which clattered and rolled everywhere.

All the commotion stopped. Everyone looked down at the stones. And then up at Devin.

There was nothing to say now.

"They're not *yours*," Kyali said, managing, in the surprise of the moment, to wrench free. She knelt to gather up the stones, which were rolling all over. Devin just watched, mute, his whole face flushed and his throat almost too tight to swallow.

"What isn't whose?" asked their father. He stood in the

threshold of the big front doors like a statue of a king, his arms folded and the metal from his vambraces shining in the sunlight. He wore some of his armor nearly all the time, and would tell anyone who asked that it kept him used to the weight. Devin imagined it was also to make people wish to do what he said, as a man in armor looked like a man who should be giving orders, and a man whose orders shouldn't be ignored.

Father definitely looked like a man who should not be ignored.

Right now he also looked frightening. Devin bowed along with everyone else on the porch. Except for Kyali, who was crawling after wishstones and leaving trails of mud everywhere: she only bobbed her head.

"Where did these come from?" Father asked, while people were still bent in their bows. His eyes unerringly found Devin.

He knew his bright red face was giving him away, but he also suspected that his brat of a sister was pointing at him behind his back. "I thought—I just—I just wanted to—"

He was going to cry, right out here in front of everyone. He stumbled into silence, unable to meet anyone's eye.

"He *took* them," Kyali said. Devin wondered if he could get away with kicking her, just once, if he did it very fast. And then she added, utterly surprising him: "But I knocked them over first. They're Ellan's."

He could feel Father staring at the top of his head. He nodded at his boots, agreeing with his little sister, and wondered if he was in enough trouble to be banished to his room for the rest of the day. The thought filled him with panic. Two stupid tears slid out of his eyes and down his face.

"Give us a moment," Father said, sounding not precisely angry, but perhaps a little confused. Faryn and Meryn and the soldiers from the watchtower all left the porch. The door guards settled back into their posts, doing a good job of pretending not to see anything, which was, Devin supposed, much of their duty.

He wished they really *couldn't* see anything. He suspected the next few moments would not be pleasant.

"Boy," Father said then, stern and short. Behind him the door guards stiffened to attention as though that tone were aimed at them. "Devin, what were you about? You two are forbidden to go into the soldiers' quarters, you know that. What possessed you?"

Devin cast a quick glance about for his sister. She appeared, and dumped a brimming double handful of wishstones into Father's hastily cupped hands.

"She ran in first," Devin mumbled, mostly to the porch, but managing little peeks up at his father. "And I hit her with a pillow and she fell and we knocked over Ellan's cot, and these came out of it, and... and..."

Father scowled darkly. Even Kyali shrank a little.

"You *stole?*" Father said, going cold and yet colder. "Devin Corwynall, is this the truth? You stole from a soldier? Did you shame this House so?"

It was difficult to breathe now, let alone speak. Devin opened his mouth, but his voice stayed lodged in his throat. Father drew a large breath.

"He took them for Mama," Kyali said quietly.

Father's mouth stayed open a moment. He looked down at the wishstones in his hands. His shoulders fell, and the breath sighed out of him, and his face moved into an unfamiliar, complicated kind of unhappiness that scared Devin far, far, worse than the threat of shouting and punishment. Kyali made a small, worried noise and backed up a step, right into him. Devin caught her shoulder. She curled two small fingers into his dirty sleeve. Father cast a dubious glance back at the door guards, moving like he didn't know what he wanted to do, which was even more frightening, because Father always knew.

Then he knelt down, the stones cupped in his hands. Kyali froze like a hare in a thicket. Devin held his breath. Father looked at them from this lesser height, the sun shining on the new lines that had appeared on his face in the last weeks, and he sighed again.

"That may be too much to ask of a stone, I'm afraid," he said, as quiet as Kyali had been.

The door guards were not doing nearly as good a job of pretending now.

Father opened his arms, looking oddly uncertain. After a moment of shock they both pelted forward into him at once, and he gave a surprised grunt and dropped most of the stones. His armored arms closed about them. Devin took an unsteady breath and bit his lip, determined not to shame himself any worse. It felt as though he were shaking apart inside. His nose was running. Kyali's muddy hair was in his mouth. She was rigid next to him, shoulders hunched up around her ears. He patted her head. The wishstones scattered all around the three of them in a muted clatter, just rocks after all.

"I see," Father said, more quietly still. "I do see. She's beyond wishes now, though, and very soon she will be beyond pain, and that is a blessing, however little it looks like one from where we stand. You will have to be brave."

"I don't *want* to be brave," Kyali gasped into Father's chest. Her thin fingers knotted over Devin's wrist, scraping the welts of the nettle plant. He could feel her trembling.

"Neither do I," Father said, shocking them both into stillness. He hugged them a little harder, then set them back. His face looked strange up close, stranger still without the frown he often wore: more worried, more surprised, less stern. "That's when being brave counts most."

Kyali hugged her middle, staring back at Father, her own scowl falling away, her face like a small mirror of Father's. "I don't know how," she said.

"Your brother can teach you."

She bit her lip; nodded, looking unsure of that. Devin could hardly blame her. He wasn't particularly sure of it either.

Father stood, unfolding like a tall metal bird. He cast another glance at the door guards, who were looking anywhere but at the three of them, and his mouth moved in a tiny, wry smile. He lifted one shoulder, let it drop, then settled a buckle on his armor with studious care.

"Pass the sergeant a message to see me this evening," he said, never looking up from the buckle. "My children will need a closer and more expert watch than the House staff can manage just now."

"Aye, sir."

Devin picked up a stone and rubbed his thumb over the marking scratched into it, then wiped his nose with his sleeve. He eyed the mess that made, and prudently wiped his eyes with the other sleeve. Kyali just peeled away the filthy overlayer of her skirt and blew her nose on it. Devin snorted messy, miserable laughter, wiped his face a second time, and knelt to collect the rest of the wishstones.

"I'll bring them back to Ellan," he said.

"Yes, boy, you will, and beg his forgiveness. Ellan is in the fields helping with the carts now, and I'll not have either one of you showing your faces outside again until you've bathed. Tonight is soon enough for you to make your apologies. You'll both help to clean the guardroom for the next fortnight, too."

That didn't even feel unfair, though he was certain it would later. He looked up as Father set a hand first on his head, and then on Kyali's. His face was calm again, but his eyes were tired and sad.

"Before all that, I think you must come in, and bid her goodbye," he said. "She doesn't have long."

Devin looked toward Kyali: his own misery suddenly seemed much smaller. She stood stiffly, her ruined dress clutched in her fists, her face ashen. He dropped the wishstones back into his father's palms and took his little sister's clenched hands in his.

"Come on," he said. "I'll be brave if you will."

She sniffed, and scowled, and finally nodded.

They followed Father over the threshold, into the dimness of the house.

Acknowledgments

No writer is an island: we just look like them, from a safe distance. Up close, if you can get past the mountain of spent pens and dirty coffee mugs and crumpled pages, you will find a complicated web of family and friends, editors and publishers, teachers, coworkers, peers... and the occasional total stranger who, through some overheard snippet of conversation, exceptionally strange action, or nothing in particular, triggered That Idea— and then politely ignored the wild-eyed eureka moment that followed.

Books don't happen without these people.

Thanks I owe to my husband, for his patience and support among so many other things; to my family, for their enthusiasm, deserved and not; to my friends, for listening to me babble endlessly about characters and themes and plot points; to my fantabulous betas Julie, Tracey, Eleanor, Steph, Jude, and Alice; to my editor Kate, for medieval Lamaze classes. And to my beloved Purgies, for the wisdom, the debates, the sympathy, the cheers, the hilarity, and the all-knowing, all-seeing L of the J.

About the Author

Amy Bai has been, by order of neither chronology nor preference, a barista, a numbers-cruncher, a paper-pusher, and a farmhand. She likes thunderstorms, the enthusiasm of dogs, tall boots and long jackets, cinnamon basil, margaritas, and being surprised by the weirdness of her fellow humans. She lives in New England with her husband and her dog. When she's not writing in hermit-like solitude or plotting world domination via a silly-string war, you can catch her procrastinating here: www.amy-bai.com.

CONGRATULATIONS!

If you're reading this you've just finished another marvelous book from Candlemark & Gleam (*Purveyors of Fine Fantastika!*) — or you've skipped to the back pages to find out what we keep here, which is also perfectly fine.

Because what we keep back here, among other things, is

A SPECIAL OFFER!

Yes indeed! Through the miracle of Modern Science, we can offer you a way to take this book with you wherever you go without the expense and inconvenience of strapping a library to your back (although we encourage you to consider this for your future Hallowe'en costume needs.)

For if you have purchased this print edition of the novel, you can buy the digital edition for only **99 cents.** Yes! For slightly less than a dollar, a nigh-infinitely portable, DRM-free version of this very book can be yours!

Just go to **www.candlemarkandgleam.com** and use this special print discount code at checkout when selecting your digital edition:

SWSP0215

Candlemark & Gleam
BOOKS UNBOUNDED.

The ADVENTURE
CONTINUES ONLINE

VISIT THE CANDLEMARK & GLEAM WEBSITE TO

Find out about new releases

Read free sample chapters

Catch up on the latest news and author events

Buy books! All purchases on the Candlemark & Gleam site are DRM-free and paperbacks come with a free digital version!

Meet flying monkey-creatures from beyond the stars!*

WWW.CANDLEMARKANDGLEAM.COM

*Space monkeys may not be available in your area. Some restrictions may apply.
This offer is only available for a limited time and is in fact a complete lie.

CPSIA information can be obtained at www.ICGtesting.com
Printed in the USA
LVOW10s1209120415

434269LV00005BA/872/P